NGOZI UKAZU

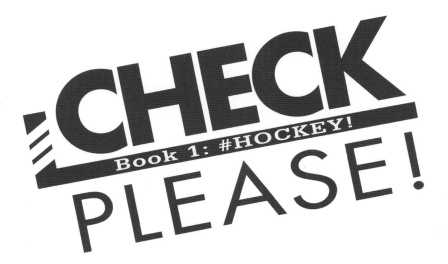

CHECK
Book 1: #HOCKEY!
PLEASE!

:01

First Second
New York

TABLE OF CONTENTS

FOREWORD

FOR A SCREENPLAY-WRITING SEMINAR during my senior year of college, I had every intention of creating some Very Serious Art™. You know—something dramatic, important, critical of various institutions, and obviously very gritty. So, enter *Hardy*, a 120-page screenplay about a hockey player who tragically falls for his best friend—a dude.

But being a Texan, a woman, and a first-generation Nigerian, I knew that writing about a white, Boston-born hockey bro would require weeks of intense anthropological study. (For starters, I could barely ice skate!) So I checked out books on hockey, attended every Yale hockey game, interviewed hockey players, their roommates, and their girlfriends, and immersed myself in the world of bro-dom. And when I emerged, not only was *Hardy* done (and surprise, it wasn't very serious art at all—it had, like, three fart jokes) but I had suffered an unintended side effect.

I had become obsessed with hockey.

The minute I began research, hockey suddenly transformed into this fast-paced, explosive, wild, and beautiful game, with a culture filled with strange rituals and cute nicknames and intense yet stoic men and women who strap knives to their boots and chase around slabs of vulcanized rubber. I had uncovered something weird and exciting and I had to tell the world. I still wanted to create, but this time something lighter and fun and much less serious. And that's how *Check, Please!* began.

The graphic novel you're about to read is a love letter to college hockey, the bonds you form in undergrad, and self-acceptance. And in a way, Eric "Bitty" Bittle is my answer to Hardy. Bitty just wants to bake, vlog, listen to pop music, and eventually learn to love himself (even if he doesn't know it yet). I don't consider this comic Very Serious Art™ at all, but I do consider it to be something even better: fun. Whether you love baking or hockey or neither or both, I hope you have fun reading Bitty's story.

Thanks, y'all!

NGOZI!

FRESHMAN YEAR

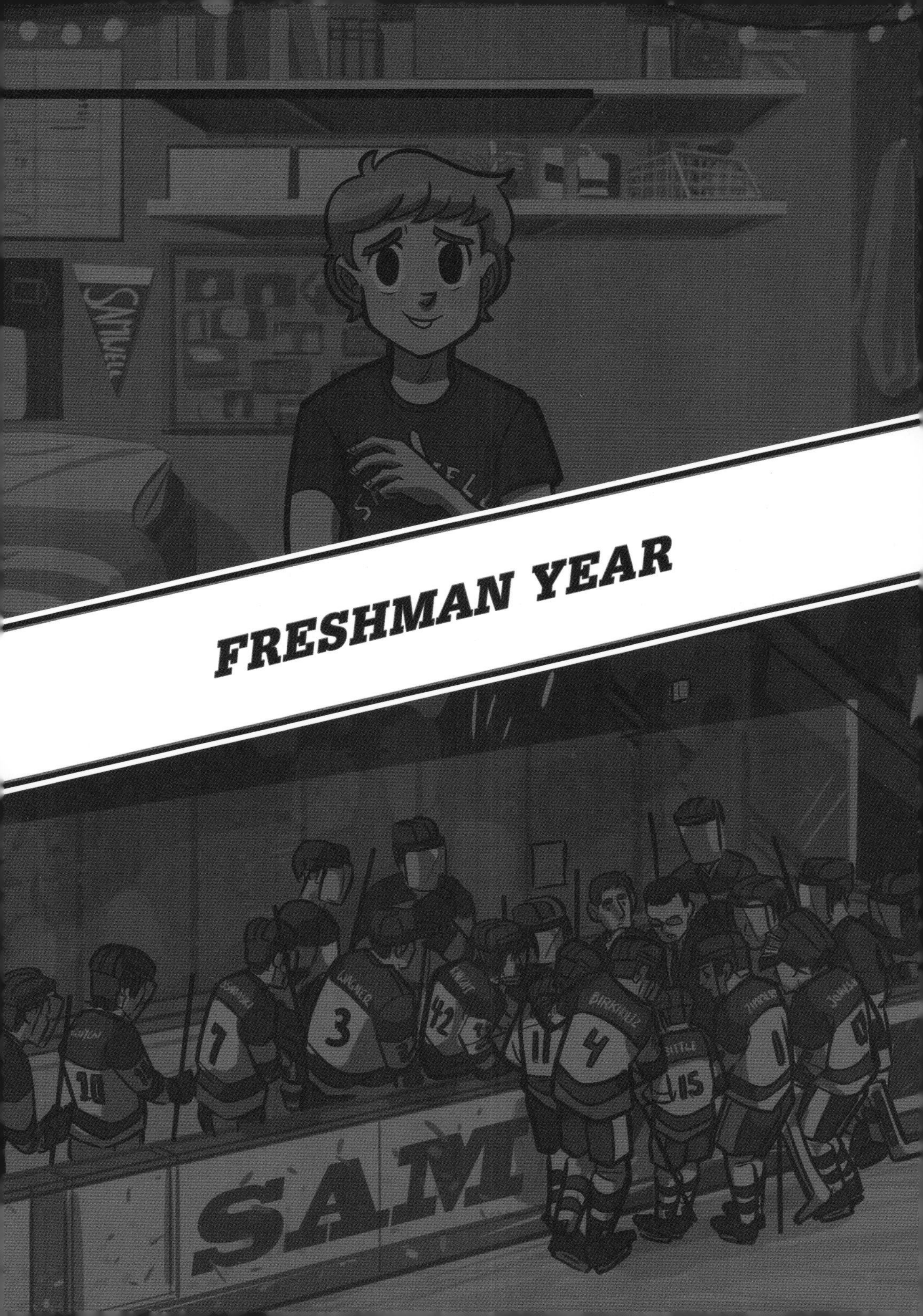

SAM

1

MEET ERIC BITTLE

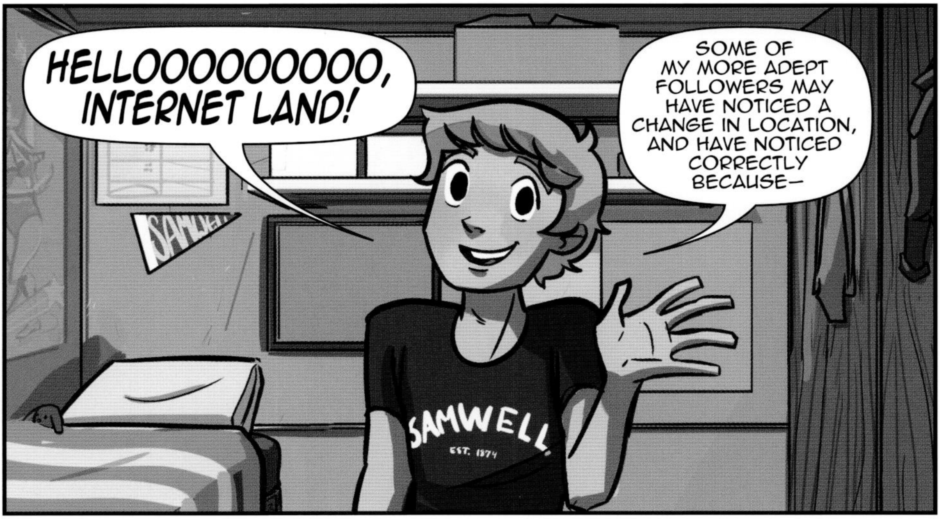
HELLOOOOOOOOO, INTERNET LAND!
SOME OF MY MORE ADEPT FOLLOWERS MAY HAVE NOTICED A CHANGE IN LOCATION, AND HAVE NOTICED CORRECTLY BECAUSE—
SAMWELL
SAMWELL EST. 1874

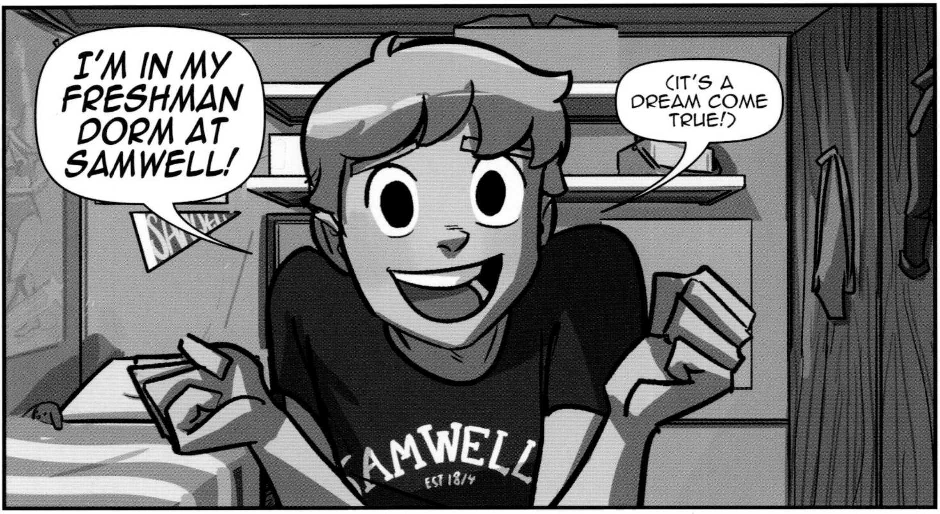
I'M IN MY FRESHMAN DORM AT SAMWELL!
(IT'S A DREAM COME TRUE!)
SAMWELL
SAMWELL
EST 1814

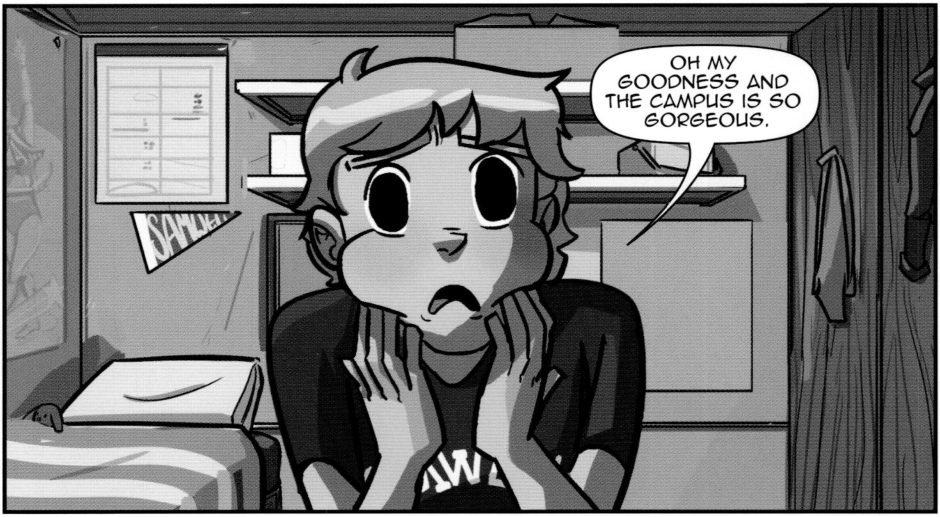
OH MY GOODNESS AND THE CAMPUS IS SO GORGEOUS.

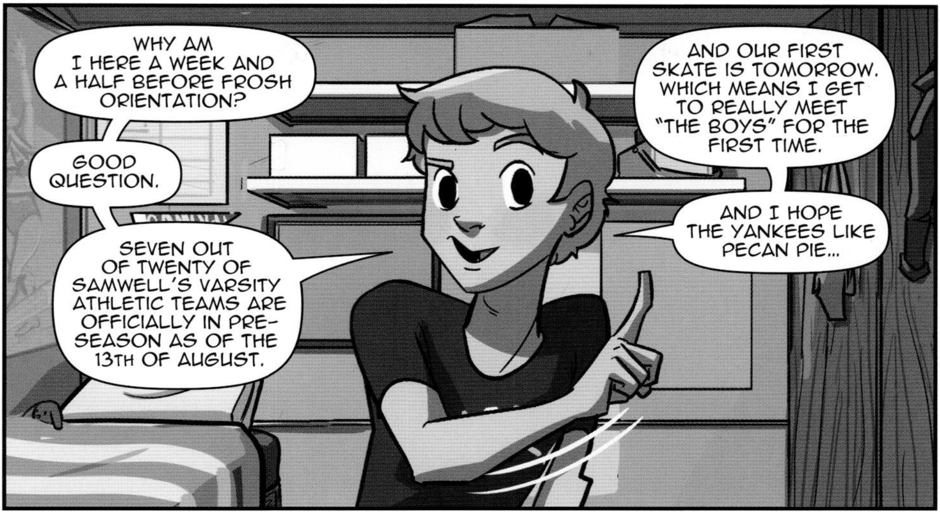
WHY AM I HERE A WEEK AND A HALF BEFORE FROSH ORIENTATION?
GOOD QUESTION.
SEVEN OUT OF TWENTY OF SAMWELL'S VARSITY ATHLETIC TEAMS ARE OFFICIALLY IN PRE-SEASON AS OF THE 13TH OF AUGUST.
AND OUR FIRST SKATE IS TOMORROW. WHICH MEANS I GET TO REALLY MEET "THE BOYS" FOR THE FIRST TIME.
AND I HOPE THE YANKEES LIKE PECAN PIE...

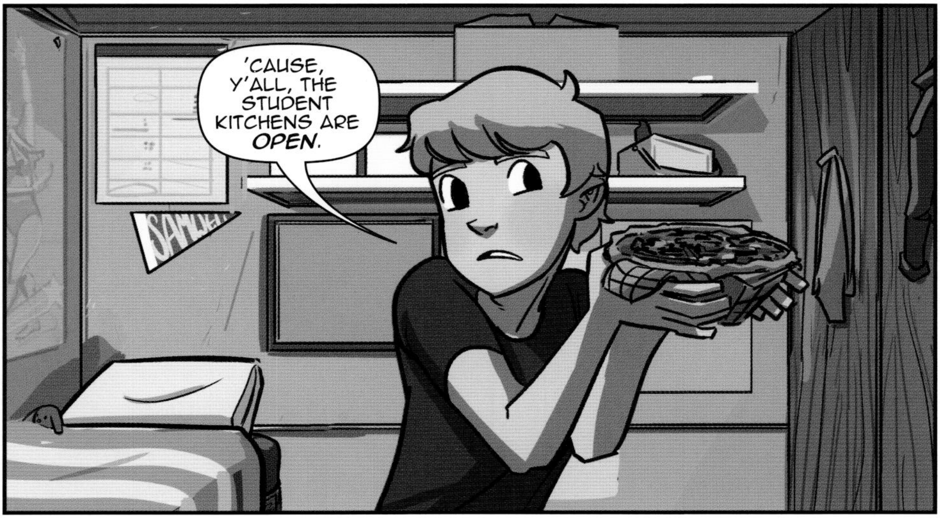
'CAUSE, Y'ALL, THE STUDENT KITCHENS ARE *OPEN*.

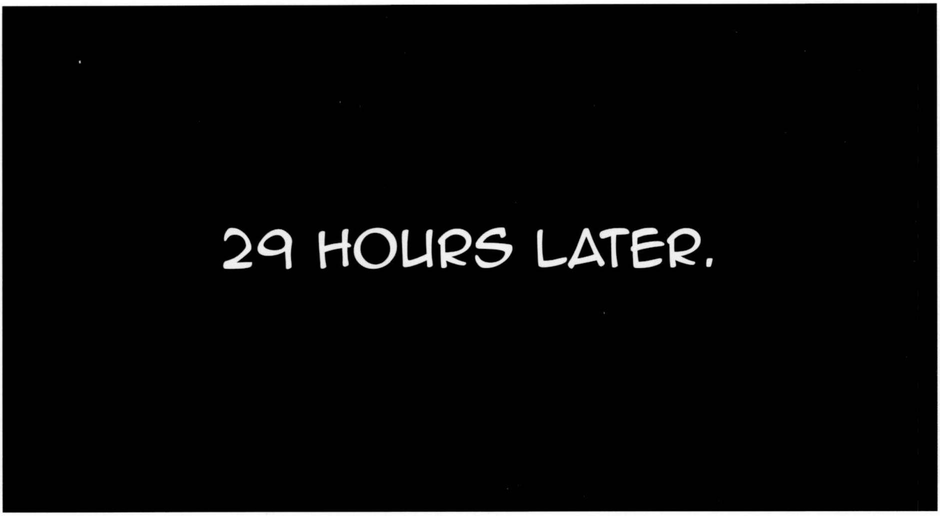
29 HOURS LATER.

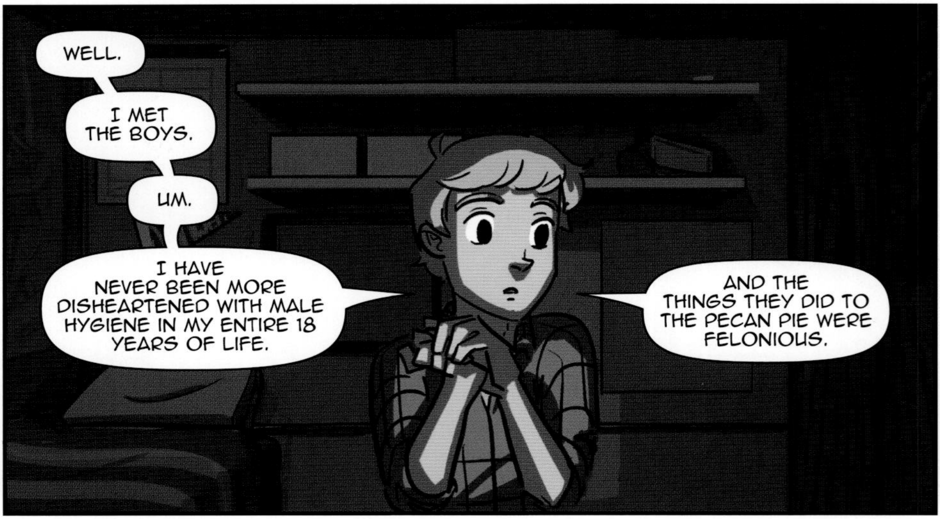
WELL.
I MET THE BOYS.
UM.
I HAVE NEVER BEEN MORE DISHEARTENED WITH MALE HYGIENE IN MY ENTIRE 18 YEARS OF LIFE.
AND THE THINGS THEY DID TO THE PECAN PIE WERE FELONIOUS.

2

MEET THE BOYS

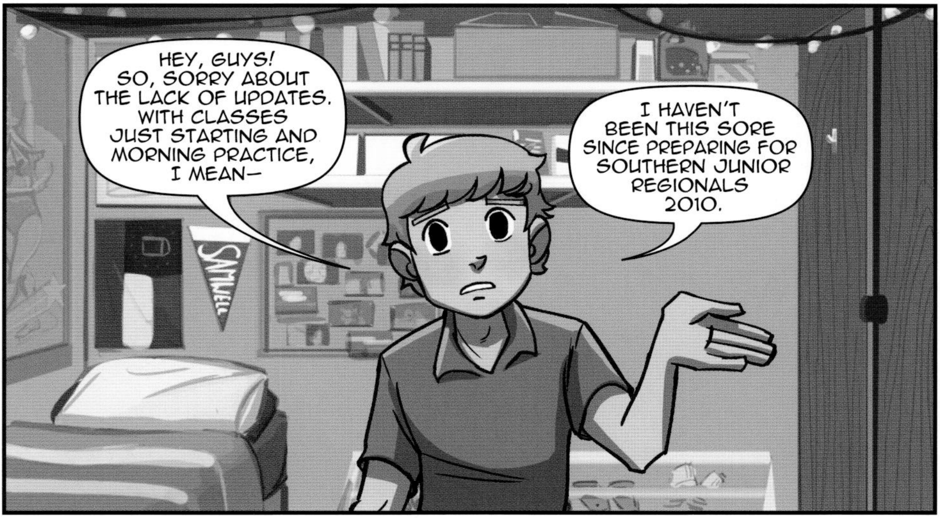

HEY, GUYS! SO, SORRY ABOUT THE LACK OF UPDATES. WITH CLASSES JUST STARTING AND MORNING PRACTICE, I MEAN—
I HAVEN'T BEEN THIS SORE SINCE PREPARING FOR SOUTHERN JUNIOR REGIONALS 2010.

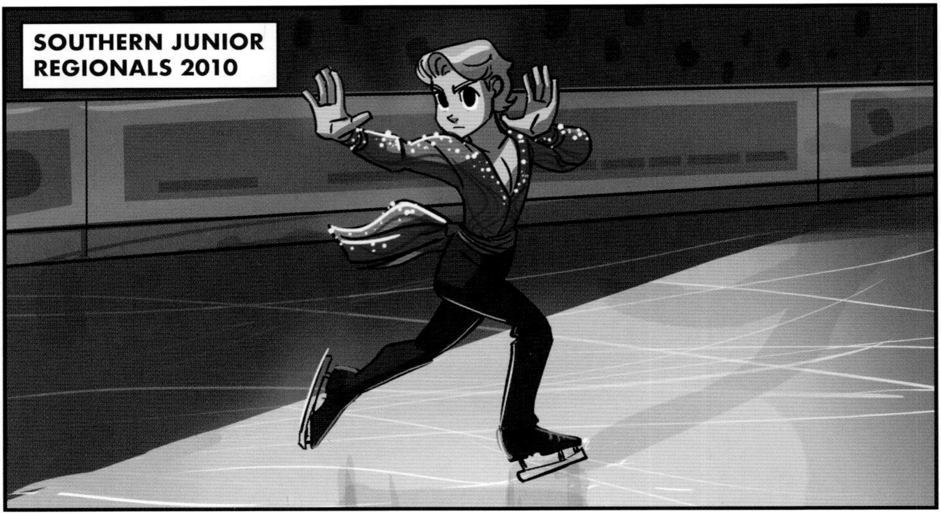
SOUTHERN JUNIOR REGIONALS 2010

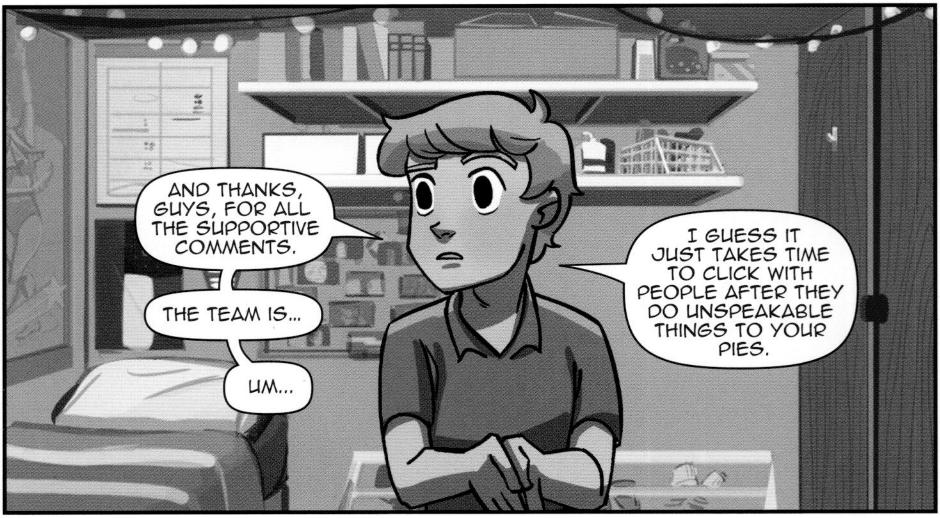
AND THANKS, GUYS, FOR ALL THE SUPPORTIVE COMMENTS.
THE TEAM IS...
UM...
I GUESS IT JUST TAKES TIME TO CLICK WITH PEOPLE AFTER THEY DO UNSPEAKABLE THINGS TO YOUR PIES.

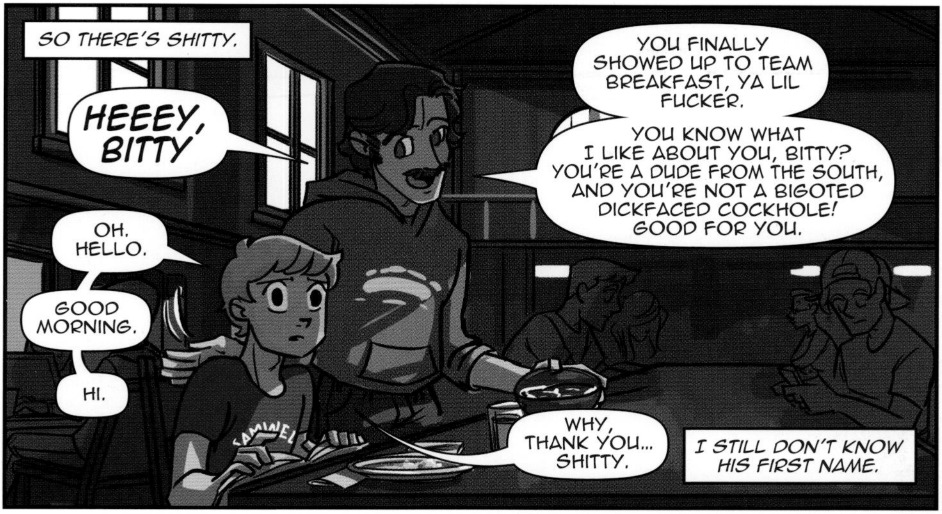
SO THERE'S SHITTY.
HEEEY, BITTY
YOU FINALLY SHOWED UP TO TEAM BREAKFAST, YA LIL FUCKER.
YOU KNOW WHAT I LIKE ABOUT YOU, BITTY? YOU'RE A DUDE FROM THE SOUTH, AND YOU'RE NOT A BIGOTED DICKFACED COCKHOLE! GOOD FOR YOU.
OH. HELLO.
GOOD MORNING.
HI.
WHY, THANK YOU... SHITTY.
I STILL DON'T KNOW HIS FIRST NAME.

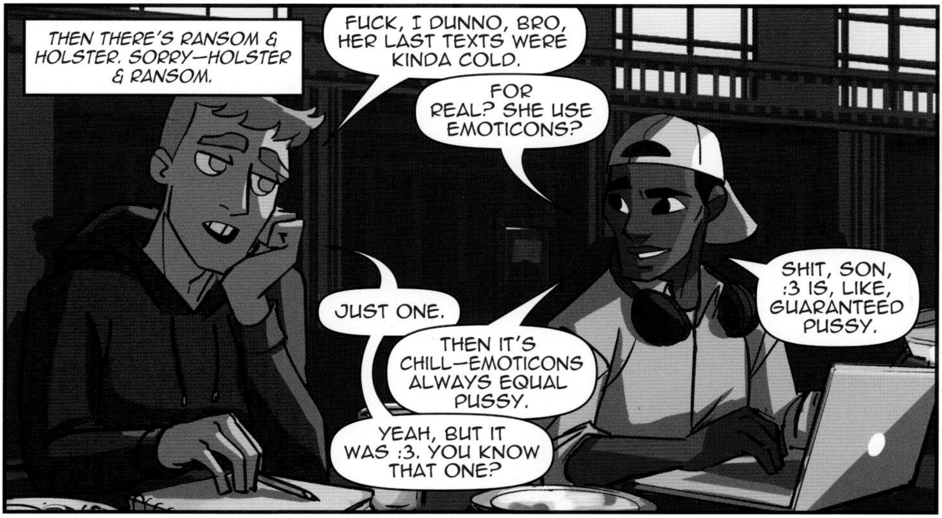
THEN THERE'S RANSOM & HOLSTER. SORRY—HOLSTER & RANSOM.
FUCK, I DUNNO, BRO, HER LAST TEXTS WERE KINDA COLD.
FOR REAL? SHE USE EMOTICONS?
JUST ONE.
THEN IT'S CHILL—EMOTICONS ALWAYS EQUAL PUSSY.
YEAH, BUT IT WAS :3. YOU KNOW THAT ONE?
SHIT, SON, :3 IS, LIKE, GUARANTEED PUSSY.

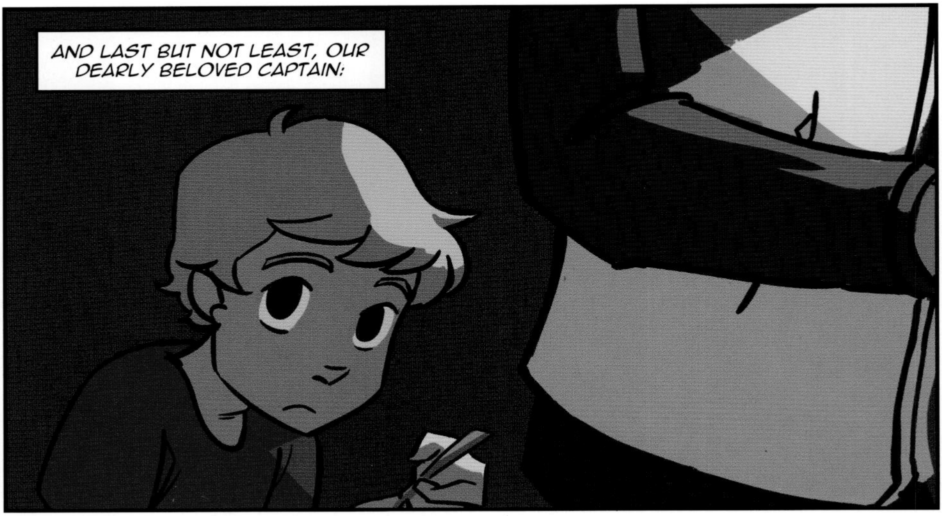
AND LAST BUT NOT LEAST, OUR DEARLY BELOVED CAPTAIN:

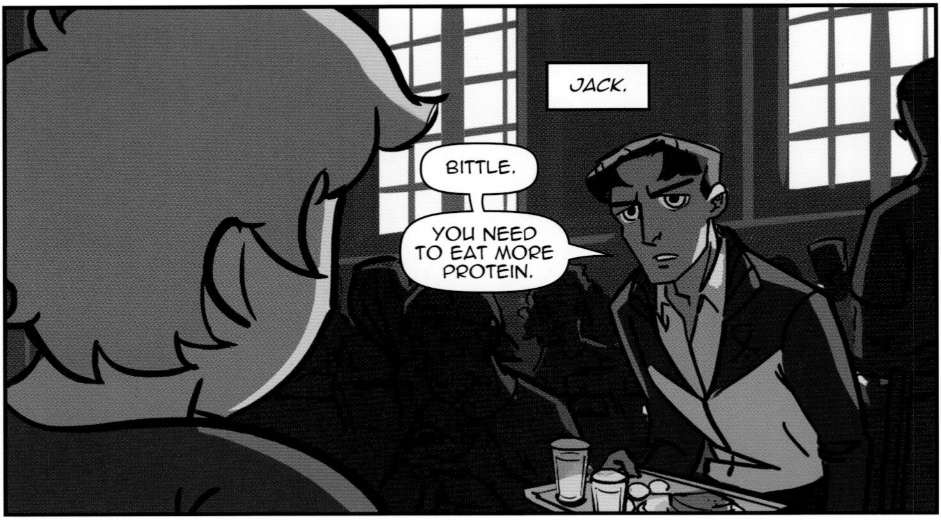
JACK.
BITTLE.
YOU NEED TO EAT MORE PROTEIN.

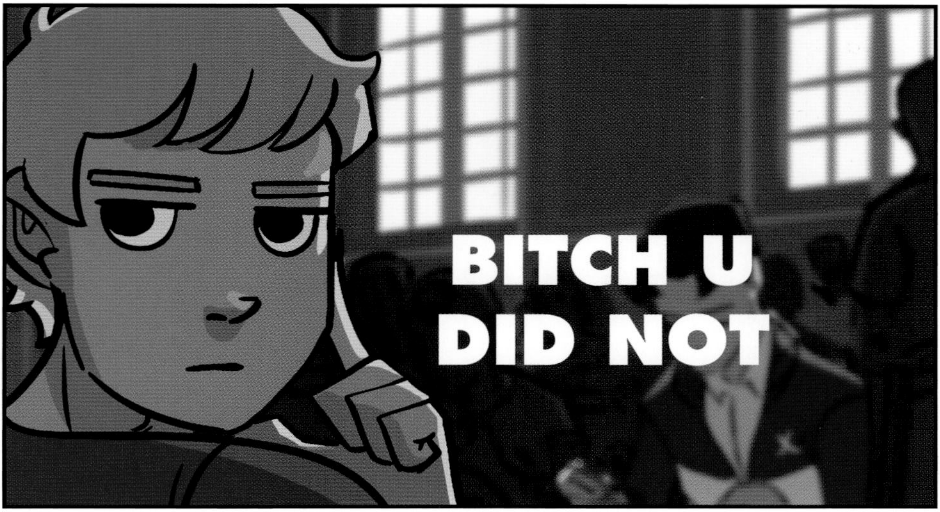
BITCH U
DID NOT

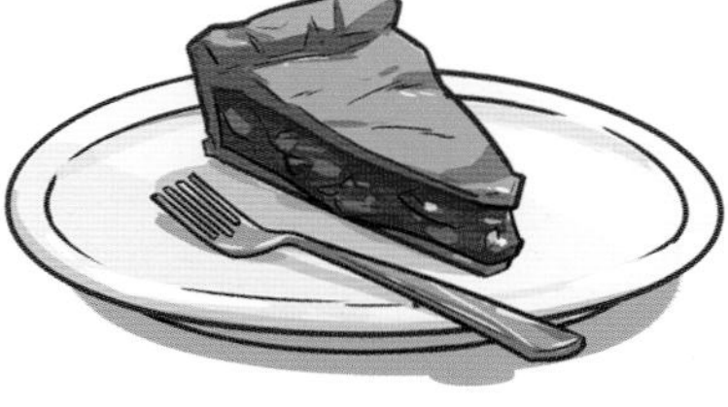

3

THE COACHES

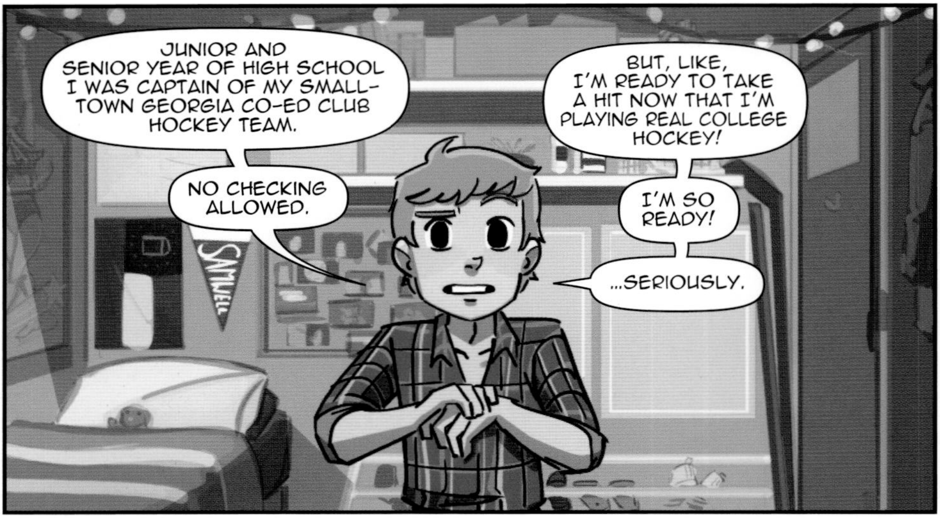

JUNIOR AND SENIOR YEAR OF HIGH SCHOOL I WAS CAPTAIN OF MY SMALL-TOWN GEORGIA CO-ED CLUB HOCKEY TEAM.
NO CHECKING ALLOWED.
BUT, LIKE, I'M READY TO TAKE A HIT NOW THAT I'M PLAYING REAL COLLEGE HOCKEY!
I'M SO READY!
...SERIOUSLY.
SAMWELL

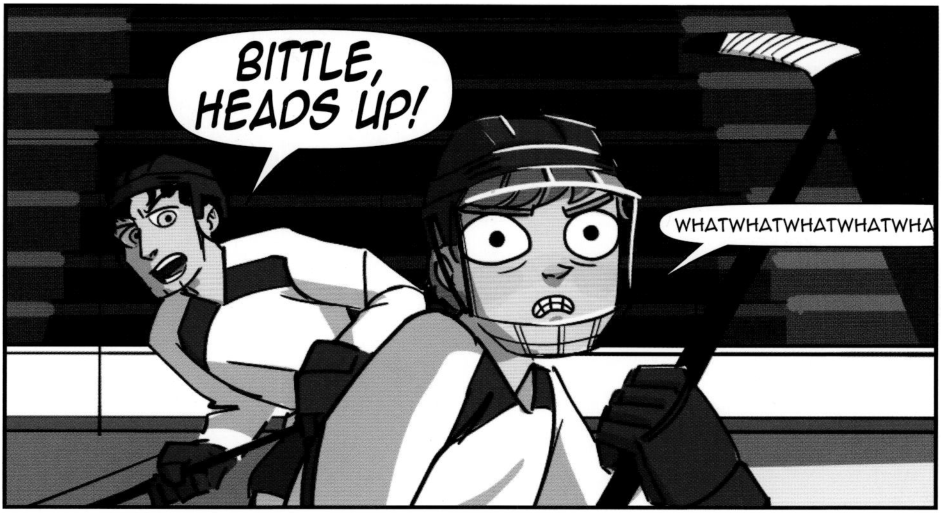
BITTLE, HEADS UP!
WHATWHATWHATWHATWHA

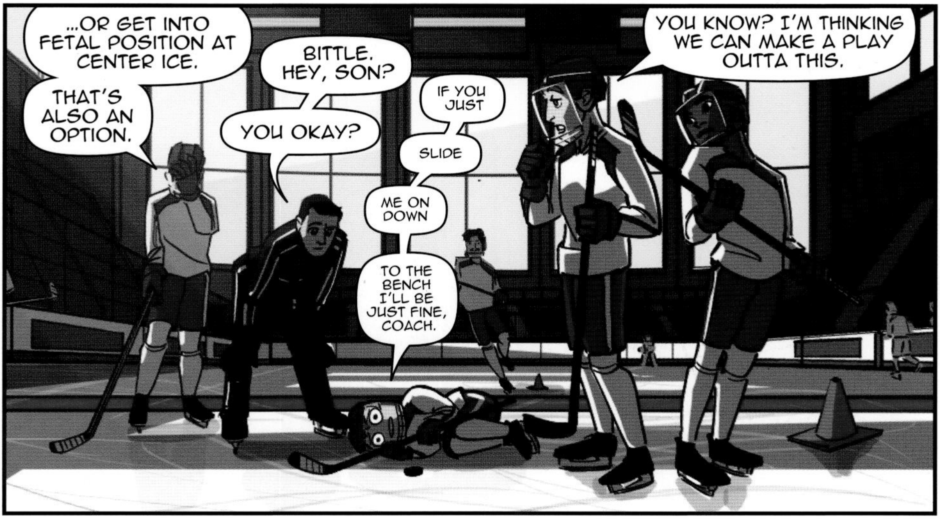
...OR GET INTO FETAL POSITION AT CENTER ICE.
THAT'S ALSO AN OPTION.
BITTLE. HEY, SON?
YOU OKAY?
IF YOU JUST
SLIDE
ME ON DOWN
TO THE BENCH I'LL BE JUST FINE, COACH.
YOU KNOW? I'M THINKING WE CAN MAKE A PLAY OUTTA THIS.

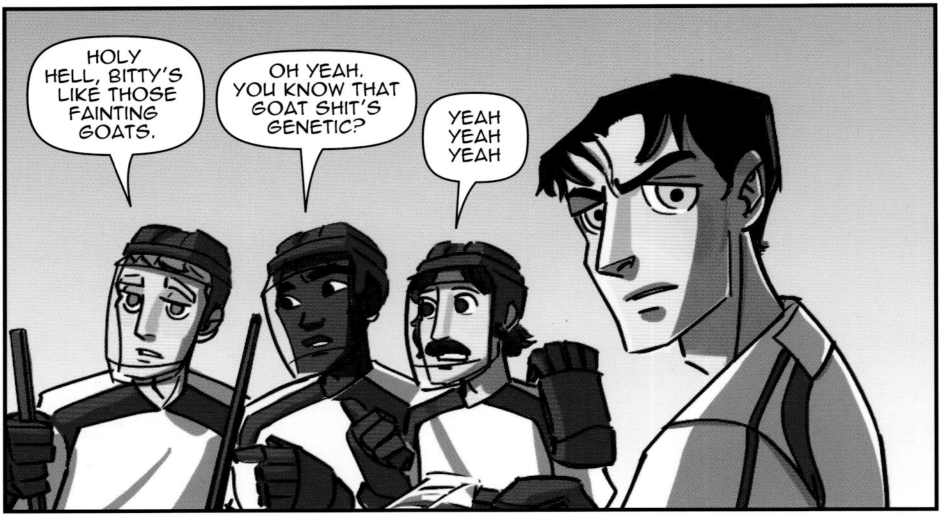
HOLY HELL, BITTY'S LIKE THOSE FAINTING GOATS.
OH YEAH. YOU KNOW THAT GOAT SHIT'S GENETIC?
YEAH YEAH YEAH

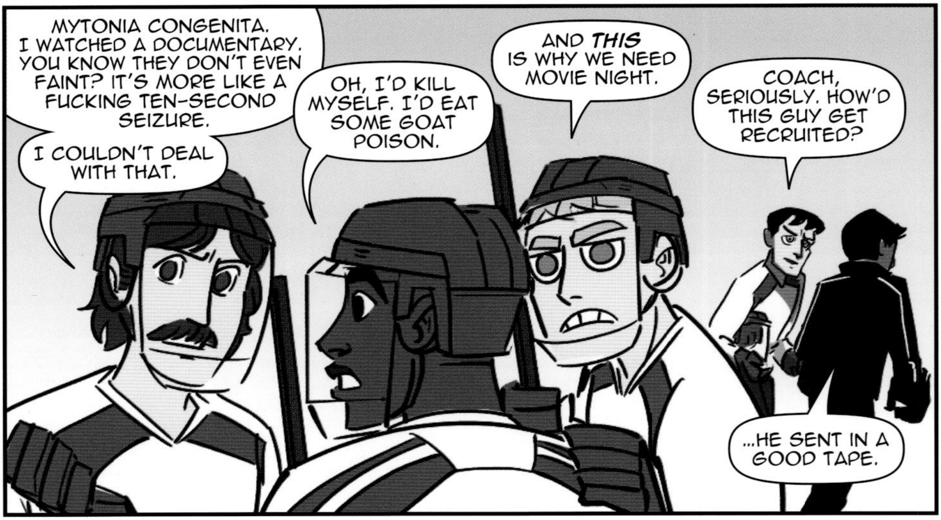
MYTONIA CONGENITA. I WATCHED A DOCUMENTARY. YOU KNOW THEY DON'T EVEN FAINT? IT'S MORE LIKE A FUCKING TEN-SECOND SEIZURE.
I COULDN'T DEAL WITH THAT.
OH, I'D KILL MYSELF. I'D EAT SOME GOAT POISON.
AND *THIS* IS WHY WE NEED MOVIE NIGHT.
COACH, SERIOUSLY. HOW'D THIS GUY GET RECRUITED?
...HE SENT IN A GOOD TAPE.

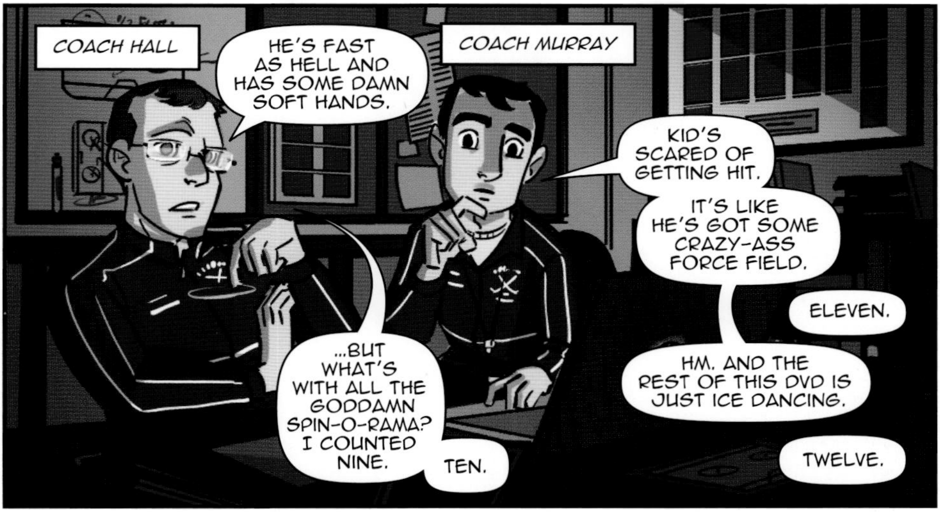
COACH HALL
HE'S FAST AS HELL AND HAS SOME DAMN SOFT HANDS.
COACH MURRAY
KID'S SCARED OF GETTING HIT.
IT'S LIKE HE'S GOT SOME CRAZY-ASS FORCE FIELD.
...BUT WHAT'S WITH ALL THE GODDAMN SPIN-O-RAMA? I COUNTED NINE.
TEN.
ELEVEN.
HM. AND THE REST OF THIS DVD IS JUST ICE DANCING.
TWELVE.

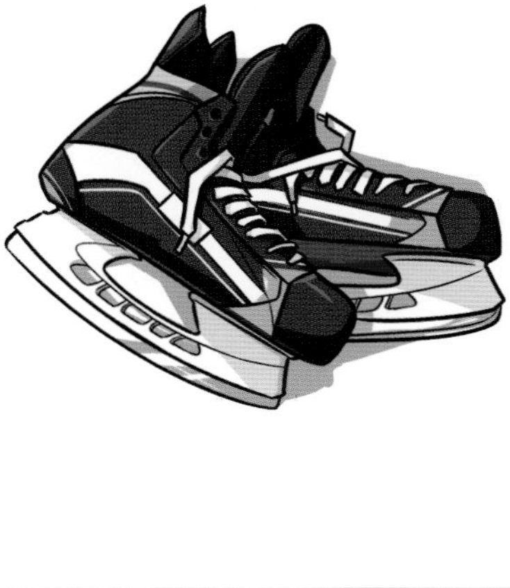

4

THE HAUS

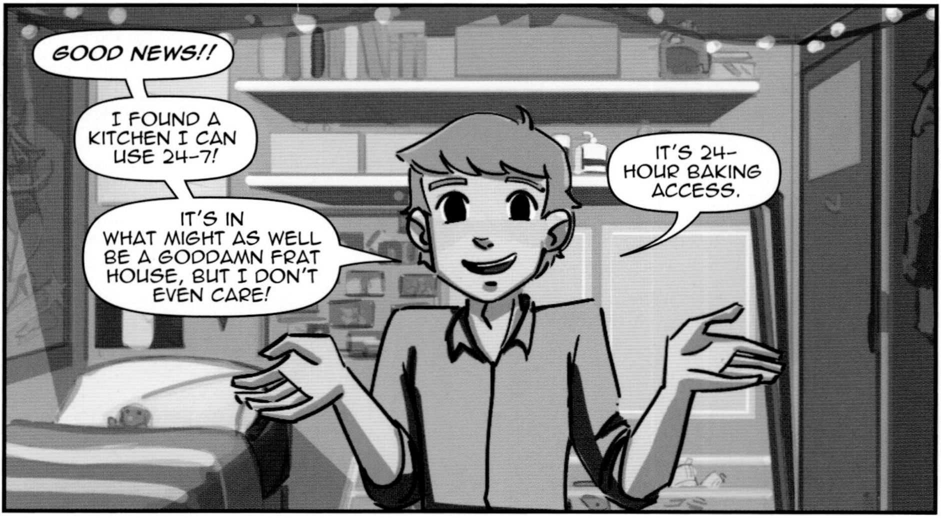
GOOD NEWS!!
I FOUND A KITCHEN I CAN USE 24-7!
IT'S IN WHAT MIGHT AS WELL BE A GODDAMN FRAT HOUSE, BUT I DON'T EVEN CARE!
IT'S 24-HOUR BAKING ACCESS.

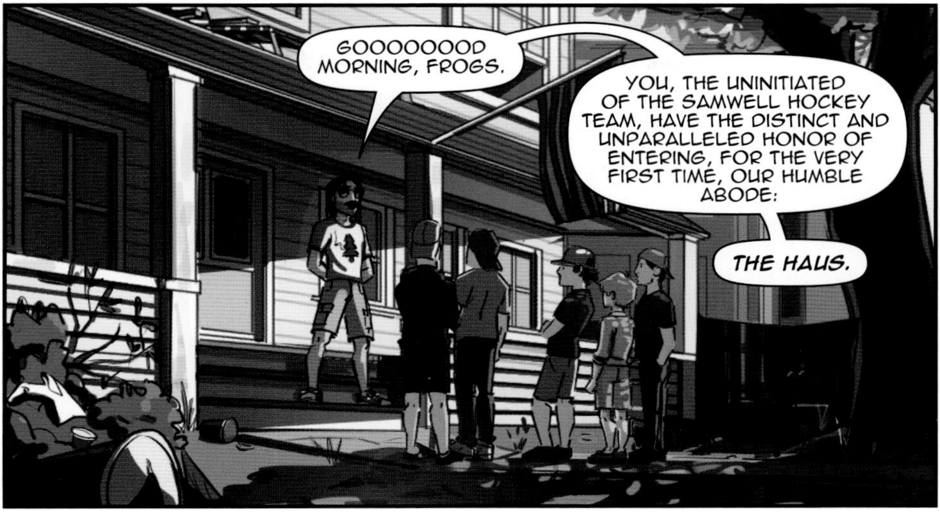
GOOOOOOOD MORNING, FROGS.
YOU, THE UNINITIATED OF THE SAMWELL HOCKEY TEAM, HAVE THE DISTINCT AND UNPARALLELED HONOR OF ENTERING, FOR THE VERY FIRST TIME, OUR HUMBLE ABODE:
THE HAUS.

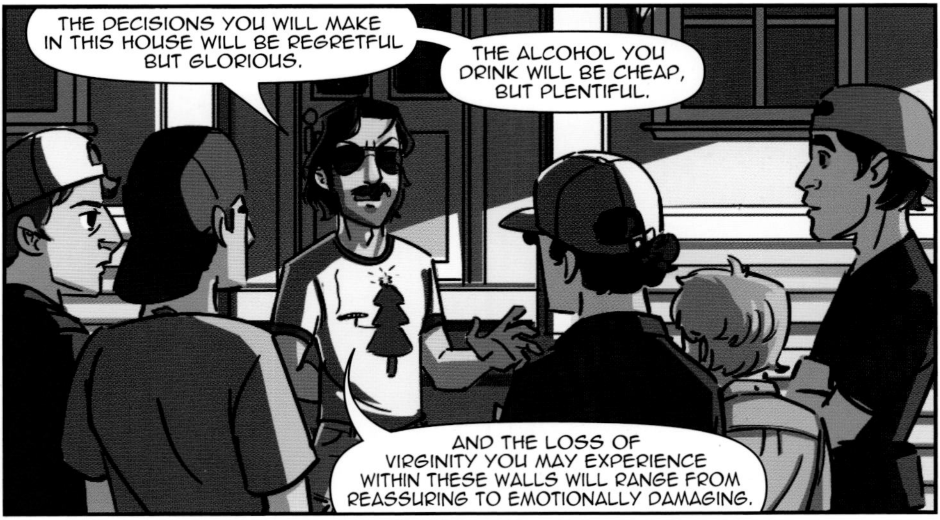
THE DECISIONS YOU WILL MAKE IN THIS HOUSE WILL BE REGRETFUL BUT GLORIOUS.
THE ALCOHOL YOU DRINK WILL BE CHEAP, BUT PLENTIFUL.
AND THE LOSS OF VIRGINITY YOU MAY EXPERIENCE WITHIN THESE WALLS WILL RANGE FROM REASSURING TO EMOTIONALLY DAMAGING.

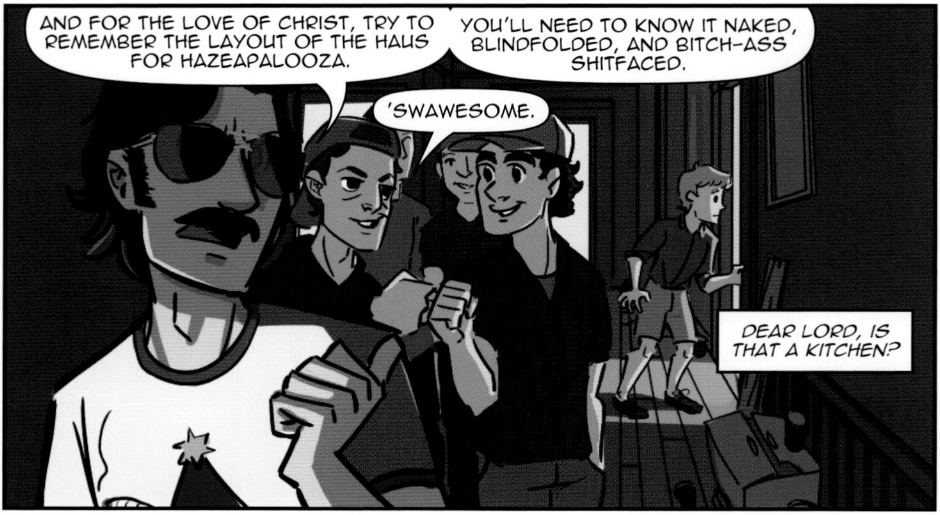
AND FOR THE LOVE OF CHRIST, TRY TO REMEMBER THE LAYOUT OF THE HAUS FOR HAZEAPALOOZA.
YOU'LL NEED TO KNOW IT NAKED, BLINDFOLDED, AND BITCH-ASS SHITFACED.
'SWAWESOME.
DEAR LORD, IS THAT A KITCHEN?

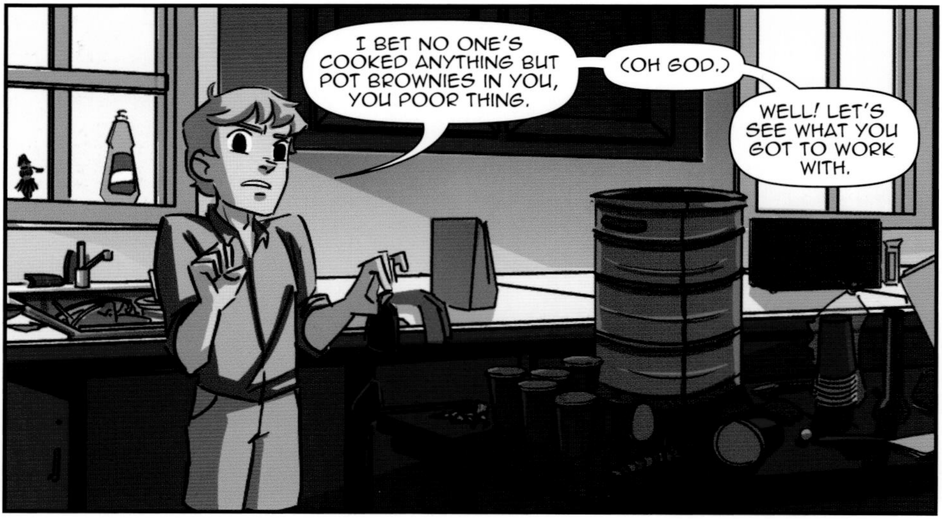
I BET NO ONE'S COOKED ANYTHING BUT POT BROWNIES IN YOU, YOU POOR THING.
(OH GOD.)
WELL! LET'S SEE WHAT YOU GOT TO WORK WITH.

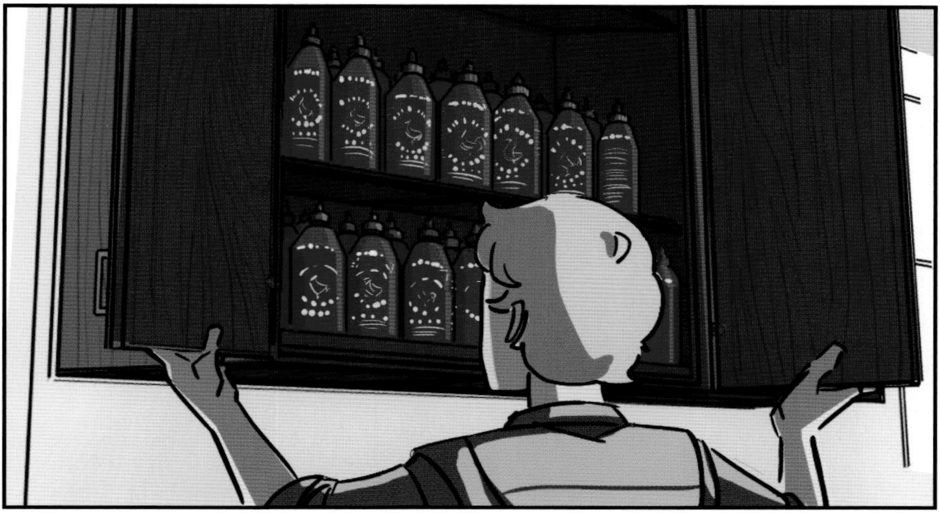

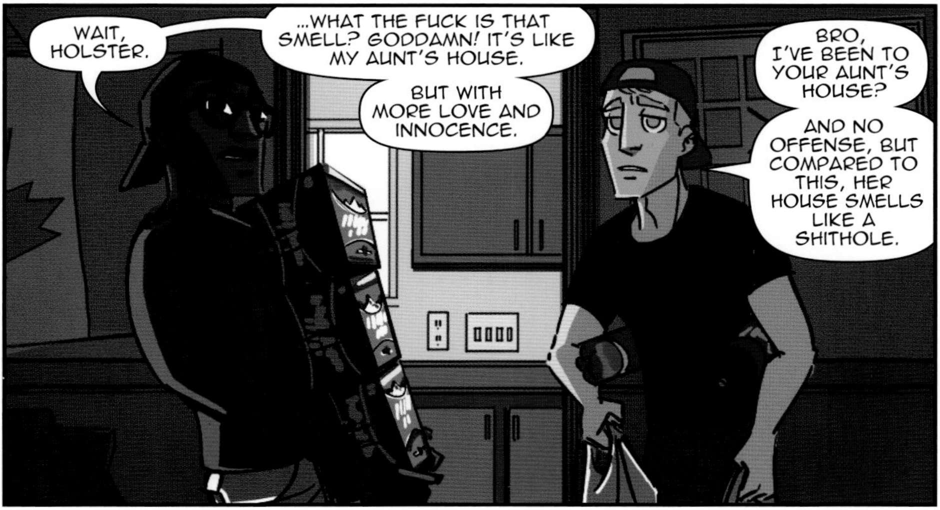
WAIT, HOLSTER.
...WHAT THE FUCK IS THAT SMELL? GODDAMN! IT'S LIKE MY AUNT'S HOUSE.
BUT WITH MORE LOVE AND INNOCENCE.
BRO, I'VE BEEN TO YOUR AUNT'S HOUSE?
AND NO OFFENSE, BUT COMPARED TO THIS, HER HOUSE SMELLS LIKE A SHITHOLE.

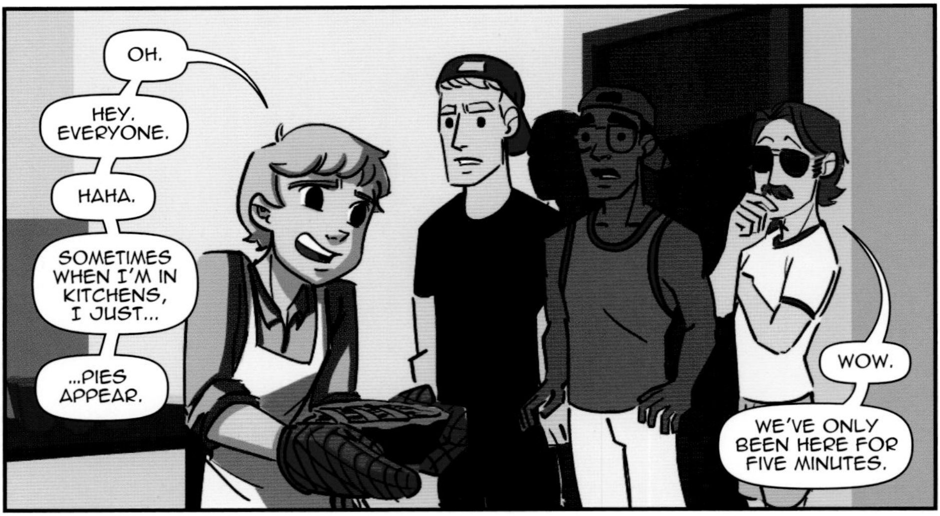
OH.
HEY. EVERYONE.
HAHA.
SOMETIMES WHEN I'M IN KITCHENS, I JUST...
...PIES APPEAR.
WOW.
WE'VE ONLY BEEN HERE FOR FIVE MINUTES.

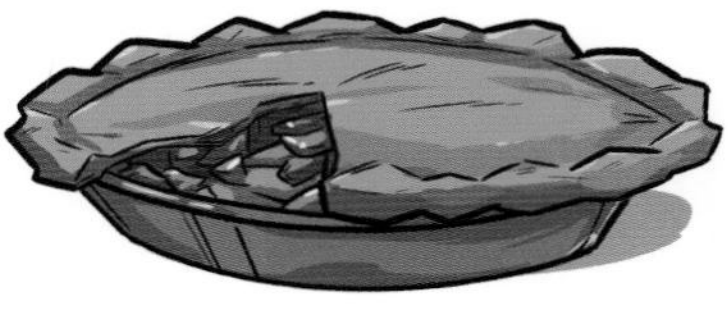

5

BAD BOB ZIMMERMANN

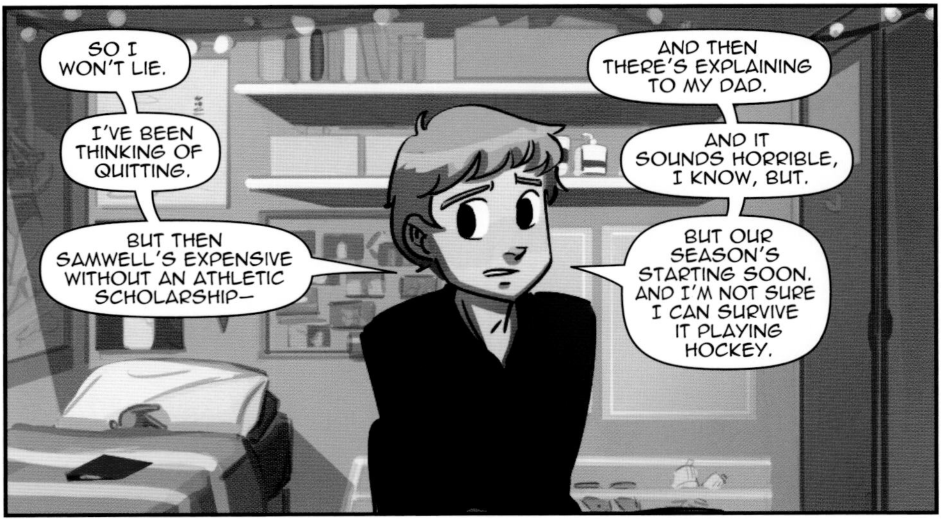
SO I WON'T LIE.
I'VE BEEN THINKING OF QUITTING.
BUT THEN SAMWELL'S EXPENSIVE WITHOUT AN ATHLETIC SCHOLARSHIP—
AND THEN THERE'S EXPLAINING TO MY DAD.
AND IT SOUNDS HORRIBLE, I KNOW, BUT.
BUT OUR SEASON'S STARTING SOON. AND I'M NOT SURE I CAN SURVIVE IT PLAYING HOCKEY.

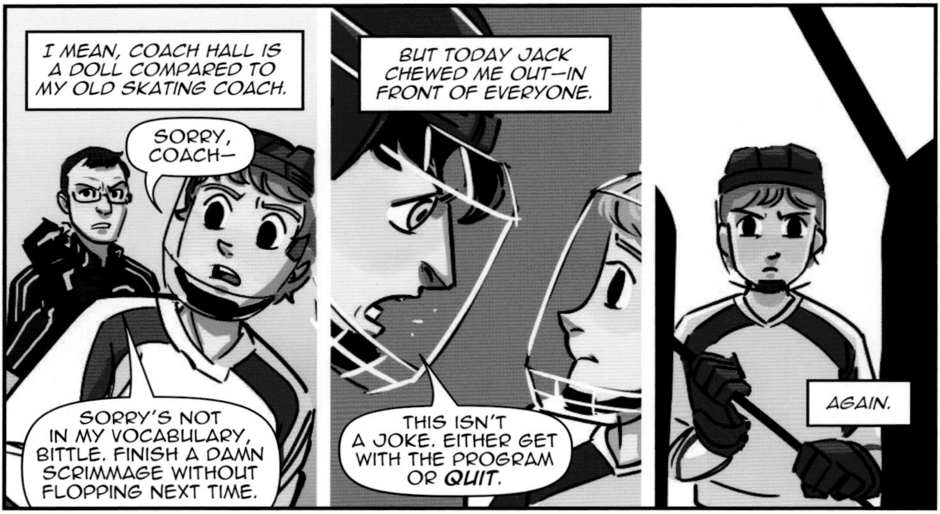
I MEAN, COACH HALL IS A DOLL COMPARED TO MY OLD SKATING COACH.
SORRY, COACH—
SORRY'S NOT IN MY VOCABULARY, BITTLE. FINISH A DAMN SCRIMMAGE WITHOUT FLOPPING NEXT TIME.
BUT TODAY JACK CHEWED ME OUT—IN FRONT OF EVERYONE.
THIS ISN'T A JOKE. EITHER GET WITH THE PROGRAM OR **QUIT**.
AGAIN.

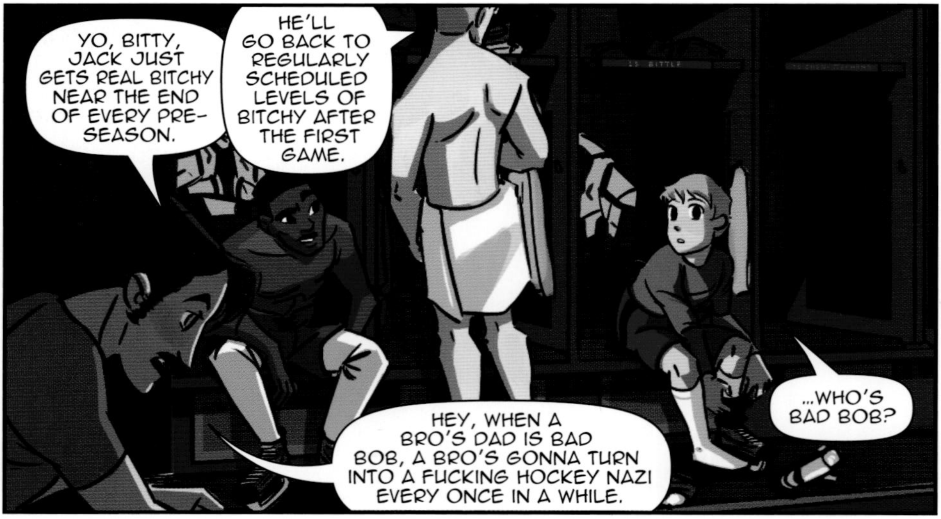
YO, BITTY, JACK JUST GETS REAL BITCHY NEAR THE END OF EVERY PRE-SEASON.
HE'LL GO BACK TO REGULARLY SCHEDULED LEVELS OF BITCHY AFTER THE FIRST GAME.
HEY, WHEN A BRO'S DAD IS BAD BOB, A BRO'S GONNA TURN INTO A FUCKING HOCKEY NAZI EVERY ONCE IN A WHILE.
...WHO'S BAD BOB?

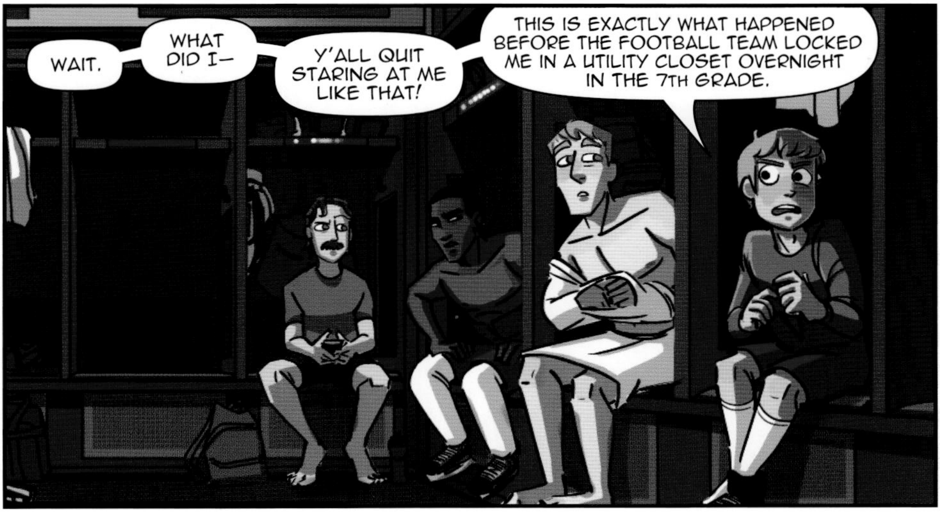
WAIT.
WHAT DID I—
Y'ALL QUIT STARING AT ME LIKE THAT!
THIS IS EXACTLY WHAT HAPPENED BEFORE THE FOOTBALL TEAM LOCKED ME IN A UTILITY CLOSET OVERNIGHT IN THE 7TH GRADE.

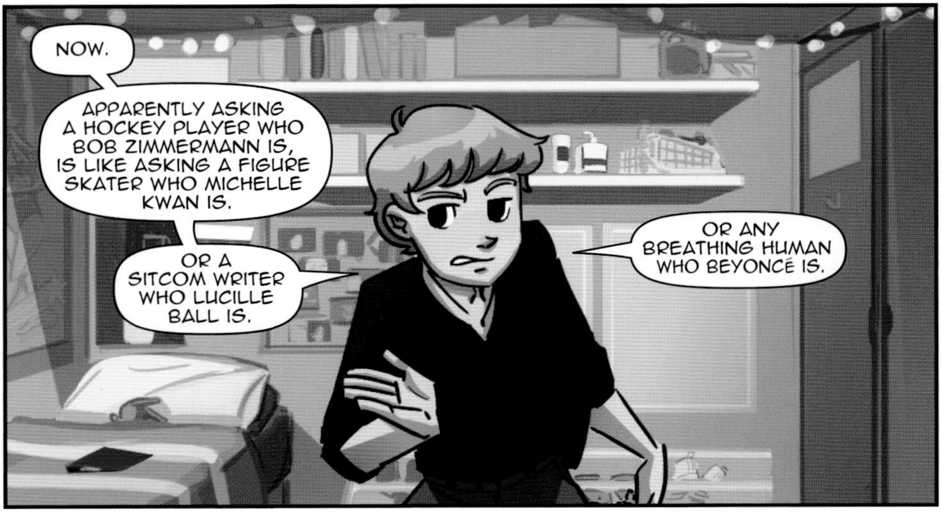
NOW.
APPARENTLY ASKING A HOCKEY PLAYER WHO BOB ZIMMERMANN IS, IS LIKE ASKING A FIGURE SKATER WHO MICHELLE KWAN IS.
OR A SITCOM WRITER WHO LUCILLE BALL IS.
OR ANY BREATHING HUMAN WHO BEYONCÉ IS.

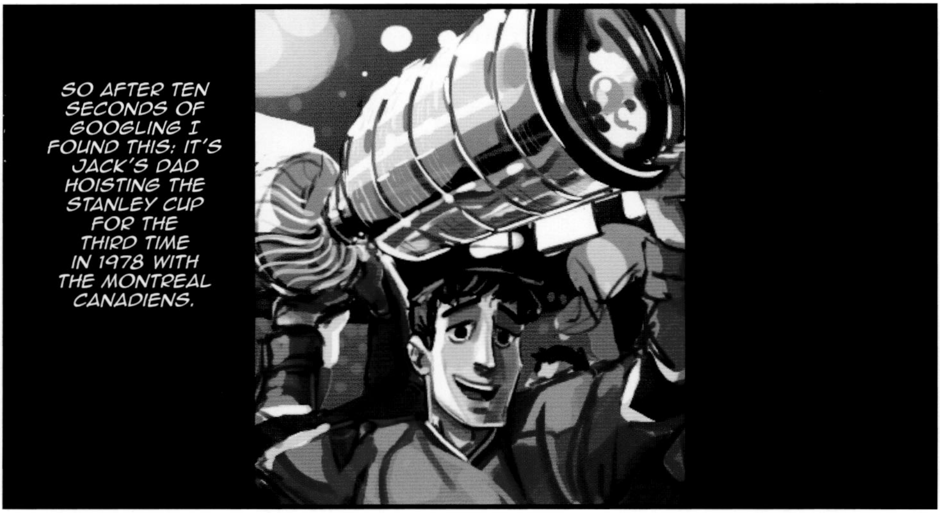
SO AFTER TEN SECONDS OF GOOGLING I FOUND THIS: IT'S JACK'S DAD HOISTING THE STANLEY CUP FOR THE THIRD TIME IN 1978 WITH THE MONTREAL CANADIENS.

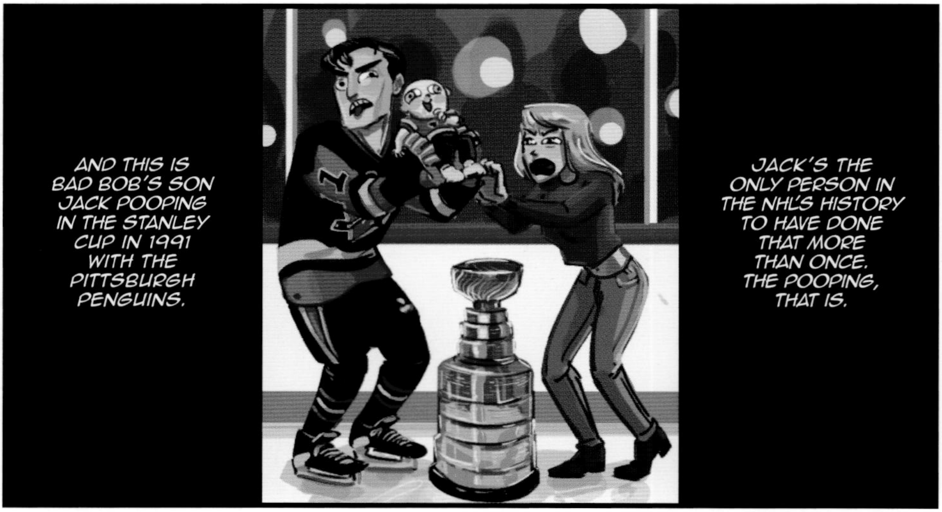
AND THIS IS BAD BOB'S SON JACK POOPING IN THE STANLEY CUP IN 1991 WITH THE PITTSBURGH PENGUINS.
JACK'S THE ONLY PERSON IN THE NHL'S HISTORY TO HAVE DONE THAT MORE THAN ONCE. THE POOPING, THAT IS.

6

THE HOCKEY PRINCE

Once upon a time there was a prince.

From a young age he knew he was destined for greatness, for he knew that one day he would inherit the kingdom from his father.

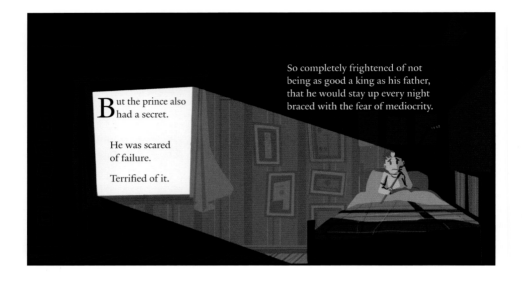

But the prince also had a secret.

He was scared of failure.

Terrified of it.

So completely frightened of not being as good a king as his father, that he would stay up every night braced with the fear of mediocrity.

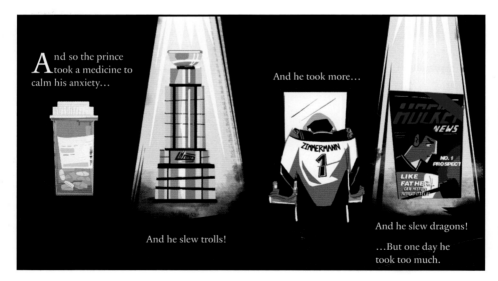

And so the prince took a medicine to calm his anxiety...

And he took more...

And he slew trolls!

ZIMMERMANN
1

HULK NEWS

NO. 1 PROSPECT

LIKE FATHER

And he slew dragons!

...But one day he took too much.

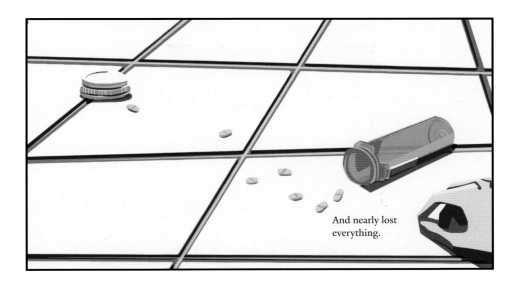

And nearly lost everything.

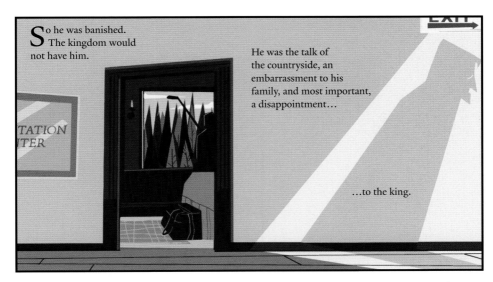

So he was banished. The kingdom would not have him.

He was the talk of the countryside, an embarrassment to his family, and most important, a disappointment…

…to the king.

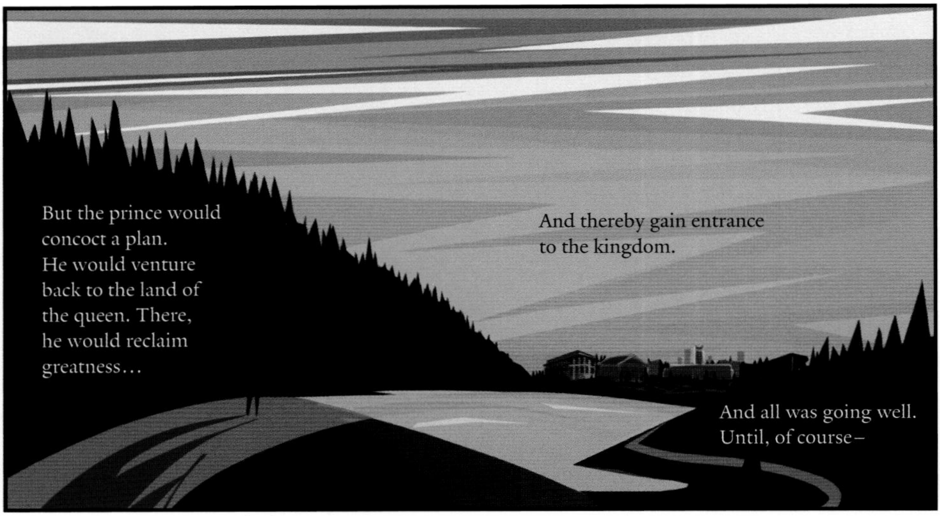
But the prince would concoct a plan. He would venture back to the land of the queen. There, he would reclaim greatness...
And thereby gain entrance to the kingdom.
And all was going well. Until, of course–

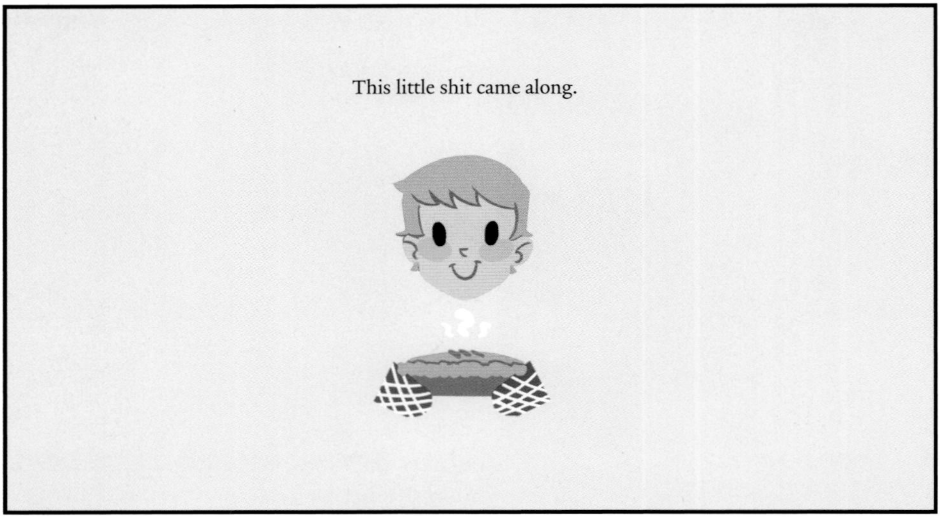
This little shit came along.

7

ASSIST!

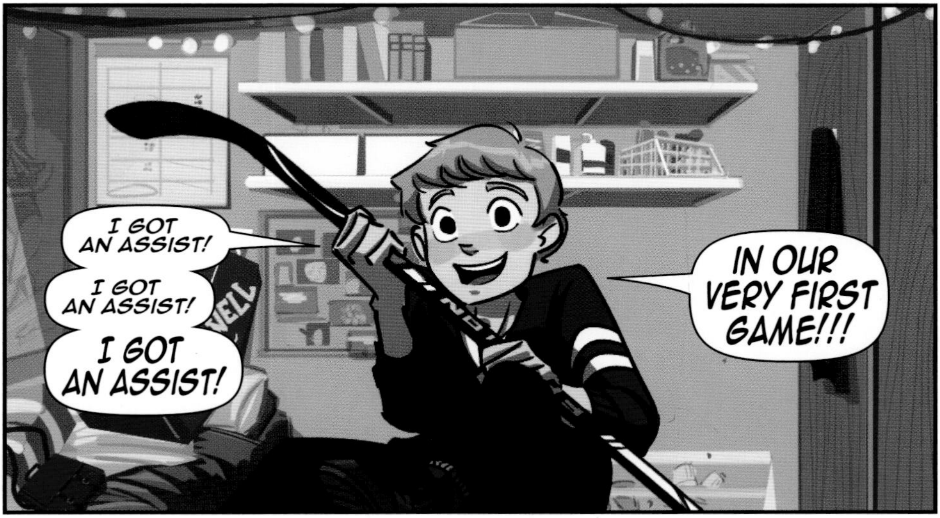
I GOT AN ASSIST!
I GOT AN ASSIST!
I GOT AN ASSIST!
IN OUR VERY FIRST GAME!!!

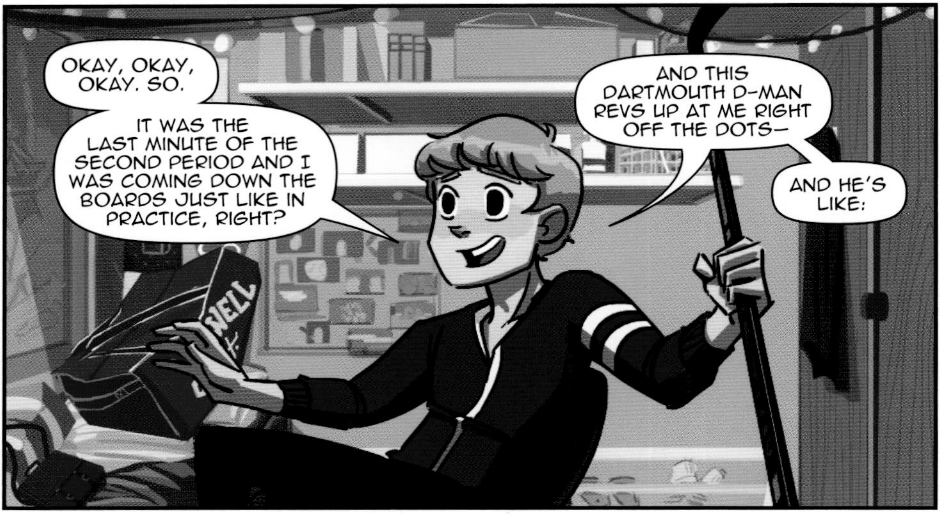
OKAY, OKAY, OKAY. SO.
IT WAS THE LAST MINUTE OF THE SECOND PERIOD AND I WAS COMING DOWN THE BOARDS JUST LIKE IN PRACTICE, RIGHT?
AND THIS DARTMOUTH D-MAN REVS UP AT ME RIGHT OFF THE DOTS—
AND HE'S LIKE:

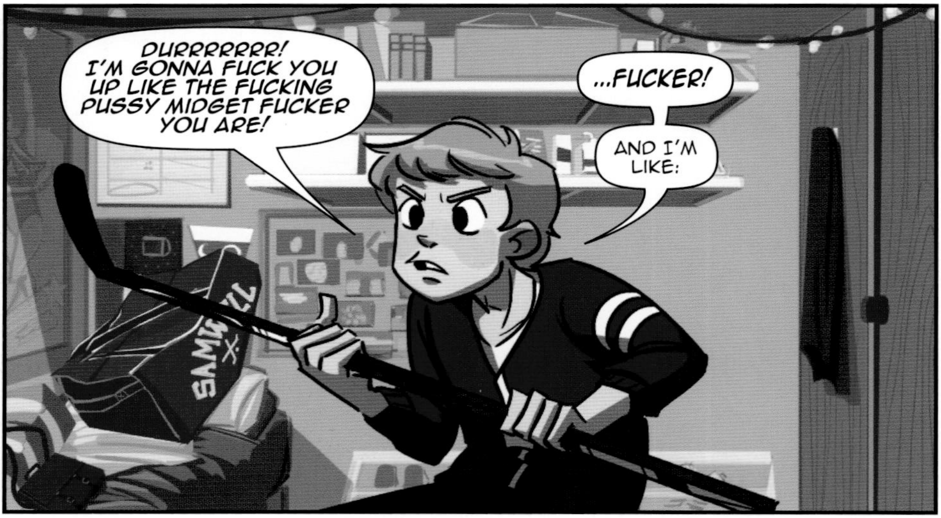
DURRRRRRR! I'M GONNA FUCK YOU UP LIKE THE FUCKING PUSSY MIDGET FUCKER YOU ARE!
...FUCKER!
AND I'M LIKE:

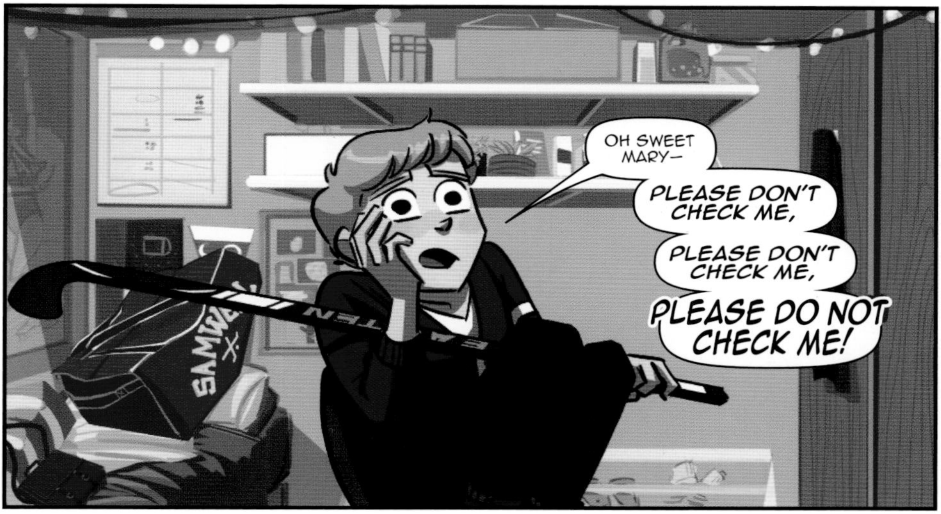
OH SWEET MARY—
PLEASE DON'T CHECK ME,
PLEASE DON'T CHECK ME,
PLEASE DO NOT CHECK ME!

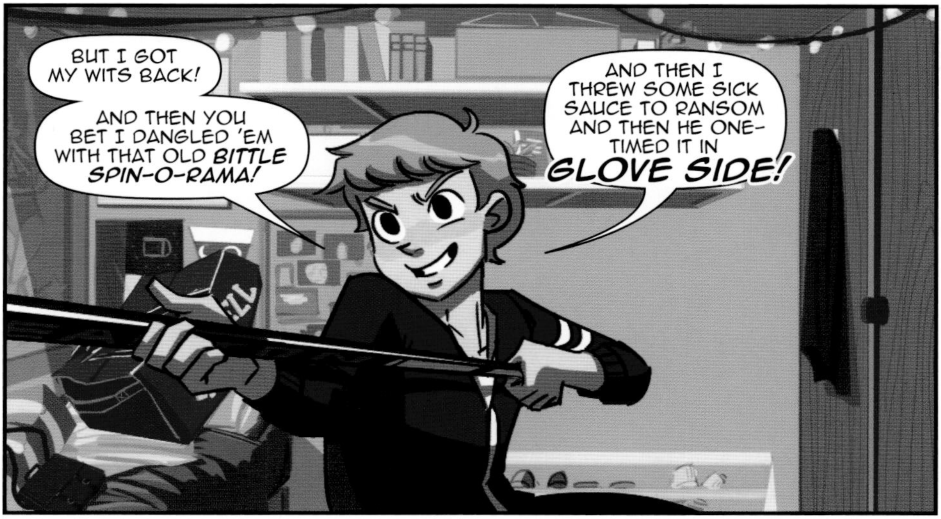
BUT I GOT MY WITS BACK!
AND THEN YOU BET I DANGLED 'EM WITH THAT OLD BITTLE SPIN-O-RAMA!
AND THEN I THREW SOME SICK SAUCE TO RANSOM AND THEN HE ONE-TIMED IT IN GLOVE SIDE!

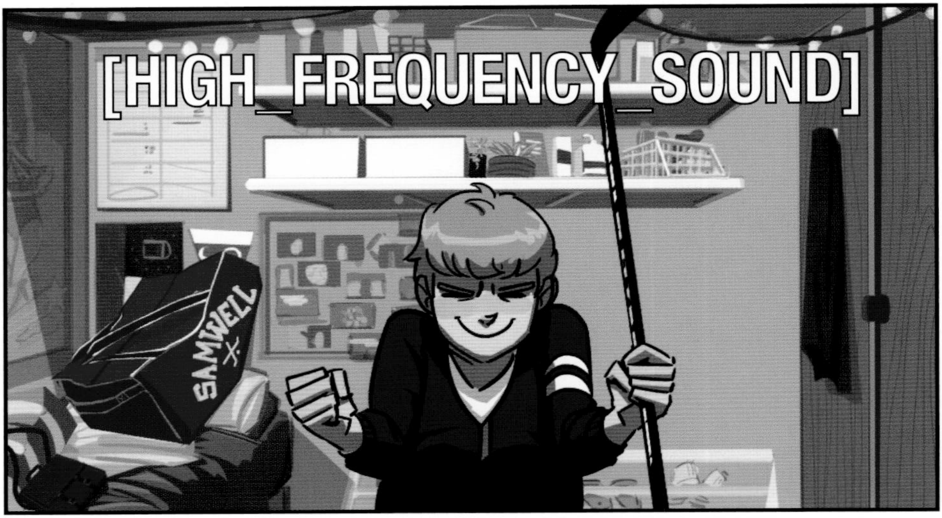
[HIGH_FREQUENCY_SOUND]
SAMWELL

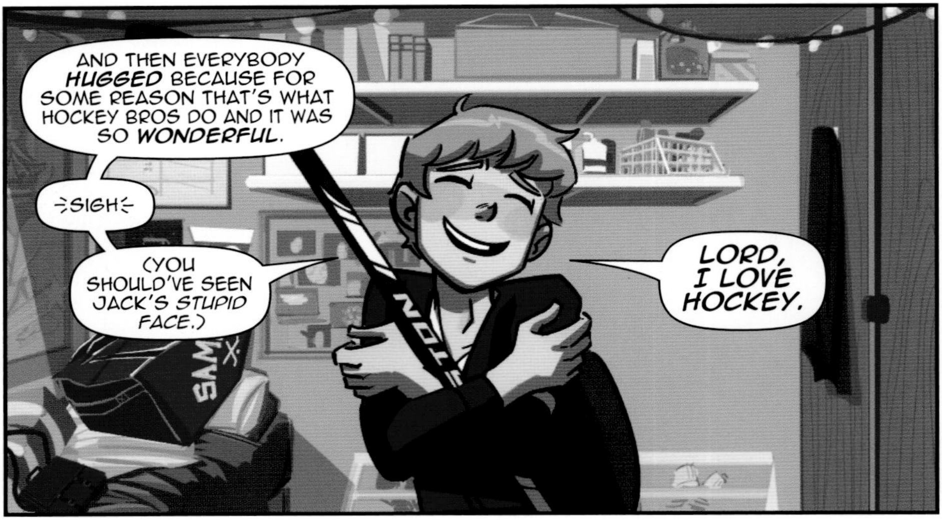
AND THEN EVERYBODY HUGGED BECAUSE FOR SOME REASON THAT'S WHAT HOCKEY BROS DO AND IT WAS SO WONDERFUL.
SIGH
(YOU SHOULD'VE SEEN JACK'S STUPID FACE.)
LORD, I LOVE HOCKEY.

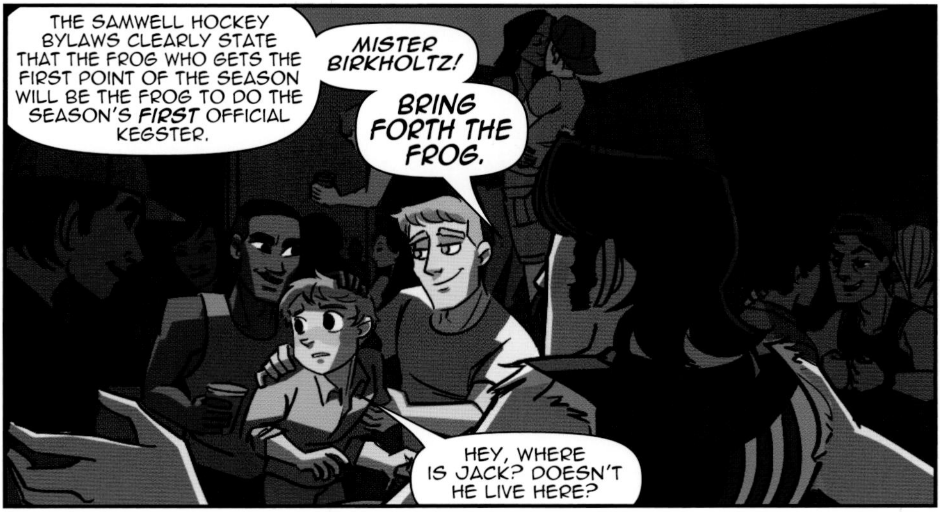
THE SAMWELL HOCKEY BYLAWS CLEARLY STATE THAT THE FROG WHO GETS THE FIRST POINT OF THE SEASON WILL BE THE FROG TO DO THE SEASON'S *FIRST* OFFICIAL KEGSTER.
MISTER BIRKHOLTZ!
BRING FORTH THE FROG.
HEY, WHERE IS JACK? DOESN'T HE LIVE HERE?

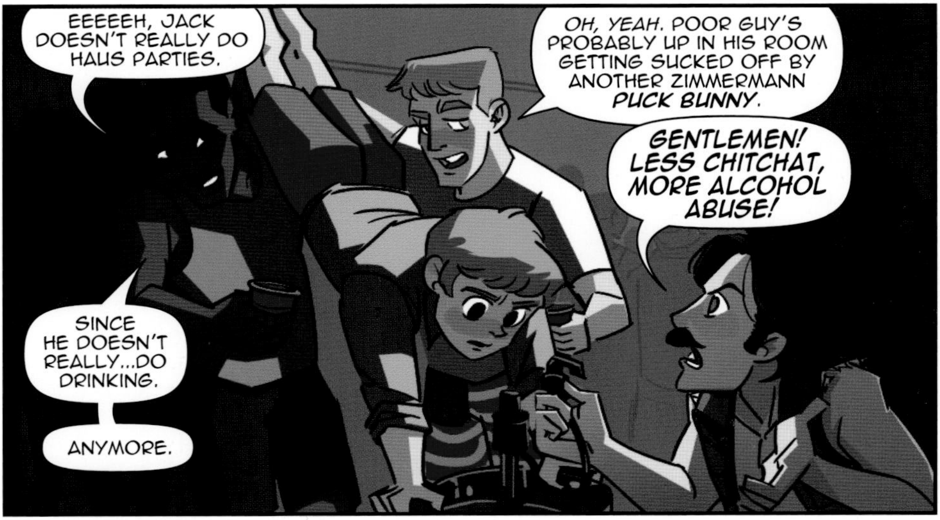
EEEEEH, JACK DOESN'T REALLY DO HAUS PARTIES.
OH, YEAH. POOR GUY'S PROBABLY UP IN HIS ROOM GETTING SUCKED OFF BY ANOTHER ZIMMERMANN *PUCK BUNNY*.
GENTLEMEN! LESS CHITCHAT, MORE ALCOHOL ABUSE!
SINCE HE DOESN'T REALLY...DO DRINKING.
ANYMORE.

8

CHECKING CLINIC

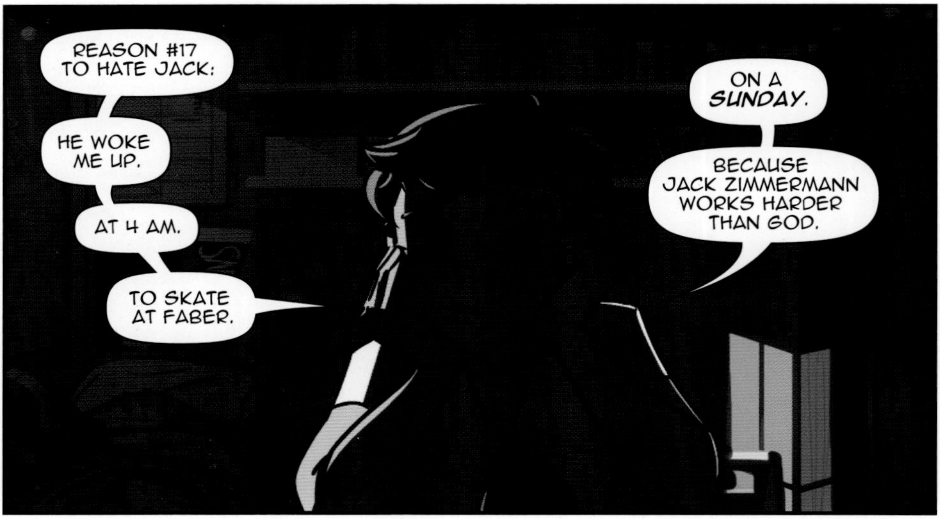
REASON #17 TO HATE JACK:
HE WOKE ME UP.
AT 4 AM.
TO SKATE AT FABER.
ON A *SUNDAY*.
BECAUSE JACK ZIMMERMANN WORKS HARDER THAN GOD.

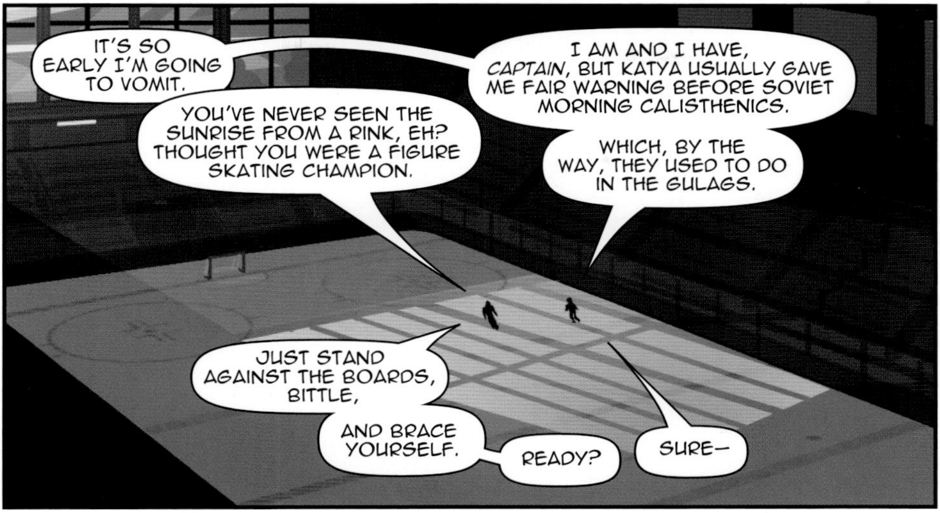
IT'S SO EARLY I'M GOING TO VOMIT.
YOU'VE NEVER SEEN THE SUNRISE FROM A RINK, EH? THOUGHT YOU WERE A FIGURE SKATING CHAMPION.
I AM AND I HAVE, *CAPTAIN*, BUT KATYA USUALLY GAVE ME FAIR WARNING BEFORE SOVIET MORNING CALISTHENICS.
WHICH, BY THE WAY, THEY USED TO DO IN THE GULAGS.
JUST STAND AGAINST THE BOARDS, BITTLE,
AND BRACE YOURSELF.
READY?
SURE—

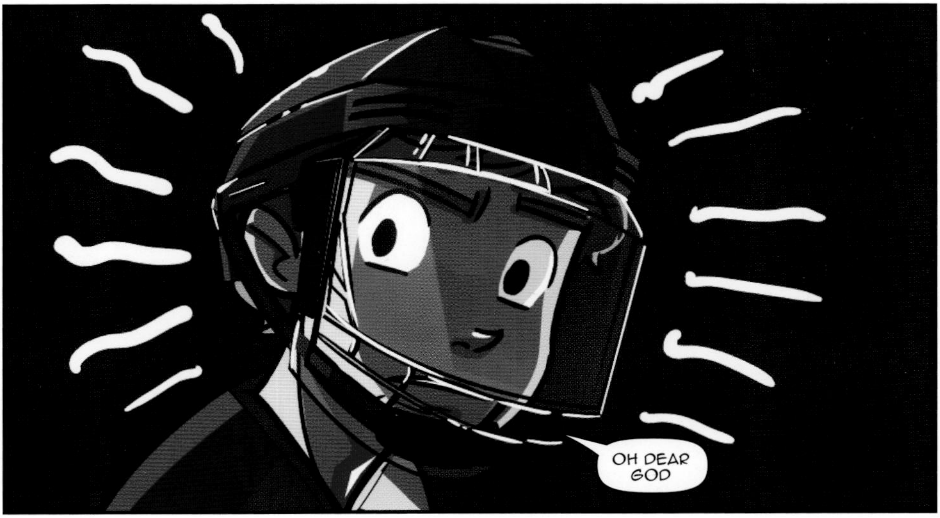
OH DEAR GOD

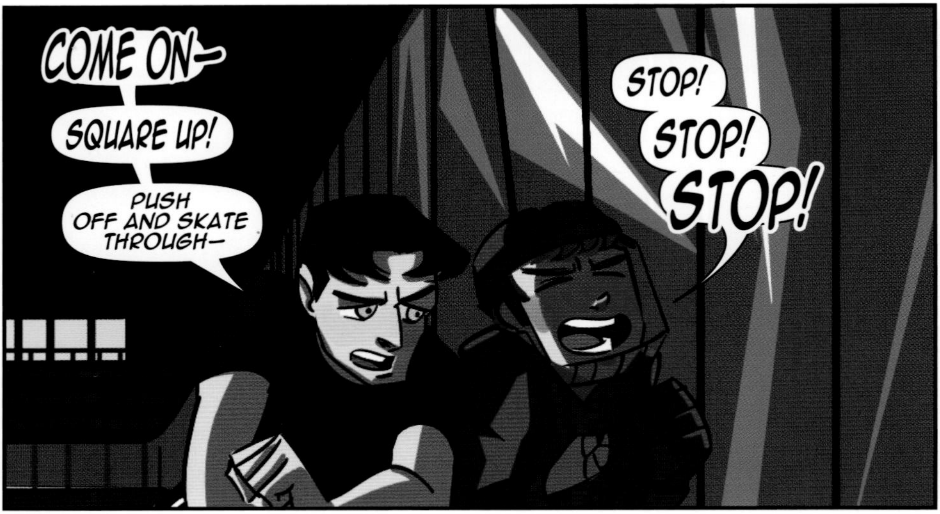
COME ON–
SQUARE UP!
PUSH OFF AND SKATE THROUGH–
STOP!
STOP!
STOP!

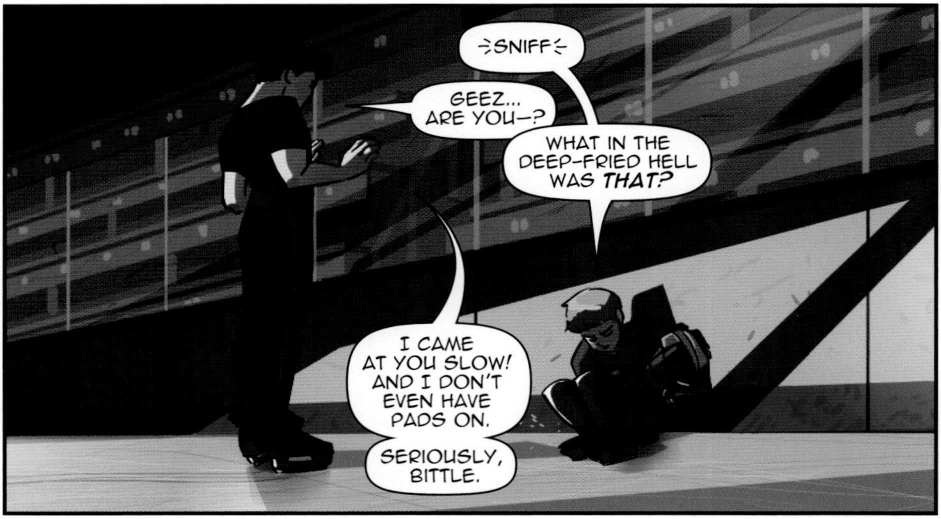
SNIFF
GEEZ... ARE YOU–?
WHAT IN THE DEEP-FRIED HELL WAS *THAT?*
I CAME AT YOU SLOW! AND I DON'T EVEN HAVE PADS ON.
SERIOUSLY, BITTLE.

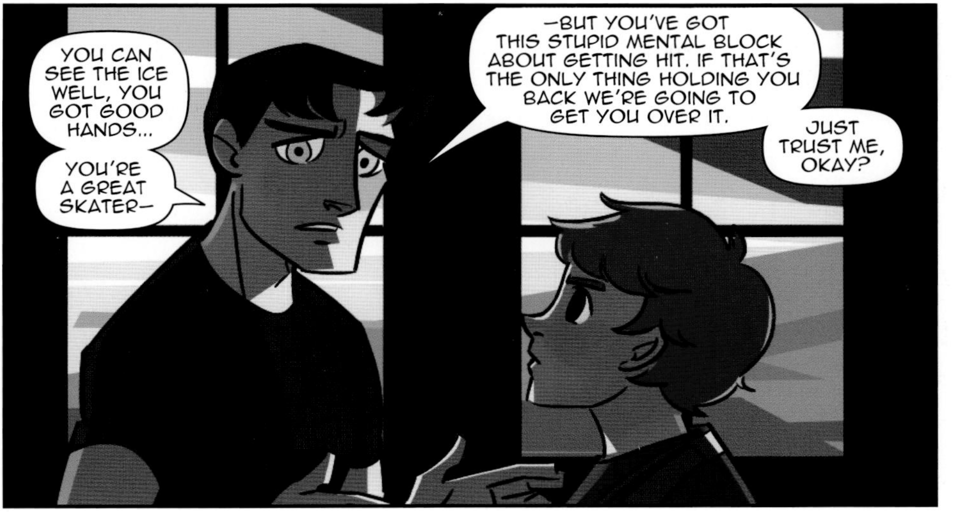
YOU CAN SEE THE ICE WELL, YOU GOT GOOD HANDS...
YOU'RE A GREAT SKATER—
—BUT YOU'VE GOT THIS STUPID MENTAL BLOCK ABOUT GETTING HIT. IF THAT'S THE ONLY THING HOLDING YOU BACK WE'RE GOING TO GET YOU OVER IT.
JUST TRUST ME, OKAY?

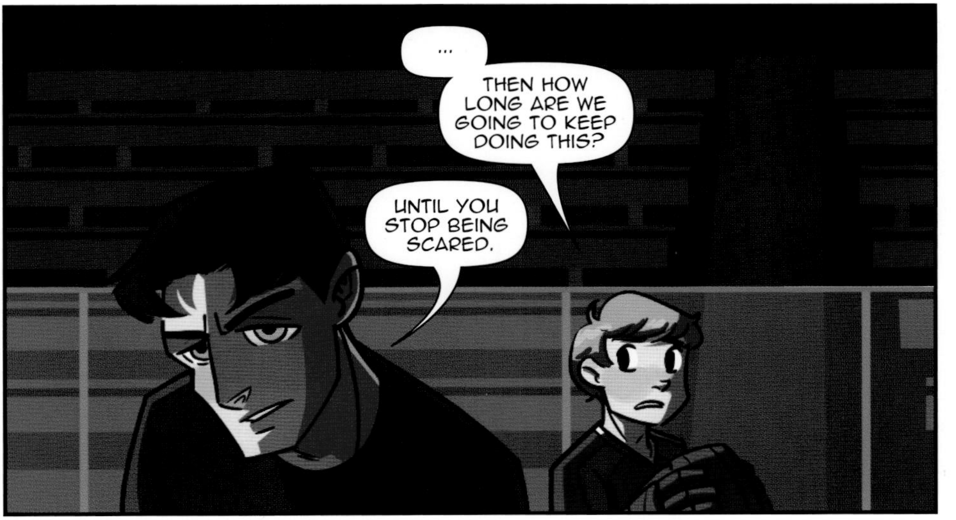
...
THEN HOW LONG ARE WE GOING TO KEEP DOING THIS?
UNTIL YOU STOP BEING SCARED.

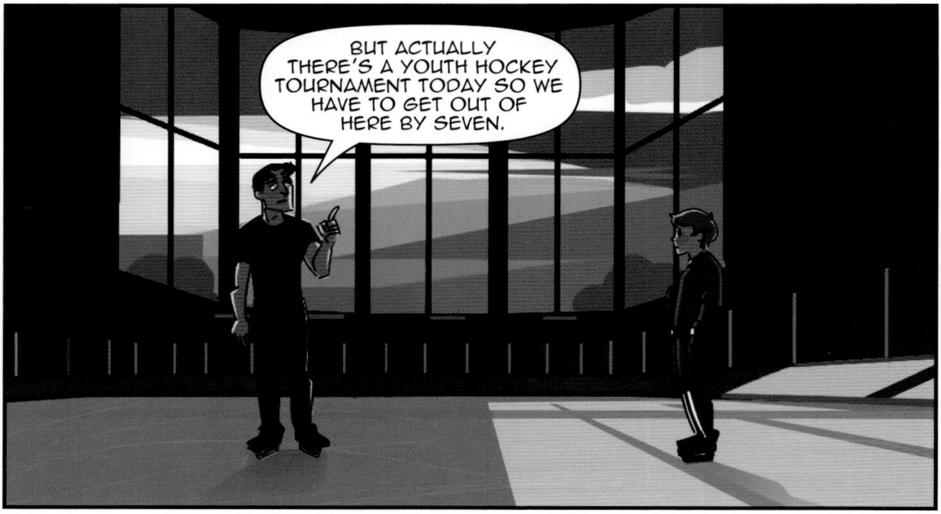
BUT ACTUALLY THERE'S A YOUTH HOCKEY TOURNAMENT TODAY SO WE HAVE TO GET OUT OF HERE BY SEVEN.

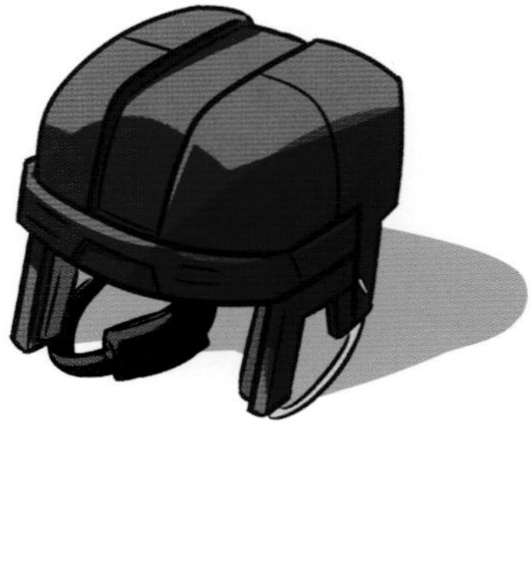

9

FAMILY WEEKEND

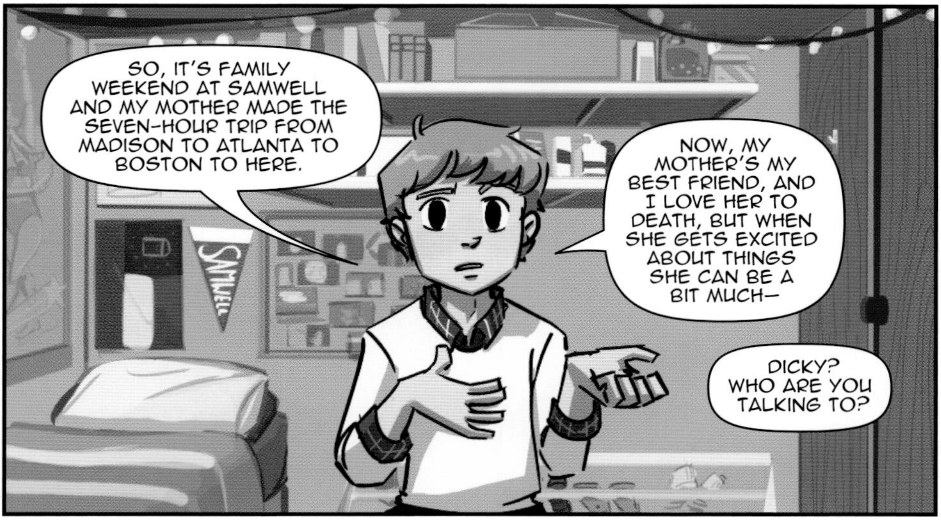
SO, IT'S FAMILY WEEKEND AT SAMWELL AND MY MOTHER MADE THE SEVEN-HOUR TRIP FROM MADISON TO ATLANTA TO BOSTON TO HERE.
NOW, MY MOTHER'S MY BEST FRIEND, AND I LOVE HER TO DEATH, BUT WHEN SHE GETS EXCITED ABOUT THINGS SHE CAN BE A BIT MUCH—
DICKY? WHO ARE YOU TALKING TO?
SAMWELL

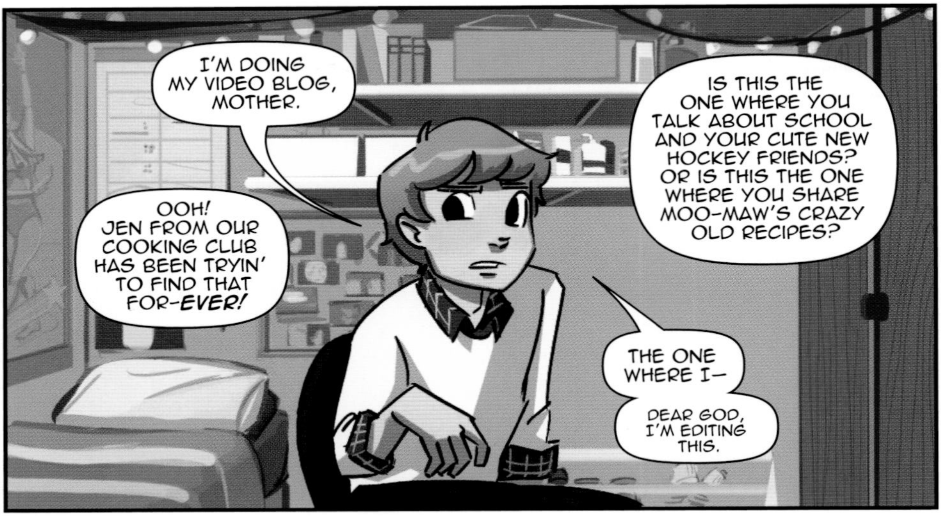
I'M DOING MY VIDEO BLOG, MOTHER.
IS THIS THE ONE WHERE YOU TALK ABOUT SCHOOL AND YOUR CUTE NEW HOCKEY FRIENDS? OR IS THIS THE ONE WHERE YOU SHARE MOO-MAW'S CRAZY OLD RECIPES?
THE ONE WHERE I—
OOH! JEN FROM OUR COOKING CLUB HAS BEEN TRYIN' TO FIND THAT FOR-*EVER!*
DEAR GOD, I'M EDITING THIS.

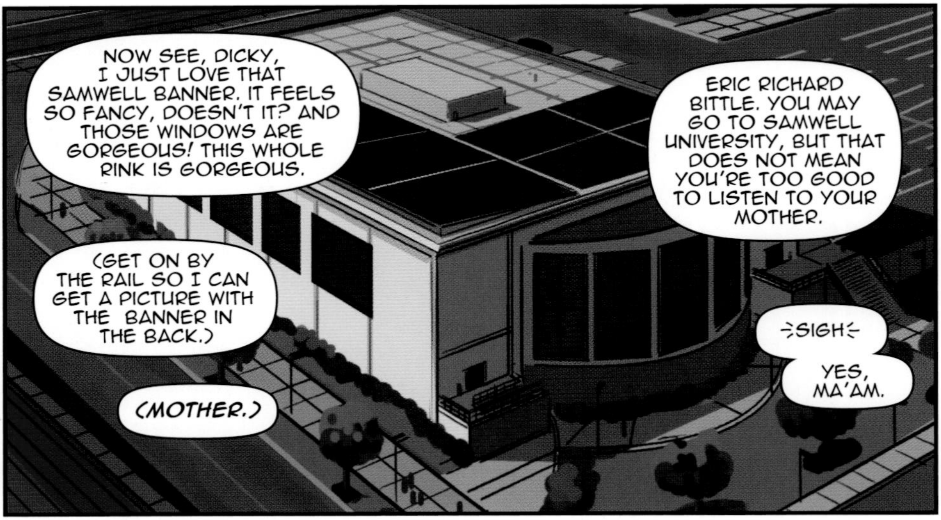
NOW SEE, DICKY, I JUST LOVE THAT SAMWELL BANNER. IT FEELS SO FANCY, DOESN'T IT? AND THOSE WINDOWS ARE GORGEOUS! THIS WHOLE RINK IS GORGEOUS.
(GET ON BY THE RAIL SO I CAN GET A PICTURE WITH THE BANNER IN THE BACK.)
(MOTHER.)
ERIC RICHARD BITTLE. YOU MAY GO TO SAMWELL UNIVERSITY, BUT THAT DOES NOT MEAN YOU'RE TOO GOOD TO LISTEN TO YOUR MOTHER.
SIGH
YES, MA'AM.

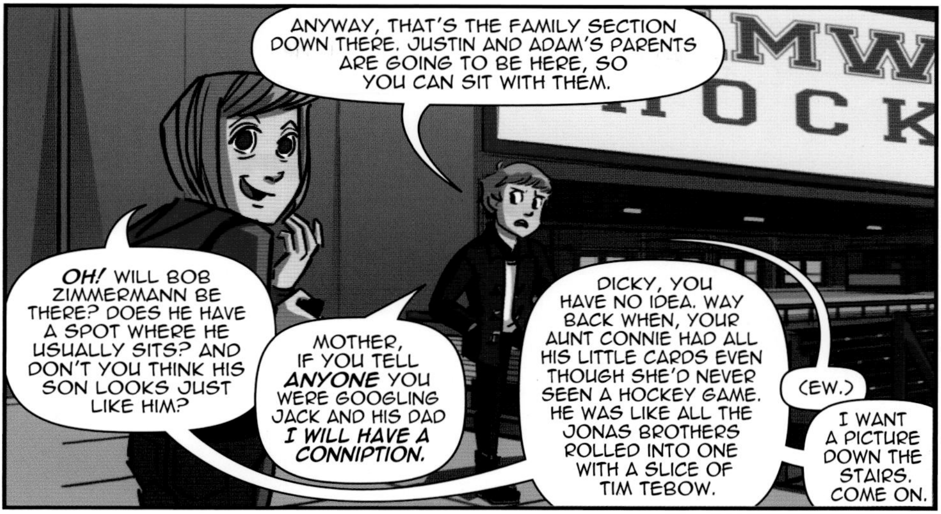
ANYWAY, THAT'S THE FAMILY SECTION DOWN THERE. JUSTIN AND ADAM'S PARENTS ARE GOING TO BE HERE, SO YOU CAN SIT WITH THEM.
OH! WILL BOB ZIMMERMANN BE THERE? DOES HE HAVE A SPOT WHERE HE USUALLY SITS? AND DON'T YOU THINK HIS SON LOOKS JUST LIKE HIM?
MOTHER, IF YOU TELL ANYONE YOU WERE GOOGLING JACK AND HIS DAD I WILL HAVE A CONNIPTION.
DICKY, YOU HAVE NO IDEA. WAY BACK WHEN, YOUR AUNT CONNIE HAD ALL HIS LITTLE CARDS EVEN THOUGH SHE'D NEVER SEEN A HOCKEY GAME. HE WAS LIKE ALL THE JONAS BROTHERS ROLLED INTO ONE WITH A SLICE OF TIM TEBOW.
(EW.)
I WANT A PICTURE DOWN THE STAIRS. COME ON.

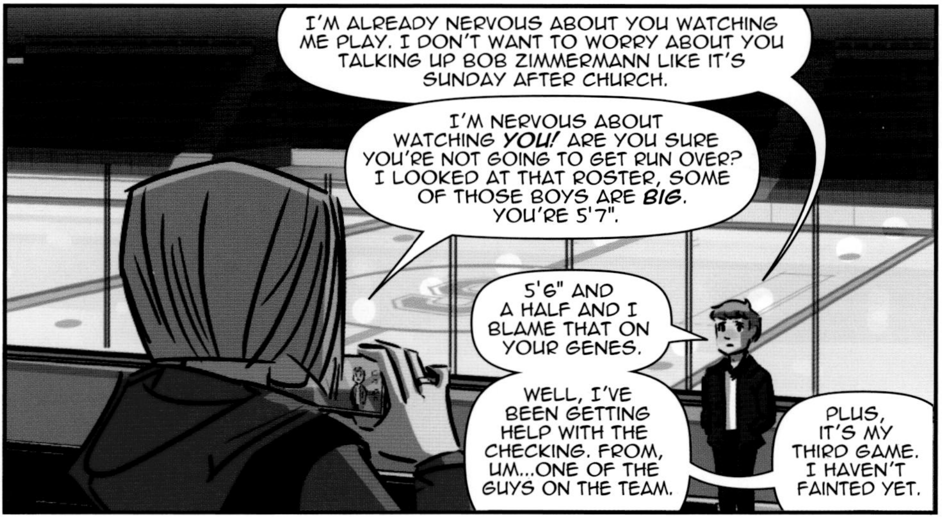
I'M ALREADY NERVOUS ABOUT YOU WATCHING ME PLAY. I DON'T WANT TO WORRY ABOUT YOU TALKING UP BOB ZIMMERMANN LIKE IT'S SUNDAY AFTER CHURCH.
I'M NERVOUS ABOUT WATCHING YOU! ARE YOU SURE YOU'RE NOT GOING TO GET RUN OVER? I LOOKED AT THAT ROSTER, SOME OF THOSE BOYS ARE BIG. YOU'RE 5'7".
5'6" AND A HALF AND I BLAME THAT ON YOUR GENES.
WELL, I'VE BEEN GETTING HELP WITH THE CHECKING. FROM, UM...ONE OF THE GUYS ON THE TEAM.
PLUS, IT'S MY THIRD GAME. I HAVEN'T FAINTED YET.

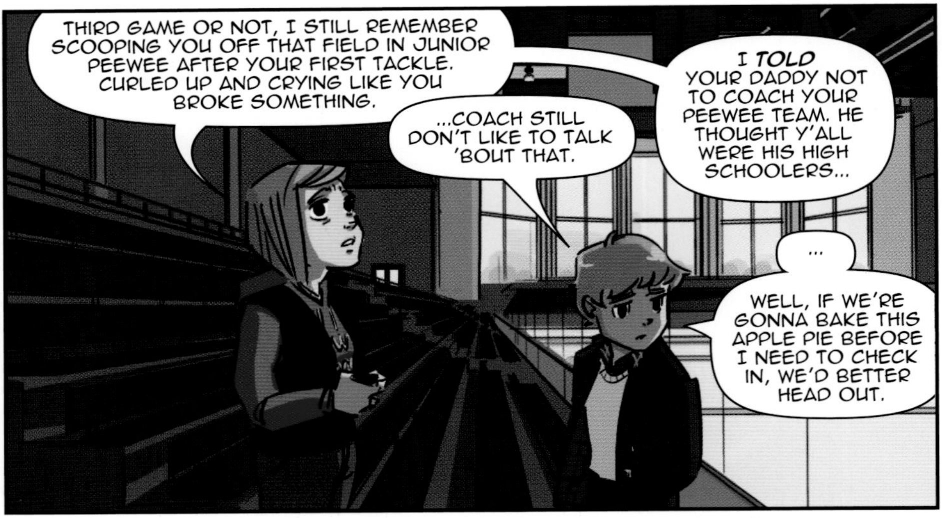
THIRD GAME OR NOT, I STILL REMEMBER SCOOPING YOU OFF THAT FIELD IN JUNIOR PEEWEE AFTER YOUR FIRST TACKLE. CURLED UP AND CRYING LIKE YOU BROKE SOMETHING.
I *TOLD* YOUR DADDY NOT TO COACH YOUR PEEWEE TEAM. HE THOUGHT Y'ALL WERE HIS HIGH SCHOOLERS...
...COACH STILL DON'T LIKE TO TALK 'BOUT THAT.
...
WELL, IF WE'RE GONNA BAKE THIS APPLE PIE BEFORE I NEED TO CHECK IN, WE'D BETTER HEAD OUT.

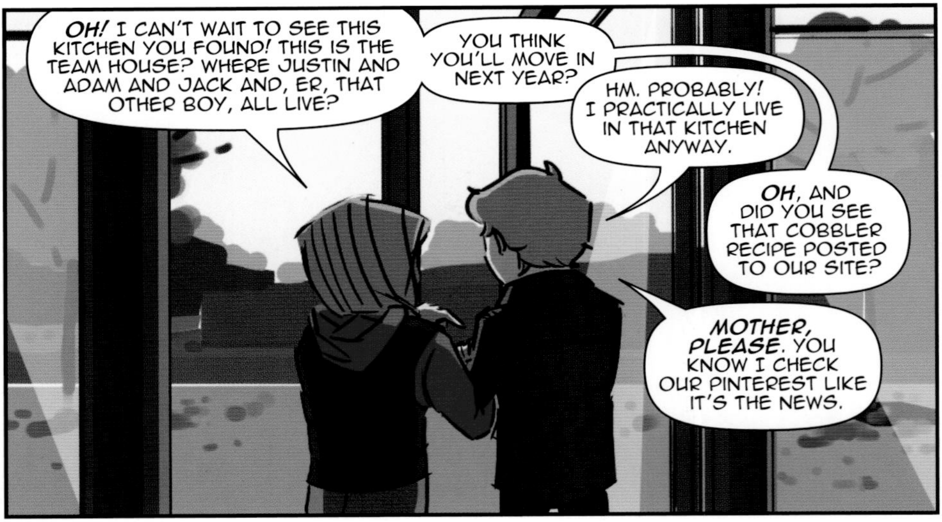
OH! I CAN'T WAIT TO SEE THIS KITCHEN YOU FOUND! THIS IS THE TEAM HOUSE? WHERE JUSTIN AND ADAM AND JACK AND, ER, THAT OTHER BOY, ALL LIVE?
YOU THINK YOU'LL MOVE IN NEXT YEAR?
HM. PROBABLY! I PRACTICALLY LIVE IN THAT KITCHEN ANYWAY.
OH, AND DID YOU SEE THAT COBBLER RECIPE POSTED TO OUR SITE?
MOTHER, PLEASE. YOU KNOW I CHECK OUR PINTEREST LIKE IT'S THE NEWS.

10

SAMWELL VS. YALE — I

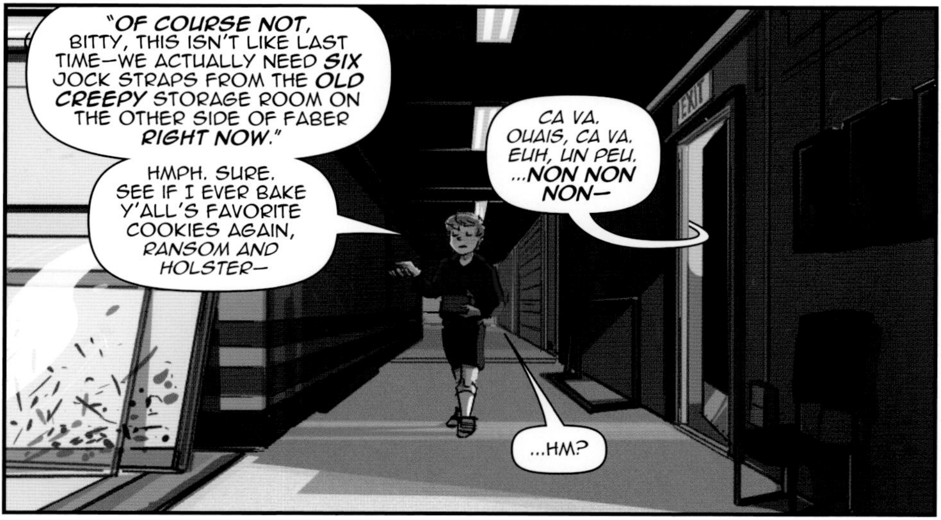
"OF COURSE NOT, BITTY, THIS ISN'T LIKE LAST TIME—WE ACTUALLY NEED SIX JOCK STRAPS FROM THE OLD CREEPY STORAGE ROOM ON THE OTHER SIDE OF FABER RIGHT NOW."
HMPH. SURE. SEE IF I EVER BAKE Y'ALL'S FAVORITE COOKIES AGAIN, RANSOM AND HOLSTER—
CA VA. OUAIS, CA VA. EUH, UN PEU. ...NON NON NON—
...HM?
EXIT

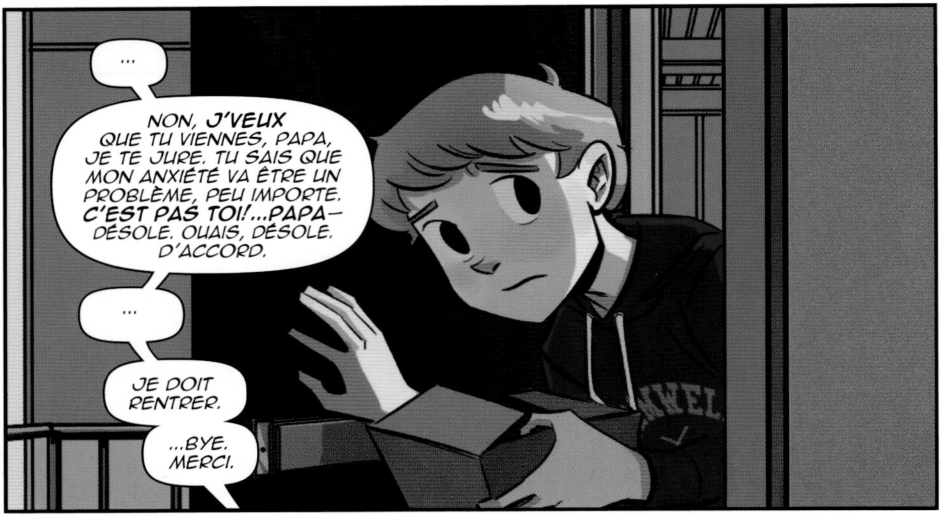
...
NON, J'VEUX QUE TU VIENNES, PAPA, JE TE JURE. TU SAIS QUE MON ANXIÉTÉ VA ÊTRE UN PROBLÈME, PEU IMPORTE. C'EST PAS TOI!...PAPA— DÉSOLE. OUAIS, DÉSOLE. D'ACCORD.
...
JE DOIT RENTRER.
...BYE. MERCI.

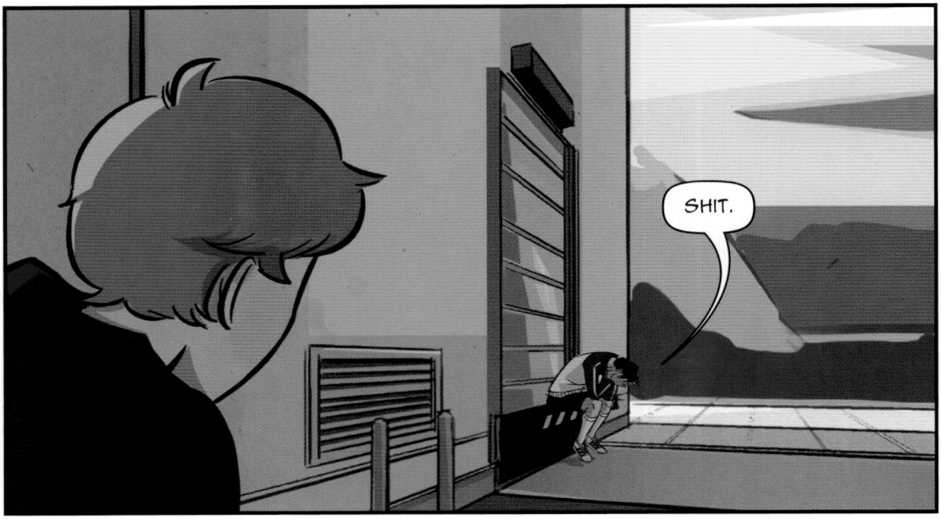
SHIT.

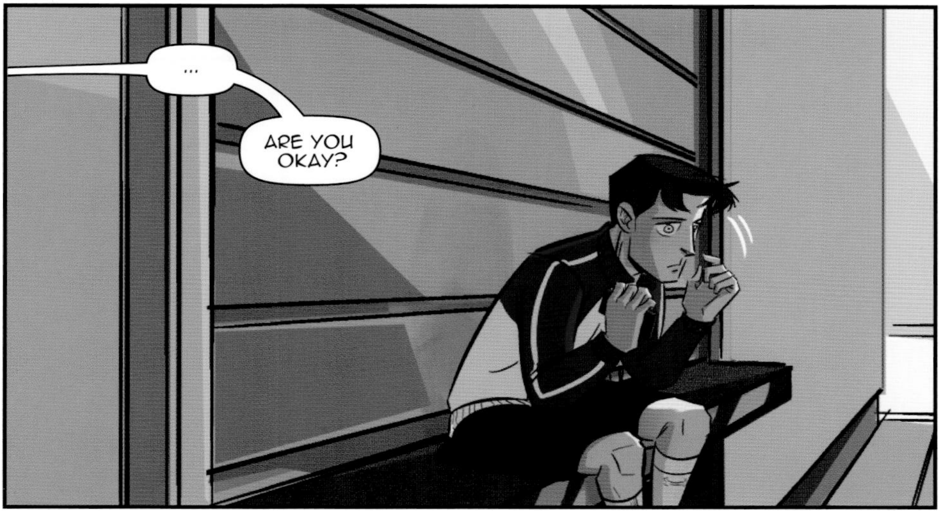
...
ARE YOU OKAY?

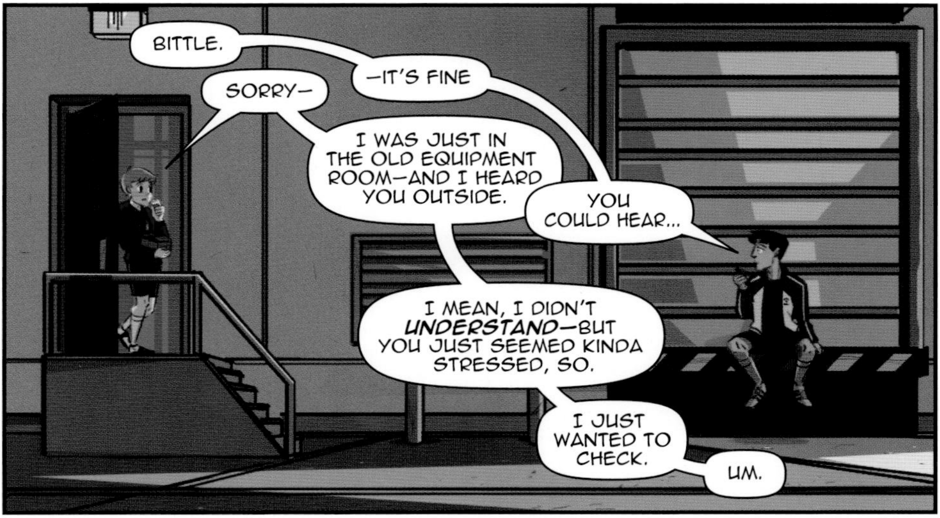
BITTLE.
SORRY—
—IT'S FINE
I WAS JUST IN THE OLD EQUIPMENT ROOM—AND I HEARD YOU OUTSIDE.
YOU COULD HEAR...
I MEAN, I DIDN'T UNDERSTAND—BUT YOU JUST SEEMED KINDA STRESSED, SO.
I JUST WANTED TO CHECK.
UM.

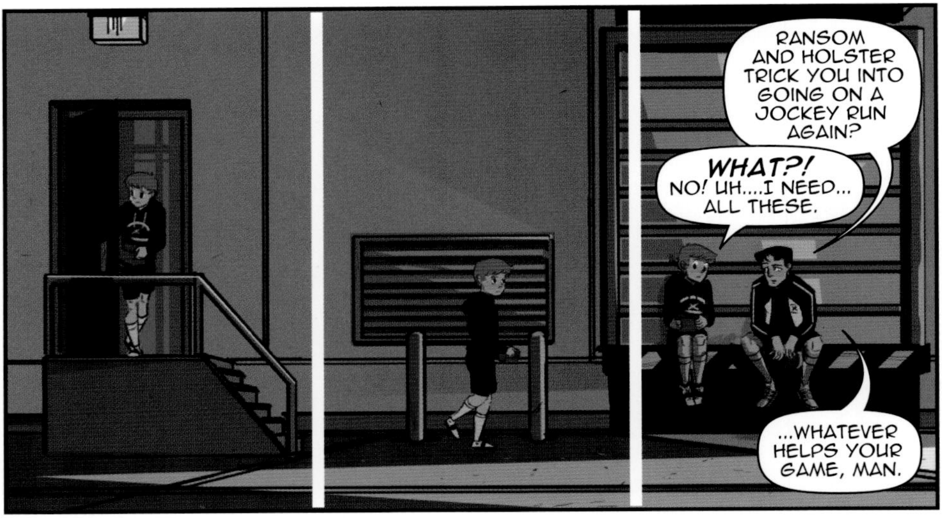
RANSOM AND HOLSTER TRICK YOU INTO GOING ON A JOCKEY RUN AGAIN?
WHAT?! NO! UH....I NEED... ALL THESE.
...WHATEVER HELPS YOUR GAME, MAN.

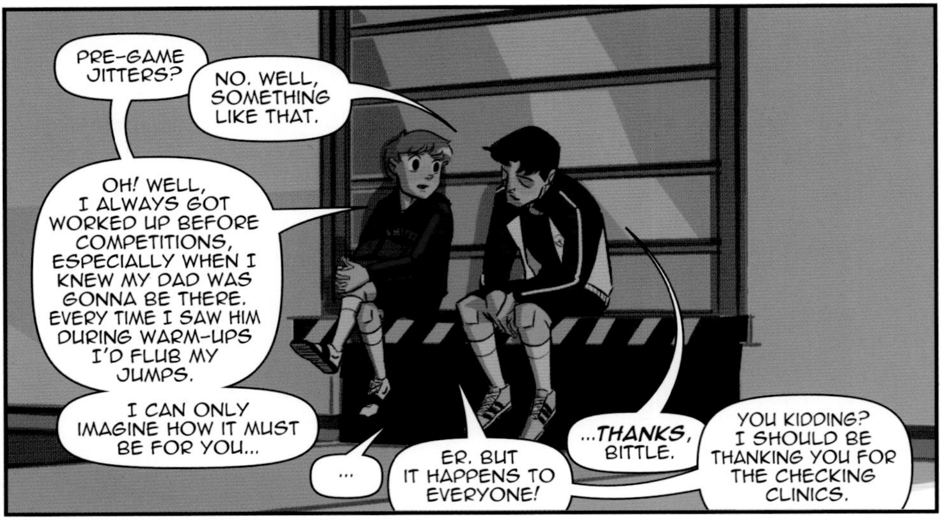
PRE-GAME JITTERS?
NO. WELL, SOMETHING LIKE THAT.
OH! WELL, I ALWAYS GOT WORKED UP BEFORE COMPETITIONS, ESPECIALLY WHEN I KNEW MY DAD WAS GONNA BE THERE. EVERY TIME I SAW HIM DURING WARM-UPS I'D FLUB MY JUMPS.
I CAN ONLY IMAGINE HOW IT MUST BE FOR YOU...
...
ER. BUT IT HAPPENS TO EVERYONE!
...THANKS, BITTLE.
YOU KIDDING? I SHOULD BE THANKING YOU FOR THE CHECKING CLINICS.

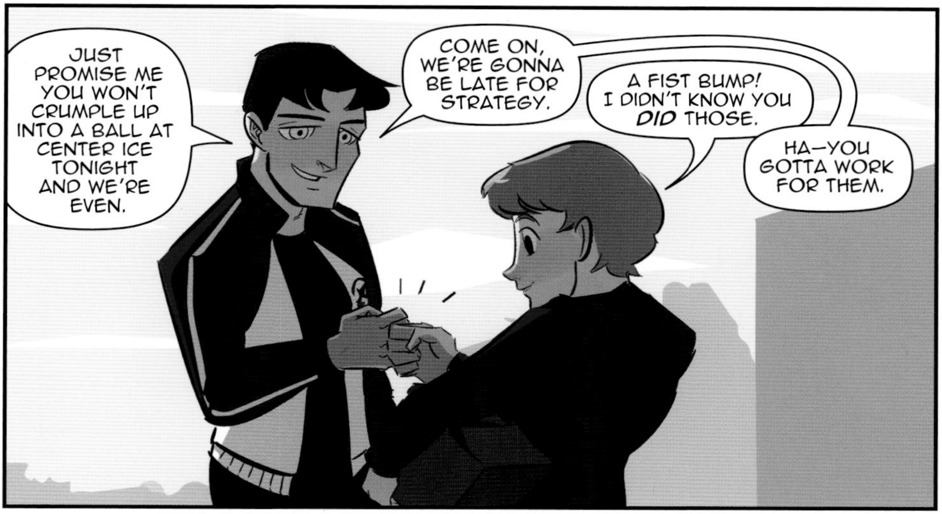
JUST PROMISE ME YOU WON'T CRUMPLE UP INTO A BALL AT CENTER ICE TONIGHT AND WE'RE EVEN.
COME ON, WE'RE GONNA BE LATE FOR STRATEGY.
A FIST BUMP! I DIDN'T KNOW YOU *DID* THOSE.
HA—YOU GOTTA WORK FOR THEM.

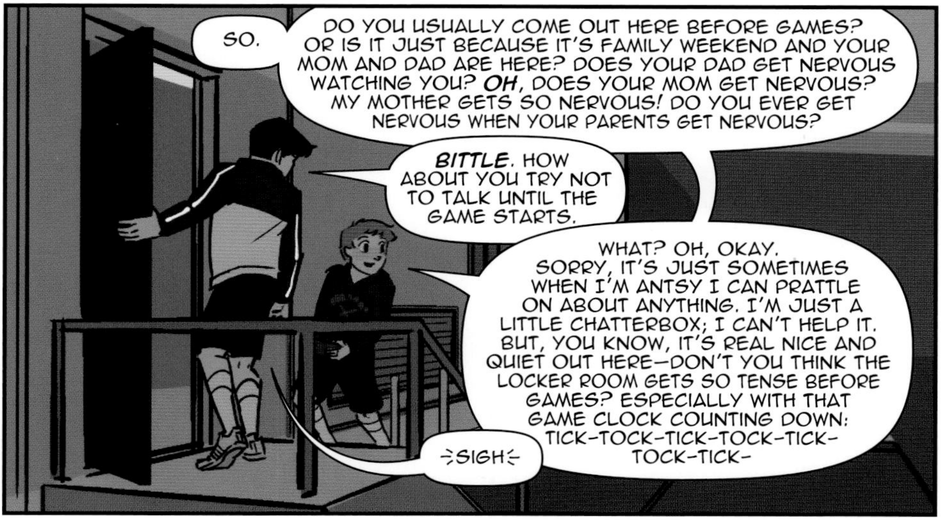
SO.
DO YOU USUALLY COME OUT HERE BEFORE GAMES? OR IS IT JUST BECAUSE IT'S FAMILY WEEKEND AND YOUR MOM AND DAD ARE HERE? DOES YOUR DAD GET NERVOUS WATCHING YOU? *OH*, DOES YOUR MOM GET NERVOUS? MY MOTHER GETS SO NERVOUS! DO YOU EVER GET NERVOUS WHEN YOUR PARENTS GET NERVOUS?
BITTLE. HOW ABOUT YOU TRY NOT TO TALK UNTIL THE GAME STARTS.
WHAT? OH, OKAY. SORRY, IT'S JUST SOMETIMES WHEN I'M ANTSY I CAN PRATTLE ON ABOUT ANYTHING. I'M JUST A LITTLE CHATTERBOX; I CAN'T HELP IT. BUT, YOU KNOW, IT'S REAL NICE AND QUIET OUT HERE—DON'T YOU THINK THE LOCKER ROOM GETS SO TENSE BEFORE GAMES? ESPECIALLY WITH THAT GAME CLOCK COUNTING DOWN: TICK-TOCK-TICK-TOCK-TICK-TOCK-TICK-
SIGH

11

SAMWELL VS. YALE — II

SAMWELL HOCKEY
SAMWELL
YALE
04:13
0
0
PERIOD 3
PLYR PENALTY
PENALTY
25 SHOTS ON GOAL 36
KNIGHT, BITTLE, WICKS—YOUR LINE.

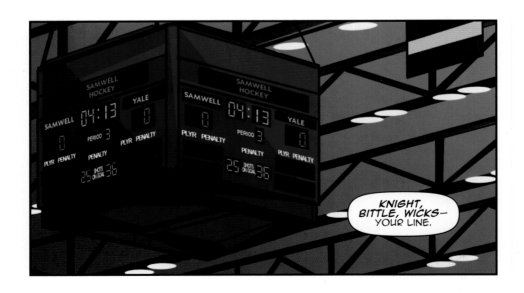

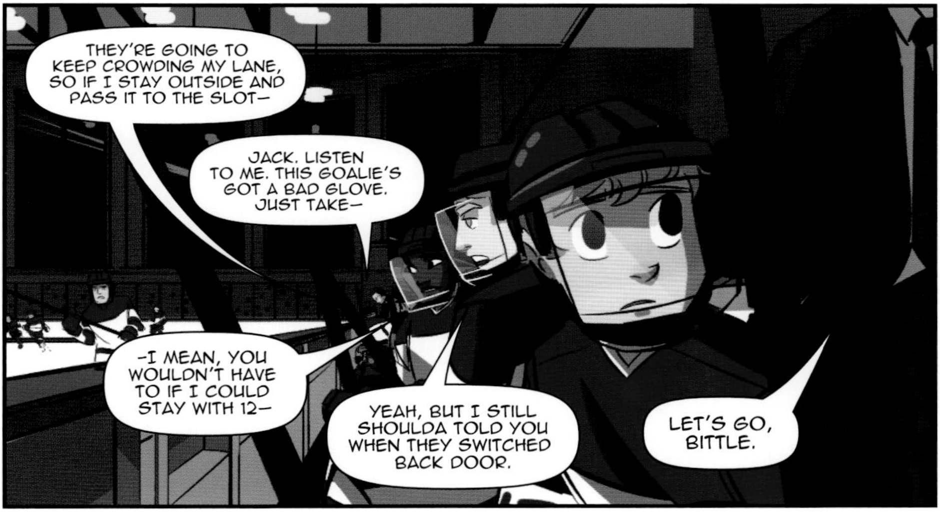
THEY'RE GOING TO KEEP CROWDING MY LANE, SO IF I STAY OUTSIDE AND PASS IT TO THE SLOT–
JACK. LISTEN TO ME. THIS GOALIE'S GOT A BAD GLOVE. JUST TAKE–
–I MEAN, YOU WOULDN'T HAVE TO IF I COULD STAY WITH 12–
YEAH, BUT I STILL SHOULDA TOLD YOU WHEN THEY SWITCHED BACK DOOR.
LET'S GO, BITTLE.

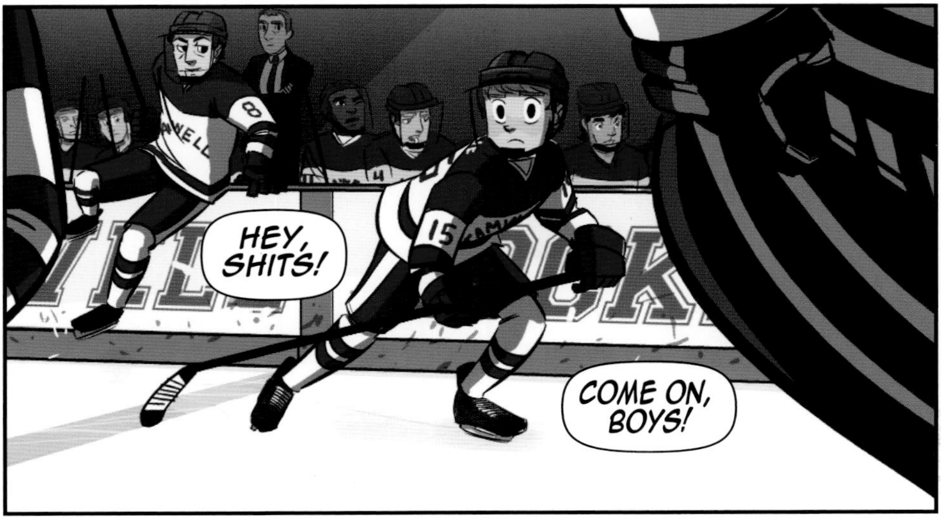
HEY, SHITS!
COME ON, BOYS!

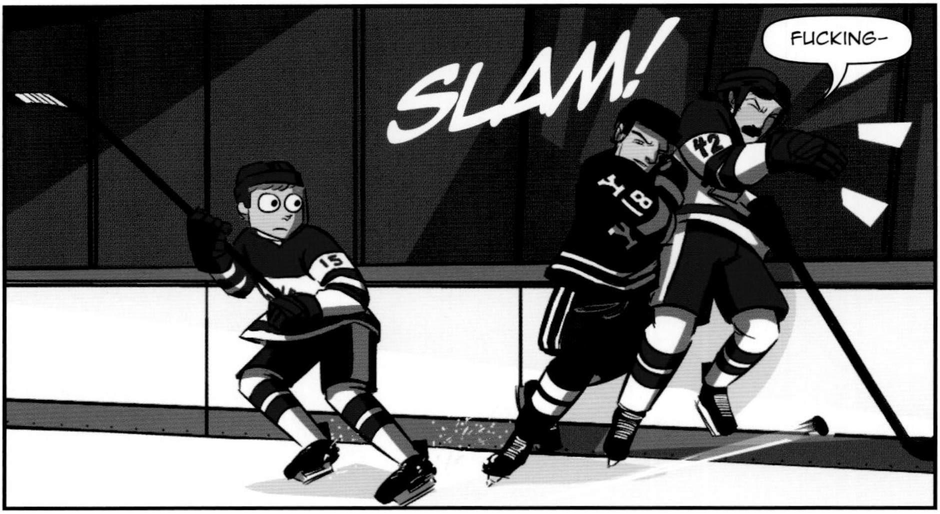
SLAM!
FUCKING-

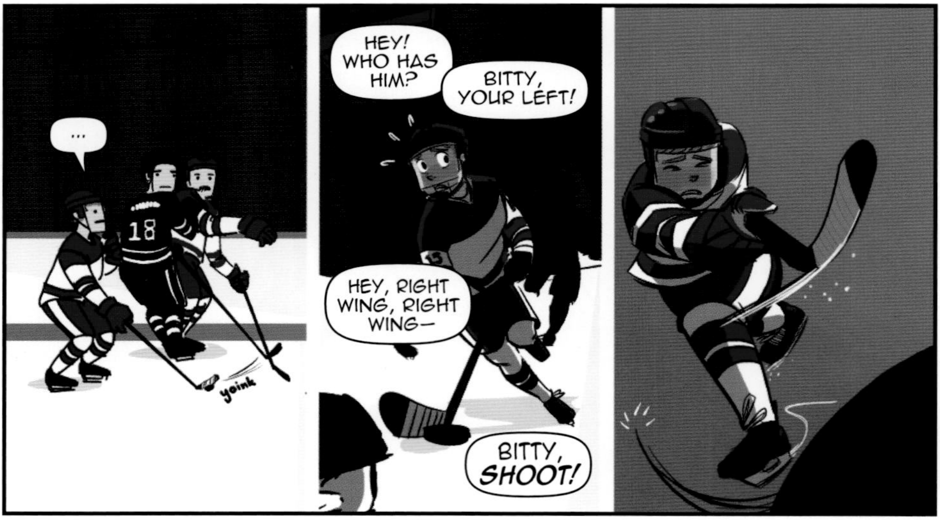
...
yoink
HEY! WHO HAS HIM?
BITTY, YOUR LEFT!
HEY, RIGHT WING, RIGHT WING—
BITTY, SHOOT!

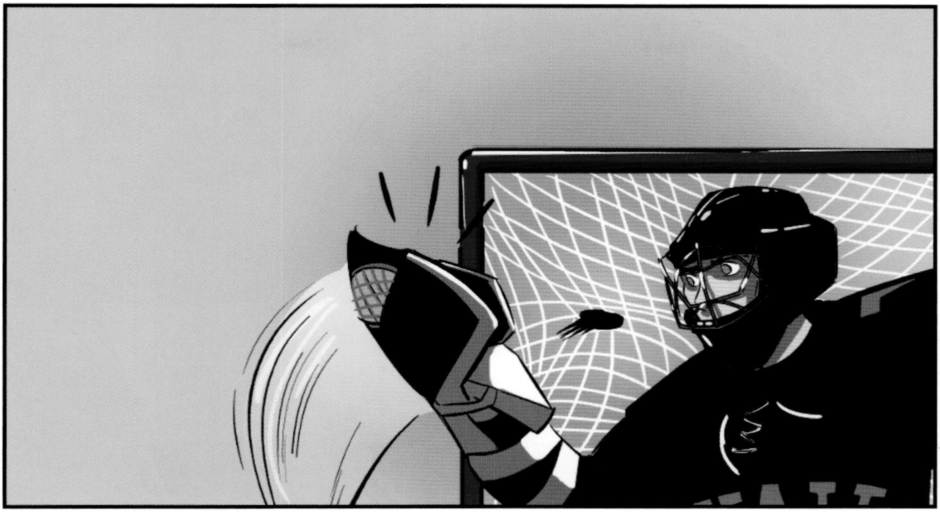

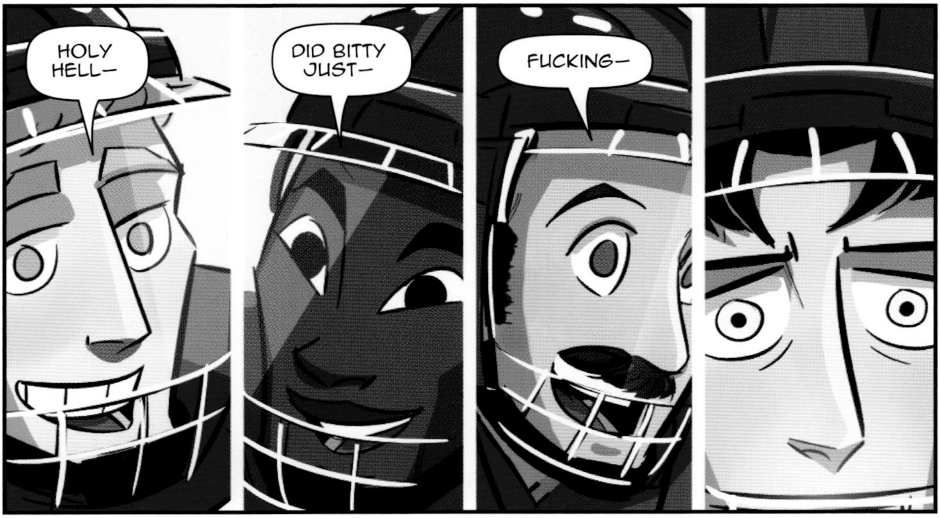
HOLY HELL–
DID BITTY JUST–
FUCKING–

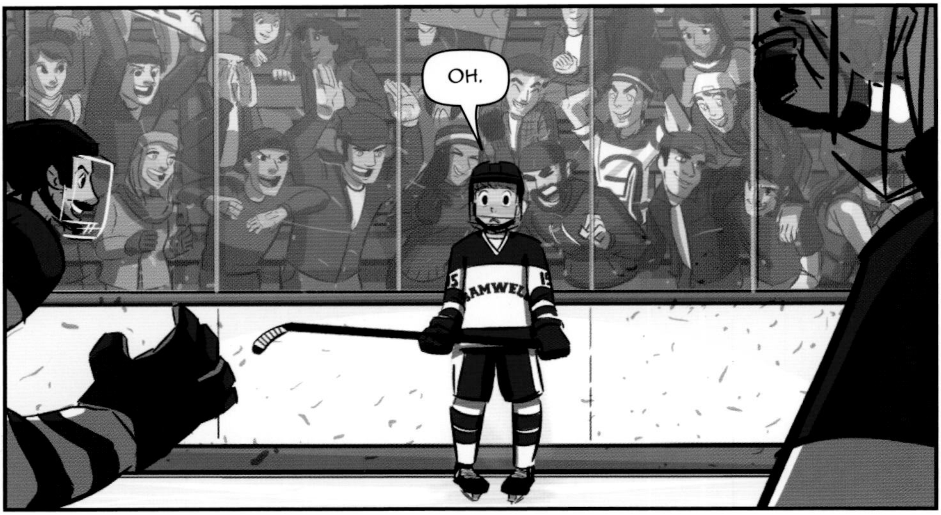
OH.

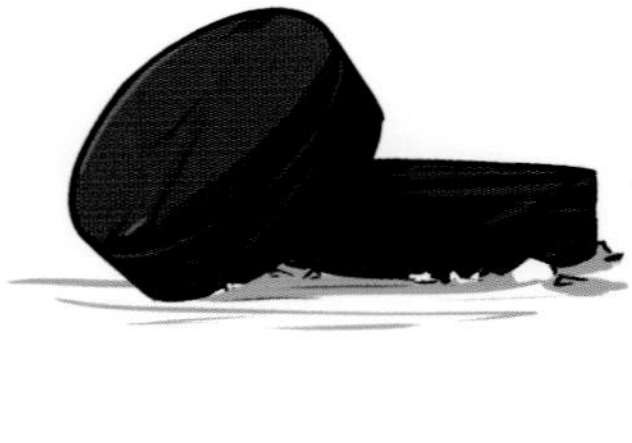

12

SAMWELL VS. YALE — III

...AND YOU SHOULD'VE SEEN ME IN THE STANDS *ALL EMOTIONAL*. SOMEONE STOPPED CHEERING TO ASK IF I WAS OKAY! DICKY, YOU WERE SO GREAT!!
THANKS. I'M JUST—I'M STILL ***IN SHOCK***. BUT I REALLY SHOULD GO SHOWER UP NOW.
OH, BEFORE YOU GO, LEMME TAKE *ONE MORE* PICTURE—

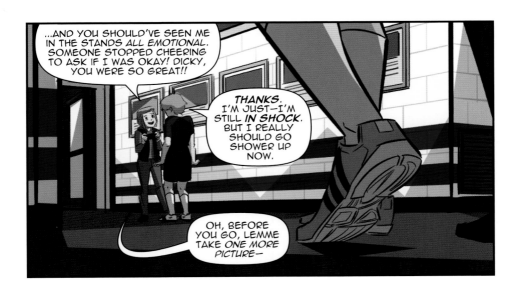

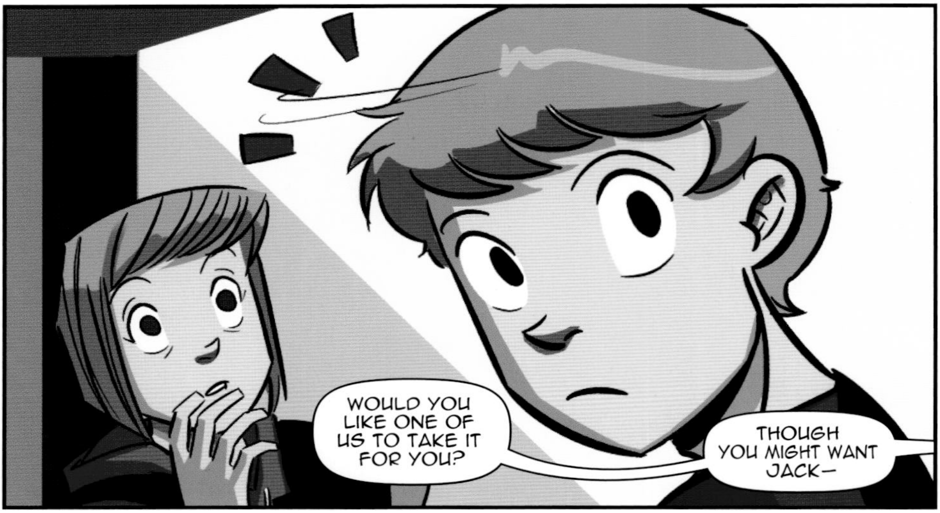
WOULD YOU LIKE ONE OF US TO TAKE IT FOR YOU?
THOUGH YOU MIGHT WANT JACK—

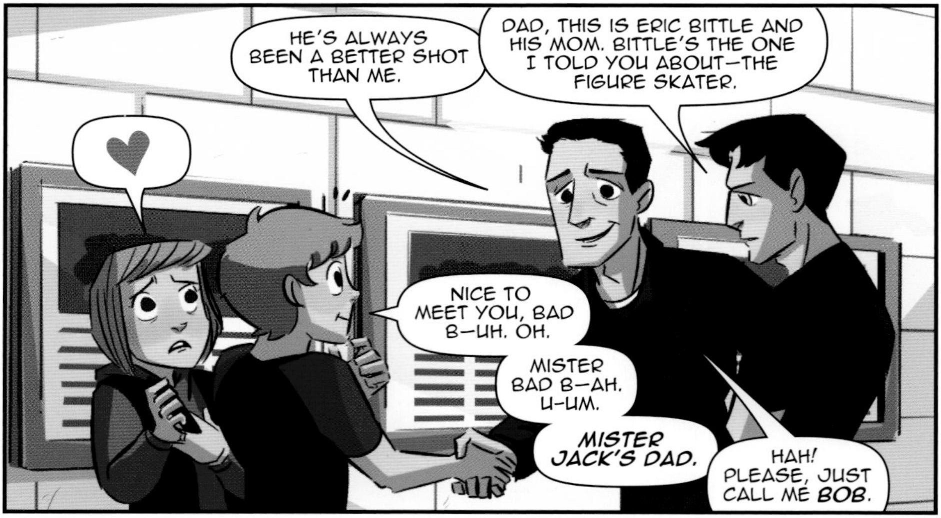
HE'S ALWAYS BEEN A BETTER SHOT THAN ME.
DAD, THIS IS ERIC BITTLE AND HIS MOM. BITTLE'S THE ONE I TOLD YOU ABOUT—THE FIGURE SKATER.
NICE TO MEET YOU, BAD B—UH. OH.
MISTER BAD B—AH. U-UM.
MISTER JACK'S DAD.
HAH! PLEASE, JUST CALL ME ***BOB***.

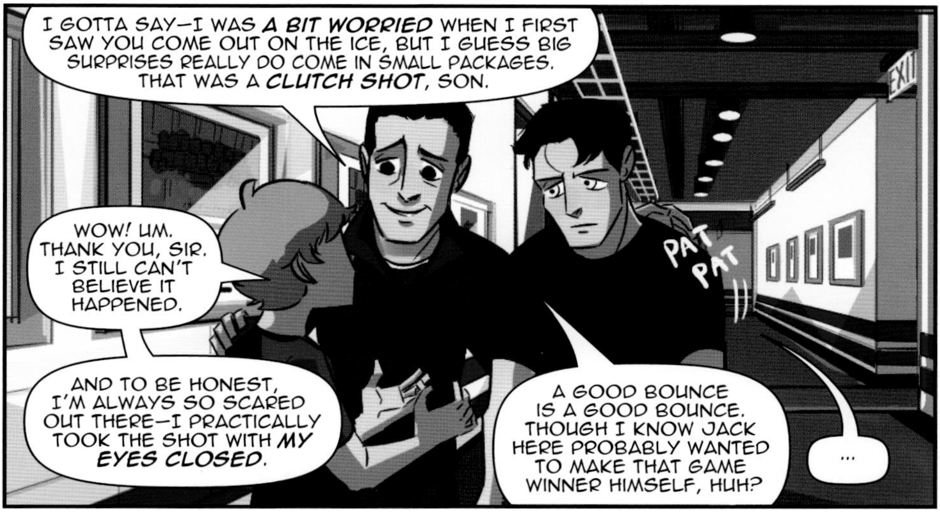
I GOTTA SAY—I WAS *A BIT WORRIED* WHEN I FIRST SAW YOU COME OUT ON THE ICE, BUT I GUESS BIG SURPRISES REALLY DO COME IN SMALL PACKAGES. THAT WAS A *CLUTCH SHOT*, SON.
WOW! UM. THANK YOU, SIR. I STILL CAN'T BELIEVE IT HAPPENED.
AND TO BE HONEST, I'M ALWAYS SO SCARED OUT THERE—I PRACTICALLY TOOK THE SHOT WITH *MY EYES CLOSED*.
PAT PAT
A GOOD BOUNCE IS A GOOD BOUNCE. THOUGH I KNOW JACK HERE PROBABLY WANTED TO MAKE THAT GAME WINNER HIMSELF, HUH?
...

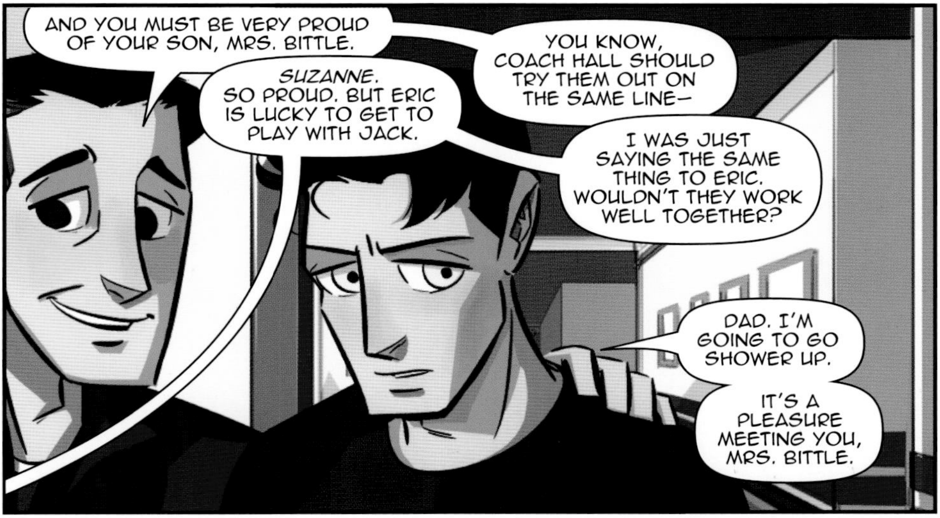
AND YOU MUST BE VERY PROUD OF YOUR SON, MRS. BITTLE.
SUZANNE. SO PROUD. BUT ERIC IS LUCKY TO GET TO PLAY WITH JACK.
YOU KNOW, COACH HALL SHOULD TRY THEM OUT ON THE SAME LINE—
I WAS JUST SAYING THE SAME THING TO ERIC. WOULDN'T THEY WORK WELL TOGETHER?
DAD. I'M GOING TO GO SHOWER UP.
IT'S A PLEASURE MEETING YOU, MRS. BITTLE.

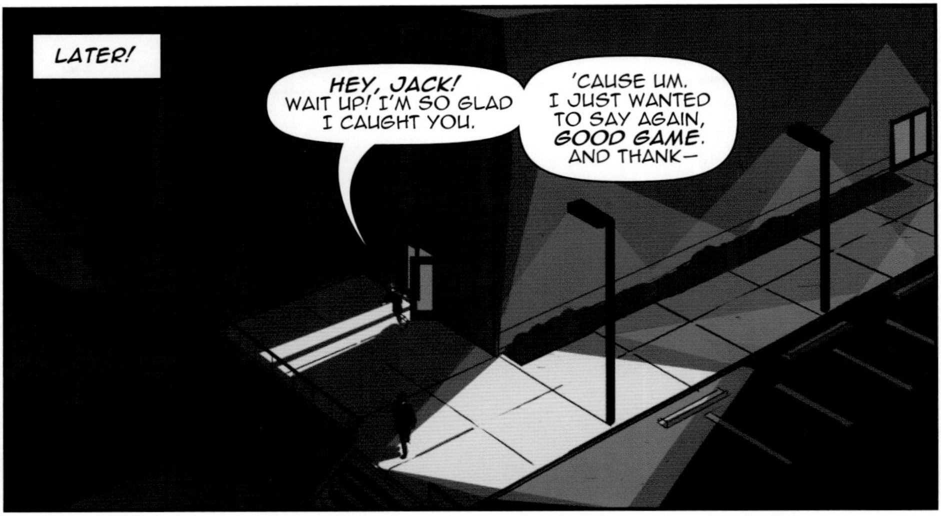
LATER!
HEY, JACK! WAIT UP! I'M SO GLAD I CAUGHT YOU.
'CAUSE UM. I JUST WANTED TO SAY AGAIN, GOOD GAME. AND THANK—

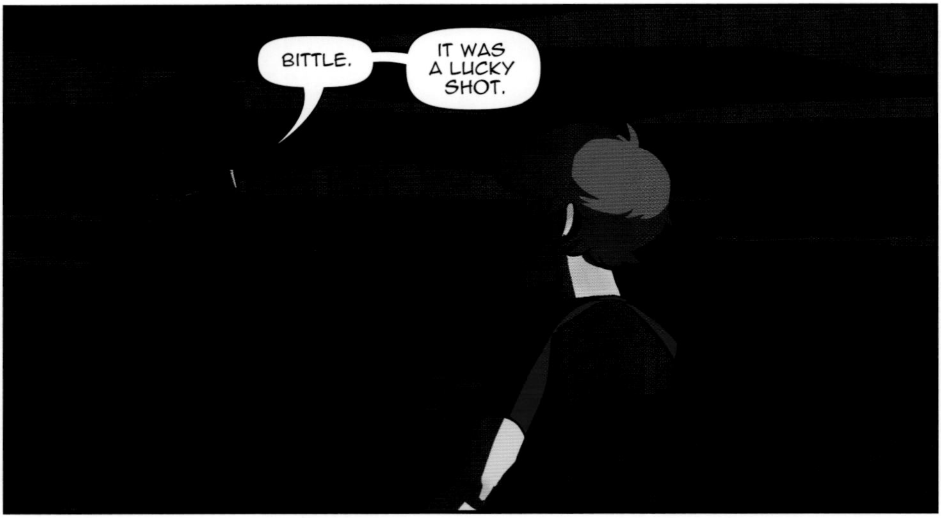
BITTLE.
IT WAS A LUCKY SHOT.

13

THE CLOSET STORY — I

ONE OF THE REASONS I WANTED TO GO TO SAMWELL WAS ITS RANKING AS U.S. NEWS & WORLD REPORT'S #1 MOST LGBTQ-FRIENDLY CAMPUS IN AMERICA FOR THE LAST THREE YEARS.
I'M FROM SMALL-TOWN GEORGIA...AND IT'S THE SOUTH...AND MY DAD'S THE COACH OF THE HIGH SCHOOL'S FOOTBALL TEAM...SO. I DIDN'T REALLY HAVE A LOT OF ROOM TO BE MYSELF.
SO I THOUGHT I COULD DO THAT HERE, EVEN IF I WAS ON THE HOCKEY TEAM.
THE ONLY THING IS... I'VE KIND OF WAITED ALL OF FALL SEMESTER TO ACTUALLY COME OUT TO MY TEAMMATES.
OOPS.

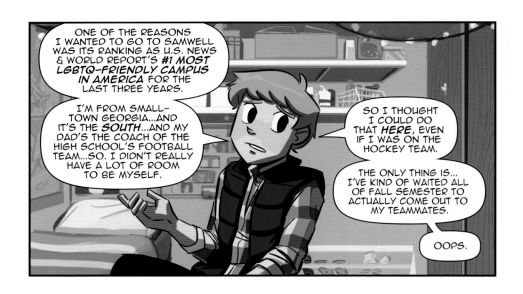

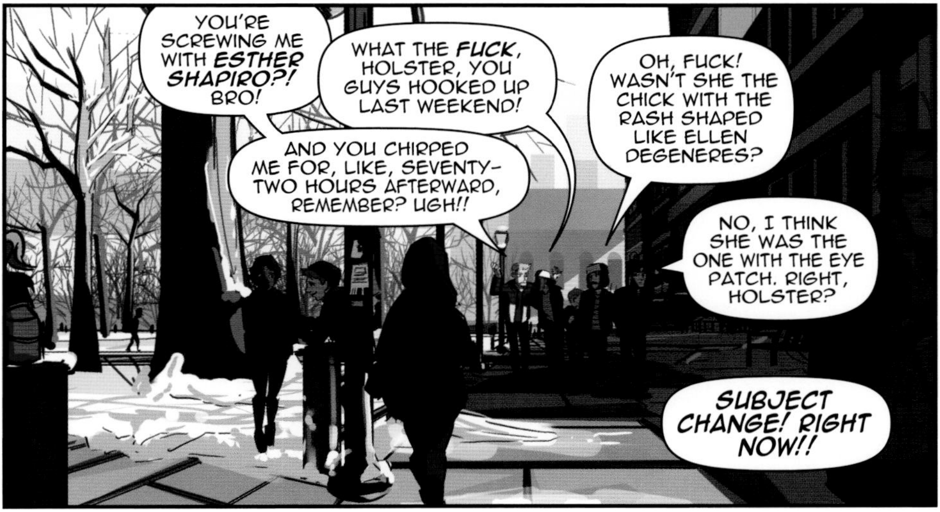
YOU'RE SCREWING ME WITH *ESTHER SHAPIRO?!* BRO!
WHAT THE *FUCK*, HOLSTER, YOU GUYS HOOKED UP LAST WEEKEND!
AND YOU CHIRPED ME FOR, LIKE, SEVENTY-TWO HOURS AFTERWARD, REMEMBER? UGH!!
OH, FUCK! WASN'T SHE THE CHICK WITH THE RASH SHAPED LIKE ELLEN DEGENERES?
NO, I THINK SHE WAS THE ONE WITH THE EYE PATCH. RIGHT, HOLSTER?
SUBJECT CHANGE! RIGHT NOW!!

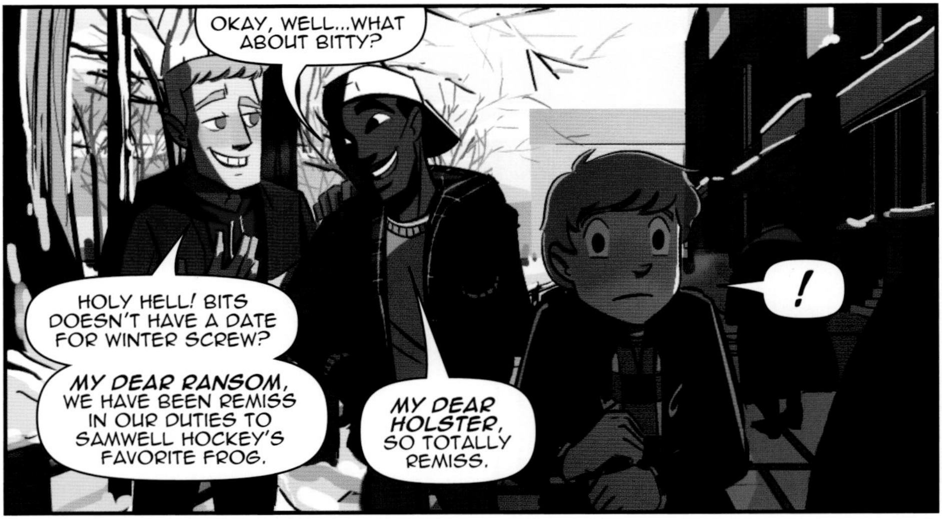
OKAY, WELL...WHAT ABOUT BITTY?
HOLY HELL! BITS DOESN'T HAVE A DATE FOR WINTER SCREW?
!
MY DEAR RANSOM, WE HAVE BEEN REMISS IN OUR DUTIES TO SAMWELL HOCKEY'S FAVORITE FROG.
MY DEAR HOLSTER, SO TOTALLY REMISS.

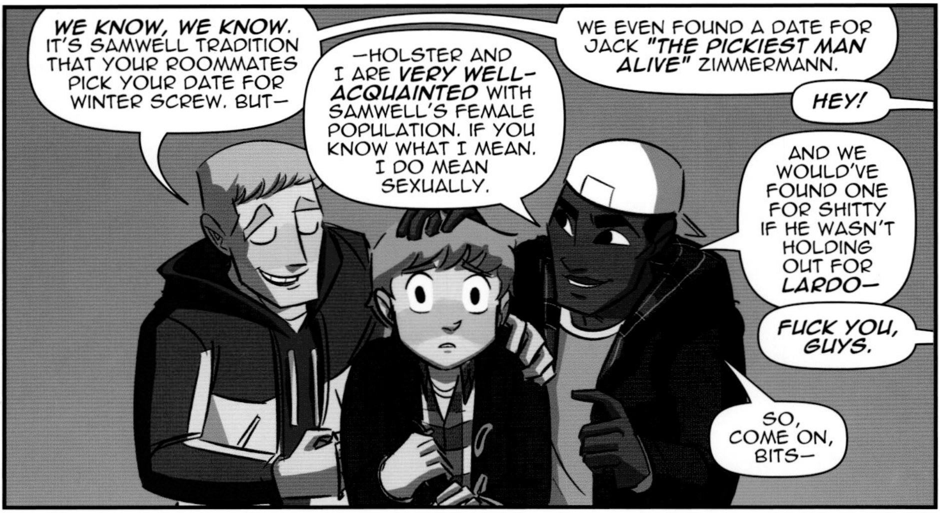
WE KNOW, WE KNOW. IT'S SAMWELL TRADITION THAT YOUR ROOMMATES PICK YOUR DATE FOR WINTER SCREW. BUT—
—HOLSTER AND I ARE VERY WELL-ACQUAINTED WITH SAMWELL'S FEMALE POPULATION. IF YOU KNOW WHAT I MEAN. I DO MEAN SEXUALLY.
WE EVEN FOUND A DATE FOR JACK "THE PICKIEST MAN ALIVE" ZIMMERMANN.
HEY!
AND WE WOULD'VE FOUND ONE FOR SHITTY IF HE WASN'T HOLDING OUT FOR LARDO—
FUCK YOU, GUYS.
SO, COME ON, BITS—

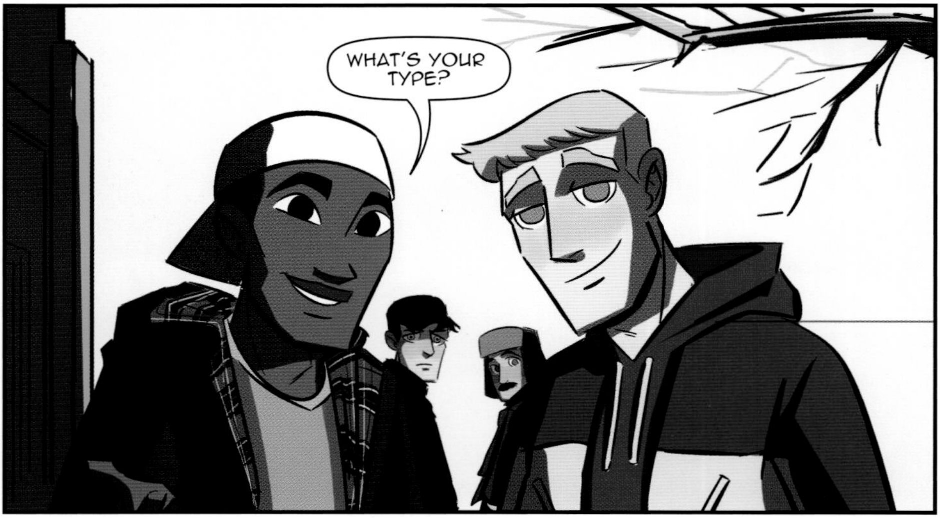
WHAT'S YOUR TYPE?

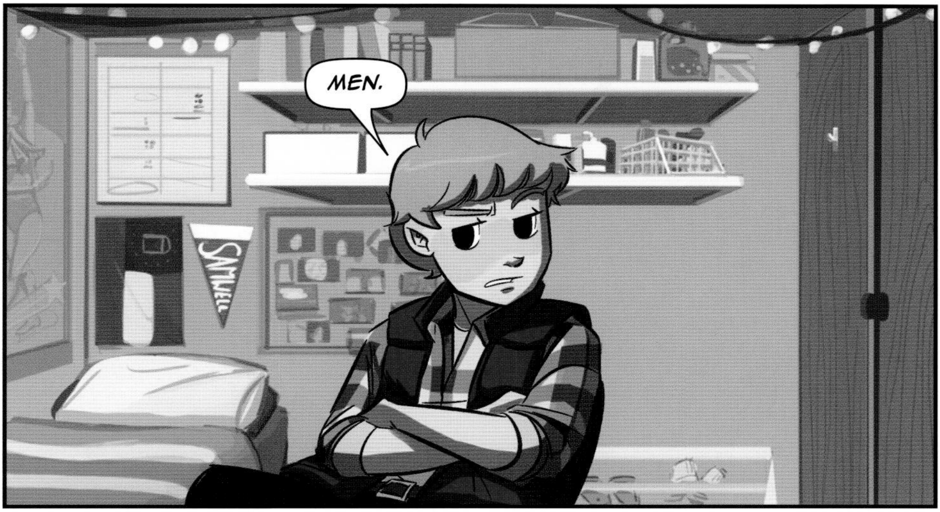
MEN.

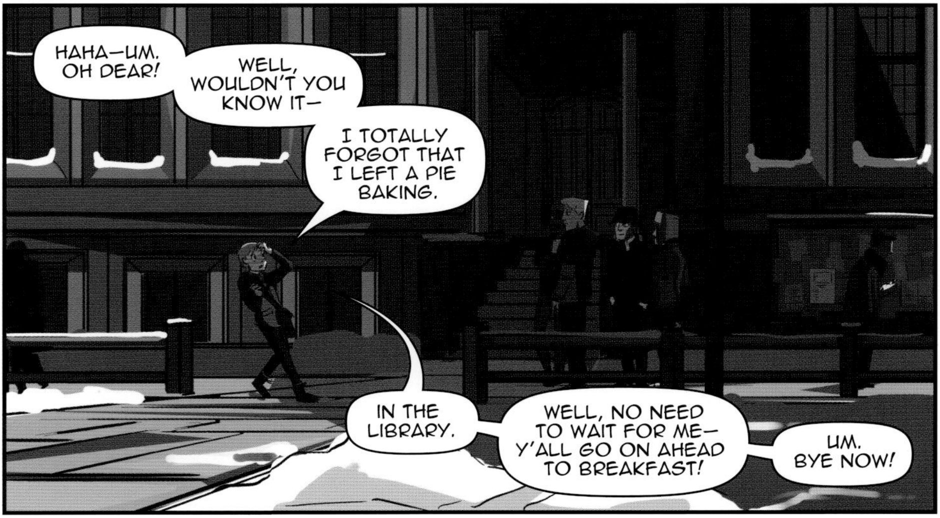
HAHA—UM. OH DEAR!
WELL, WOULDN'T YOU KNOW IT—
I TOTALLY FORGOT THAT I LEFT A PIE BAKING.
IN THE LIBRARY.
WELL, NO NEED TO WAIT FOR ME— Y'ALL GO ON AHEAD TO BREAKFAST!
UM. BYE NOW!

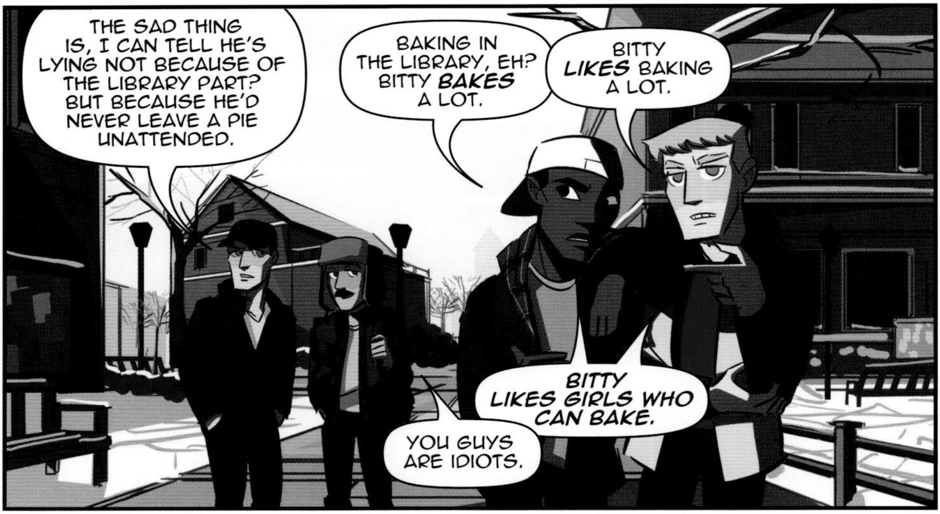
THE SAD THING IS, I CAN TELL HE'S LYING NOT BECAUSE OF THE LIBRARY PART? BUT BECAUSE HE'D NEVER LEAVE A PIE UNATTENDED.
BAKING IN THE LIBRARY, EH? BITTY **BAKES** A LOT.
BITTY **LIKES** BAKING A LOT.
BITTY LIKES GIRLS WHO CAN BAKE.
YOU GUYS ARE IDIOTS.

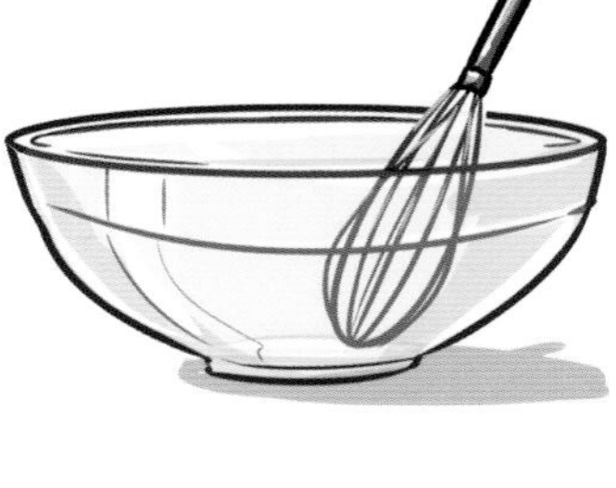

14

THE CLOSET STORY — II

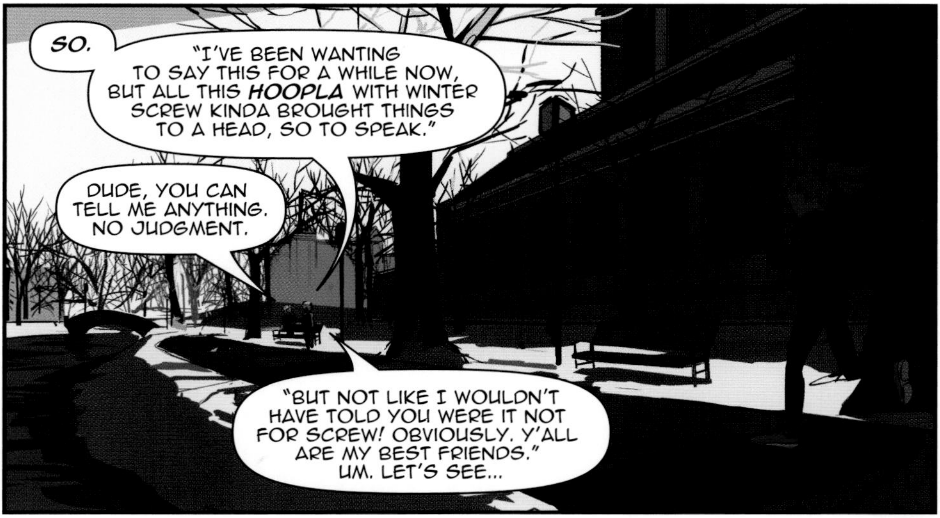
SO.
"I'VE BEEN WANTING TO SAY THIS FOR A WHILE NOW, BUT ALL THIS HOOPLA WITH WINTER SCREW KINDA BROUGHT THINGS TO A HEAD, SO TO SPEAK."
DUDE, YOU CAN TELL ME ANYTHING. NO JUDGMENT.
"BUT NOT LIKE I WOULDN'T HAVE TOLD YOU WERE IT NOT FOR SCREW! OBVIOUSLY. Y'ALL ARE MY BEST FRIENDS." UM. LET'S SEE...

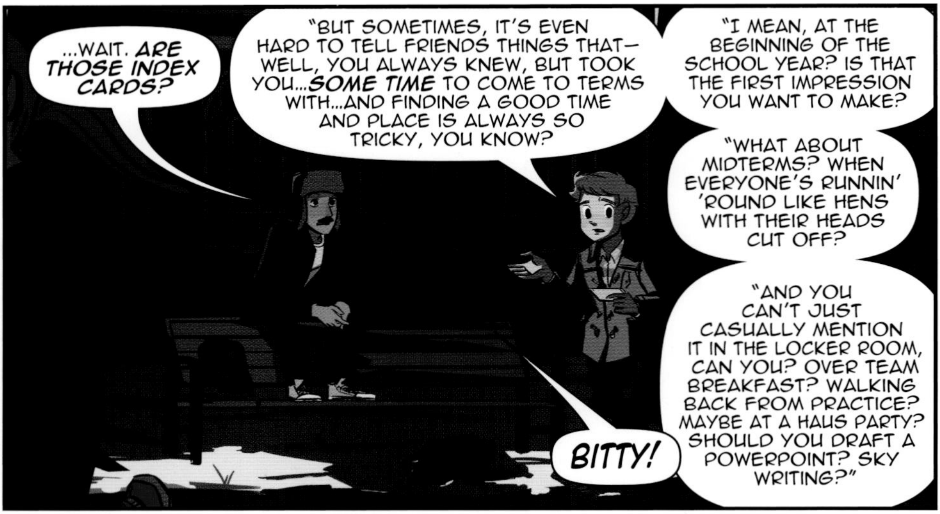
…WAIT. ARE THOSE INDEX CARDS?
"BUT SOMETIMES, IT'S EVEN HARD TO TELL FRIENDS THINGS THAT— WELL, YOU ALWAYS KNEW, BUT TOOK YOU…SOME TIME TO COME TO TERMS WITH…AND FINDING A GOOD TIME AND PLACE IS ALWAYS SO TRICKY, YOU KNOW?
"I MEAN, AT THE BEGINNING OF THE SCHOOL YEAR? IS THAT THE FIRST IMPRESSION YOU WANT TO MAKE?
"WHAT ABOUT MIDTERMS? WHEN EVERYONE'S RUNNIN' 'ROUND LIKE HENS WITH THEIR HEADS CUT OFF?
"AND YOU CAN'T JUST CASUALLY MENTION IT IN THE LOCKER ROOM, CAN YOU? OVER TEAM BREAKFAST? WALKING BACK FROM PRACTICE? MAYBE AT A HAUS PARTY? SHOULD YOU DRAFT A POWERPOINT? SKY WRITING?"
BITTY!

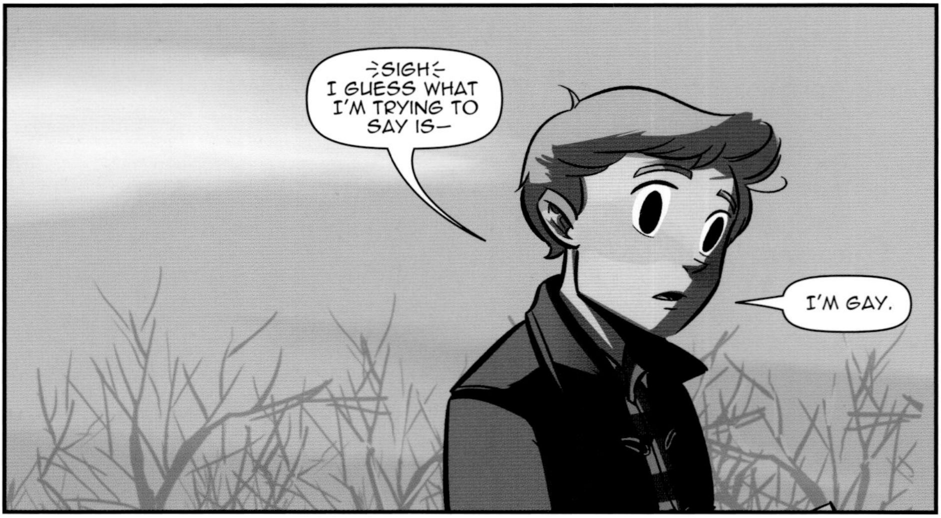
SIGH
I GUESS WHAT I'M TRYING TO SAY IS—
I'M GAY.

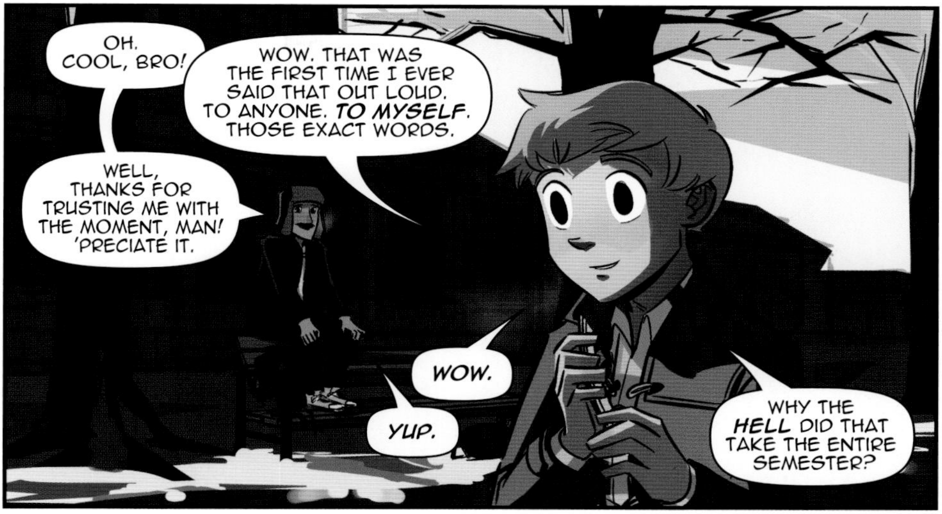
OH. COOL, BRO!
WOW. THAT WAS THE FIRST TIME I EVER SAID THAT OUT LOUD. TO ANYONE. *TO MYSELF*. THOSE EXACT WORDS.
WELL, THANKS FOR TRUSTING ME WITH THE MOMENT, MAN! 'PRECIATE IT.
WOW.
YUP.
WHY THE ***HELL*** DID THAT TAKE THE ENTIRE SEMESTER?

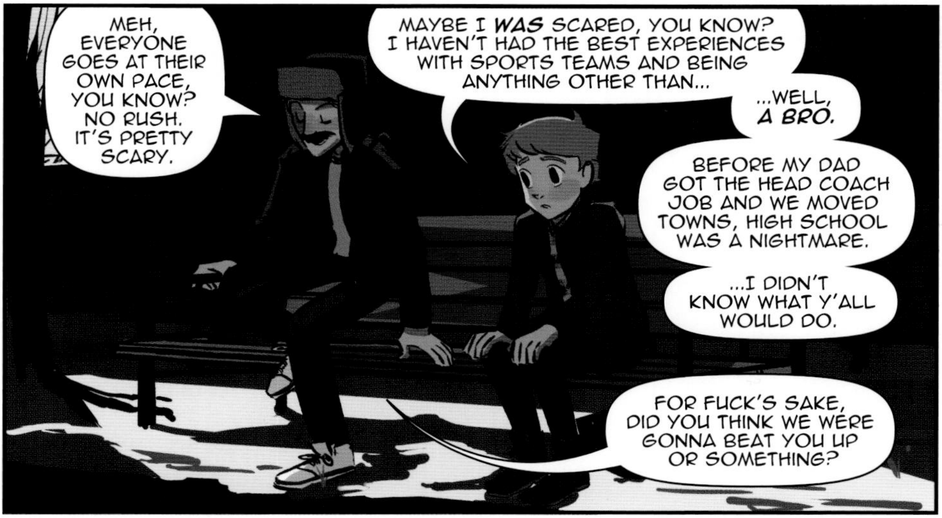
MEH, EVERYONE GOES AT THEIR OWN PACE, YOU KNOW? NO RUSH. IT'S PRETTY SCARY.
MAYBE I ***WAS*** SCARED, YOU KNOW? I HAVEN'T HAD THE BEST EXPERIENCES WITH SPORTS TEAMS AND BEING ANYTHING OTHER THAN...
...WELL, ***A BRO.***
BEFORE MY DAD GOT THE HEAD COACH JOB AND WE MOVED TOWNS, HIGH SCHOOL WAS A NIGHTMARE.
...I DIDN'T KNOW WHAT Y'ALL WOULD DO.
FOR FUCK'S SAKE, DID YOU THINK WE WERE GONNA BEAT YOU UP OR SOMETHING?

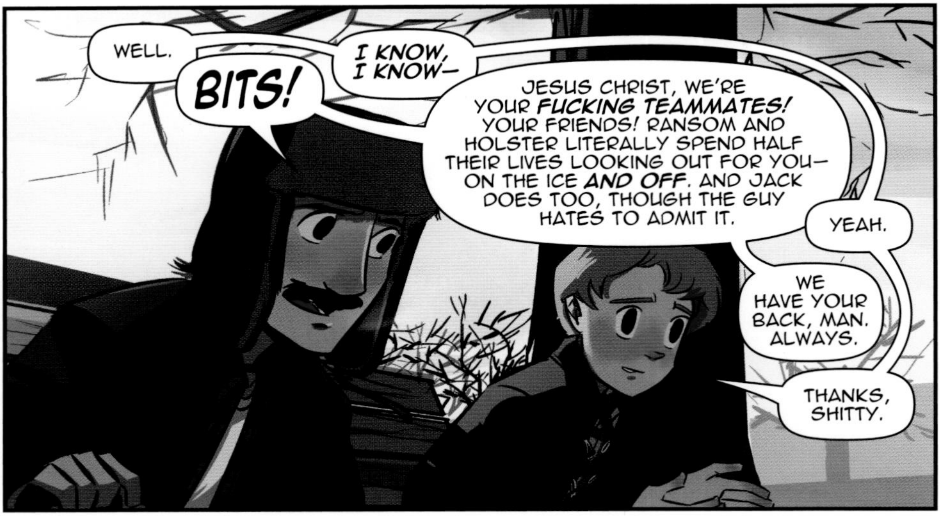
WELL.
I KNOW, I KNOW—
BITS!
JESUS CHRIST, WE'RE YOUR FUCKING TEAMMATES! YOUR FRIENDS! RANSOM AND HOLSTER LITERALLY SPEND HALF THEIR LIVES LOOKING OUT FOR YOU—ON THE ICE AND OFF. AND JACK DOES TOO, THOUGH THE GUY HATES TO ADMIT IT.
YEAH.
WE HAVE YOUR BACK, MAN. ALWAYS.
THANKS, SHITTY.

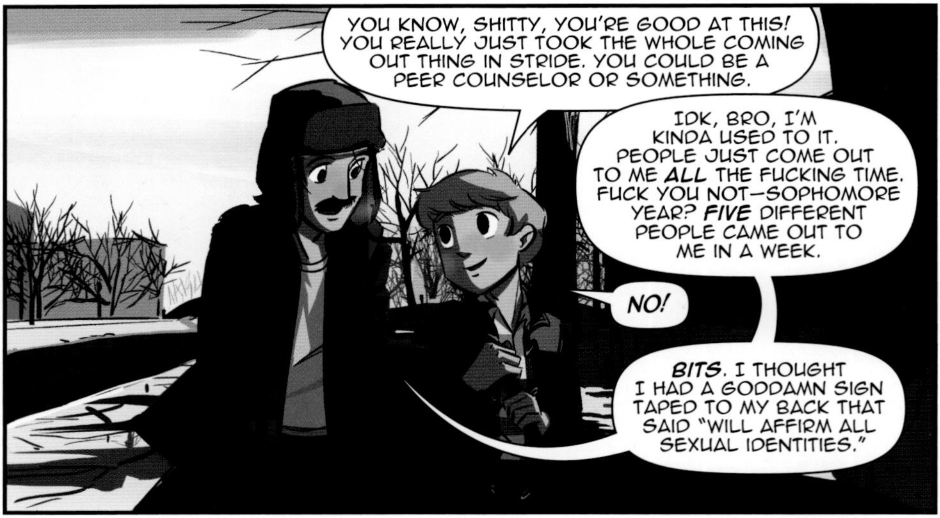
YOU KNOW, SHITTY, YOU'RE GOOD AT THIS! YOU REALLY JUST TOOK THE WHOLE COMING OUT THING IN STRIDE. YOU COULD BE A PEER COUNSELOR OR SOMETHING.
IDK, BRO, I'M KINDA USED TO IT. PEOPLE JUST COME OUT TO ME ALL THE FUCKING TIME. FUCK YOU NOT-SOPHOMORE YEAR? FIVE DIFFERENT PEOPLE CAME OUT TO ME IN A WEEK.
NO!
BITS. I THOUGHT I HAD A GODDAMN SIGN TAPED TO MY BACK THAT SAID "WILL AFFIRM ALL SEXUAL IDENTITIES."

15

LARDO

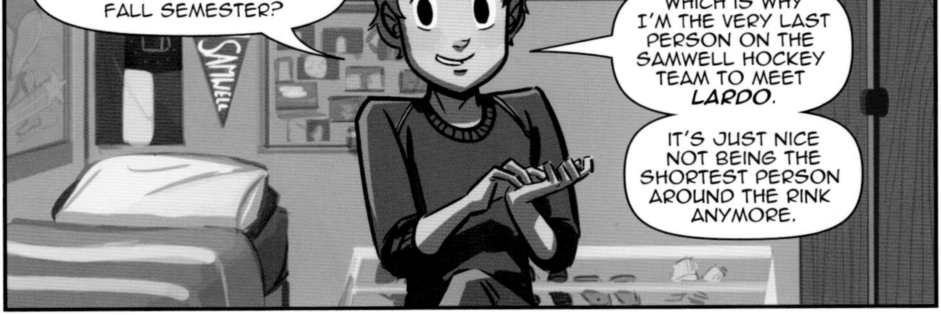
HAPPY SPRING SEMESTER!
SO MUCH IS GOING ON HERE AT SAMWELL—INCLUDING NEW FACES! SUPPOSEDLY SOPHOMORES TEND TO STUDY ABROAD FALL SEMESTER?
WHICH IS WHY I'M THE VERY LAST PERSON ON THE SAMWELL HOCKEY TEAM TO MEET LARDO.
IT'S JUST NICE NOT BEING THE SHORTEST PERSON AROUND THE RINK ANYMORE.
SAMWELL

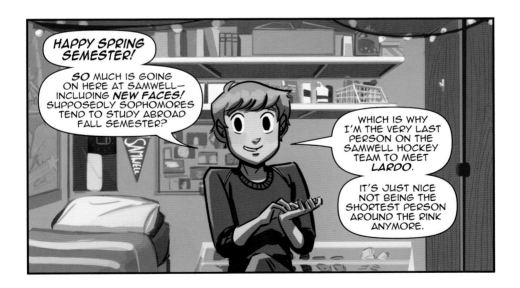

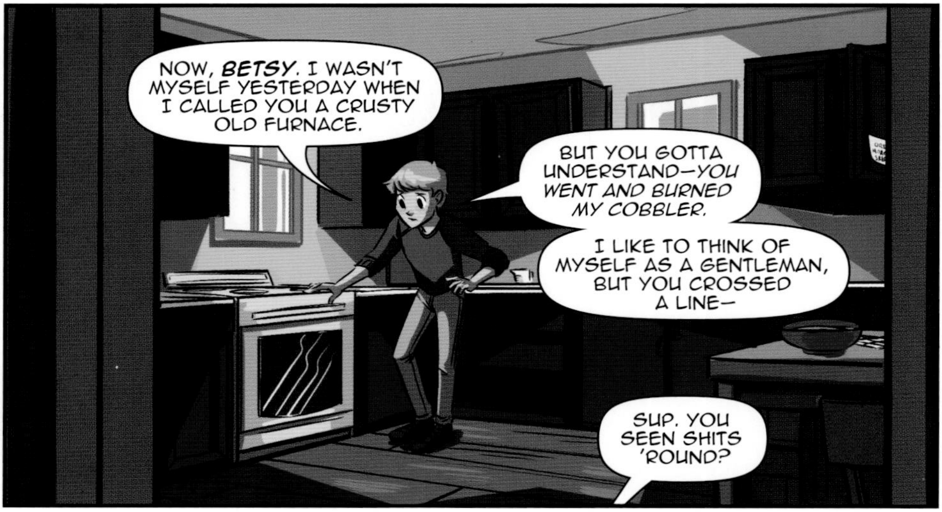
NOW, BETSY. I WASN'T MYSELF YESTERDAY WHEN I CALLED YOU A CRUSTY OLD FURNACE.
BUT YOU GOTTA UNDERSTAND—YOU WENT AND BURNED MY COBBLER.
I LIKE TO THINK OF MYSELF AS A GENTLEMAN, BUT YOU CROSSED A LINE—
SUP. YOU SEEN SHITS 'ROUND?

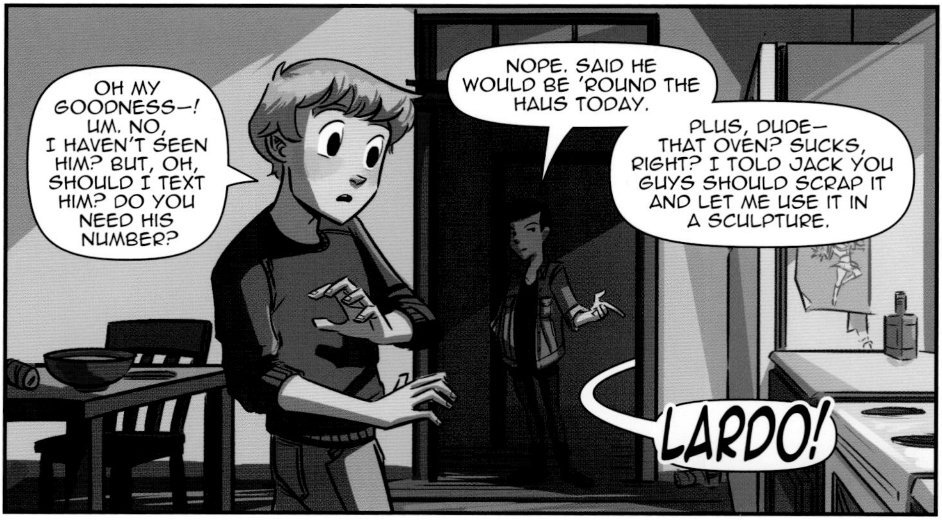
OH MY GOODNESS—! UM. NO, I HAVEN'T SEEN HIM? BUT, OH, SHOULD I TEXT HIM? DO YOU NEED HIS NUMBER?
NOPE. SAID HE WOULD BE 'ROUND THE HAUS TODAY.
PLUS, DUDE—THAT OVEN? SUCKS, RIGHT? I TOLD JACK YOU GUYS SHOULD SCRAP IT AND LET ME USE IT IN A SCULPTURE.
LARDO!

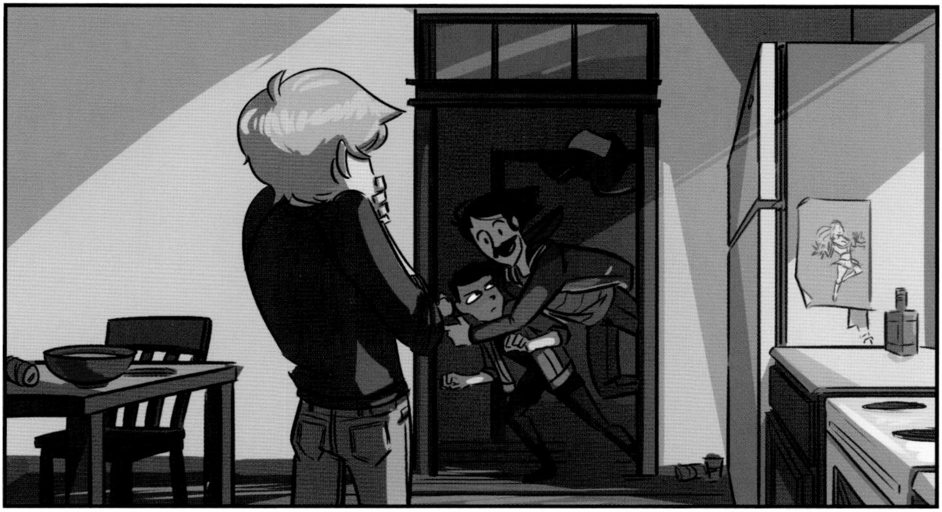

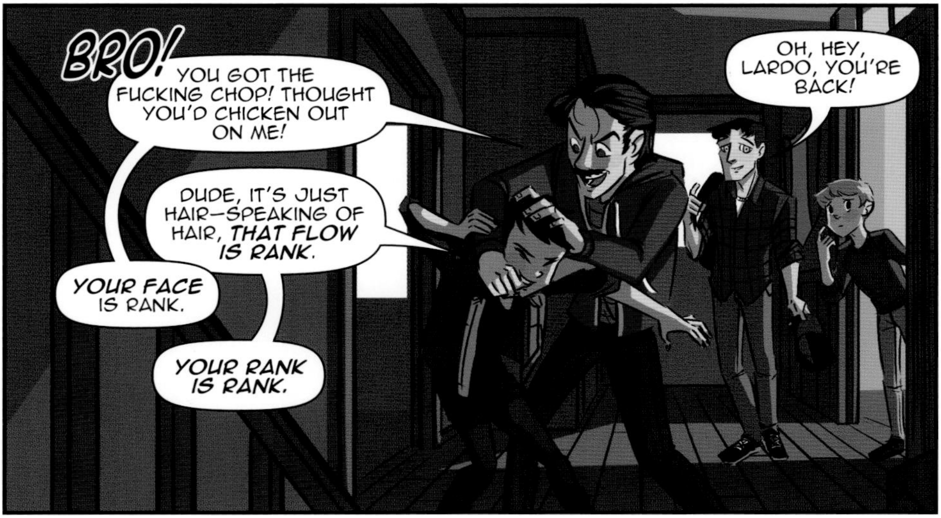
BRO! YOU GOT THE FUCKING CHOP! THOUGHT YOU'D CHICKEN OUT ON ME!
DUDE, IT'S JUST HAIR—SPEAKING OF HAIR, THAT FLOW IS RANK.
YOUR FACE IS RANK.
YOUR RANK IS RANK.
OH, HEY, LARDO, YOU'RE BACK!

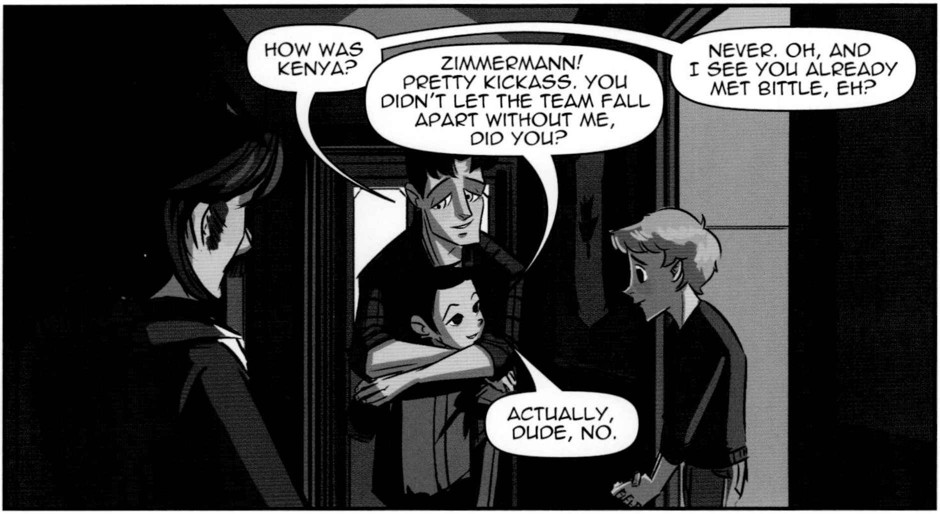
HOW WAS KENYA?
ZIMMERMANN! PRETTY KICKASS. YOU DIDN'T LET THE TEAM FALL APART WITHOUT ME, DID YOU?
NEVER. OH, AND I SEE YOU ALREADY MET BITTLE, EH?
ACTUALLY, DUDE, NO.

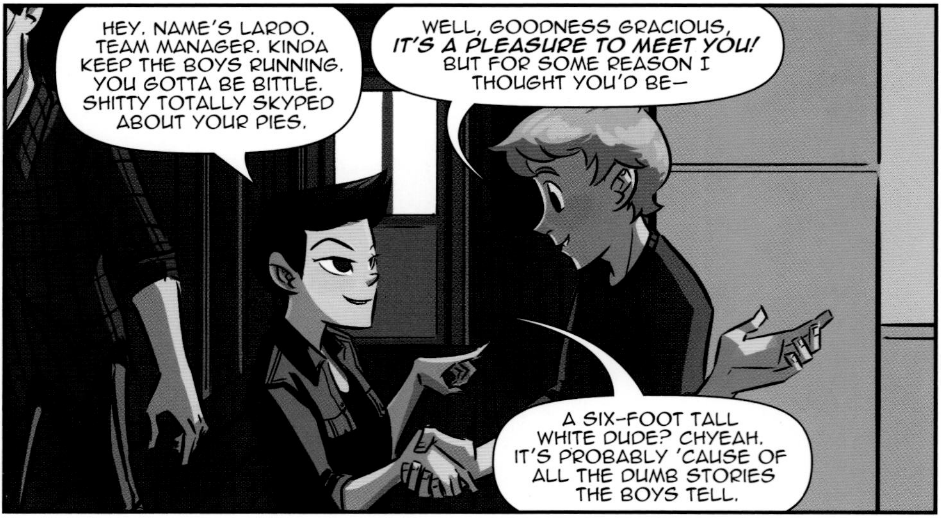
HEY. NAME'S LARDO. TEAM MANAGER. KINDA KEEP THE BOYS RUNNING. YOU GOTTA BE BITTLE. SHITTY TOTALLY SKYPED ABOUT YOUR PIES.
WELL, GOODNESS GRACIOUS, *IT'S A PLEASURE TO MEET YOU!* BUT FOR SOME REASON I THOUGHT YOU'D BE—
A SIX-FOOT TALL WHITE DUDE? CHYEAH. IT'S PROBABLY 'CAUSE OF ALL THE DUMB STORIES THE BOYS TELL.

RIGHT, RIGHT, SO HAUS RULES SAY SHOTS BEFORE LAST CUP, OKAY? AND MIND YOU THIS IS FOR *THE HAUS DOUBLES FUCKING CHAMPIONSHIP*, OKAY? SO IT'S ME AND LARDO BUT THEN LARDO DOES THE *'SWAWESOMEST* MOVE—

LIKE LARDO JUST THROWS ONE BACK AND LIKE WINKS AT ME AND HOLTZY AND JUST LIKE MURDERS OUR LAST CUP WITH SOME *MJ FADE-AWAY BULLSHIT.*

—THEN GOES AND BURPS IN HOLSTER'S FACE FOR *LIKE EIGHT SECONDS.*

I WAS DISGUSTED AT FIRST? BUT THEN I REALIZED IT WAS A SHOW OF RESPECT.

16

LINEMATES

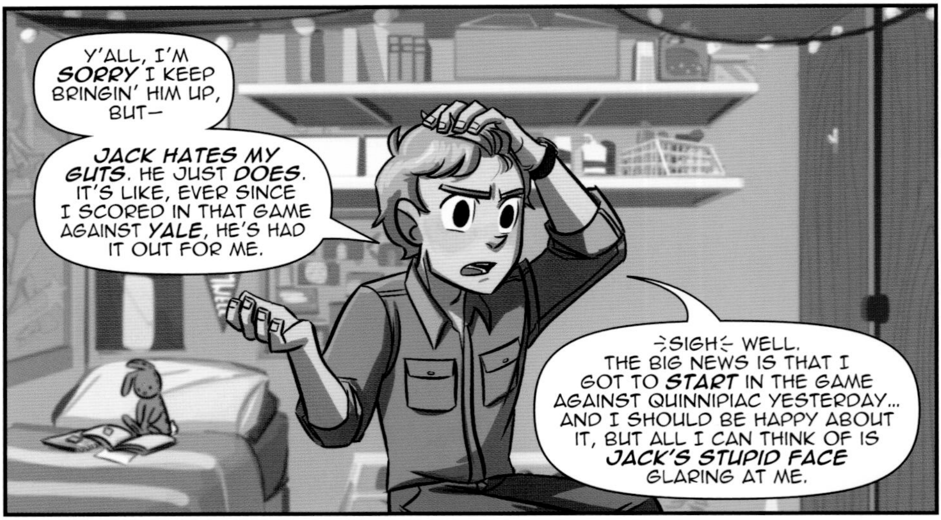
Y'ALL, I'M SORRY I KEEP BRINGIN' HIM UP, BUT—
JACK HATES MY GUTS. HE JUST DOES. IT'S LIKE, EVER SINCE I SCORED IN THAT GAME AGAINST YALE, HE'S HAD IT OUT FOR ME.
⇉SIGH⇇ WELL. THE BIG NEWS IS THAT I GOT TO START IN THE GAME AGAINST QUINNIPIAC YESTERDAY... AND I SHOULD BE HAPPY ABOUT IT, BUT ALL I CAN THINK OF IS JACK'S STUPID FACE GLARING AT ME.

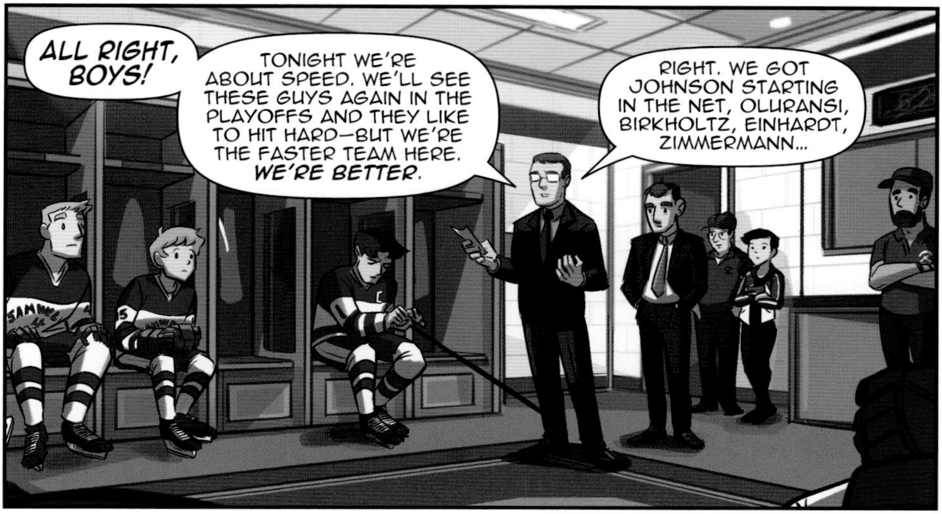
ALL RIGHT, BOYS!
TONIGHT WE'RE ABOUT SPEED. WE'LL SEE THESE GUYS AGAIN IN THE PLAYOFFS AND THEY LIKE TO HIT HARD—BUT WE'RE THE FASTER TEAM HERE. WE'RE BETTER.
RIGHT. WE GOT JOHNSON STARTING IN THE NET, OLURANSI, BIRKHOLTZ, EINHARDT, ZIMMERMANN...

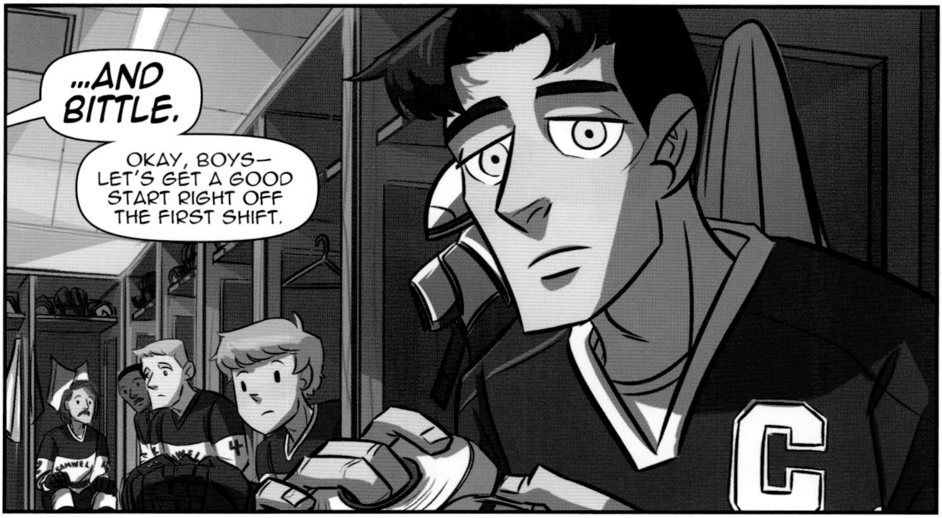
...AND BITTLE.
OKAY, BOYS—LET'S GET A GOOD START RIGHT OFF THE FIRST SHIFT.

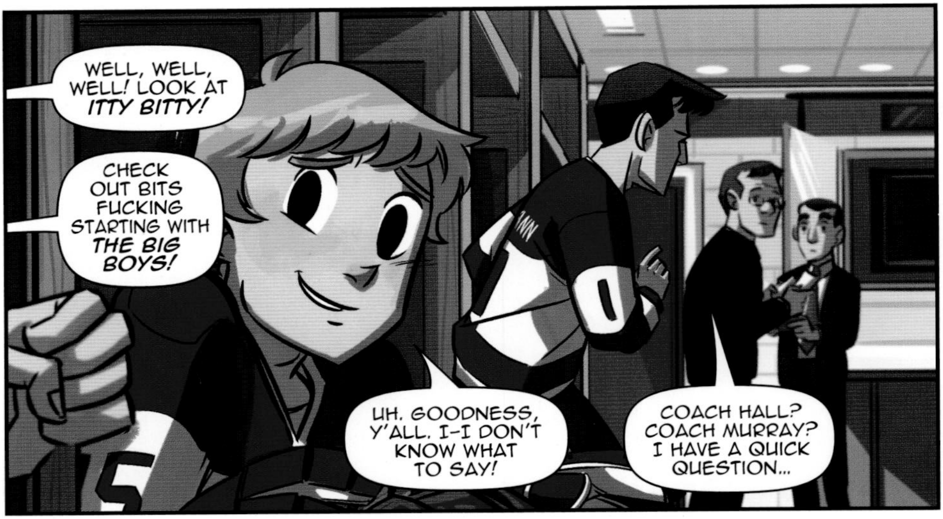
WELL, WELL, WELL! LOOK AT *ITTY BITTY!*
CHECK OUT BITS FUCKING STARTING WITH *THE BIG BOYS!*
UH. GOODNESS, Y'ALL. I-I DON'T KNOW WHAT TO SAY!
COACH HALL? COACH MURRAY? I HAVE A QUICK QUESTION...

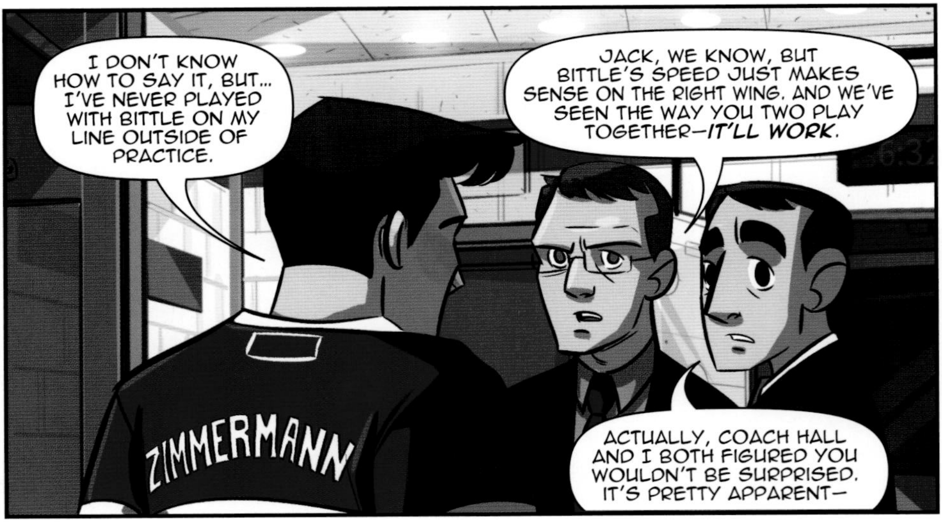
I DON'T KNOW HOW TO SAY IT, BUT... I'VE NEVER PLAYED WITH BITTLE ON MY LINE OUTSIDE OF PRACTICE.
JACK, WE KNOW, BUT BITTLE'S SPEED JUST MAKES SENSE ON THE RIGHT WING. AND WE'VE SEEN THE WAY YOU TWO PLAY TOGETHER—*IT'LL WORK*.
ZIMMERMANN
ACTUALLY, COACH HALL AND I BOTH FIGURED YOU WOULDN'T BE SURPRISED. IT'S PRETTY APPARENT—

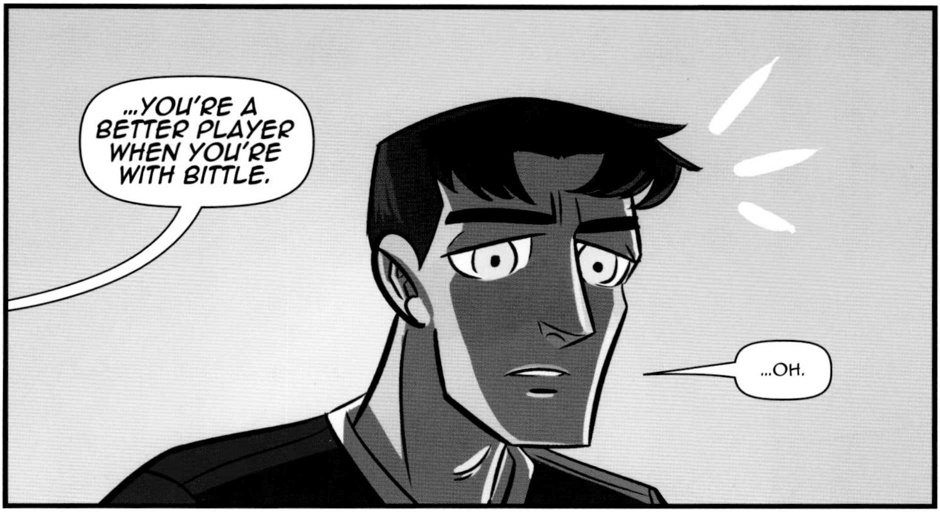
...YOU'RE A BETTER PLAYER WHEN YOU'RE WITH BITTLE.
...OH.

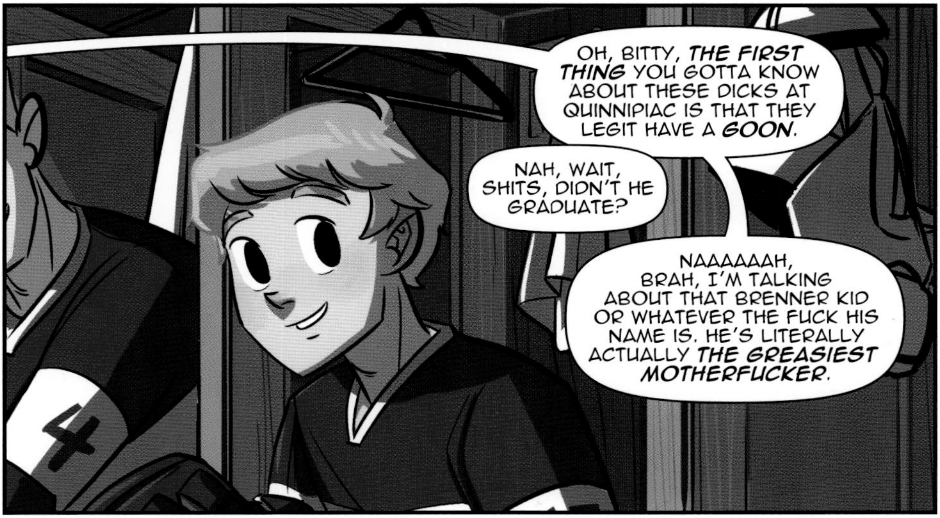
OH, BITTY, THE FIRST THING YOU GOTTA KNOW ABOUT THESE DICKS AT QUINNIPIAC IS THAT THEY LEGIT HAVE A GOON.
NAH, WAIT, SHITS, DIDN'T HE GRADUATE?
NAAAAAAH, BRAH, I'M TALKING ABOUT THAT BRENNER KID OR WHATEVER THE FUCK HIS NAME IS. HE'S LITERALLY ACTUALLY THE GREASIEST MOTHERFUCKER.

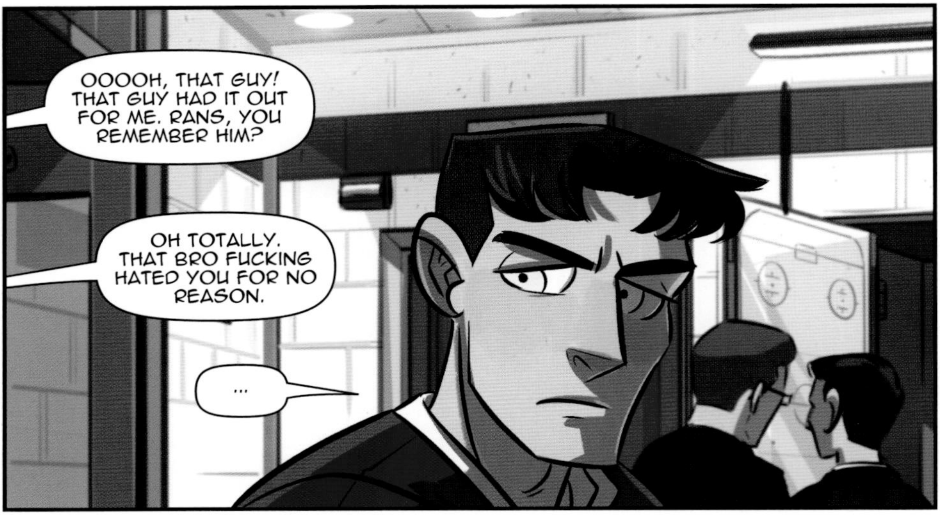
OOOOH, THAT GUY! THAT GUY HAD IT OUT FOR ME. RANS, YOU REMEMBER HIM?
OH TOTALLY. THAT BRO FUCKING HATED YOU FOR NO REASON.
...

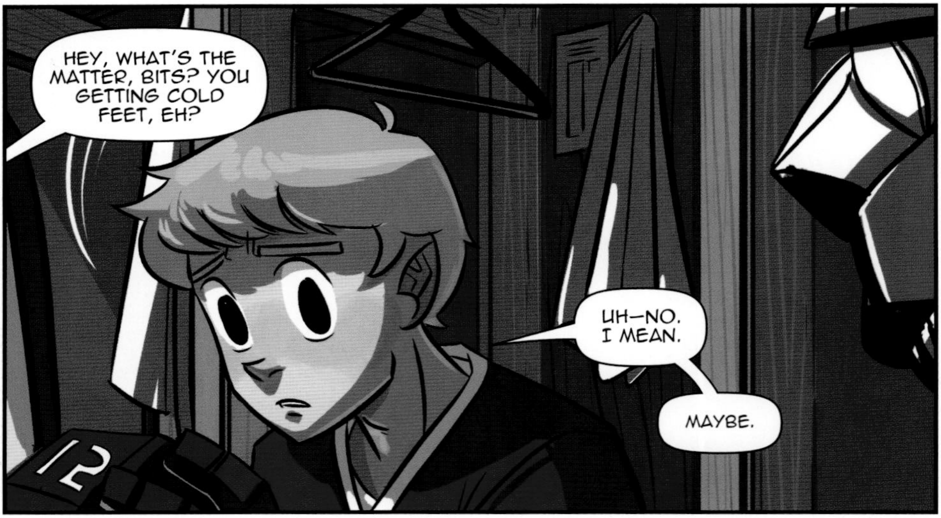
HEY, WHAT'S THE MATTER, BITS? YOU GETTING COLD FEET, EH?
UH—NO. I MEAN.
MAYBE.
12

17

TADPOLES

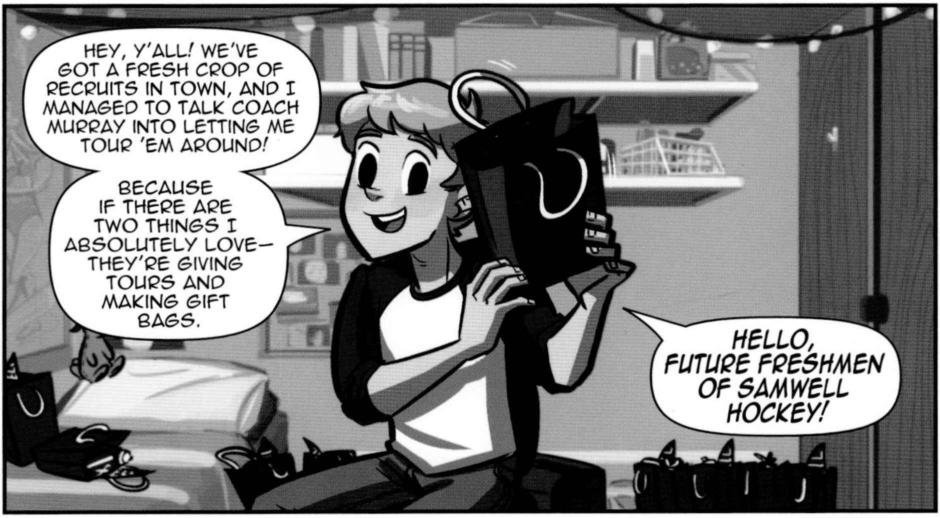
HEY, Y'ALL! WE'VE GOT A FRESH CROP OF RECRUITS IN TOWN, AND I MANAGED TO TALK COACH MURRAY INTO LETTING ME TOUR 'EM AROUND!
BECAUSE IF THERE ARE TWO THINGS I ABSOLUTELY LOVE— THEY'RE GIVING TOURS AND MAKING GIFT BAGS.
HELLO, FUTURE FRESHMEN OF SAMWELL HOCKEY!

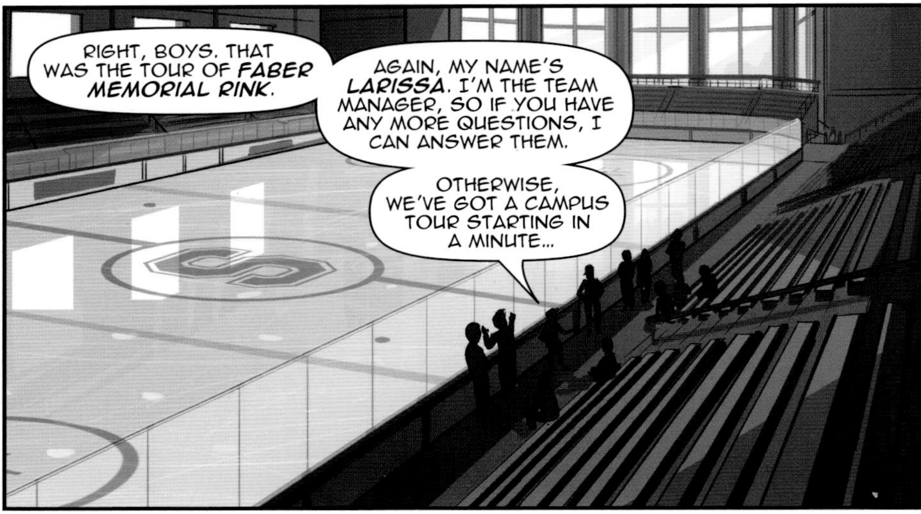
RIGHT, BOYS. THAT WAS THE TOUR OF FABER MEMORIAL RINK.
AGAIN, MY NAME'S LARISSA. I'M THE TEAM MANAGER, SO IF YOU HAVE ANY MORE QUESTIONS, I CAN ANSWER THEM.
OTHERWISE, WE'VE GOT A CAMPUS TOUR STARTING IN A MINUTE...

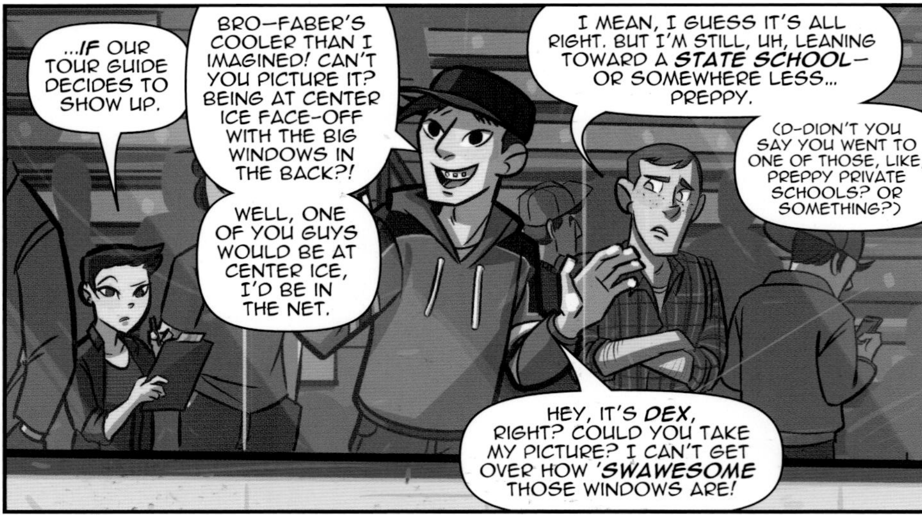
...IF OUR TOUR GUIDE DECIDES TO SHOW UP.
BRO—FABER'S COOLER THAN I IMAGINED! CAN'T YOU PICTURE IT? BEING AT CENTER ICE FACE-OFF WITH THE BIG WINDOWS IN THE BACK?!
WELL, ONE OF YOU GUYS WOULD BE AT CENTER ICE, I'D BE IN THE NET.
I MEAN, I GUESS IT'S ALL RIGHT. BUT I'M STILL, UH, LEANING TOWARD A STATE SCHOOL— OR SOMEWHERE LESS... PREPPY.
(D-DIDN'T YOU SAY YOU WENT TO ONE OF THOSE, LIKE, PREPPY PRIVATE SCHOOLS? OR SOMETHING?)
HEY, IT'S DEX, RIGHT? COULD YOU TAKE MY PICTURE? I CAN'T GET OVER HOW 'SWAWESOME THOSE WINDOWS ARE!

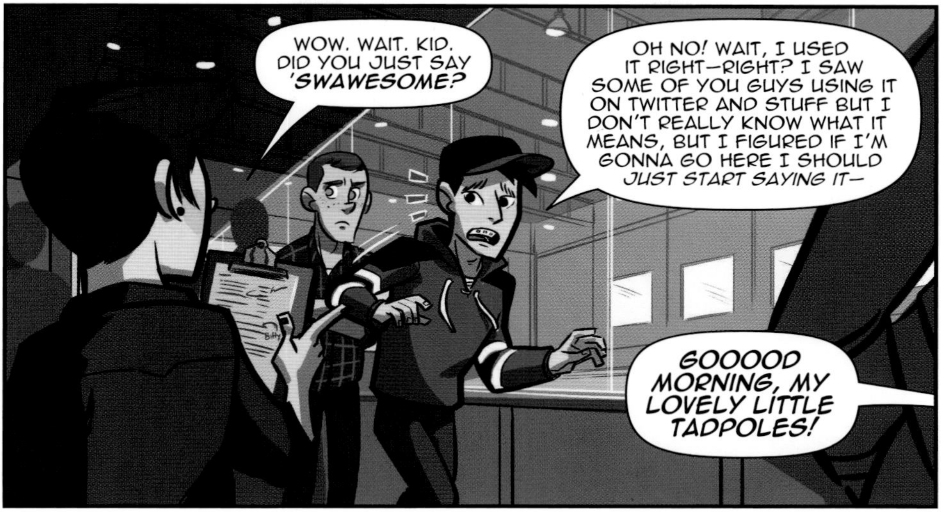
WOW. WAIT. KID. DID YOU JUST SAY 'SWAWESOME?
OH NO! WAIT, I USED IT RIGHT—RIGHT? I SAW SOME OF YOU GUYS USING IT ON TWITTER AND STUFF BUT I DON'T REALLY KNOW WHAT IT MEANS, BUT I FIGURED IF I'M GONNA GO HERE I SHOULD JUST START SAYING IT—
GOOOOD MORNING, MY LOVELY LITTLE TADPOLES!

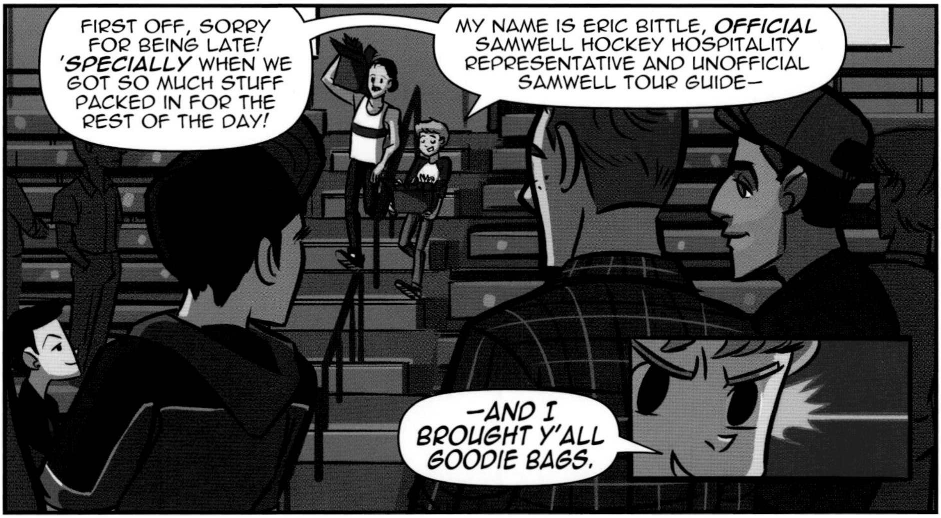
FIRST OFF, SORRY FOR BEING LATE! 'SPECIALLY WHEN WE GOT SO MUCH STUFF PACKED IN FOR THE REST OF THE DAY!
MY NAME IS ERIC BITTLE, OFFICIAL SAMWELL HOCKEY HOSPITALITY REPRESENTATIVE AND UNOFFICIAL SAMWELL TOUR GUIDE—
—AND I BROUGHT Y'ALL GOODIE BAGS.

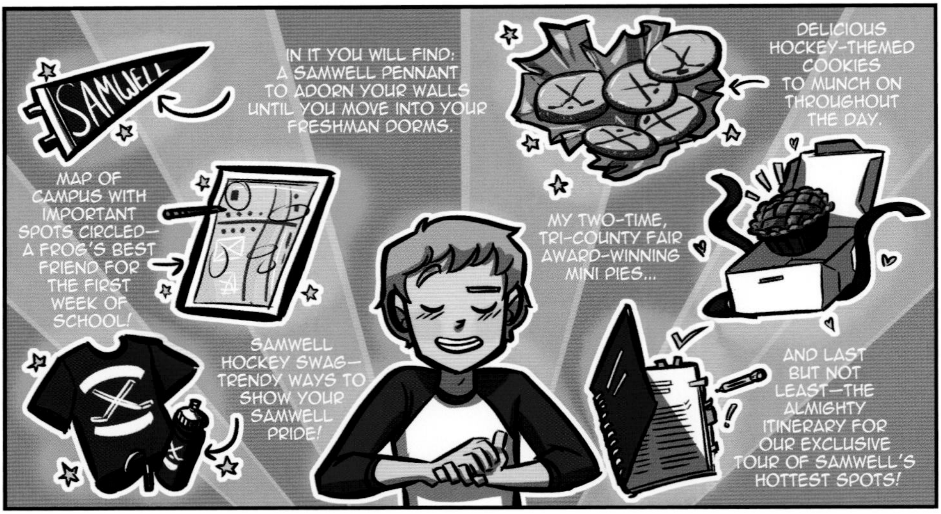
IN IT YOU WILL FIND: A SAMWELL PENNANT TO ADORN YOUR WALLS UNTIL YOU MOVE INTO YOUR FRESHMAN DORMS.
SAMWELL
DELICIOUS HOCKEY-THEMED COOKIES TO MUNCH ON THROUGHOUT THE DAY.
MAP OF CAMPUS WITH IMPORTANT SPOTS CIRCLED— A FROG'S BEST FRIEND FOR THE FIRST WEEK OF SCHOOL!
MY TWO-TIME, TRI-COUNTY FAIR AWARD-WINNING MINI PIES...
SAMWELL HOCKEY SWAG— TRENDY WAYS TO SHOW YOUR SAMWELL PRIDE!
AND LAST BUT NOT LEAST—THE ALMIGHTY ITINERARY FOR OUR EXCLUSIVE TOUR OF SAMWELL'S HOTTEST SPOTS!

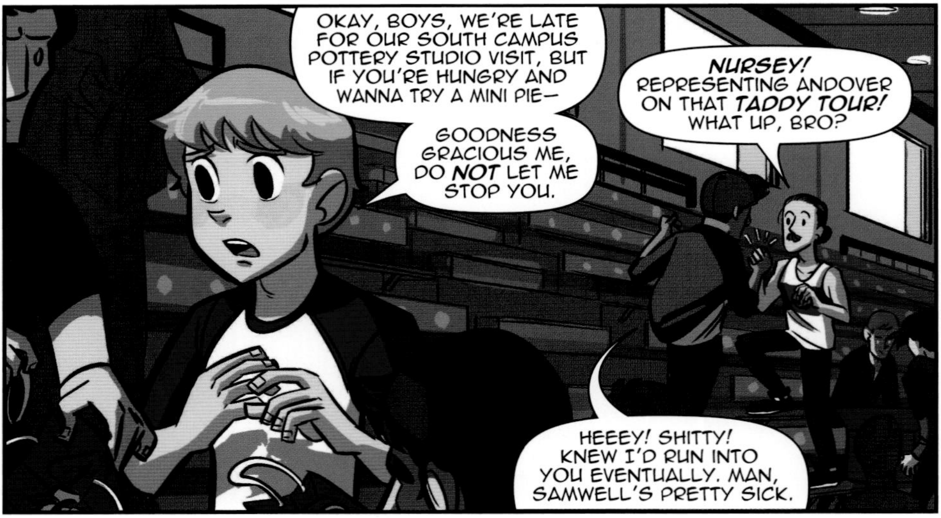
OKAY, BOYS, WE'RE LATE FOR OUR SOUTH CAMPUS POTTERY STUDIO VISIT, BUT IF YOU'RE HUNGRY AND WANNA TRY A MINI PIE—
GOODNESS GRACIOUS ME, DO **NOT** LET ME STOP YOU.
NURSEY! REPRESENTING ANDOVER ON THAT ***TADDY TOUR!*** WHAT UP, BRO?
HEEEY! SHITTY! KNEW I'D RUN INTO YOU EVENTUALLY. MAN, SAMWELL'S PRETTY SICK.

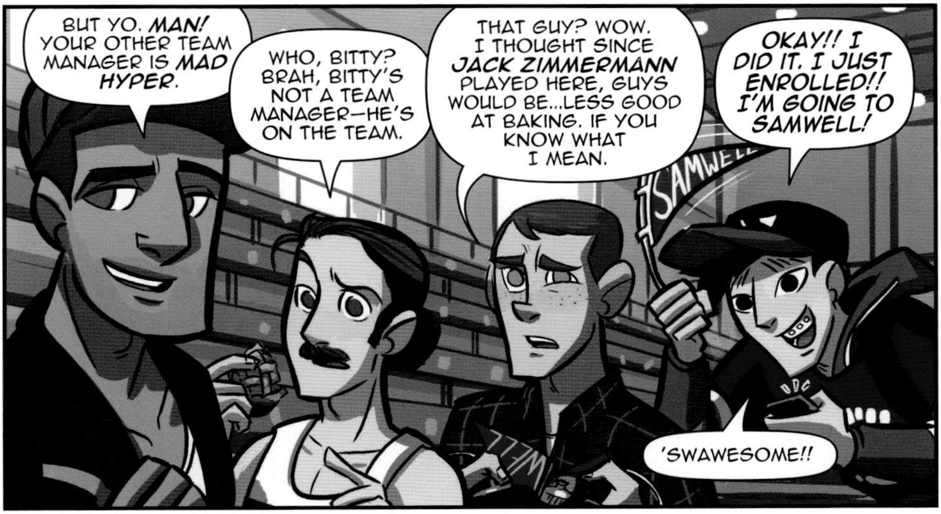
BUT YO. MAN! YOUR OTHER TEAM MANAGER IS MAD HYPER.
WHO, BITTY? BRAH, BITTY'S NOT A TEAM MANAGER—HE'S ON THE TEAM.
THAT GUY? WOW. I THOUGHT SINCE JACK ZIMMERMANN PLAYED HERE, GUYS WOULD BE...LESS GOOD AT BAKING. IF YOU KNOW WHAT I MEAN.
OKAY!! I DID IT. I JUST ENROLLED!! I'M GOING TO SAMWELL!
'SWAWESOME!!
SAMWELL

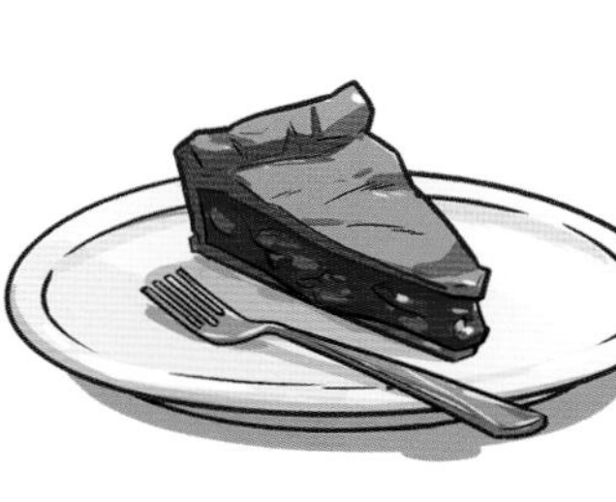

18

PLAYOFFS — I

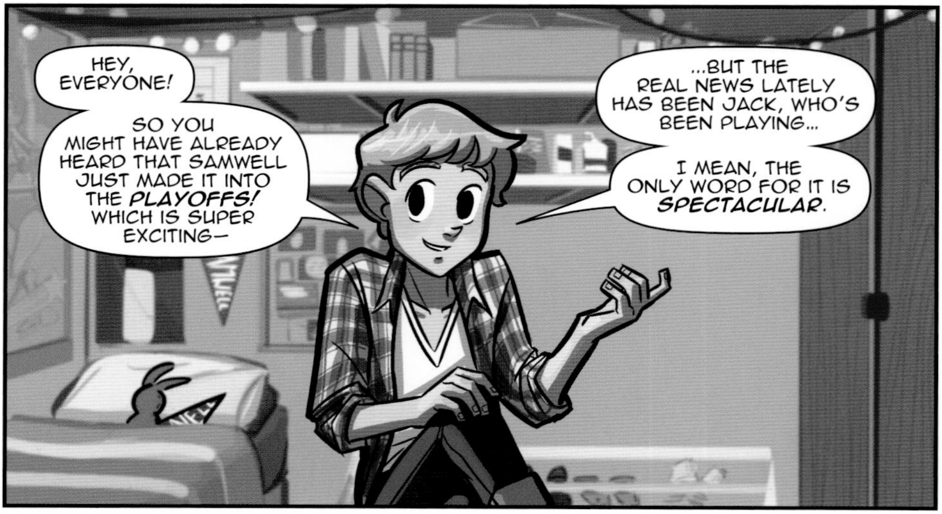
HEY, EVERYONE!
SO YOU MIGHT HAVE ALREADY HEARD THAT SAMWELL JUST MADE IT INTO THE *PLAYOFFS!* WHICH IS SUPER EXCITING—
...BUT THE REAL NEWS LATELY HAS BEEN JACK, WHO'S BEEN PLAYING...
I MEAN, THE ONLY WORD FOR IT IS *SPECTACULAR*.

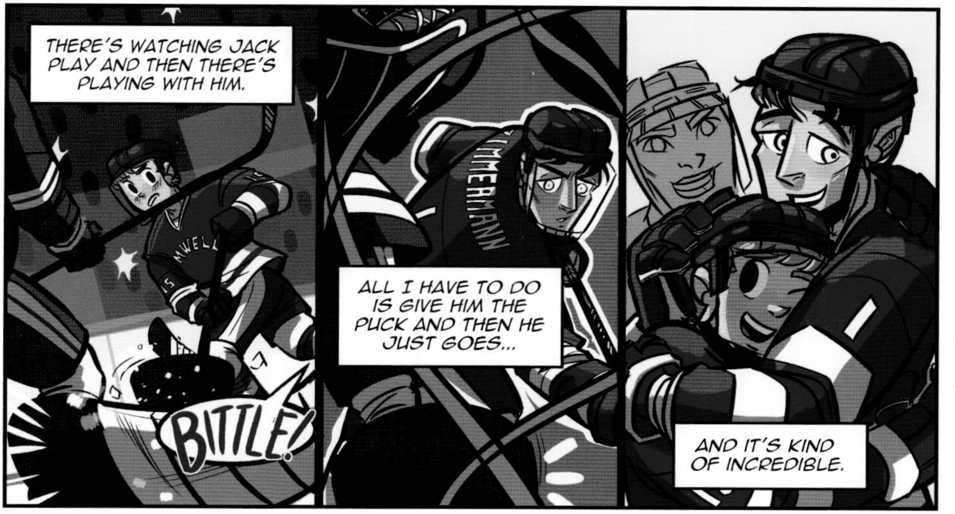
THERE'S WATCHING JACK PLAY AND THEN THERE'S PLAYING WITH HIM.
BITTLE!
ALL I HAVE TO DO IS GIVE HIM THE PUCK AND THEN HE JUST GOES...
AND IT'S KIND OF INCREDIBLE.

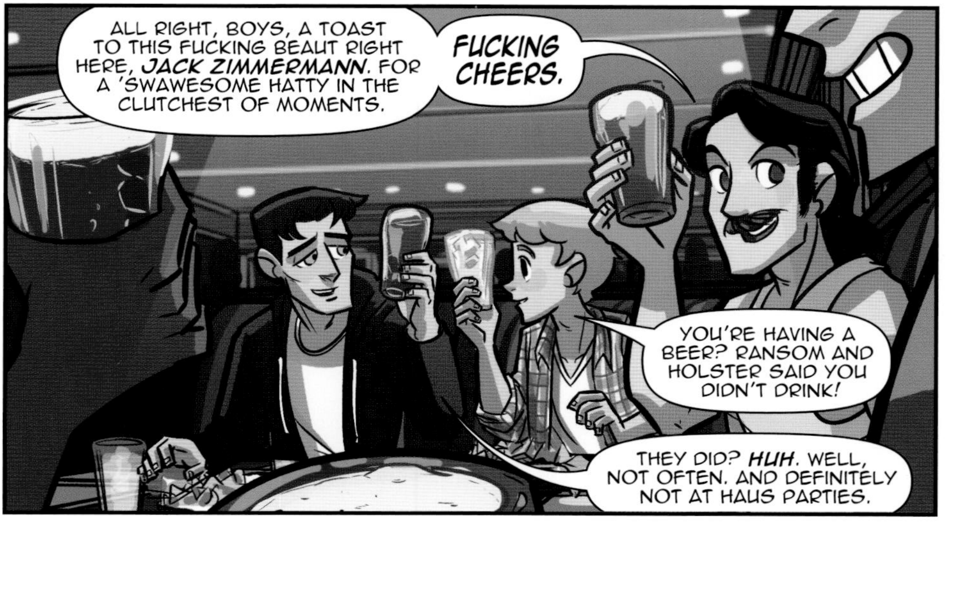
ALL RIGHT, BOYS, A TOAST TO THIS FUCKING BEAUT RIGHT HERE, JACK ZIMMERMANN. FOR A 'SWAWESOME HATTY IN THE CLUTCHEST OF MOMENTS.
FUCKING CHEERS.
YOU'RE HAVING A BEER? RANSOM AND HOLSTER SAID YOU DIDN'T DRINK!
THEY DID? HUH. WELL, NOT OFTEN. AND DEFINITELY NOT AT HAUS PARTIES.

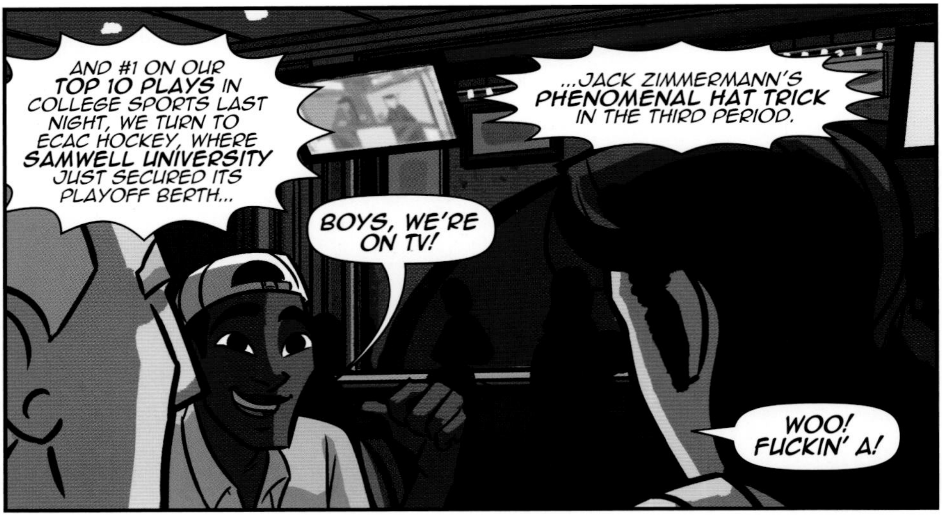
AND #1 ON OUR TOP 10 PLAYS IN COLLEGE SPORTS LAST NIGHT, WE TURN TO ECAC HOCKEY, WHERE SAMWELL UNIVERSITY JUST SECURED ITS PLAYOFF BERTH...
...JACK ZIMMERMANN'S PHENOMENAL HAT TRICK IN THE THIRD PERIOD.
BOYS, WE'RE ON TV!
WOO! FUCKIN' A!

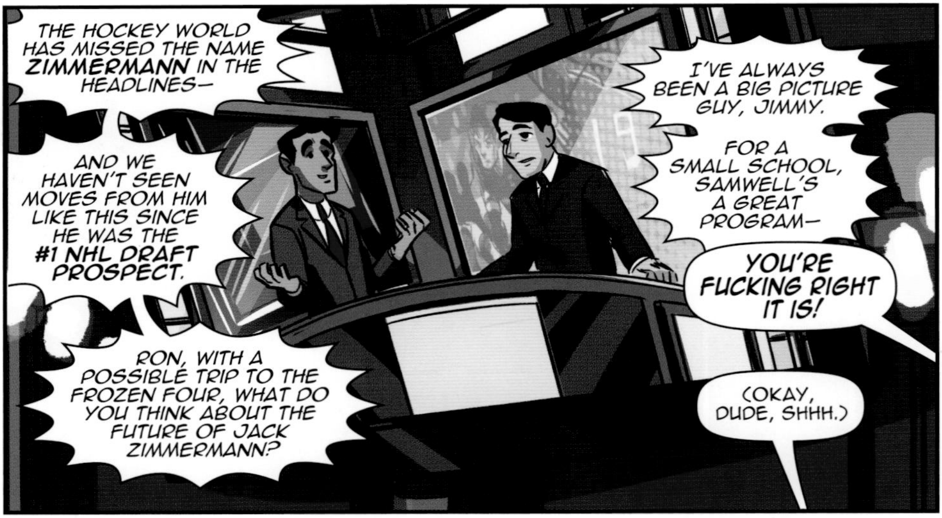
THE HOCKEY WORLD HAS MISSED THE NAME ZIMMERMANN IN THE HEADLINES—
AND WE HAVEN'T SEEN MOVES FROM HIM LIKE THIS SINCE HE WAS THE #1 NHL DRAFT PROSPECT.
RON, WITH A POSSIBLE TRIP TO THE FROZEN FOUR, WHAT DO YOU THINK ABOUT THE FUTURE OF JACK ZIMMERMANN?
I'VE ALWAYS BEEN A BIG PICTURE GUY, JIMMY.
FOR A SMALL SCHOOL, SAMWELL'S A GREAT PROGRAM—
YOU'RE FUCKING RIGHT IT IS!
(OKAY, DUDE, SHHH.)

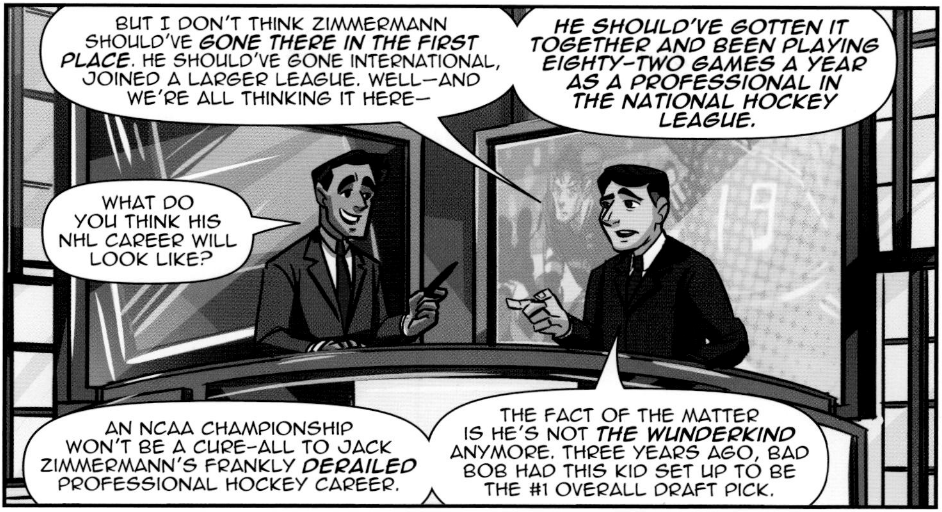
BUT I DON'T THINK ZIMMERMANN SHOULD'VE GONE THERE IN THE FIRST PLACE. HE SHOULD'VE GONE INTERNATIONAL, JOINED A LARGER LEAGUE. WELL—AND WE'RE ALL THINKING IT HERE—
HE SHOULD'VE GOTTEN IT TOGETHER AND BEEN PLAYING EIGHTY-TWO GAMES A YEAR AS A PROFESSIONAL IN THE NATIONAL HOCKEY LEAGUE.
WHAT DO YOU THINK HIS NHL CAREER WILL LOOK LIKE?
AN NCAA CHAMPIONSHIP WON'T BE A CURE-ALL TO JACK ZIMMERMANN'S FRANKLY DERAILED PROFESSIONAL HOCKEY CAREER.
THE FACT OF THE MATTER IS HE'S NOT THE WUNDERKIND ANYMORE. THREE YEARS AGO, BAD BOB HAD THIS KID SET UP TO BE THE #1 OVERALL DRAFT PICK.

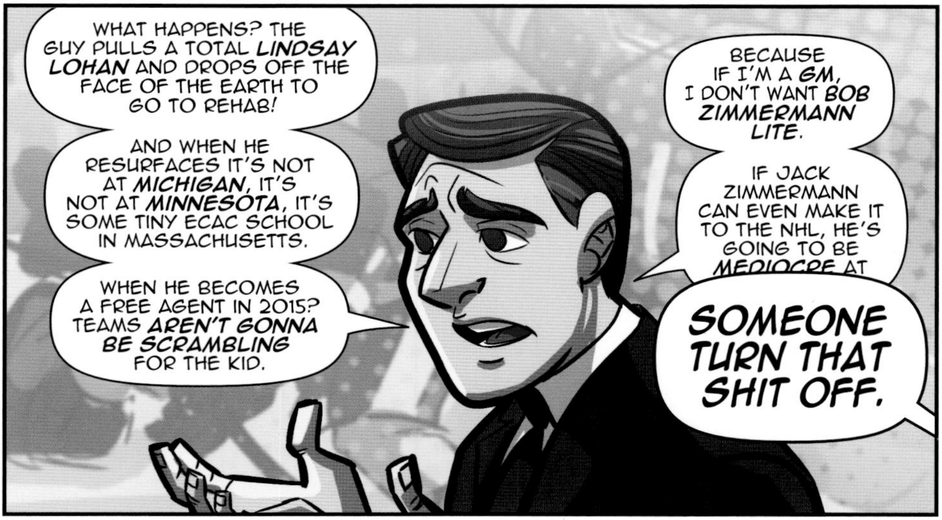
WHAT HAPPENS? THE GUY PULLS A TOTAL LINDSAY LOHAN AND DROPS OFF THE FACE OF THE EARTH TO GO TO REHAB!
AND WHEN HE RESURFACES IT'S NOT AT MICHIGAN, IT'S NOT AT MINNESOTA, IT'S SOME TINY ECAC SCHOOL IN MASSACHUSETTS.
WHEN HE BECOMES A FREE AGENT IN 2015? TEAMS AREN'T GONNA BE SCRAMBLING FOR THE KID.
BECAUSE IF I'M A GM, I DON'T WANT BOB ZIMMERMANN LITE.
IF JACK ZIMMERMANN CAN EVEN MAKE IT TO THE NHL, HE'S GOING TO BE
SOMEONE TURN THAT SHIT OFF.

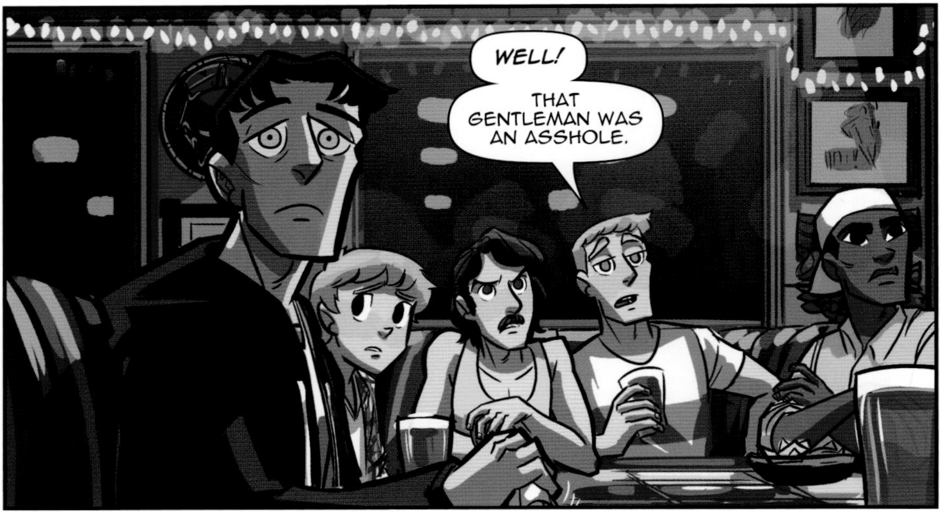
WELL!
THAT GENTLEMAN WAS AN ASSHOLE.

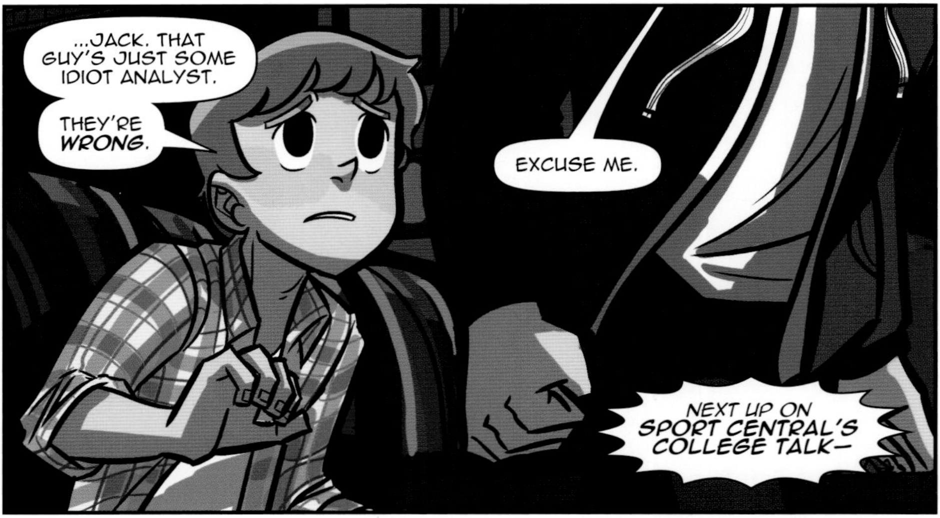
...JACK. THAT GUY'S JUST SOME IDIOT ANALYST.
THEY'RE WRONG.
EXCUSE ME.
NEXT UP ON SPORT CENTRAL'S COLLEGE TALK—

19

PLAYOFFS — II

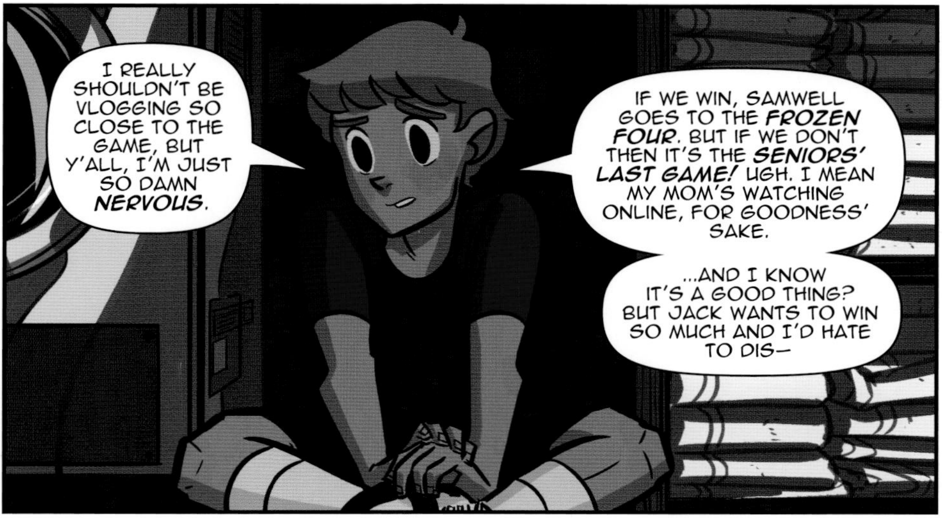
I REALLY SHOULDN'T BE VLOGGING SO CLOSE TO THE GAME, BUT Y'ALL, I'M JUST SO DAMN ***NERVOUS***.
IF WE WIN, SAMWELL GOES TO THE ***FROZEN FOUR***. BUT IF WE DON'T THEN IT'S THE ***SENIORS' LAST GAME!*** UGH. I MEAN MY MOM'S WATCHING ONLINE, FOR GOODNESS' SAKE.
...AND I KNOW IT'S A GOOD THING? BUT JACK WANTS TO WIN SO MUCH AND I'D HATE TO DIS—

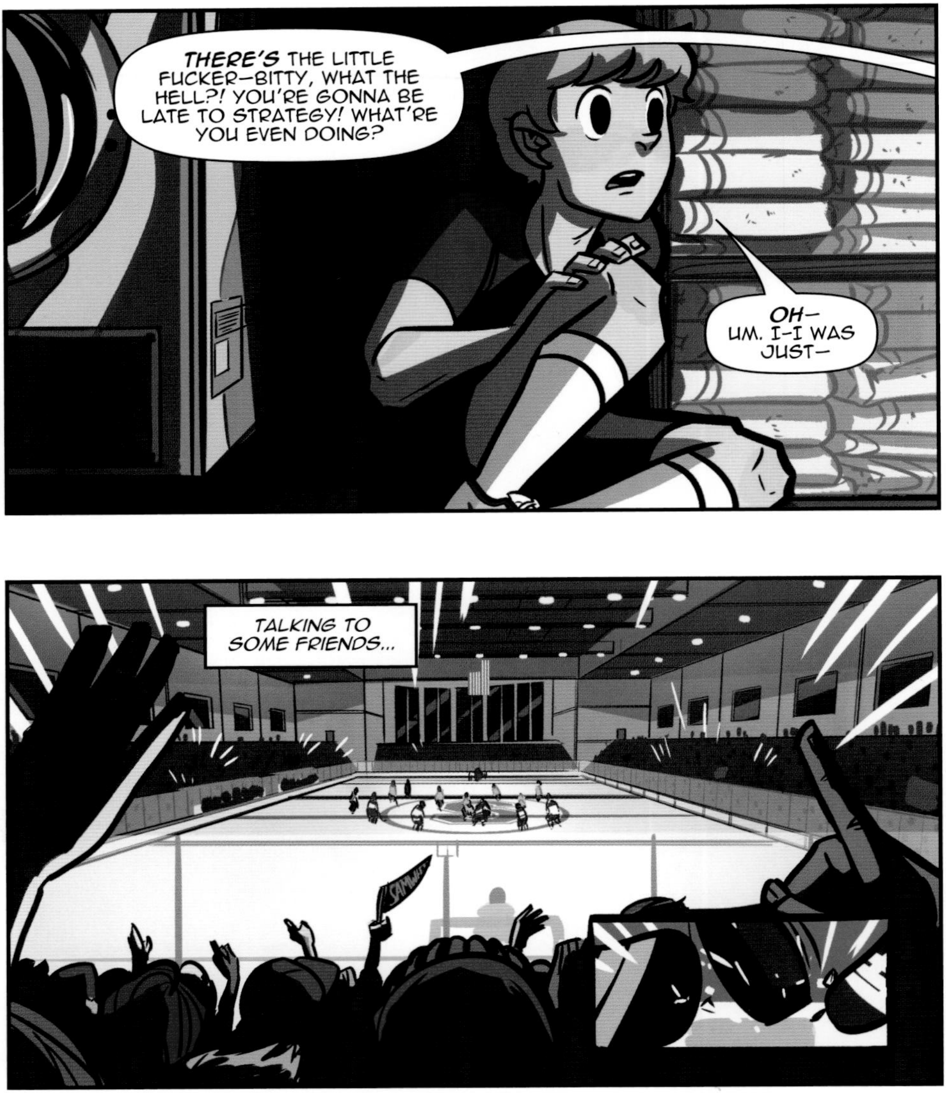
THERE'S THE LITTLE FUCKER—BITTY, WHAT THE HELL?! YOU'RE GONNA BE LATE TO STRATEGY! WHAT'RE YOU EVEN DOING?
OH— UM. I-I WAS JUST—
TALKING TO SOME FRIENDS...

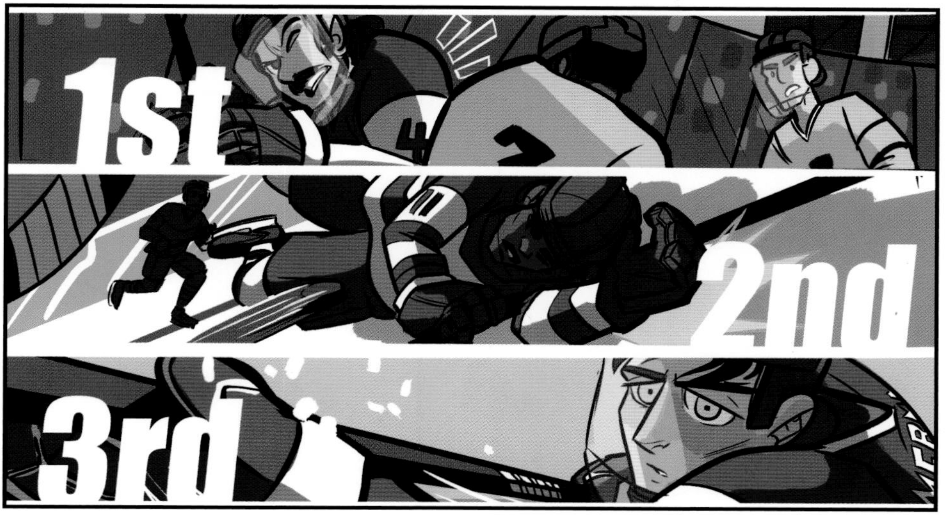
1st
2nd
3rd

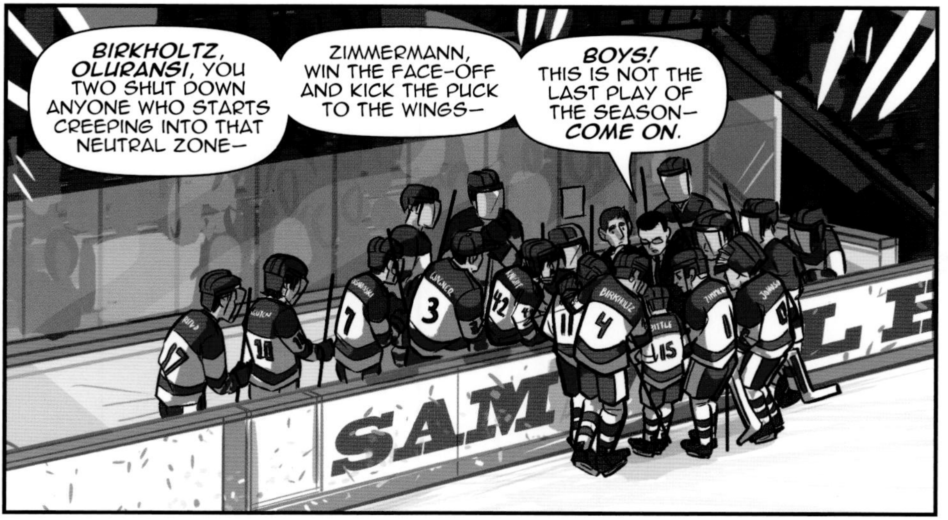
BIRKHOLTZ, OLURANSI, YOU TWO SHUT DOWN ANYONE WHO STARTS CREEPING INTO THAT NEUTRAL ZONE—
ZIMMERMANN, WIN THE FACE-OFF AND KICK THE PUCK TO THE WINGS—
BOYS! THIS IS NOT THE LAST PLAY OF THE SEASON— COME ON.
SAM

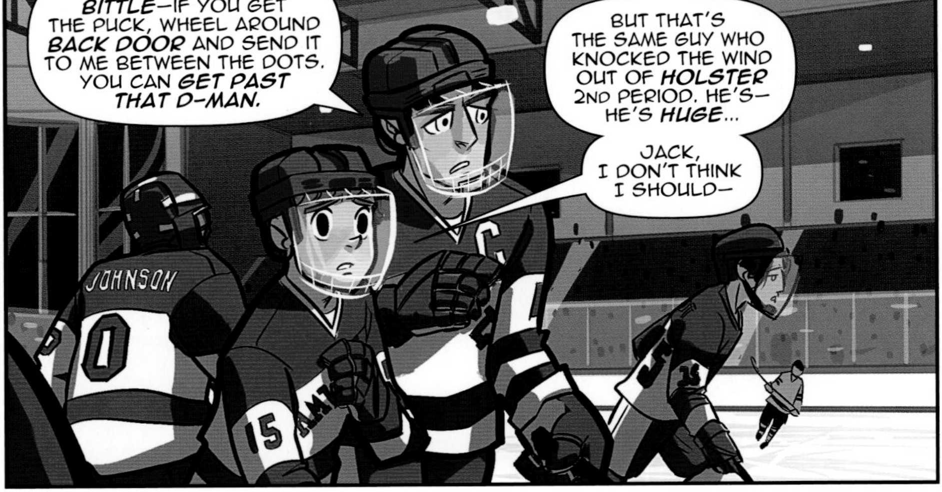
BITTLE—IF YOU GET THE PUCK, WHEEL AROUND BACK DOOR AND SEND IT TO ME BETWEEN THE DOTS. YOU CAN GET PAST THAT D-MAN.
BUT THAT'S THE SAME GUY WHO KNOCKED THE WIND OUT OF HOLSTER 2ND PERIOD. HE'S— HE'S HUGE...
JACK, I DON'T THINK I SHOULD—
JOHNSON

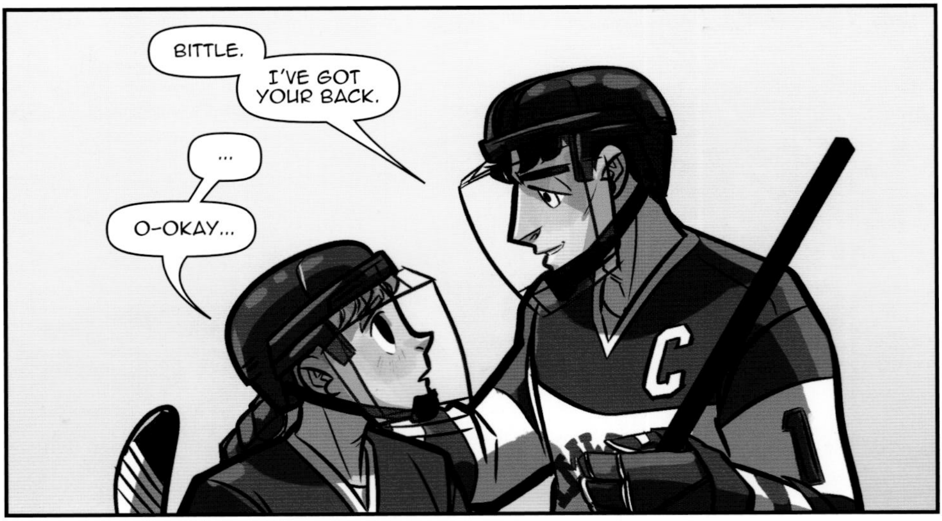
BITTLE.
I'VE GOT YOUR BACK.
...
O-OKAY...

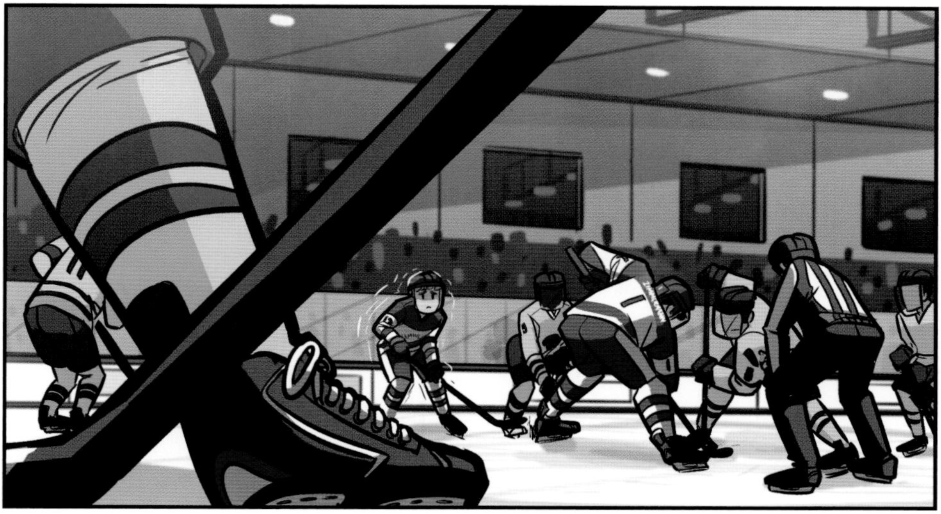

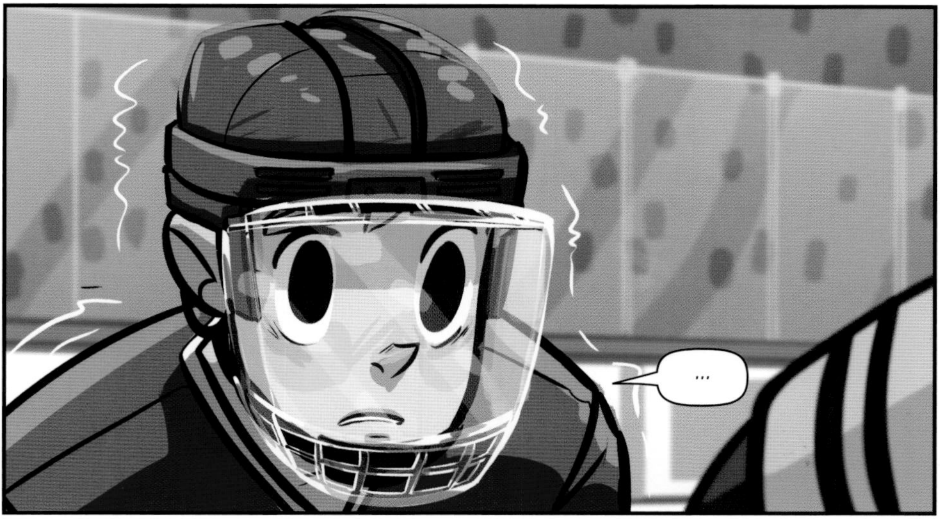
...

20

PLAYOFFS — III

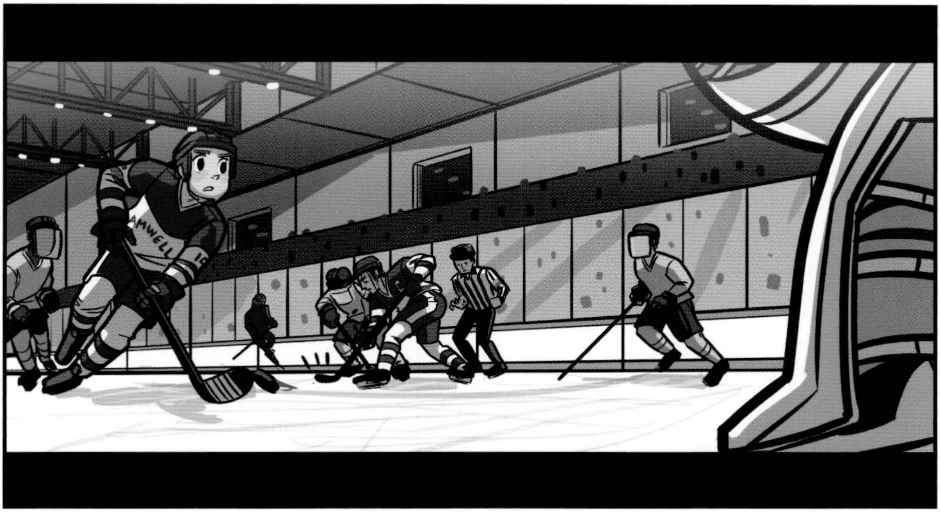

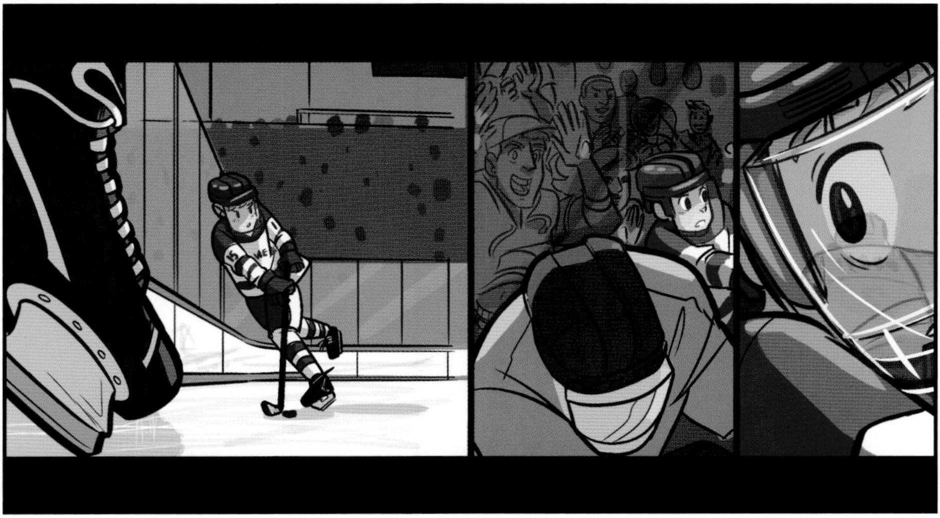

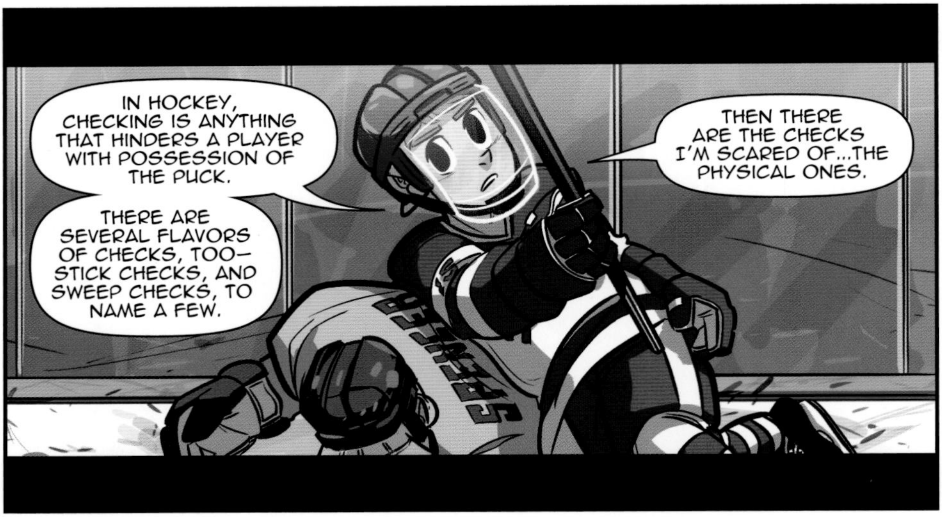
IN HOCKEY, CHECKING IS ANYTHING THAT HINDERS A PLAYER WITH POSSESSION OF THE PUCK.
THERE ARE SEVERAL FLAVORS OF CHECKS, TOO—STICK CHECKS, AND SWEEP CHECKS, TO NAME A FEW.
THEN THERE ARE THE CHECKS I'M SCARED OF...THE PHYSICAL ONES.

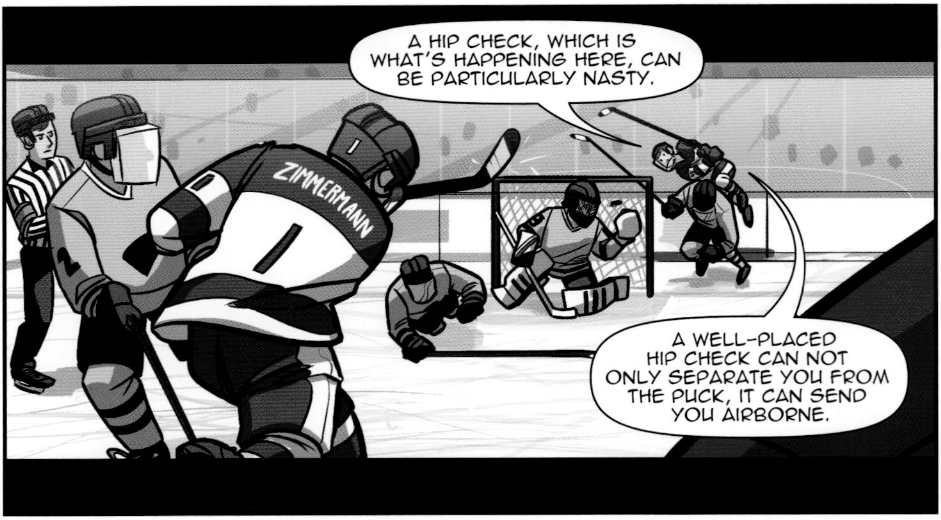
A HIP CHECK, WHICH IS WHAT'S HAPPENING HERE, CAN BE PARTICULARLY NASTY.
ZIMMERMANN
A WELL-PLACED HIP CHECK CAN NOT ONLY SEPARATE YOU FROM THE PUCK, IT CAN SEND YOU AIRBORNE.

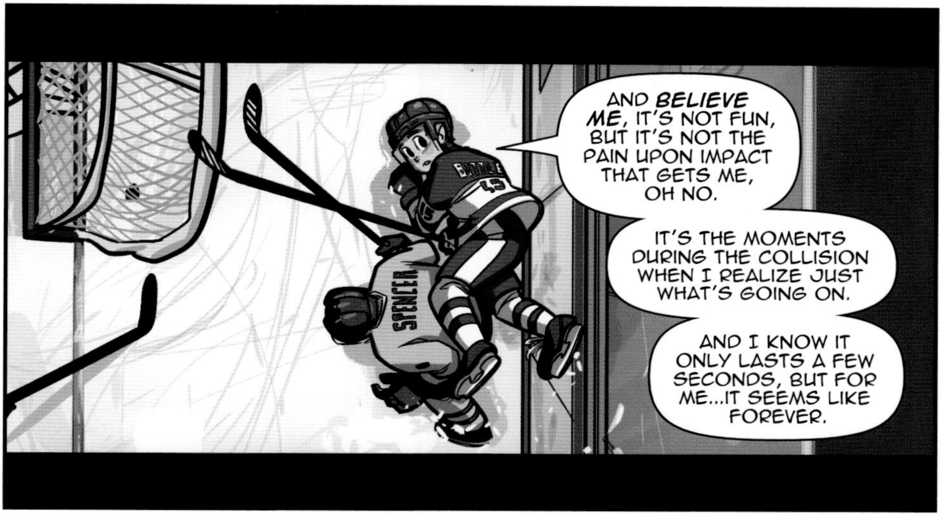
AND **BELIEVE ME**, IT'S NOT FUN, BUT IT'S NOT THE PAIN UPON IMPACT THAT GETS ME, OH NO.
IT'S THE MOMENTS DURING THE COLLISION WHEN I REALIZE JUST WHAT'S GOING ON.
AND I KNOW IT ONLY LASTS A FEW SECONDS, BUT FOR ME...IT SEEMS LIKE FOREVER.
SPENCER

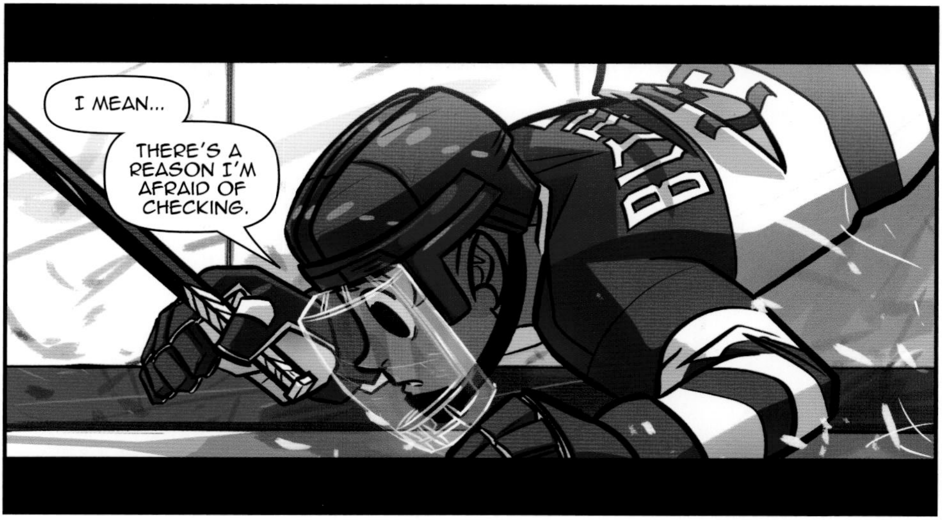
I MEAN...
THERE'S A REASON I'M AFRAID OF CHECKING.

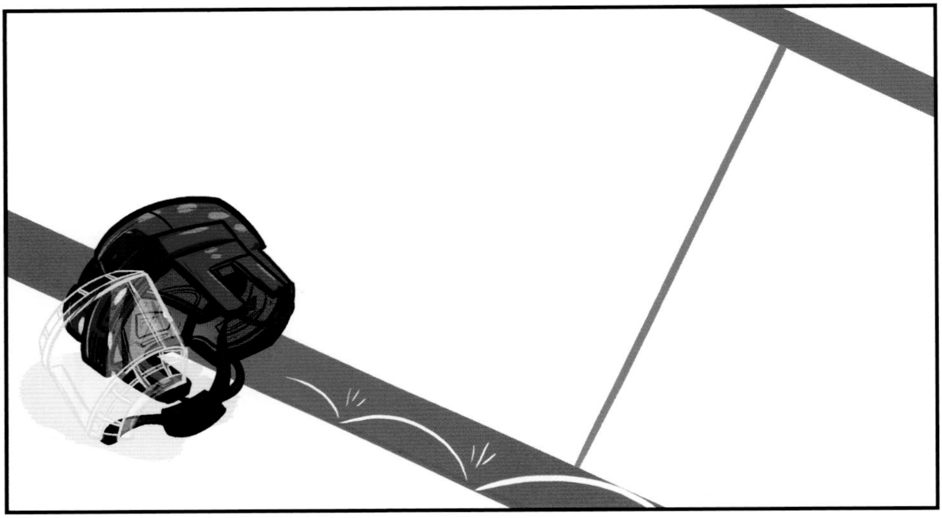

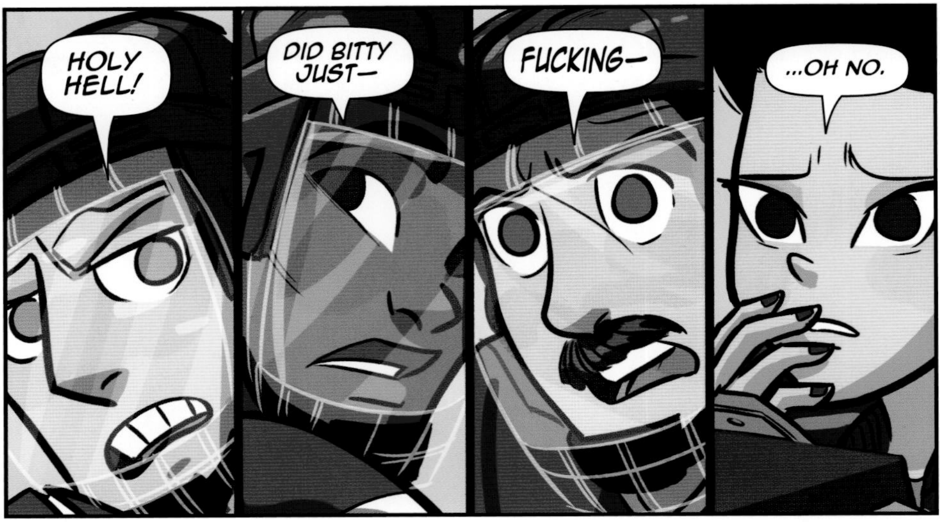
HOLY HELL!
DID BITTY JUST—
FUCKING—
...OH NO.

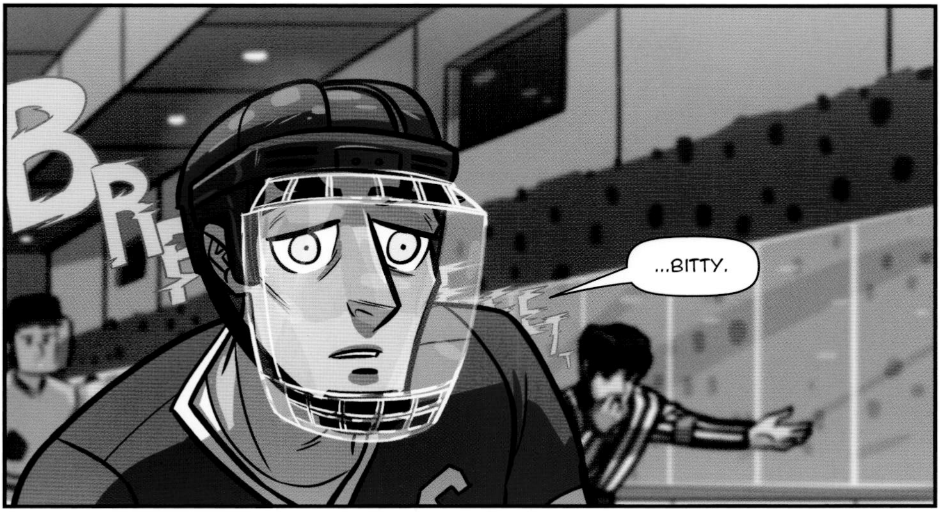
...BITTY.

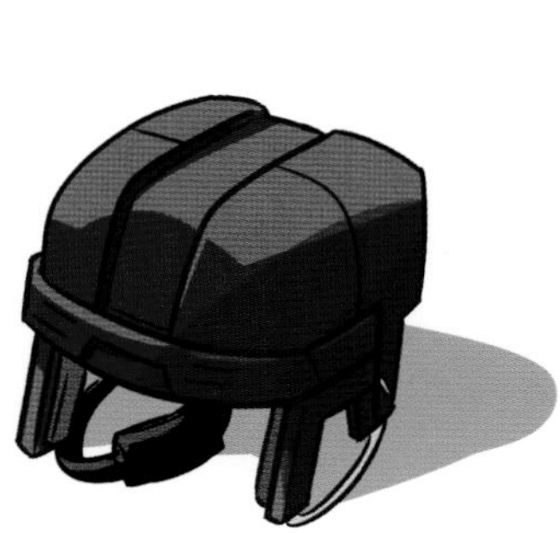

21

BANQUET

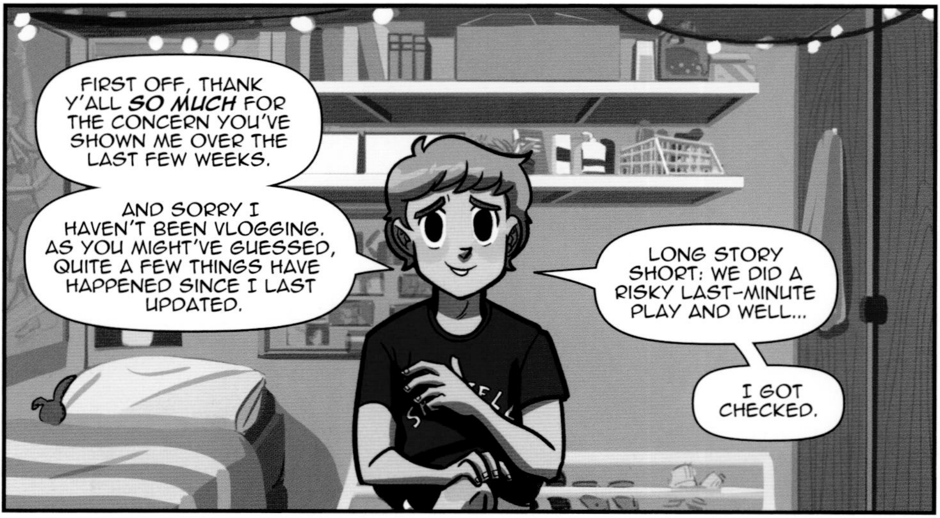
FIRST OFF, THANK Y'ALL *SO MUCH* FOR THE CONCERN YOU'VE SHOWN ME OVER THE LAST FEW WEEKS.
AND SORRY I HAVEN'T BEEN VLOGGING. AS YOU MIGHT'VE GUESSED, QUITE A FEW THINGS HAVE HAPPENED SINCE I LAST UPDATED.
LONG STORY SHORT: WE DID A RISKY LAST-MINUTE PLAY AND WELL...
I GOT CHECKED.

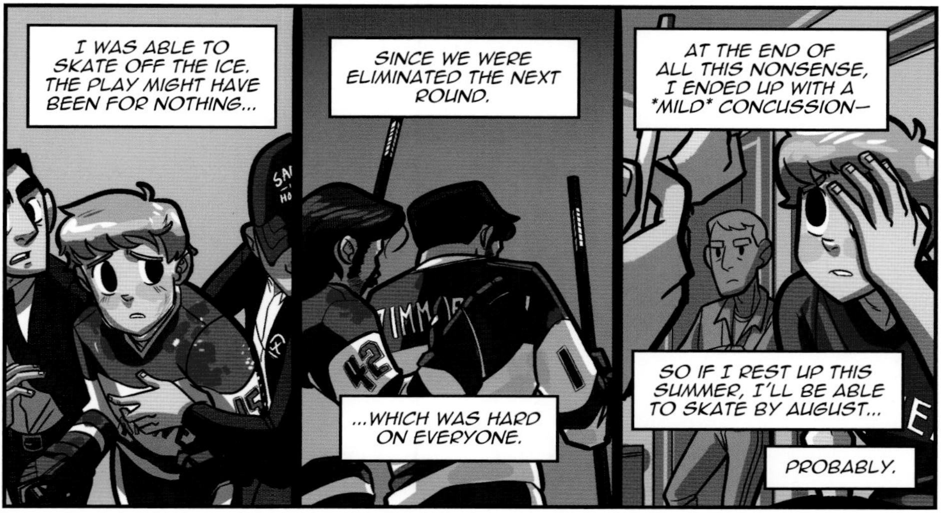
I WAS ABLE TO SKATE OFF THE ICE. THE PLAY MIGHT HAVE BEEN FOR NOTHING...
SINCE WE WERE ELIMINATED THE NEXT ROUND.
...WHICH WAS HARD ON EVERYONE.
AT THE END OF ALL THIS NONSENSE, I ENDED UP WITH A *MILD* CONCUSSION—
SO IF I REST UP THIS SUMMER, I'LL BE ABLE TO SKATE BY AUGUST...
PROBABLY.

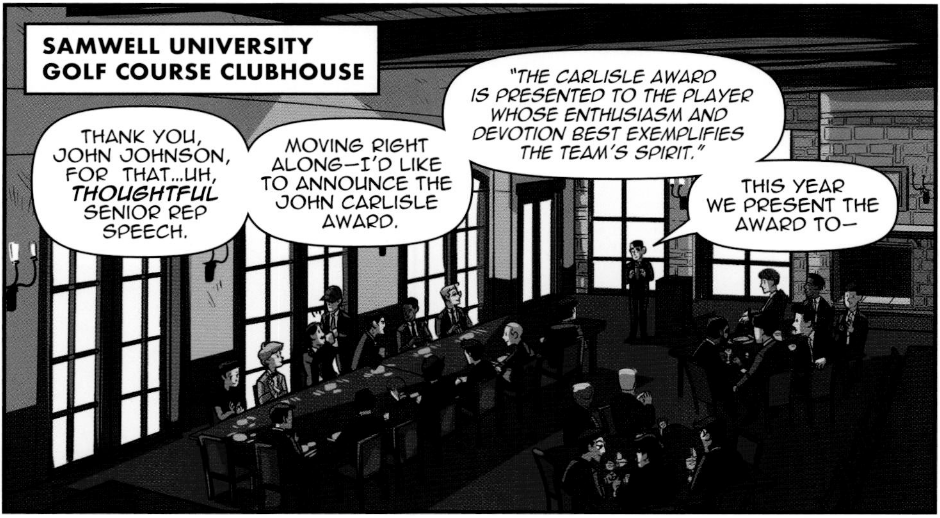
SAMWELL UNIVERSITY GOLF COURSE CLUBHOUSE
THANK YOU, JOHN JOHNSON, FOR THAT...UH, THOUGHTFUL SENIOR REP SPEECH.
MOVING RIGHT ALONG—I'D LIKE TO ANNOUNCE THE JOHN CARLISLE AWARD.
"THE CARLISLE AWARD IS PRESENTED TO THE PLAYER WHOSE ENTHUSIASM AND DEVOTION BEST EXEMPLIFIES THE TEAM'S SPIRIT."
THIS YEAR WE PRESENT THE AWARD TO—

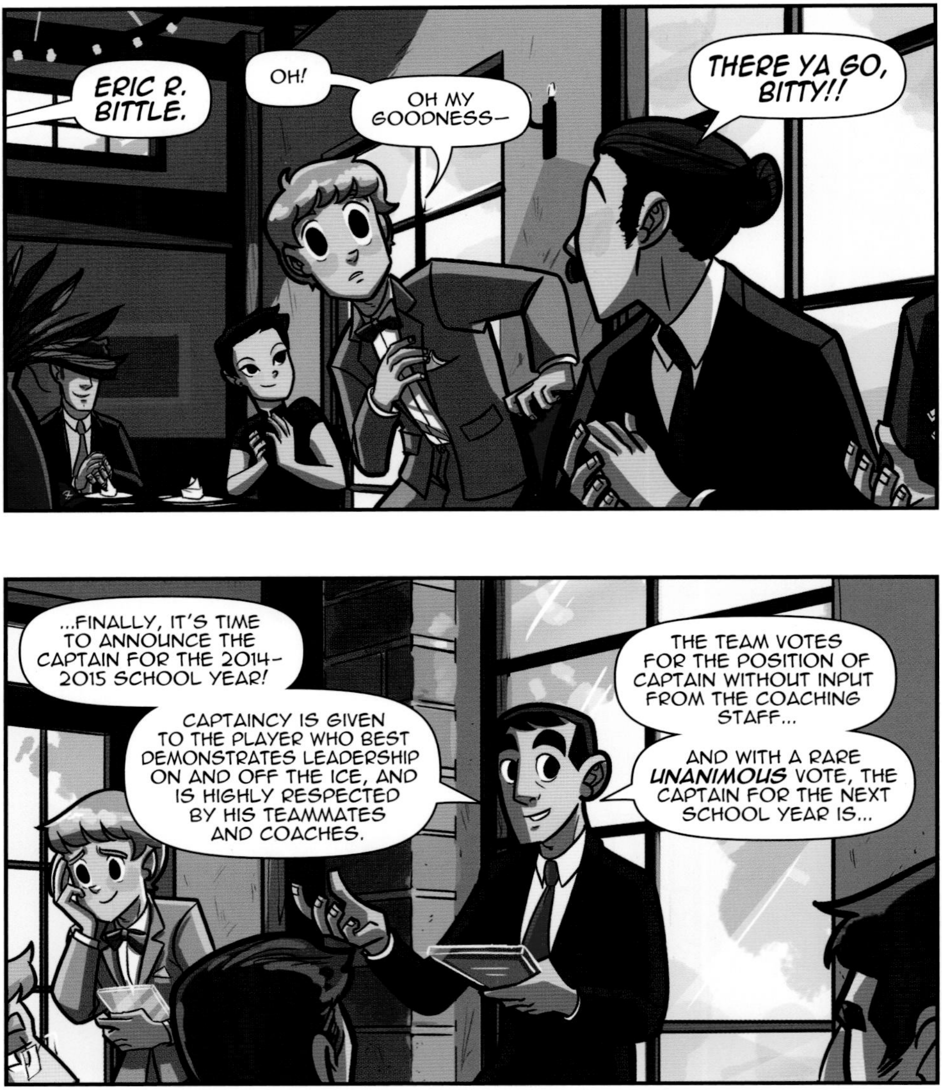
ERIC R. BITTLE.
OH!
OH MY GOODNESS—
THERE YA GO, BITTY!!
...FINALLY, IT'S TIME TO ANNOUNCE THE CAPTAIN FOR THE 2014-2015 SCHOOL YEAR!
CAPTAINCY IS GIVEN TO THE PLAYER WHO BEST DEMONSTRATES LEADERSHIP ON AND OFF THE ICE, AND IS HIGHLY RESPECTED BY HIS TEAMMATES AND COACHES.
THE TEAM VOTES FOR THE POSITION OF CAPTAIN WITHOUT INPUT FROM THE COACHING STAFF...
AND WITH A RARE UNANIMOUS VOTE, THE CAPTAIN FOR THE NEXT SCHOOL YEAR IS...

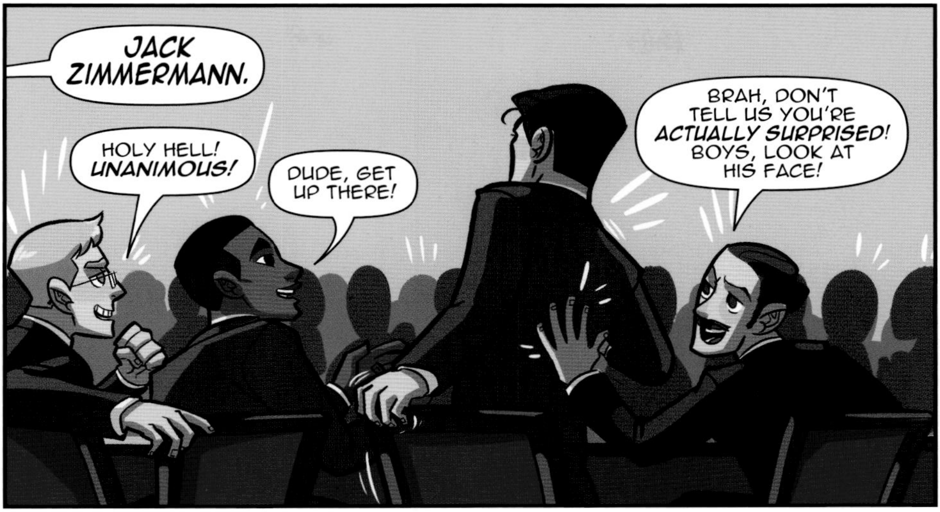
JACK ZIMMERMANN.
HOLY HELL! UNANIMOUS!
DUDE, GET UP THERE!
BRAH, DON'T TELL US YOU'RE ACTUALLY SURPRISED! BOYS, LOOK AT HIS FACE!

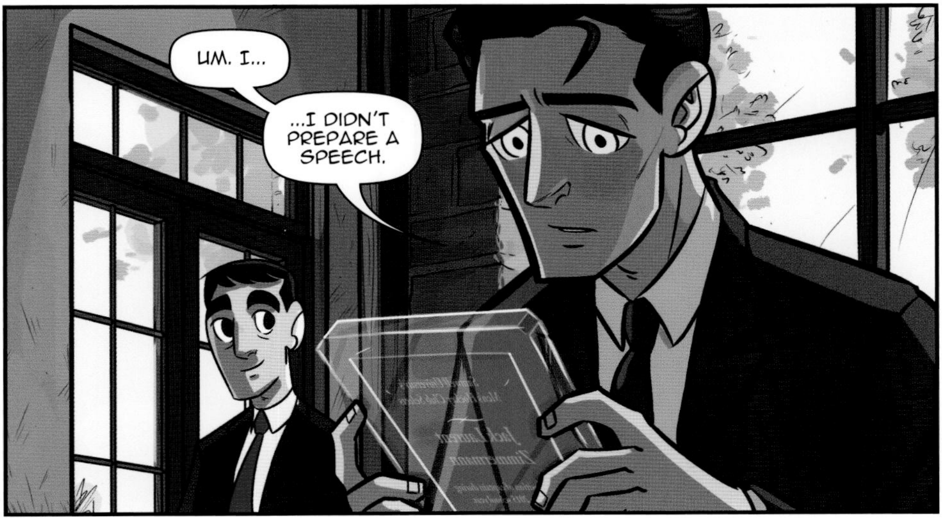
UM. I...
...I DIDN'T PREPARE A SPEECH.

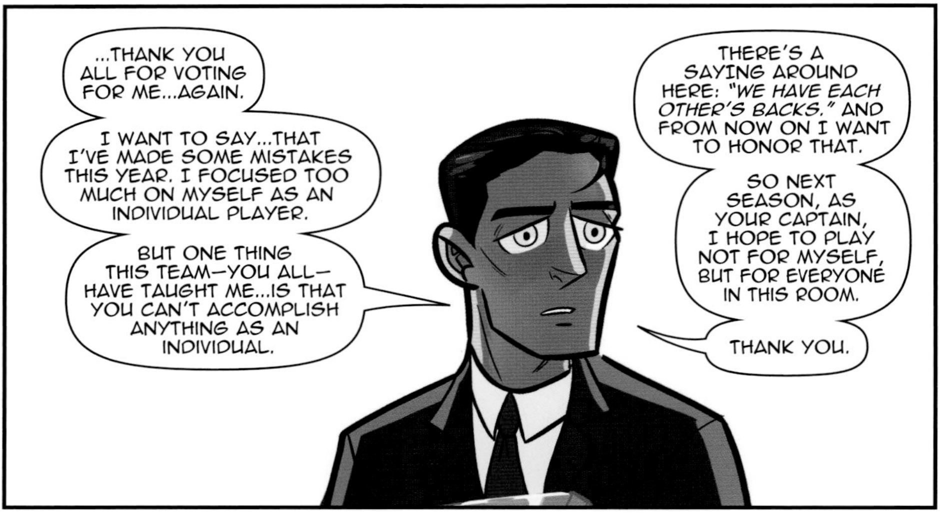
...THANK YOU ALL FOR VOTING FOR ME...AGAIN.
I WANT TO SAY...THAT I'VE MADE SOME MISTAKES THIS YEAR. I FOCUSED TOO MUCH ON MYSELF AS AN INDIVIDUAL PLAYER.
BUT ONE THING THIS TEAM—YOU ALL—HAVE TAUGHT ME...IS THAT YOU CAN'T ACCOMPLISH ANYTHING AS AN INDIVIDUAL.
THERE'S A SAYING AROUND HERE: *"WE HAVE EACH OTHER'S BACKS."* AND FROM NOW ON I WANT TO HONOR THAT.
SO NEXT SEASON, AS YOUR CAPTAIN, I HOPE TO PLAY NOT FOR MYSELF, BUT FOR EVERYONE IN THIS ROOM.
THANK YOU.

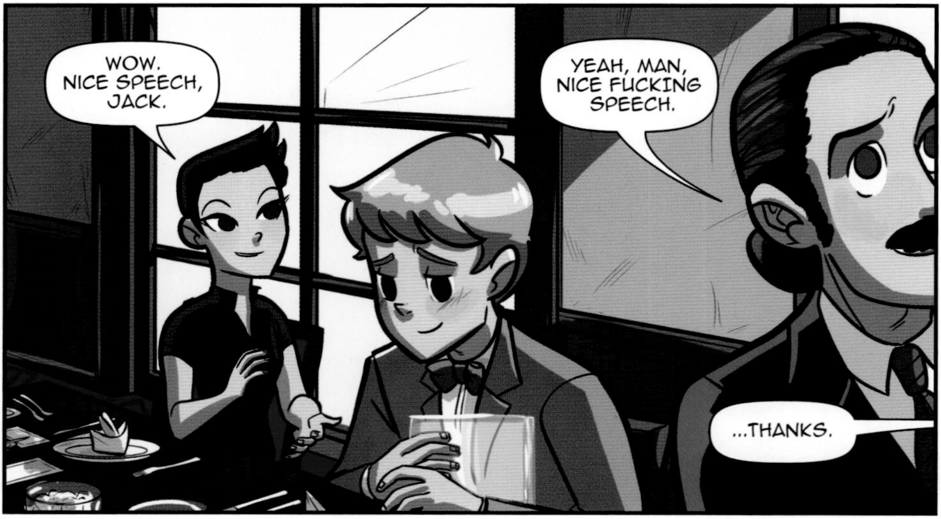
WOW. NICE SPEECH, JACK.
YEAH, MAN, NICE FUCKING SPEECH.
...THANKS.

22

GOODBYE FOR THE SUMMER

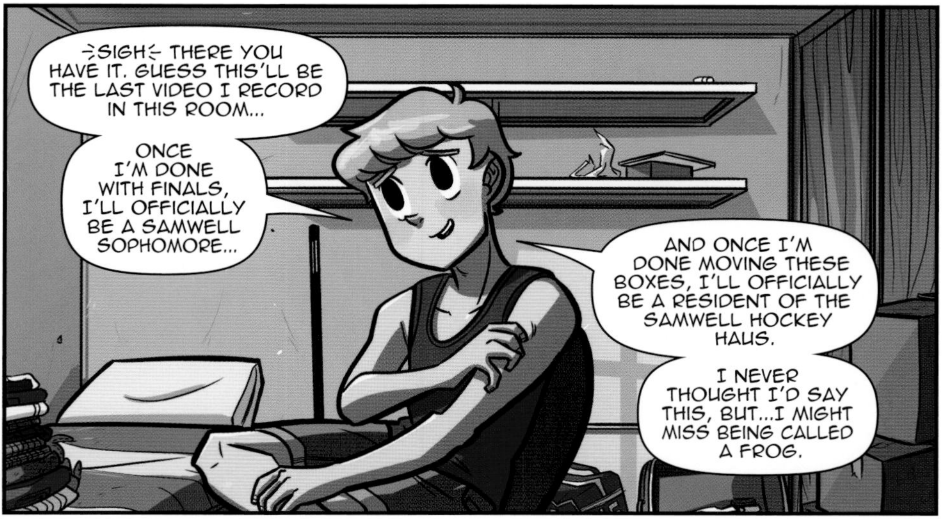

=SIGH= THERE YOU HAVE IT. GUESS THIS'LL BE THE LAST VIDEO I RECORD IN THIS ROOM...
ONCE I'M DONE WITH FINALS, I'LL OFFICIALLY BE A SAMWELL SOPHOMORE...
AND ONCE I'M DONE MOVING THESE BOXES, I'LL OFFICIALLY BE A RESIDENT OF THE SAMWELL HOCKEY HAUS.
I NEVER THOUGHT I'D SAY THIS, BUT...I MIGHT MISS BEING CALLED A FROG.

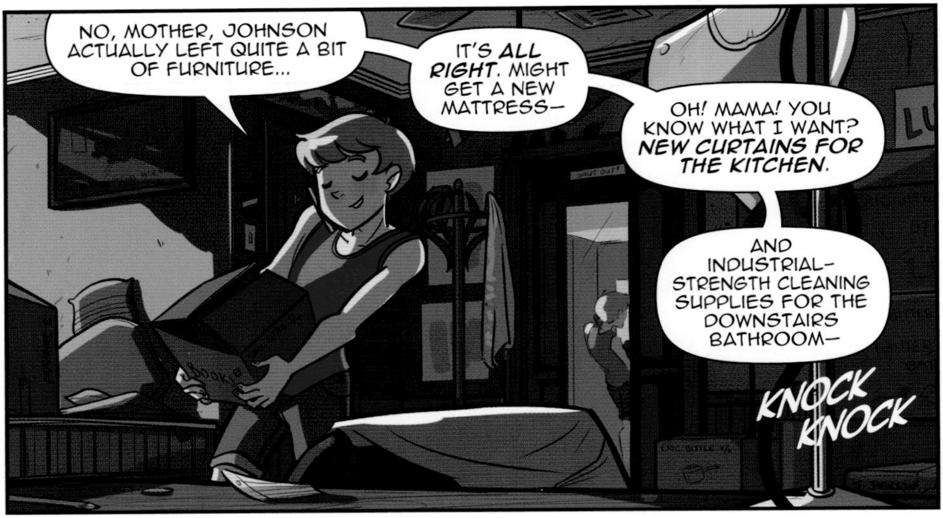
NO, MOTHER, JOHNSON ACTUALLY LEFT QUITE A BIT OF FURNITURE...
IT'S **ALL RIGHT**. MIGHT GET A NEW MATTRESS—
OH! MAMA! YOU KNOW WHAT I WANT? ***NEW CURTAINS FOR THE KITCHEN.***
AND INDUSTRIAL-STRENGTH CLEANING SUPPLIES FOR THE DOWNSTAIRS BATHROOM—
KNOCK KNOCK

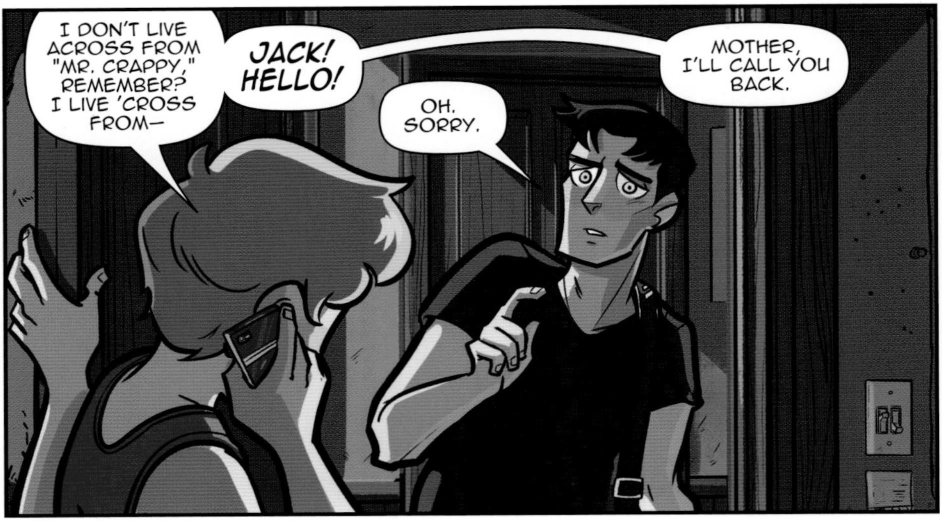
I DON'T LIVE ACROSS FROM "MR. CRAPPY," REMEMBER? I LIVE 'CROSS FROM—
JACK! HELLO!
MOTHER, I'LL CALL YOU BACK.
OH. SORRY.

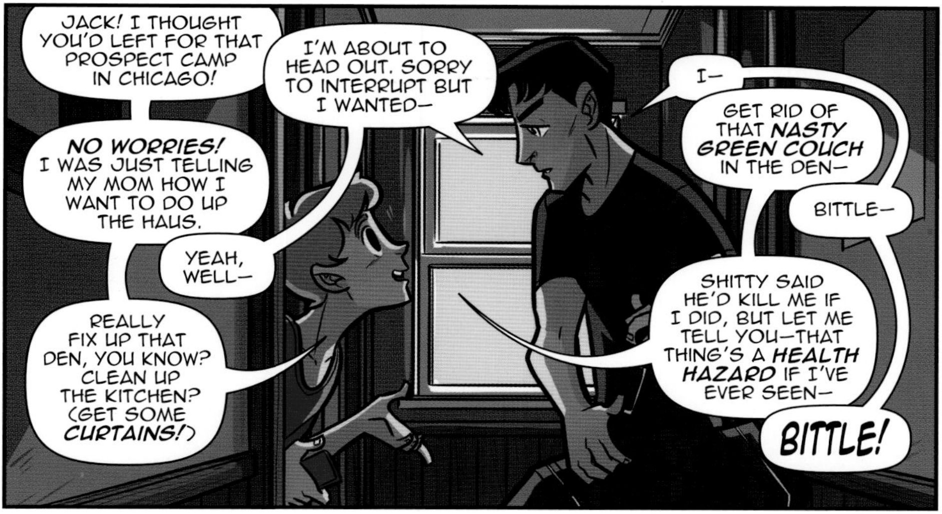
JACK! I THOUGHT YOU'D LEFT FOR THAT PROSPECT CAMP IN CHICAGO!
I'M ABOUT TO HEAD OUT. SORRY TO INTERRUPT BUT I WANTED—
NO WORRIES! I WAS JUST TELLING MY MOM HOW I WANT TO DO UP THE HAUS.
YEAH, WELL—
REALLY FIX UP THAT DEN, YOU KNOW? CLEAN UP THE KITCHEN? (GET SOME CURTAINS!)
I—
GET RID OF THAT NASTY GREEN COUCH IN THE DEN—
BITTLE—
SHITTY SAID HE'D KILL ME IF I DID, BUT LET ME TELL YOU—THAT THING'S A HEALTH HAZARD IF I'VE EVER SEEN—
BITTLE!

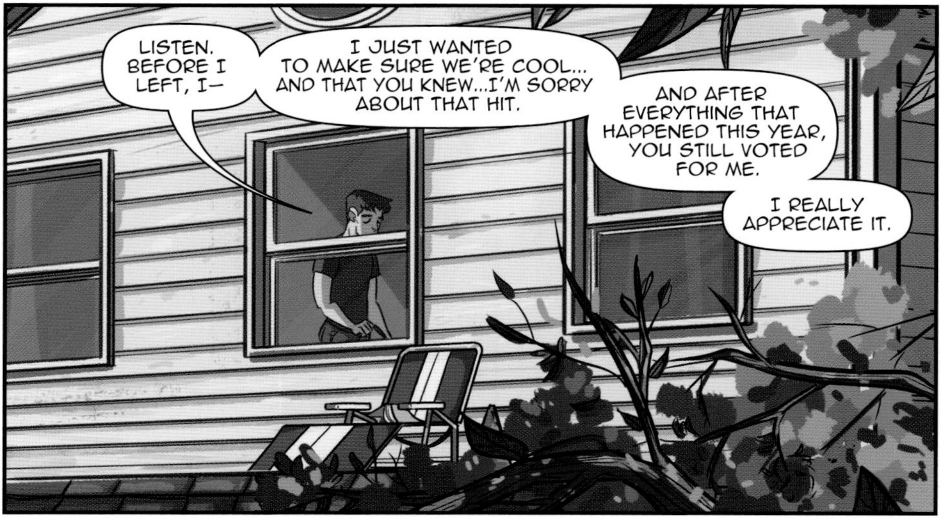
LISTEN. BEFORE I LEFT, I—
I JUST WANTED TO MAKE SURE WE'RE COOL... AND THAT YOU KNEW...I'M SORRY ABOUT THAT HIT.
AND AFTER EVERYTHING THAT HAPPENED THIS YEAR, YOU STILL VOTED FOR ME.
I REALLY APPRECIATE IT.

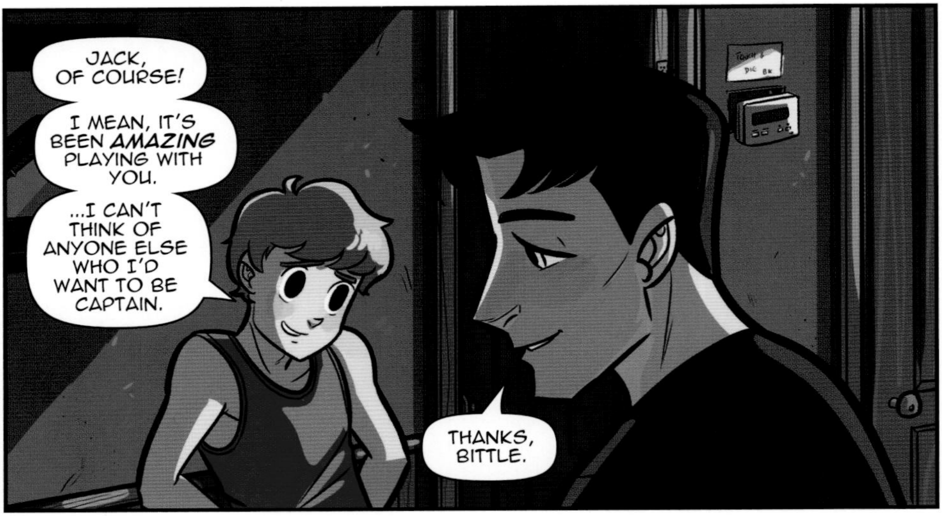
JACK, OF COURSE!
I MEAN, IT'S BEEN *AMAZING* PLAYING WITH YOU.
...I CAN'T THINK OF ANYONE ELSE WHO I'D WANT TO BE CAPTAIN.
THANKS, BITTLE.

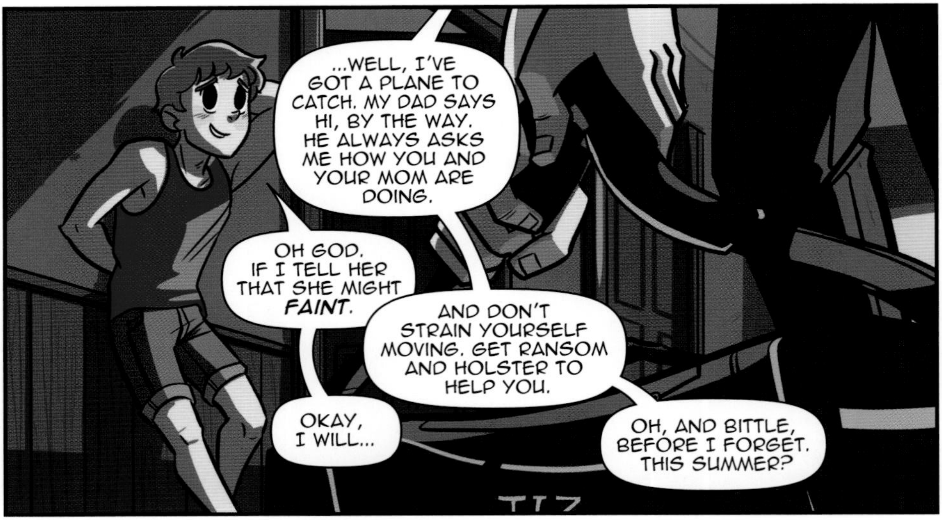
...WELL, I'VE GOT A PLANE TO CATCH. MY DAD SAYS HI, BY THE WAY. HE ALWAYS ASKS ME HOW YOU AND YOUR MOM ARE DOING.
OH GOD. IF I TELL HER THAT SHE MIGHT *FAINT*.
AND DON'T STRAIN YOURSELF MOVING. GET RANSOM AND HOLSTER TO HELP YOU.
OKAY, I WILL...
OH, AND BITTLE, BEFORE I FORGET. THIS SUMMER?

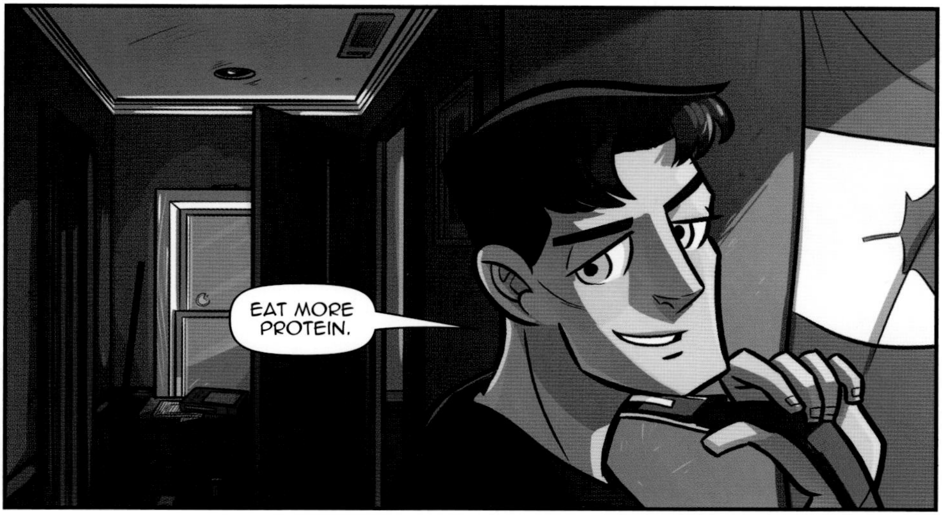
EAT MORE PROTEIN.

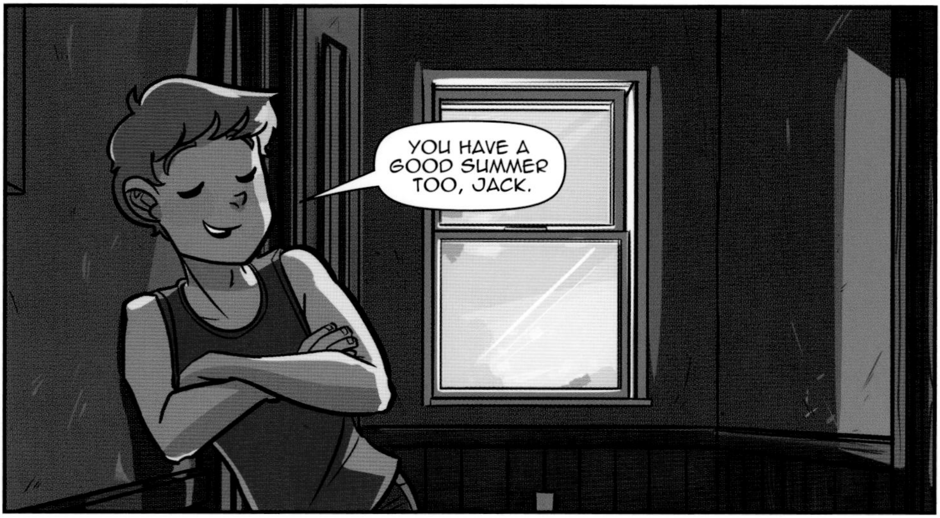
YOU HAVE A GOOD SUMMER TOO, JACK.

SOPHOMORE YEAR

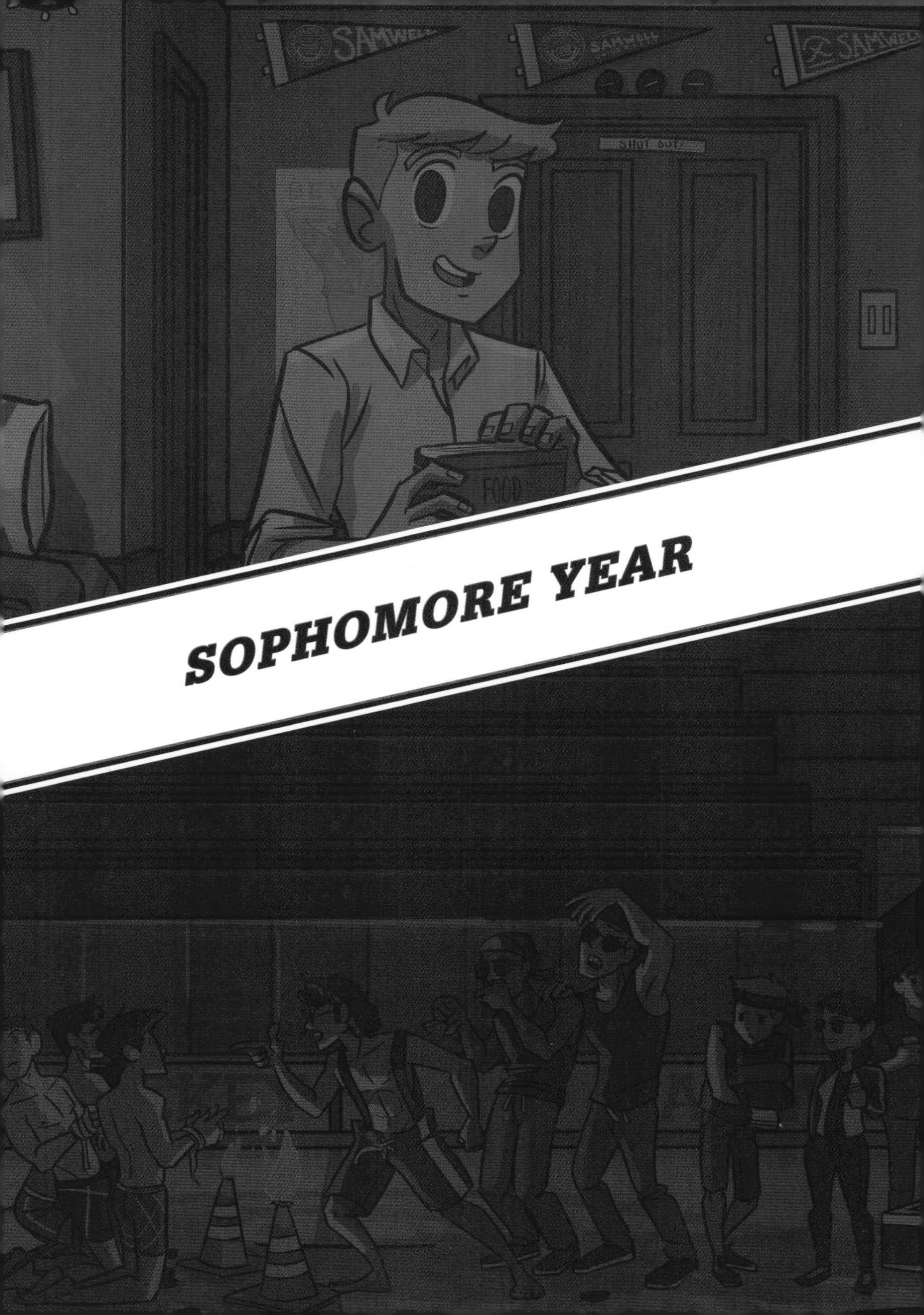

SAMWELL
SAMWELL
SAMWELL
SHUT OUT!
FOOD

1

MOVED IN

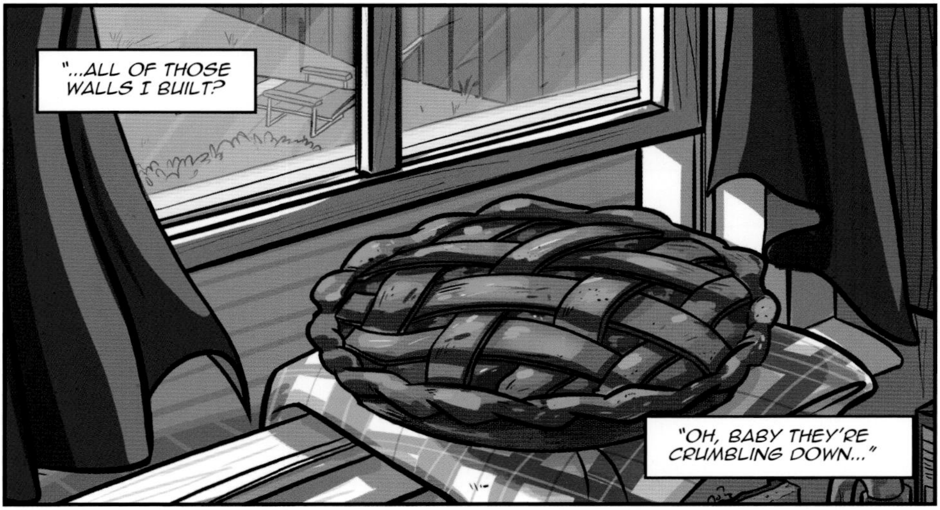
"...ALL OF THOSE WALLS I BUILT?
"OH, BABY THEY'RE CRUMBLING DOWN..."

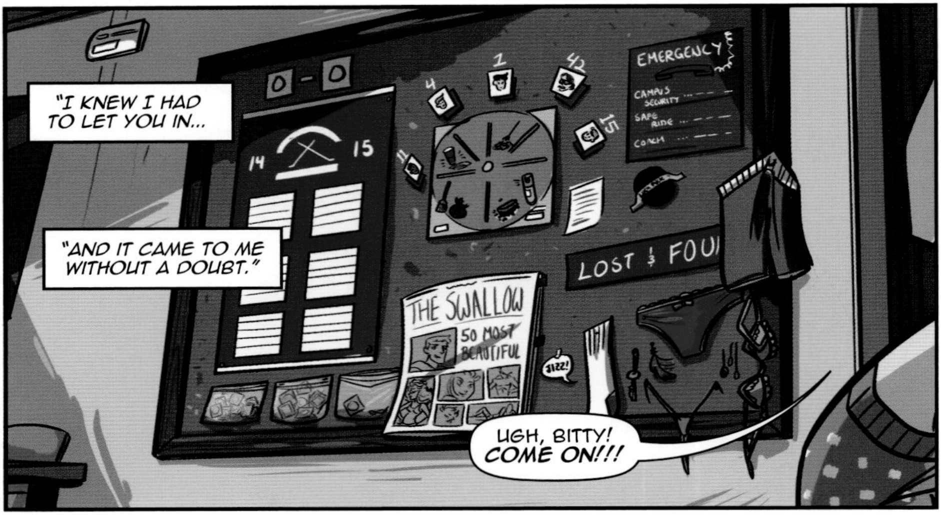
"I KNEW I HAD TO LET YOU IN...
"AND IT CAME TO ME WITHOUT A DOUBT."
0-0
14
15
EMERGENCY
CAMPUS SECURITY
SAFE RIDE
COACH
LOST & FOU
THE SWALLOW
50 MOST BEAUTIFUL
UGH, BITTY! COME ON!!!

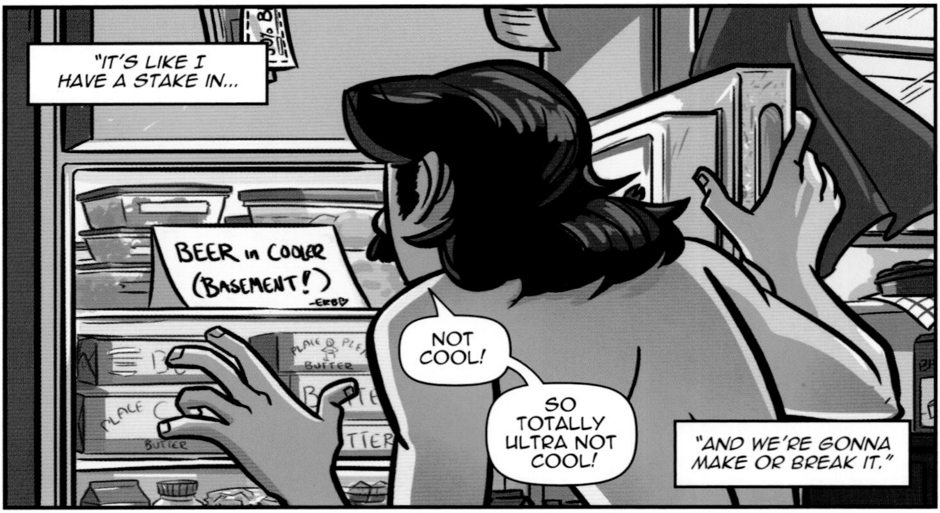
"IT'S LIKE I HAVE A STAKE IN...
BEER in COOLER (BASEMENT!)
NOT COOL!
SO TOTALLY ULTRA NOT COOL!
"AND WE'RE GONNA MAKE OR BREAK IT."

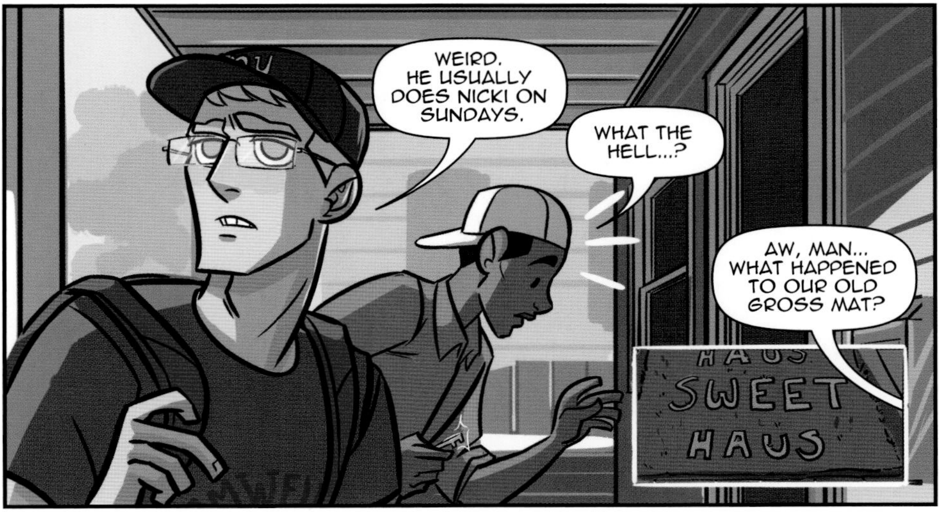
WEIRD. HE USUALLY DOES NICKI ON SUNDAYS.
WHAT THE HELL...?
AW, MAN... WHAT HAPPENED TO OUR OLD GROSS MAT?
HAUS SWEET HAUS

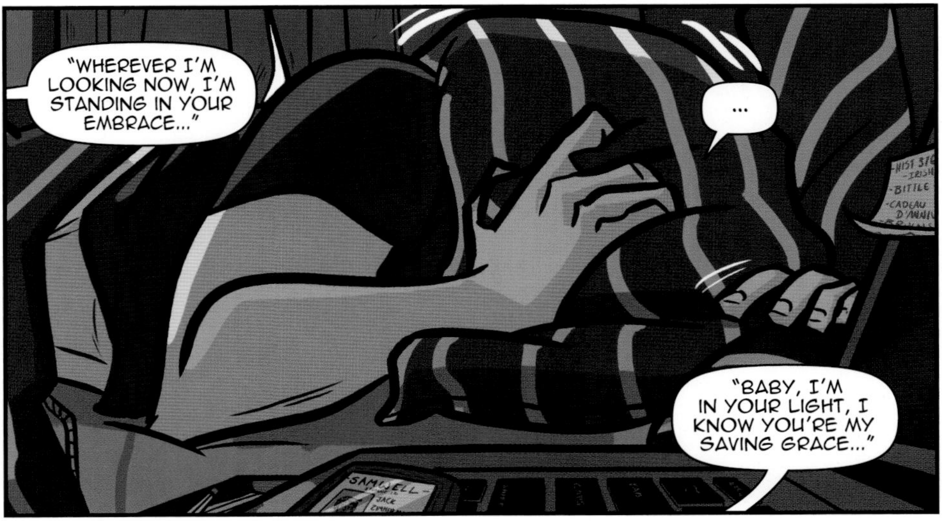
"WHEREVER I'M LOOKING NOW, I'M STANDING IN YOUR EMBRACE..."
...
"BABY, I'M IN YOUR LIGHT, I KNOW YOU'RE MY SAVING GRACE..."

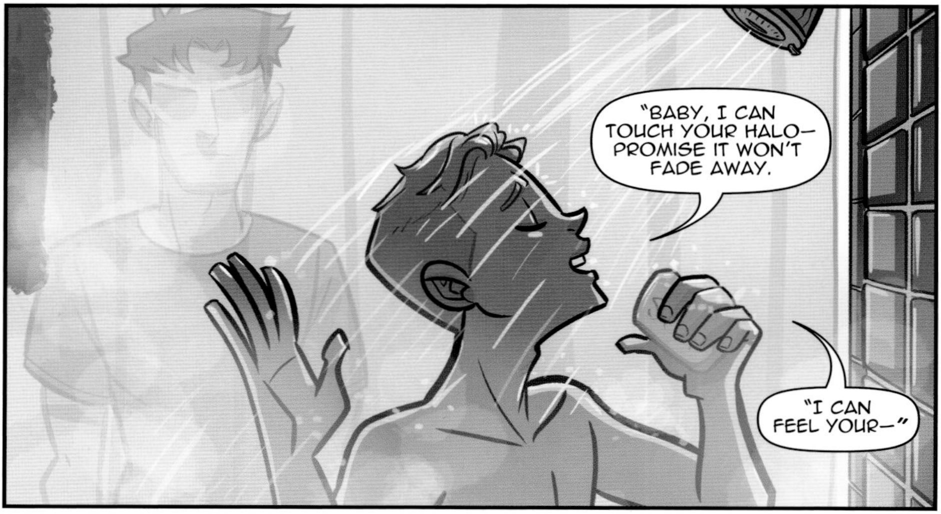
"BABY, I CAN TOUCH YOUR HALO— PROMISE IT WON'T FADE AWAY.
"I CAN FEEL YOUR—"

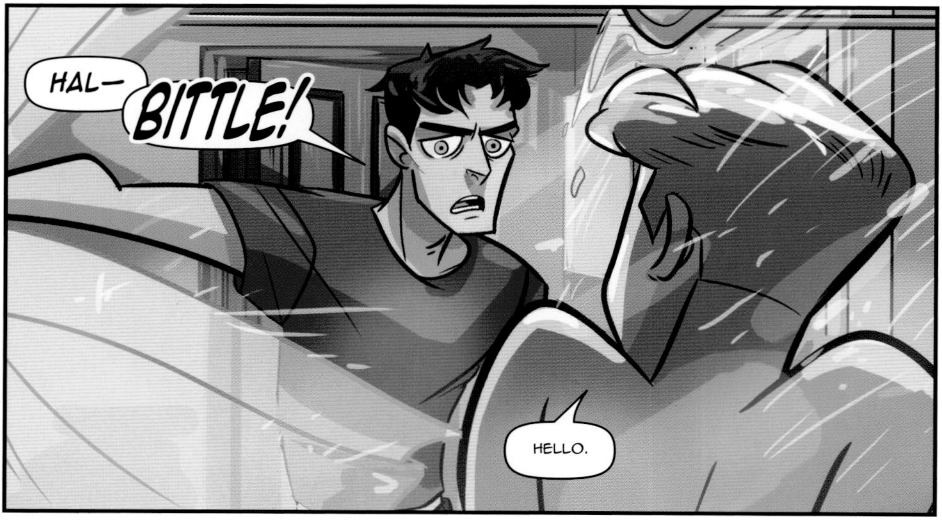
HAL—
BITTLE!
HELLO.

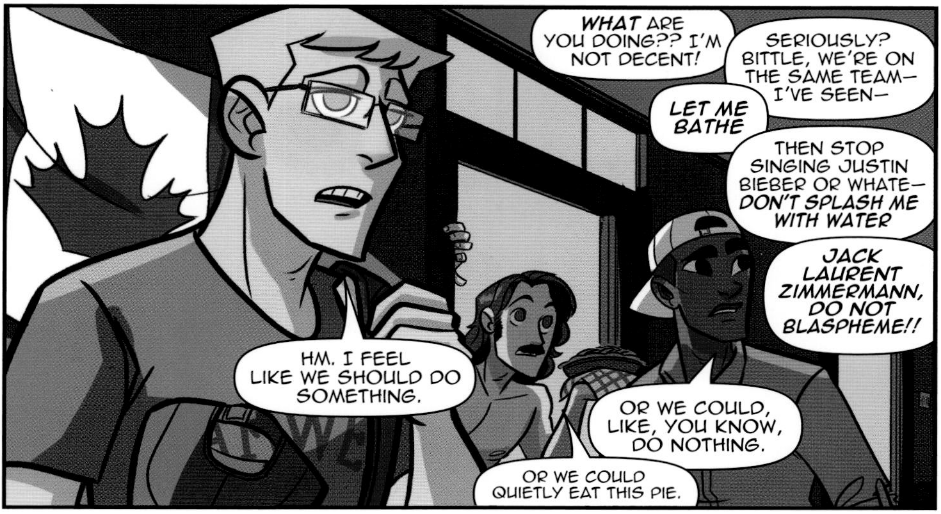
WHAT ARE YOU DOING?? I'M NOT DECENT!
SERIOUSLY? BITTLE, WE'RE ON THE SAME TEAM— I'VE SEEN—
LET ME BATHE
THEN STOP SINGING JUSTIN BIEBER OR WHATE— DON'T SPLASH ME WITH WATER
JACK LAURENT ZIMMERMANN, DO NOT BLASPHEME!!
HM. I FEEL LIKE WE SHOULD DO SOMETHING.
OR WE COULD, LIKE, YOU KNOW, DO NOTHING.
OR WE COULD QUIETLY EAT THIS PIE.

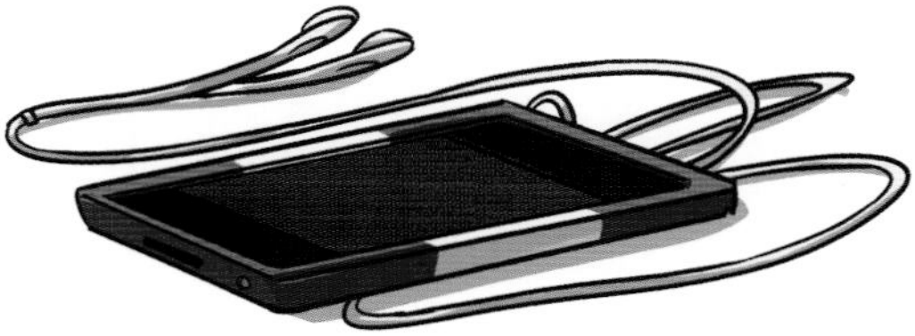

2

SQUARE ONE

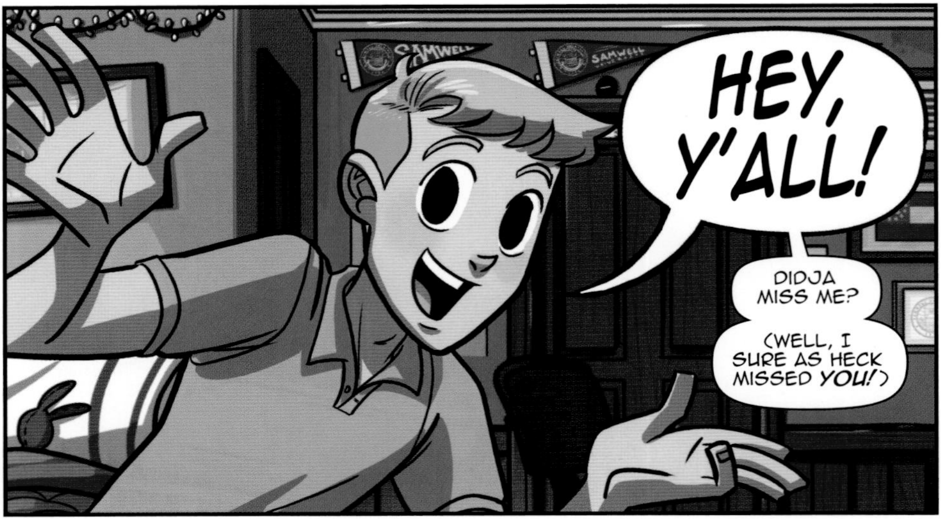
HEY, Y'ALL!
DIDJA MISS ME?
(WELL, I SURE AS HECK MISSED YOU!)

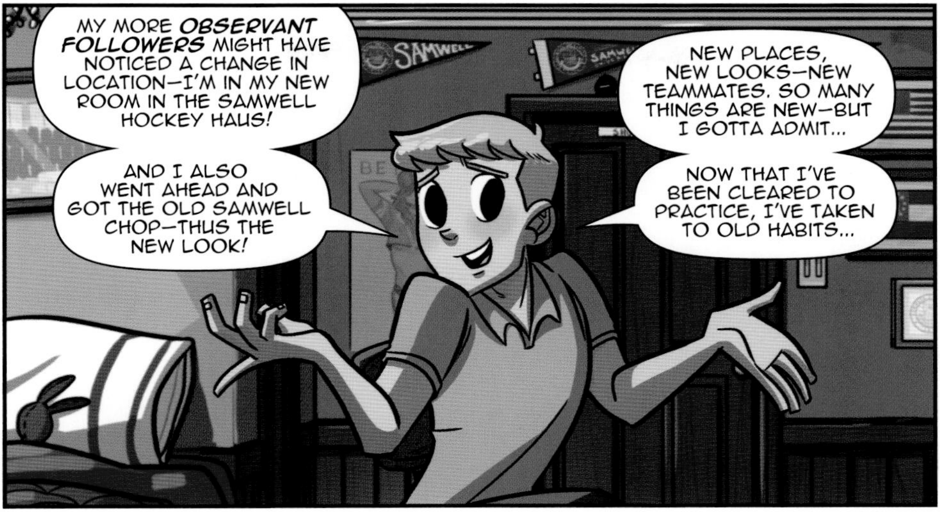
MY MORE OBSERVANT FOLLOWERS MIGHT HAVE NOTICED A CHANGE IN LOCATION—I'M IN MY NEW ROOM IN THE SAMWELL HOCKEY HAUS!
AND I ALSO WENT AHEAD AND GOT THE OLD SAMWELL CHOP—THUS THE NEW LOOK!
NEW PLACES, NEW LOOKS—NEW TEAMMATES. SO MANY THINGS ARE NEW—BUT I GOTTA ADMIT...
NOW THAT I'VE BEEN CLEARED TO PRACTICE, I'VE TAKEN TO OLD HABITS...
SAMWELL

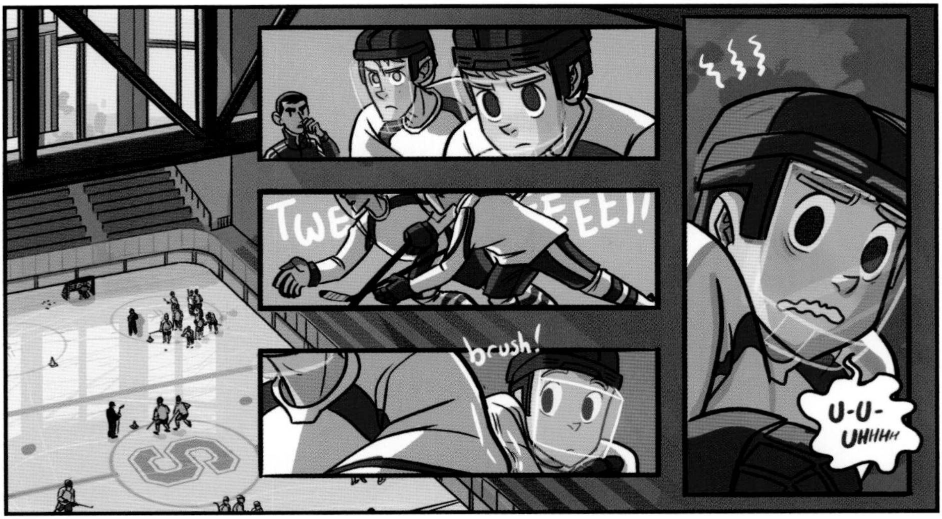
TWE EEET!!
brush!
U-U-UHHHH

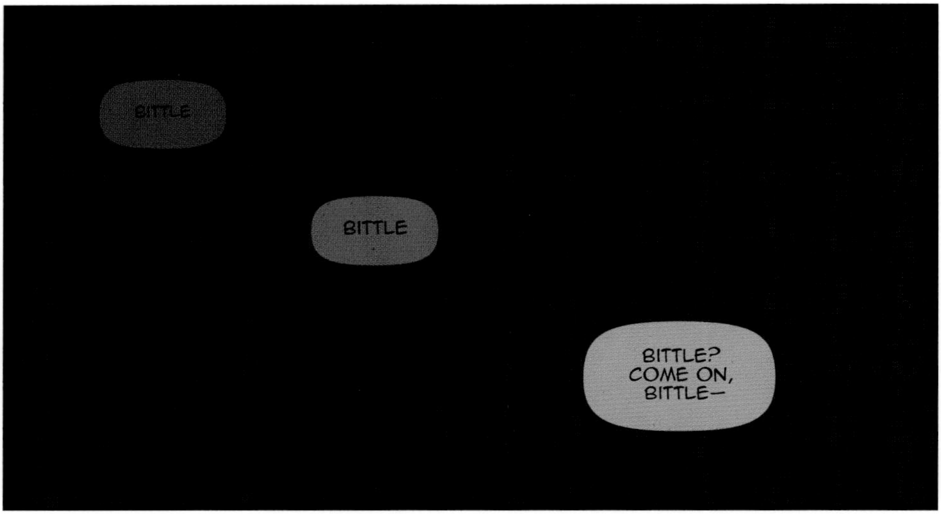
BITTLE
BITTLE
BITTLE? COME ON, BITTLE—

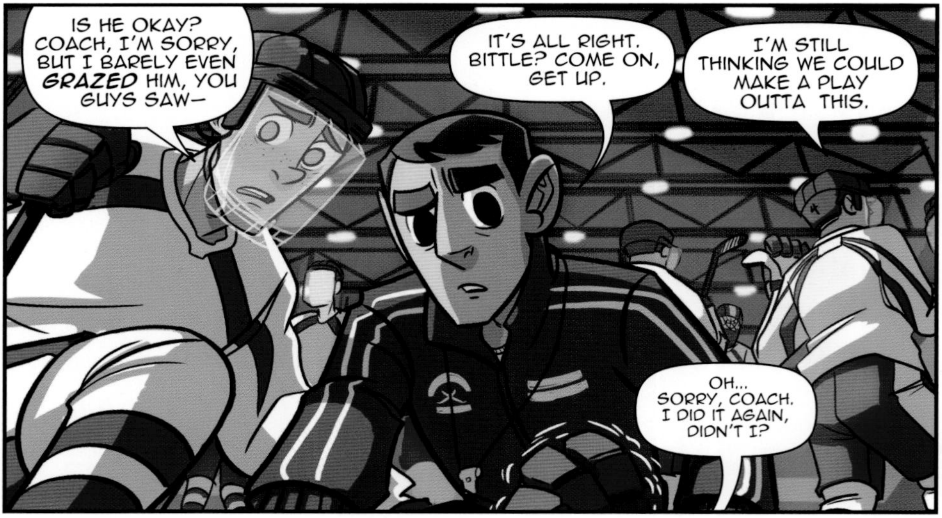
IS HE OKAY? COACH, I'M SORRY, BUT I BARELY EVEN GRAZED HIM, YOU GUYS SAW—
IT'S ALL RIGHT. BITTLE? COME ON, GET UP.
I'M STILL THINKING WE COULD MAKE A PLAY OUTTA THIS.
OH... SORRY, COACH. I DID IT AGAIN, DIDN'T I?

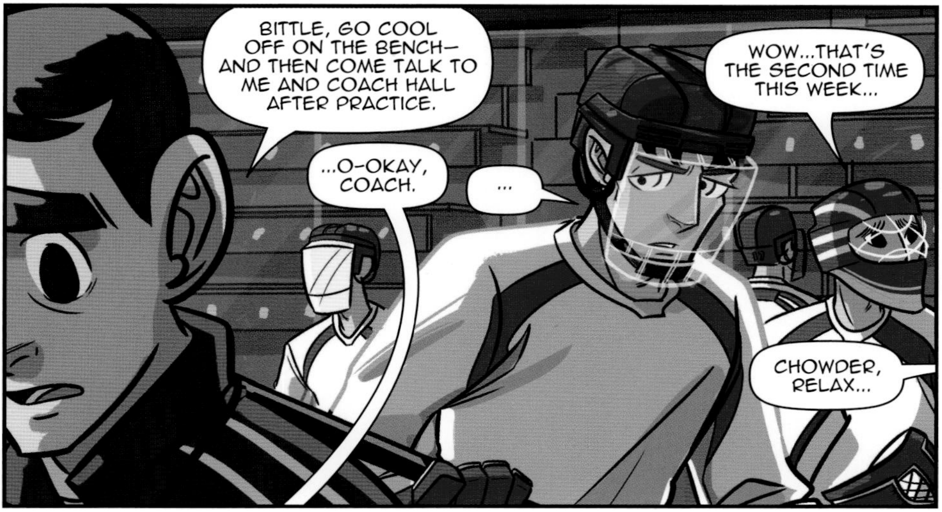
BITTLE, GO COOL OFF ON THE BENCH—AND THEN COME TALK TO ME AND COACH HALL AFTER PRACTICE.
...O-OKAY, COACH.
...
WOW...THAT'S THE SECOND TIME THIS WEEK...
CHOWDER, RELAX...

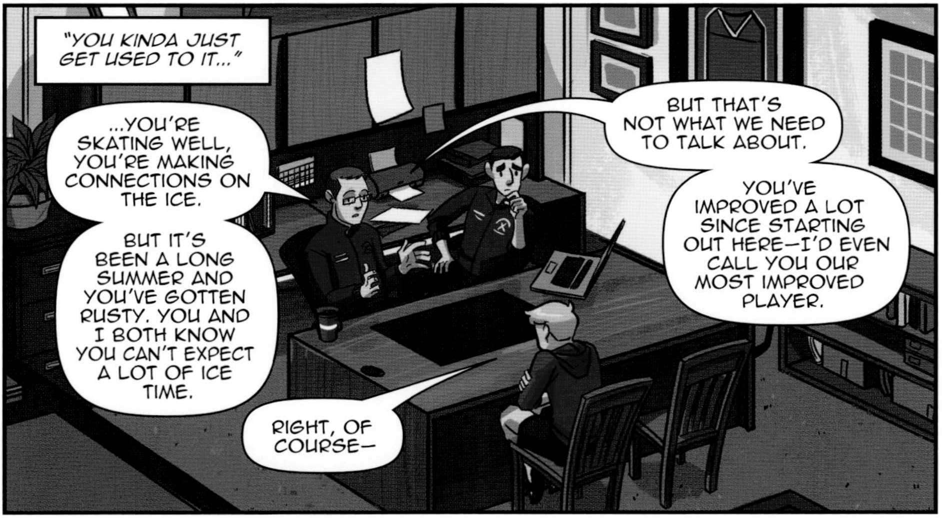
"YOU KINDA JUST GET USED TO IT..."
...YOU'RE SKATING WELL, YOU'RE MAKING CONNECTIONS ON THE ICE.
BUT IT'S BEEN A LONG SUMMER AND YOU'VE GOTTEN RUSTY. YOU AND I BOTH KNOW YOU CAN'T EXPECT A LOT OF ICE TIME.
RIGHT, OF COURSE—
BUT THAT'S NOT WHAT WE NEED TO TALK ABOUT.
YOU'VE IMPROVED A LOT SINCE STARTING OUT HERE—I'D EVEN CALL YOU OUR MOST IMPROVED PLAYER.

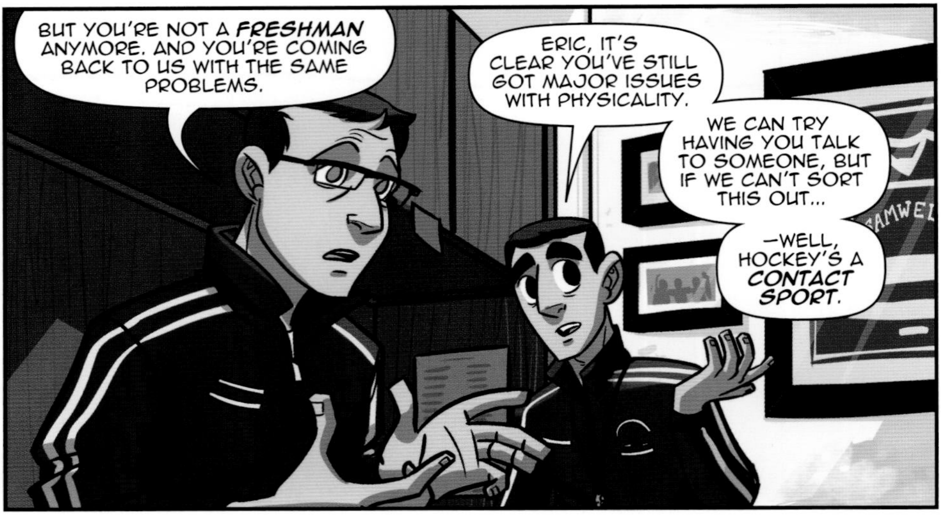
BUT YOU'RE NOT A FRESHMAN ANYMORE. AND YOU'RE COMING BACK TO US WITH THE SAME PROBLEMS.
ERIC, IT'S CLEAR YOU'VE STILL GOT MAJOR ISSUES WITH PHYSICALITY.
WE CAN TRY HAVING YOU TALK TO SOMEONE, BUT IF WE CAN'T SORT THIS OUT...
—WELL, HOCKEY'S A CONTACT SPORT.

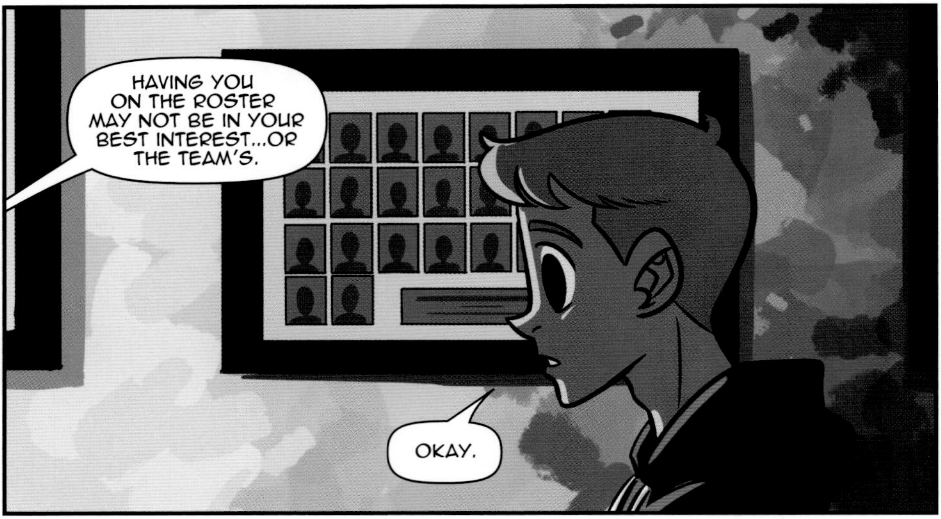
HAVING YOU ON THE ROSTER MAY NOT BE IN YOUR BEST INTEREST...OR THE TEAM'S.
OKAY.

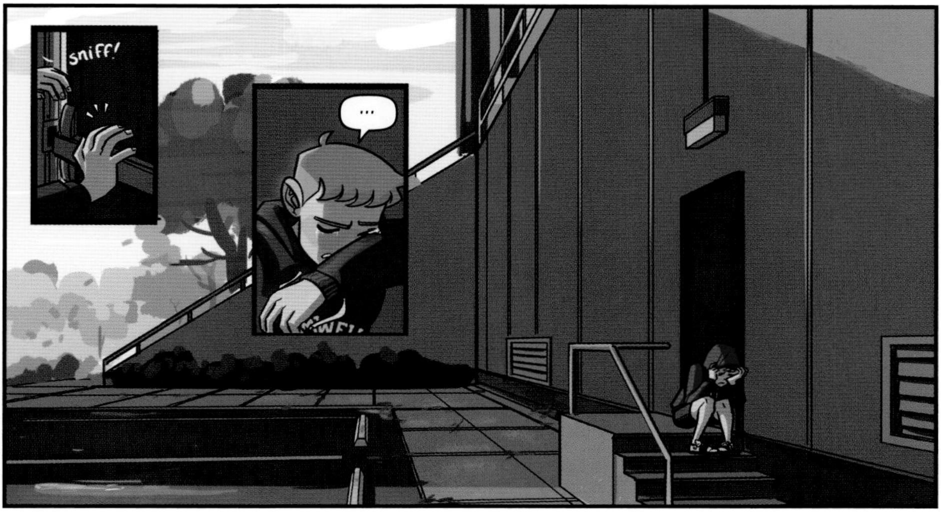
sniff!
...
MWELL

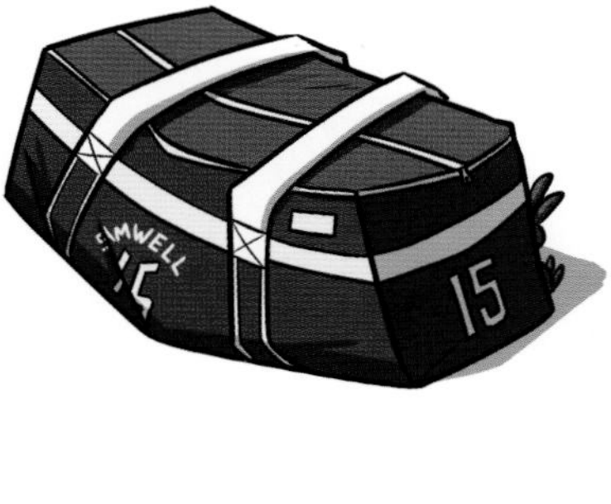
IMWELL
15
15

3

MEET THE FROGS

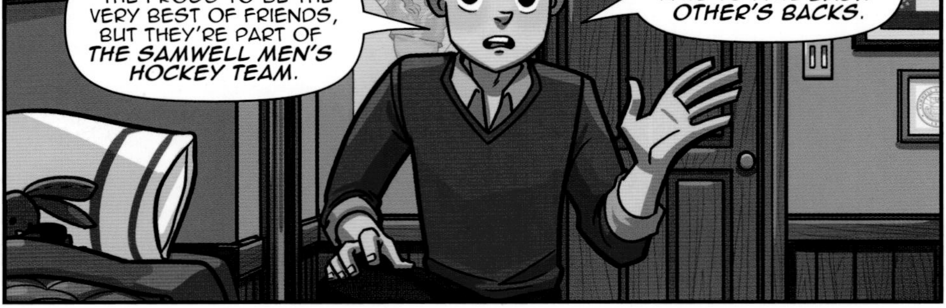
SO, Y'ALL GO AHEAD AND QUIT YOUR REGULARLY SCHEDULED WORRYING OVER ME—AND LET'S TALK ABOUT THESE *FRESHMEN*.
I DON'T EXPECT THE FROGS TO BE THE VERY BEST OF FRIENDS, BUT THEY'RE PART OF *THE SAMWELL MEN'S HOCKEY TEAM*.
AND THAT MEANS EVEN IF THEY *HATE* EACH OTHER—THEY HAVE TO HAVE *EACH OTHER'S BACKS*.
SAMWELL
SAMWELL
SAMWELL

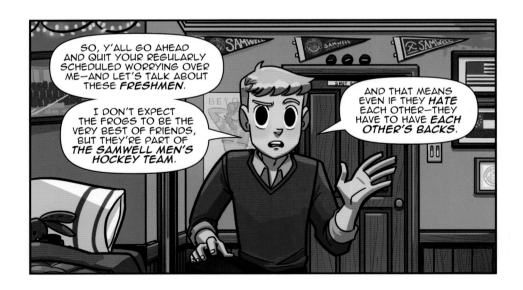

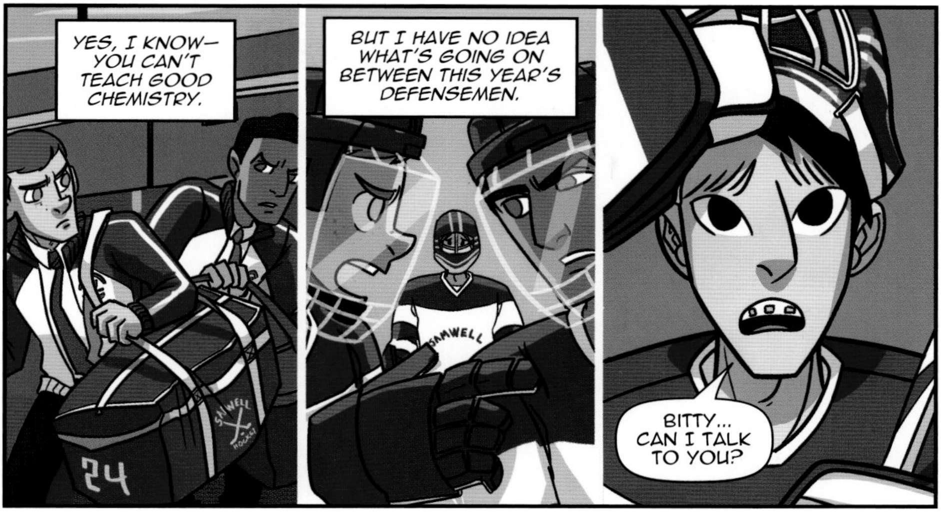
YES, I KNOW—YOU CAN'T TEACH GOOD CHEMISTRY.
BUT I HAVE NO IDEA WHAT'S GOING ON BETWEEN THIS YEAR'S DEFENSEMEN.
BITTY... CAN I TALK TO YOU?

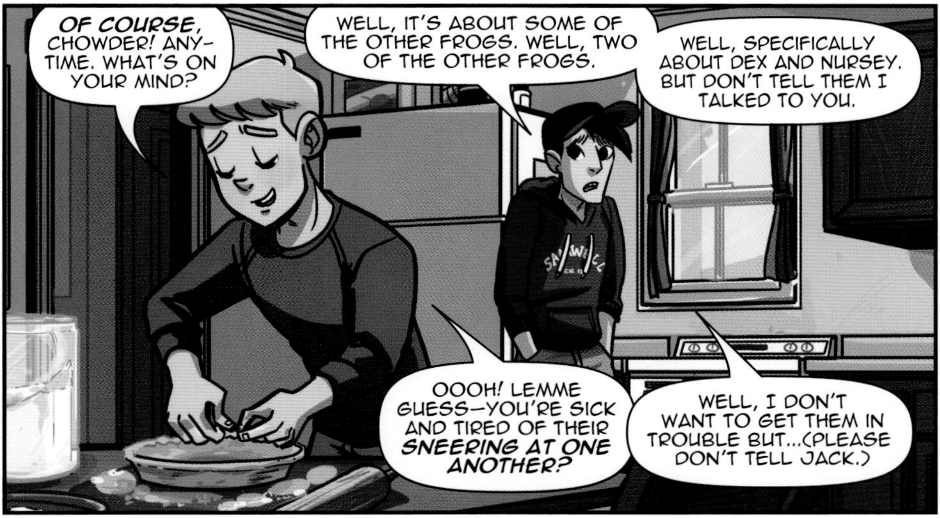
OF COURSE, CHOWDER! ANY-TIME. WHAT'S ON YOUR MIND?
WELL, IT'S ABOUT SOME OF THE OTHER FROGS. WELL, TWO OF THE OTHER FROGS.
WELL, SPECIFICALLY ABOUT DEX AND NURSEY. BUT DON'T TELL THEM I TALKED TO YOU.
OOOH! LEMME GUESS—YOU'RE SICK AND TIRED OF THEIR SNEERING AT ONE ANOTHER?
WELL, I DON'T WANT TO GET THEM IN TROUBLE BUT...(PLEASE DON'T TELL JACK.)

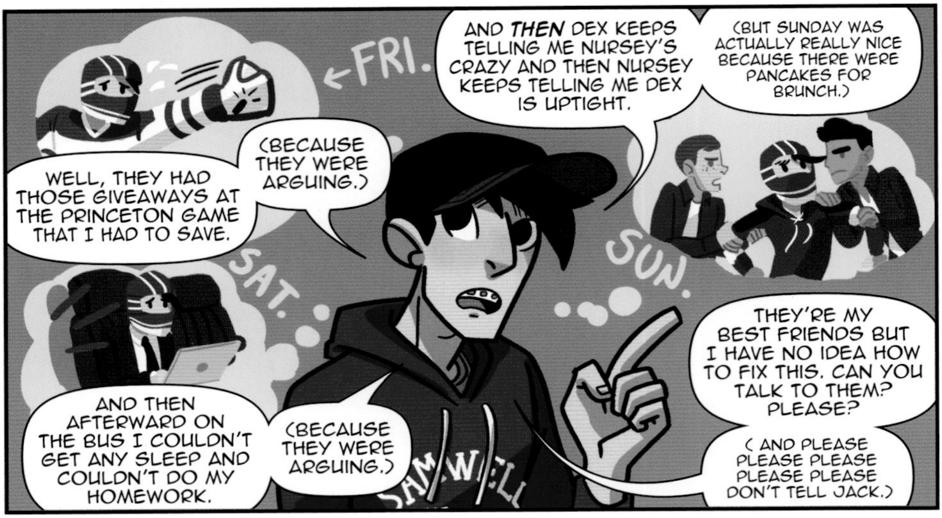
FRI.
SAT.
SUN.
WELL, THEY HAD THOSE GIVEAWAYS AT THE PRINCETON GAME THAT I HAD TO SAVE.
(BECAUSE THEY WERE ARGUING.)
AND THEN AFTERWARD ON THE BUS I COULDN'T GET ANY SLEEP AND COULDN'T DO MY HOMEWORK.
(BECAUSE THEY WERE ARGUING.)
AND THEN DEX KEEPS TELLING ME NURSEY'S CRAZY AND THEN NURSEY KEEPS TELLING ME DEX IS UPTIGHT.
(BUT SUNDAY WAS ACTUALLY REALLY NICE BECAUSE THERE WERE PANCAKES FOR BRUNCH.)
THEY'RE MY BEST FRIENDS BUT I HAVE NO IDEA HOW TO FIX THIS. CAN YOU TALK TO THEM? PLEASE?
(AND PLEASE PLEASE PLEASE PLEASE PLEASE DON'T TELL JACK.)
SAMWELL

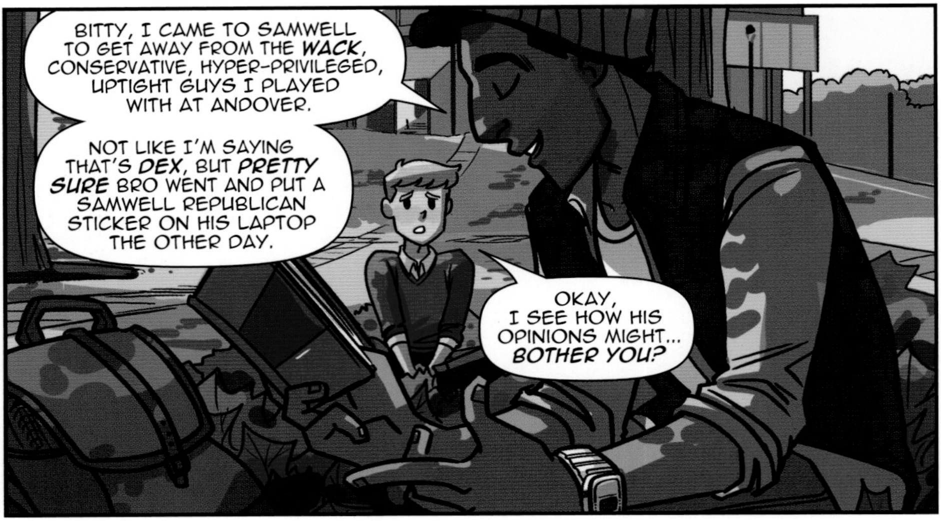
BITTY, I CAME TO SAMWELL TO GET AWAY FROM THE WACK, CONSERVATIVE, HYPER-PRIVILEGED, UPTIGHT GUYS I PLAYED WITH AT ANDOVER.
NOT LIKE I'M SAYING THAT'S DEX, BUT PRETTY SURE BRO WENT AND PUT A SAMWELL REPUBLICAN STICKER ON HIS LAPTOP THE OTHER DAY.
OKAY, I SEE HOW HIS OPINIONS MIGHT... BOTHER YOU?

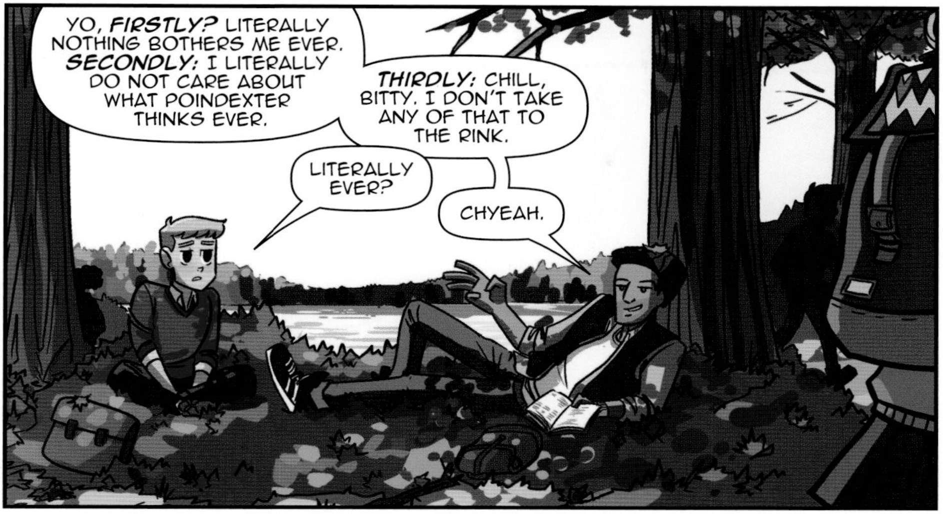
YO, FIRSTLY? LITERALLY NOTHING BOTHERS ME EVER. SECONDLY: I LITERALLY DO NOT CARE ABOUT WHAT POINDEXTER THINKS EVER.
THIRDLY: CHILL, BITTY. I DON'T TAKE ANY OF THAT TO THE RINK.
LITERALLY EVER?
CHYEAH.

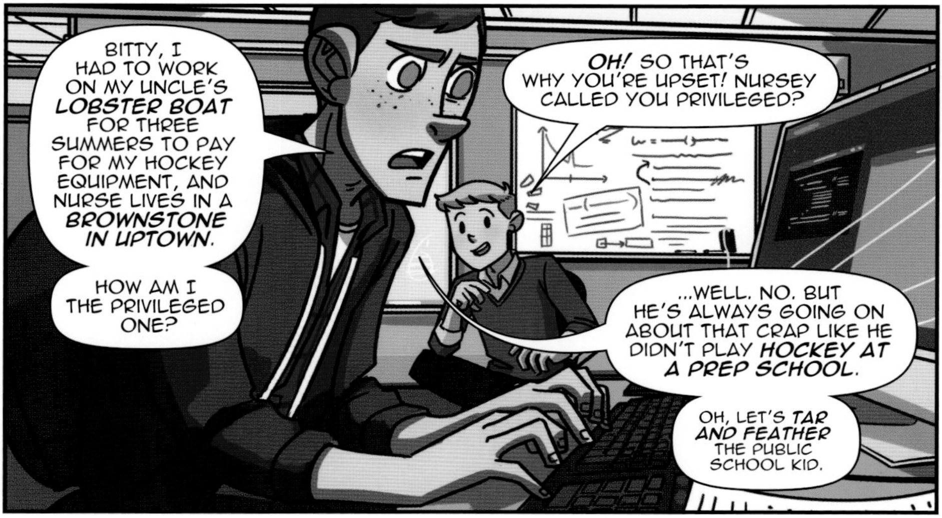
BITTY, I HAD TO WORK ON MY UNCLE'S LOBSTER BOAT FOR THREE SUMMERS TO PAY FOR MY HOCKEY EQUIPMENT, AND NURSE LIVES IN A BROWNSTONE IN UPTOWN.
HOW AM I THE PRIVILEGED ONE?
OH! SO THAT'S WHY YOU'RE UPSET! NURSEY CALLED YOU PRIVILEGED?
...WELL. NO. BUT HE'S ALWAYS GOING ON ABOUT THAT CRAP LIKE HE DIDN'T PLAY HOCKEY AT A PREP SCHOOL.
OH, LET'S TAR AND FEATHER THE PUBLIC SCHOOL KID.

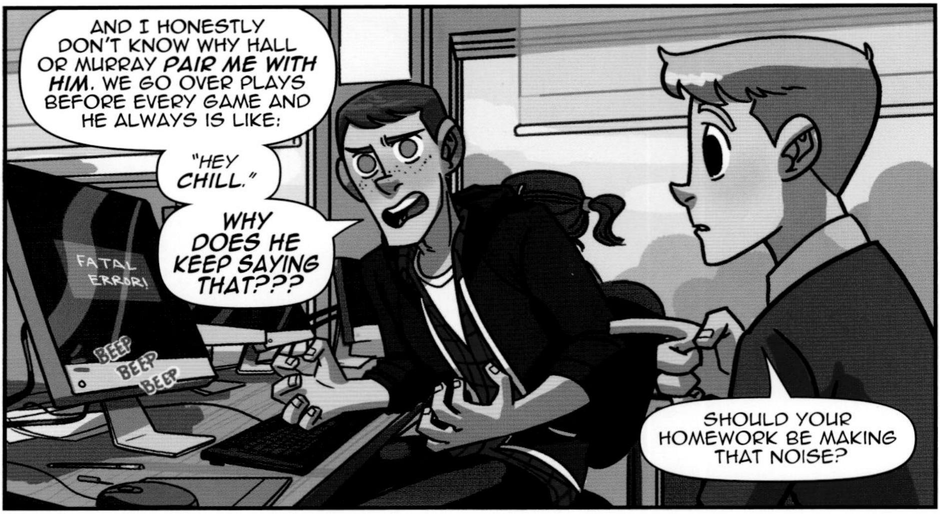
AND I HONESTLY DON'T KNOW WHY HALL OR MURRAY **PAIR ME WITH HIM**. WE GO OVER PLAYS BEFORE EVERY GAME AND HE ALWAYS IS LIKE:
"HEY **CHILL**."
WHY DOES HE KEEP SAYING THAT???
FATAL ERROR!
BEEP BEEP BEEP
SHOULD YOUR HOMEWORK BE MAKING THAT NOISE?

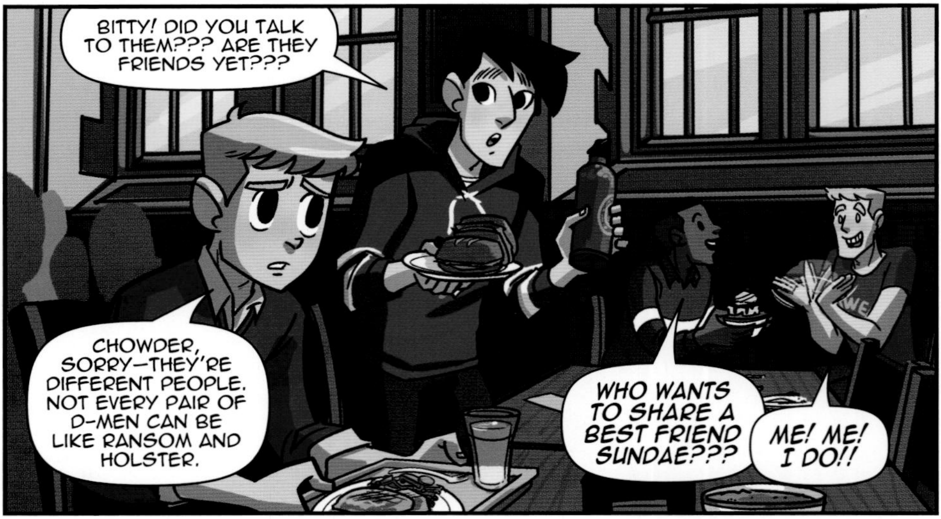
BITTY! DID YOU TALK TO THEM??? ARE THEY FRIENDS YET???
CHOWDER, SORRY—THEY'RE DIFFERENT PEOPLE. NOT EVERY PAIR OF D-MEN CAN BE LIKE RANSOM AND HOLSTER.
WHO WANTS TO SHARE A BEST FRIEND SUNDAE???
ME! ME! I DO!!

4

HAZEAPALOOZA

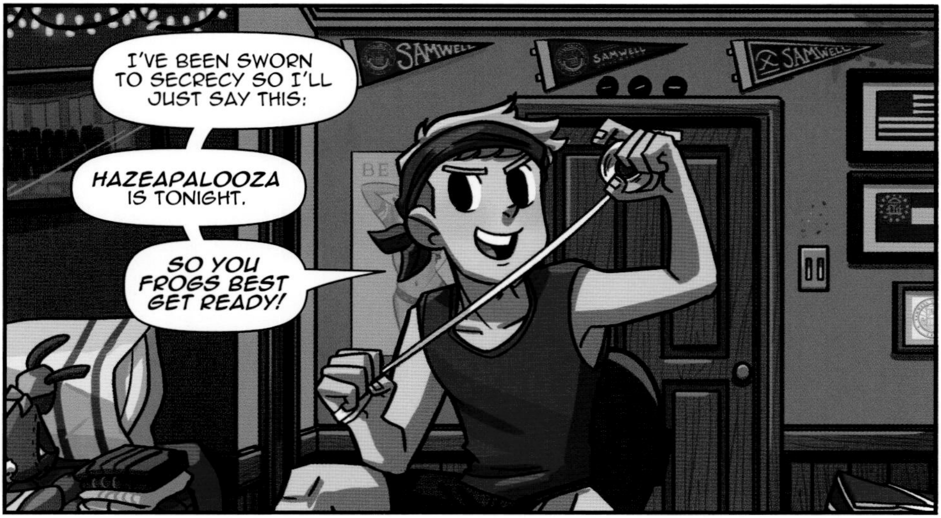

SAMWELL
SAMWELL
SAMWELL
I'VE BEEN SWORN TO SECRECY SO I'LL JUST SAY THIS:
HAZEAPALOOZA IS TONIGHT.
SO YOU FROGS BEST GET READY!

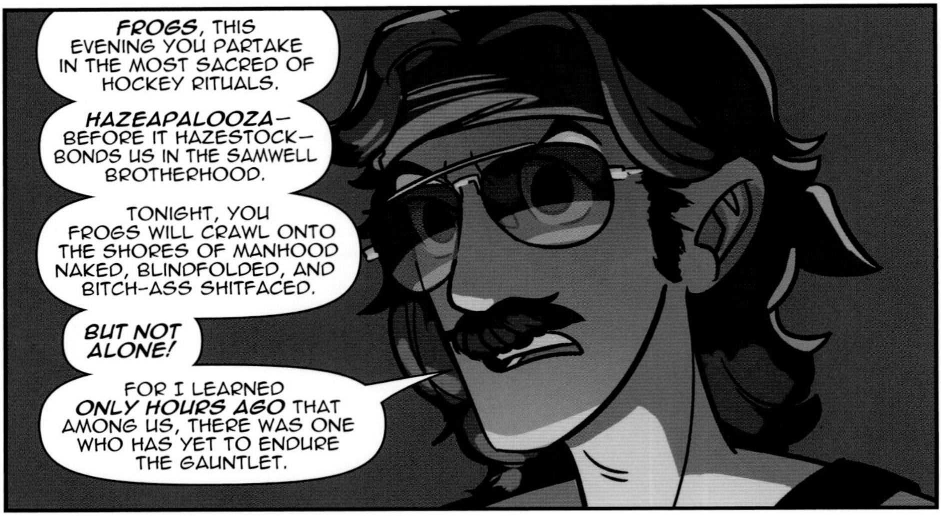
FROGS, THIS EVENING YOU PARTAKE IN THE MOST SACRED OF HOCKEY RITUALS.
HAZEAPALOOZA– BEFORE IT HAZESTOCK– BONDS US IN THE SAMWELL BROTHERHOOD.
TONIGHT, YOU FROGS WILL CRAWL ONTO THE SHORES OF MANHOOD NAKED, BLINDFOLDED, AND BITCH-ASS SHITFACED.
BUT NOT ALONE!
FOR I LEARNED ONLY HOURS AGO THAT AMONG US, THERE WAS ONE WHO HAS YET TO ENDURE THE GAUNTLET.

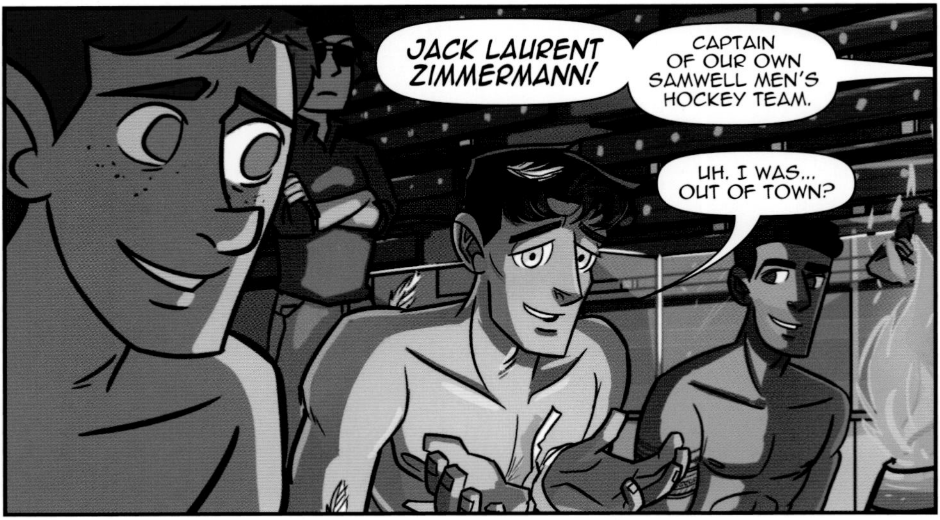
JACK LAURENT ZIMMERMANN!
CAPTAIN OF OUR OWN SAMWELL MEN'S HOCKEY TEAM.
UH. I WAS... OUT OF TOWN?

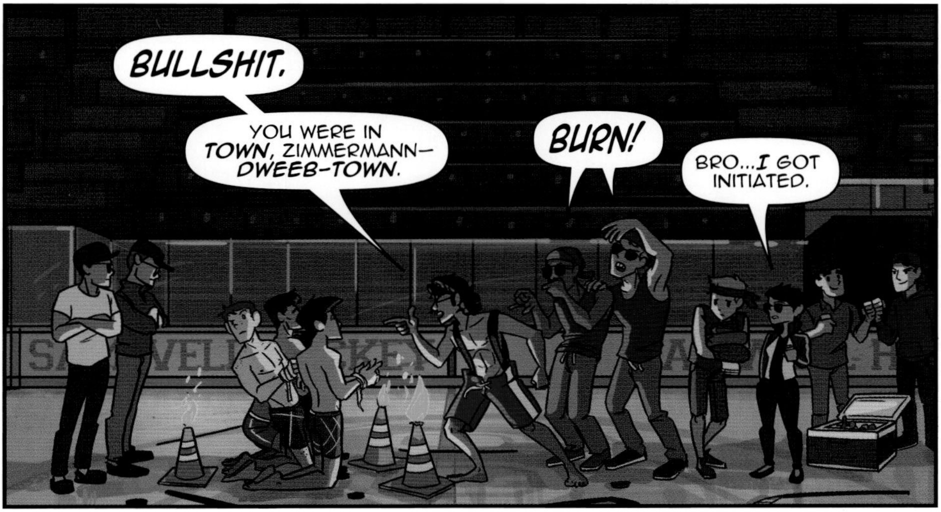
BULLSHIT.
YOU WERE IN TOWN, ZIMMERMANN—DWEEB-TOWN.
BURN!
BRO...I GOT INITIATED.

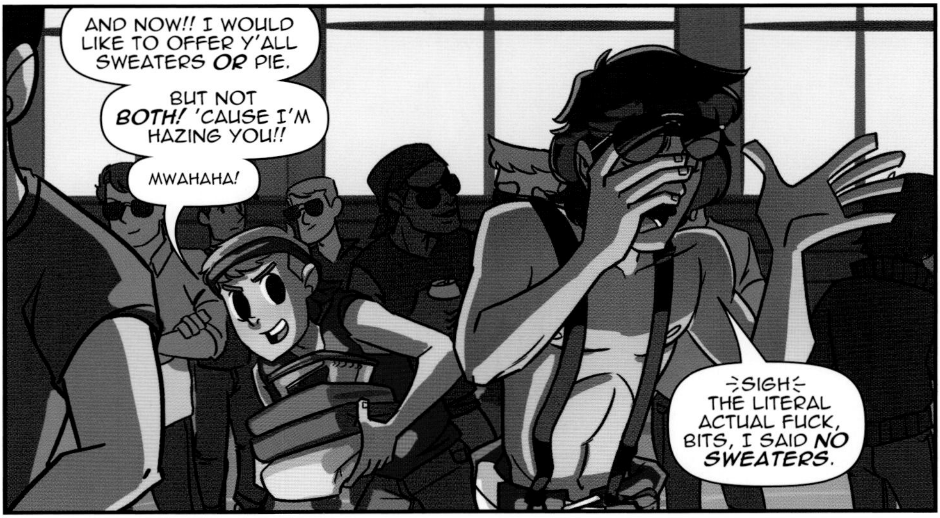
AND NOW!! I WOULD LIKE TO OFFER Y'ALL SWEATERS OR PIE.
BUT NOT BOTH! 'CAUSE I'M HAZING YOU!!
MWAHAHA!
SIGH
THE LITERAL ACTUAL FUCK, BITS, I SAID NO SWEATERS.

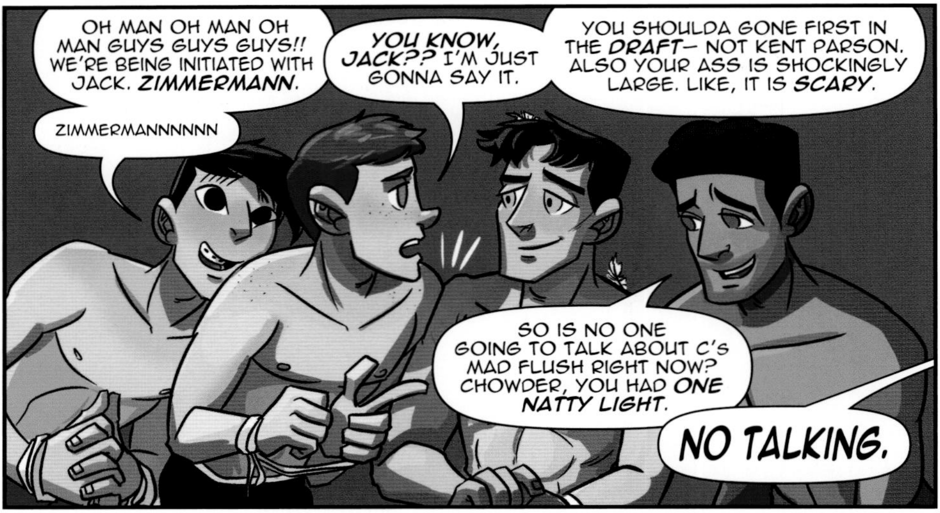
OH MAN OH MAN OH MAN GUYS GUYS GUYS!! WE'RE BEING INITIATED WITH JACK. ZIMMERMANN.
ZIMMERMANNNNNN
YOU KNOW, JACK?? I'M JUST GONNA SAY IT.
YOU SHOULDA GONE FIRST IN THE DRAFT— NOT KENT PARSON. ALSO YOUR ASS IS SHOCKINGLY LARGE. LIKE, IT IS SCARY.
SO IS NO ONE GOING TO TALK ABOUT C'S MAD FLUSH RIGHT NOW? CHOWDER, YOU HAD ONE NATTY LIGHT.
NO TALKING.

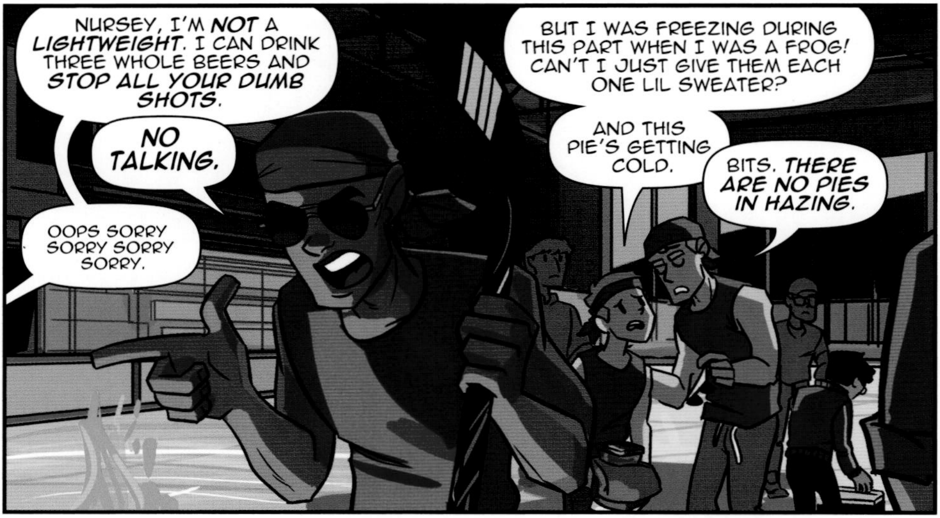
NURSEY, I'M NOT A LIGHTWEIGHT. I CAN DRINK THREE WHOLE BEERS AND STOP ALL YOUR DUMB SHOTS.
NO TALKING.
OOPS SORRY SORRY SORRY SORRY.
BUT I WAS FREEZING DURING THIS PART WHEN I WAS A FROG! CAN'T I JUST GIVE THEM EACH ONE LIL SWEATER?
AND THIS PIE'S GETTING COLD.
BITS. THERE ARE NO PIES IN HAZING.

(HA HA
HA HA HA)
ZIMMERMANN, YOU FUCKER, QUIT GIGGLING AND TAKE THIS SERIOUSLY.
AWOOOOO-OW-OW-OW!!!
UGH. JUST HOWL. NOW! FUCKING EVERYONE!
BUT IF WE'RE FROGS, SHOULDN'T WE BE... CROAKING?
ZIMMERMANN!! KEEP CRACKING WISE AND I'M DEMOTING YOU TO TADPOLE!

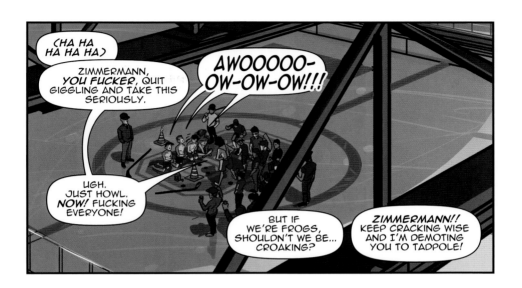

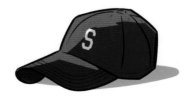

5

PROVIDENCE FALCONERS

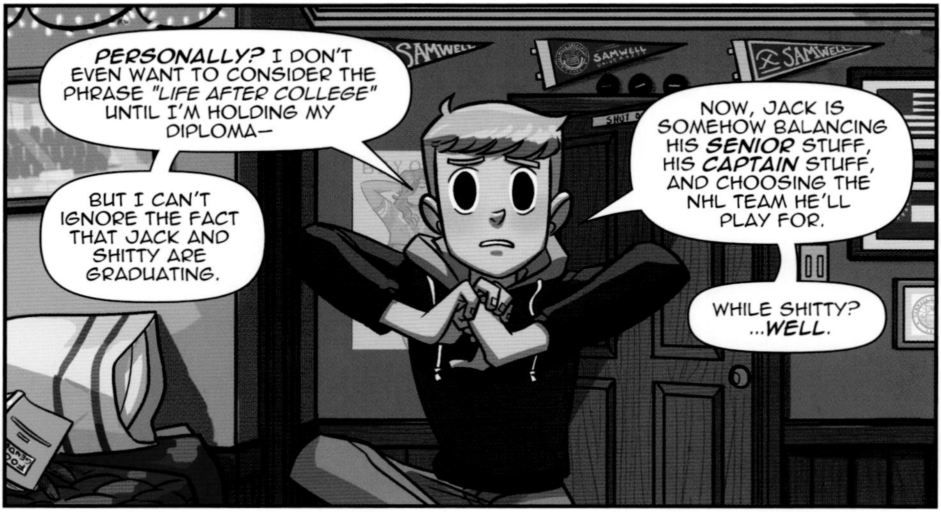

SAMWELL
SAMWELL UNIVERSITY
SAMWELL
PERSONALLY? I DON'T EVEN WANT TO CONSIDER THE PHRASE "LIFE AFTER COLLEGE" UNTIL I'M HOLDING MY DIPLOMA—
BUT I CAN'T IGNORE THE FACT THAT JACK AND SHITTY ARE GRADUATING.
NOW, JACK IS SOMEHOW BALANCING HIS SENIOR STUFF, HIS CAPTAIN STUFF, AND CHOOSING THE NHL TEAM HE'LL PLAY FOR.
WHILE SHITTY? ...WELL.

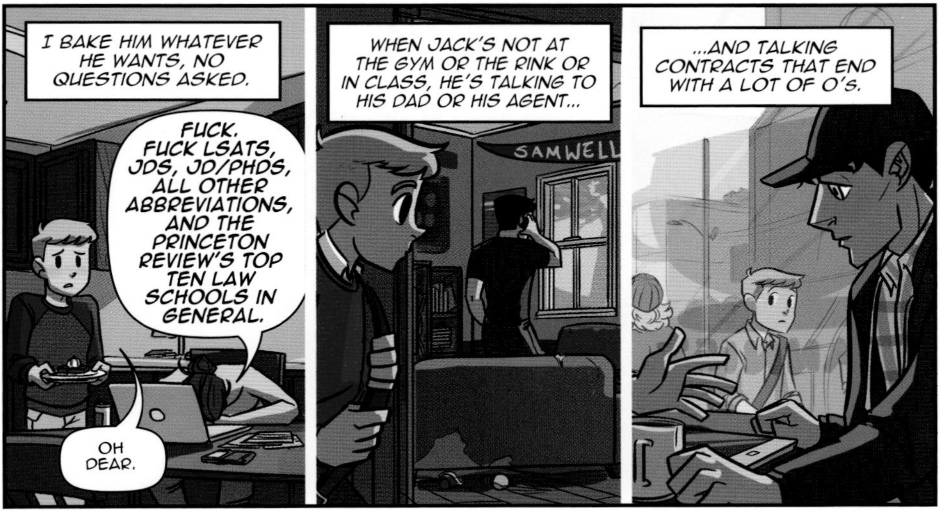
I BAKE HIM WHATEVER HE WANTS, NO QUESTIONS ASKED.
FUCK. FUCK LSATS, JDS, JD/PHDS, ALL OTHER ABBREVIATIONS, AND THE PRINCETON REVIEW'S TOP TEN LAW SCHOOLS IN GENERAL.
OH DEAR.
WHEN JACK'S NOT AT THE GYM OR THE RINK OR IN CLASS, HE'S TALKING TO HIS DAD OR HIS AGENT...
SAMWELL
...AND TALKING CONTRACTS THAT END WITH A LOT OF O's.

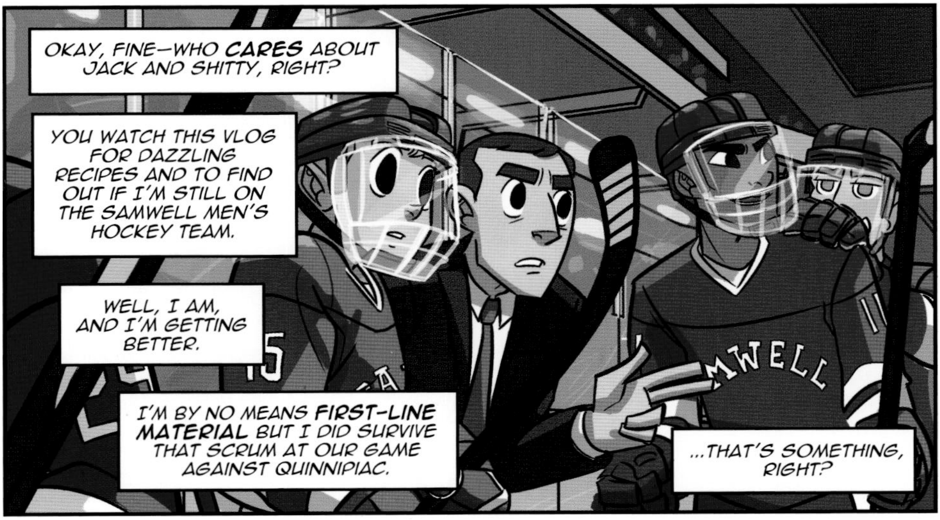
OKAY, FINE—WHO CARES ABOUT JACK AND SHITTY, RIGHT?
YOU WATCH THIS VLOG FOR DAZZLING RECIPES AND TO FIND OUT IF I'M STILL ON THE SAMWELL MEN'S HOCKEY TEAM.
WELL, I AM, AND I'M GETTING BETTER.
I'M BY NO MEANS FIRST-LINE MATERIAL BUT I DID SURVIVE THAT SCRUM AT OUR GAME AGAINST QUINNIPIAC.
...THAT'S SOMETHING, RIGHT?

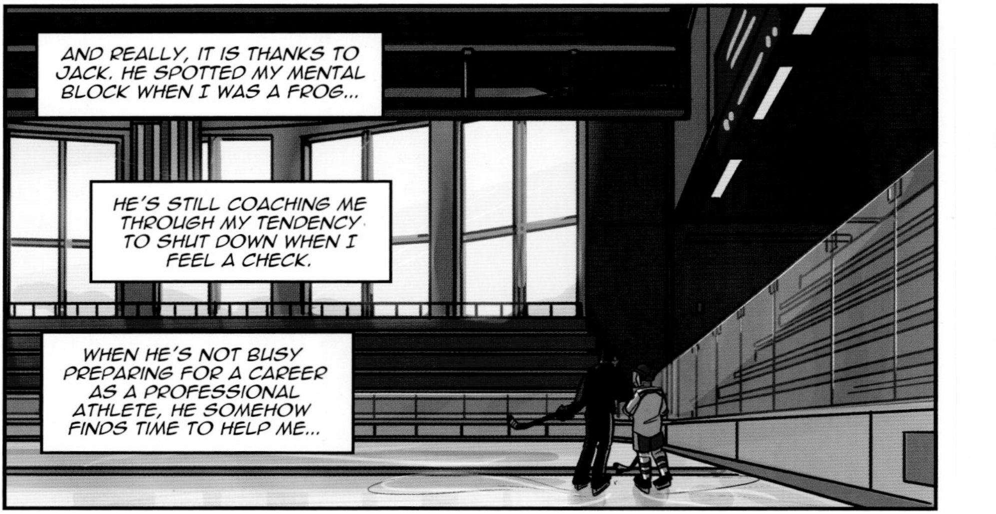
AND REALLY, IT IS THANKS TO JACK. HE SPOTTED MY MENTAL BLOCK WHEN I WAS A FROG...
HE'S STILL COACHING ME THROUGH MY TENDENCY TO SHUT DOWN WHEN I FEEL A CHECK.
WHEN HE'S NOT BUSY PREPARING FOR A CAREER AS A PROFESSIONAL ATHLETE, HE SOMEHOW FINDS TIME TO HELP ME...

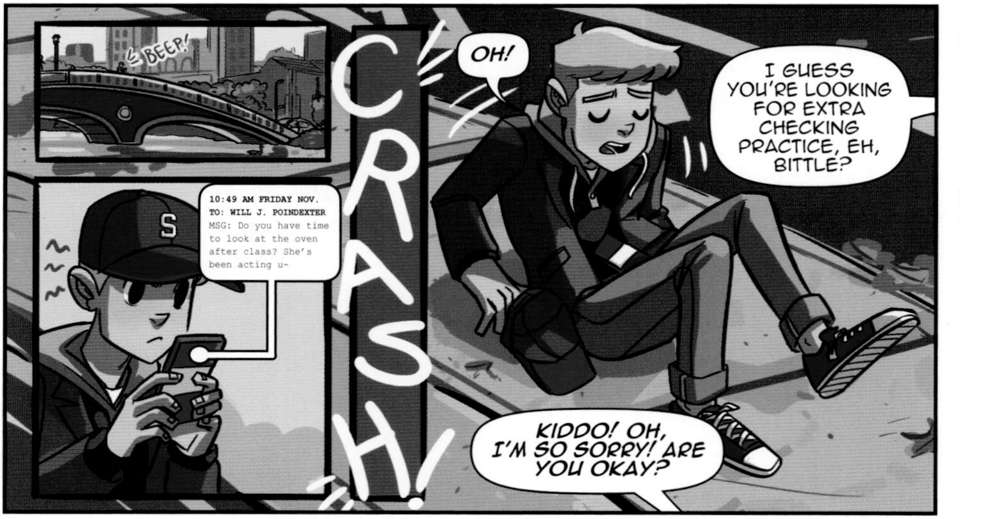
BEEP!
10:49 AM FRIDAY NOV.
TO: WILL J. POINDEXTER
MSG: Do you have time to look at the oven after class? She's been acting u-
CRASH!
OH!
I GUESS YOU'RE LOOKING FOR EXTRA CHECKING PRACTICE, EH, BITTLE?
KIDDO! OH, I'M SO SORRY! ARE YOU OKAY?

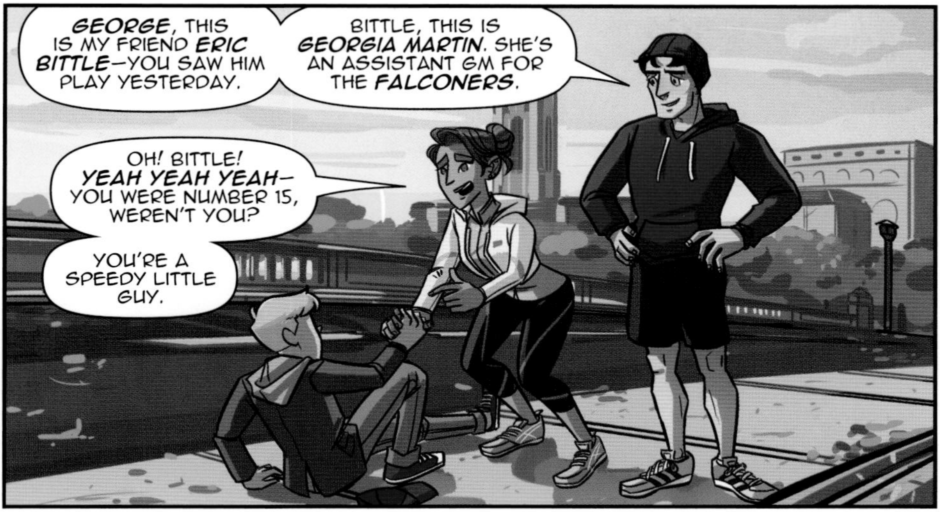
GEORGE, THIS IS MY FRIEND ERIC BITTLE—YOU SAW HIM PLAY YESTERDAY.
BITTLE, THIS IS GEORGIA MARTIN. SHE'S AN ASSISTANT GM FOR THE FALCONERS.
OH! BITTLE! YEAH YEAH YEAH— YOU WERE NUMBER 15, WEREN'T YOU?
YOU'RE A SPEEDY LITTLE GUY.

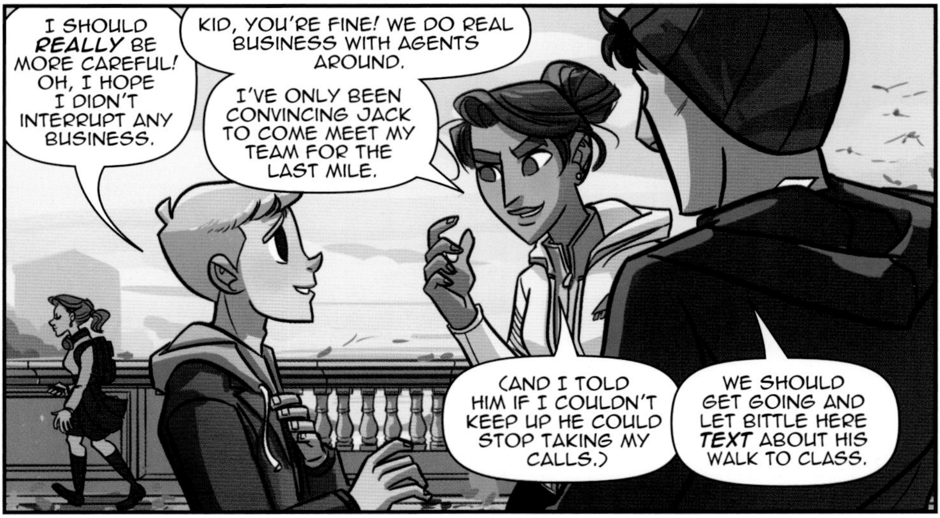
I SHOULD REALLY BE MORE CAREFUL! OH, I HOPE I DIDN'T INTERRUPT ANY BUSINESS.
KID, YOU'RE FINE! WE DO REAL BUSINESS WITH AGENTS AROUND.
I'VE ONLY BEEN CONVINCING JACK TO COME MEET MY TEAM FOR THE LAST MILE.
(AND I TOLD HIM IF I COULDN'T KEEP UP HE COULD STOP TAKING MY CALLS.)
WE SHOULD GET GOING AND LET BITTLE HERE TEXT ABOUT HIS WALK TO CLASS.

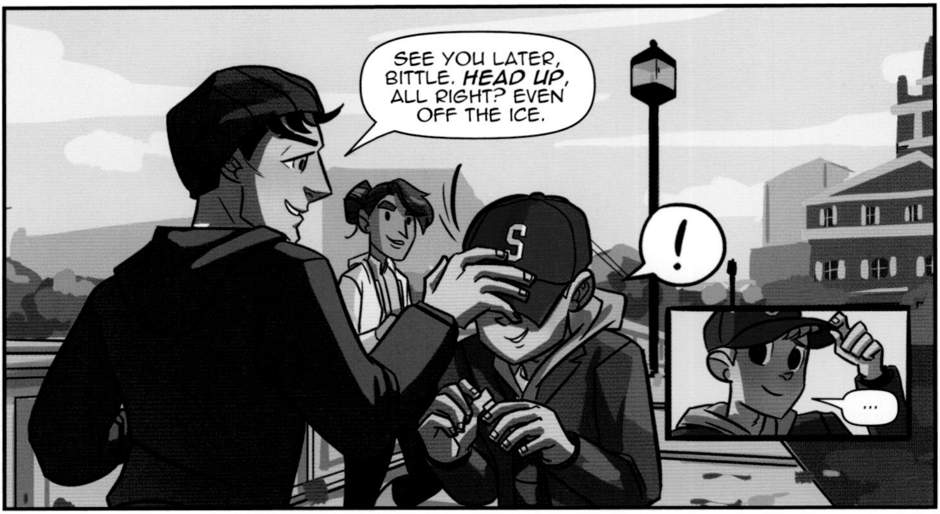
SEE YOU LATER, BITTLE. ***HEAD UP***, ALL RIGHT? EVEN OFF THE ICE.
!
...

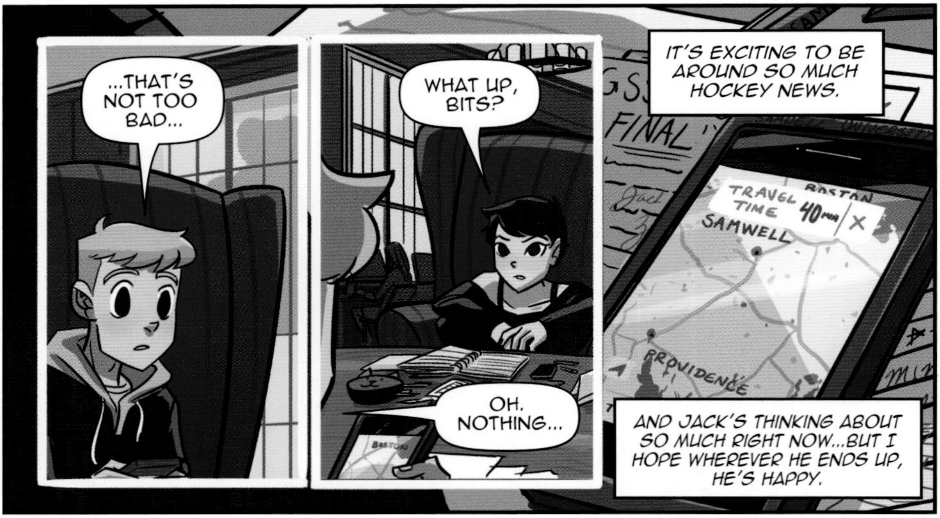
...THAT'S NOT TOO BAD...
WHAT UP, BITS?
OH. NOTHING...
IT'S EXCITING TO BE AROUND SO MUCH HOCKEY NEWS.
FINAL
TRAVEL TIME 40min
BOSTON
SAMWELL
PROVIDENCE
AND JACK'S THINKING ABOUT SO MUCH RIGHT NOW...BUT I HOPE WHEREVER HE ENDS UP, HE'S HAPPY.

6

WGSS120/HIST376: WOMEN, FOOD, AND AMERICAN CULTURE

SINCE Y'ALL TUNE IN TO HEAR EXCLUSIVE BAKING TIPS AND MY ADVENTURES IN HOCKEY, I DON'T TALK MUCH ABOUT SCHOOL.
BUT THIS SEMESTER I WORKED MY WAY INTO A SENIOR HISTORY SEMINAR: HIST376, WOMEN, FOOD, AND AMERICAN CULTURE.
AND GUESS WHO'S ONE OF MY CLASSMATES?
THREE CLUES: HE IS FRENCH-CANADIAN, LIVES 'CROSS THE HALL, AND DRAWS HOCKEY PLAYS IN HIS NOTES.
SAMWELL
SAMWELL
SAMWELL
SHUT OUT!
FOOD & US HISTORY

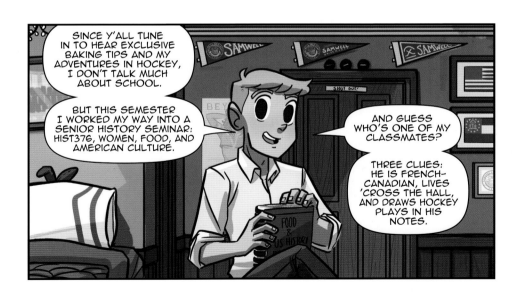

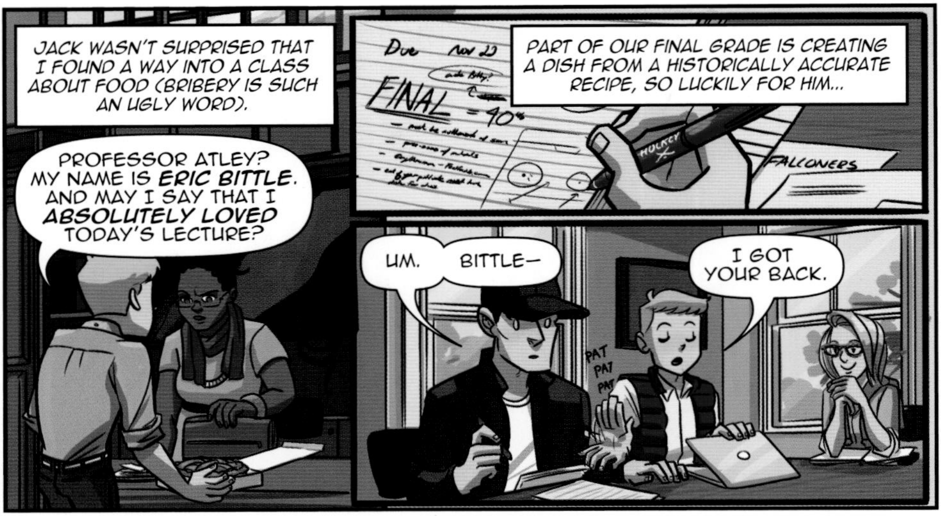
JACK WASN'T SURPRISED THAT I FOUND A WAY INTO A CLASS ABOUT FOOD (BRIBERY IS SUCH AN UGLY WORD).
PROFESSOR ATLEY? MY NAME IS ERIC BITTLE. AND MAY I SAY THAT I ABSOLUTELY LOVED TODAY'S LECTURE?
PART OF OUR FINAL GRADE IS CREATING A DISH FROM A HISTORICALLY ACCURATE RECIPE, SO LUCKILY FOR HIM...
FALCONERS
UM.
BITTLE—
I GOT YOUR BACK.
PAT PAT PAT

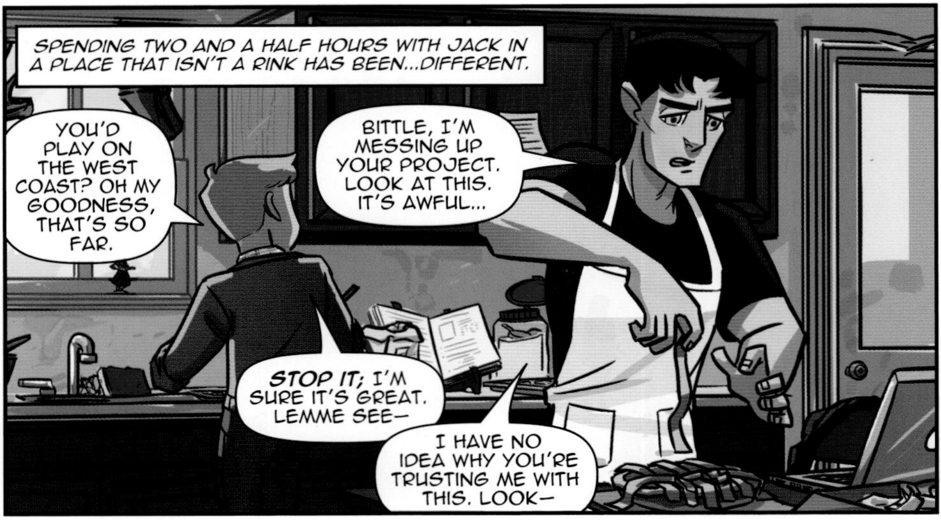
SPENDING TWO AND A HALF HOURS WITH JACK IN A PLACE THAT ISN'T A RINK HAS BEEN...DIFFERENT.
YOU'D PLAY ON THE WEST COAST? OH MY GOODNESS, THAT'S SO FAR.
BITTLE, I'M MESSING UP YOUR PROJECT. LOOK AT THIS. IT'S AWFUL...
STOP IT; I'M SURE IT'S GREAT. LEMME SEE—
I HAVE NO IDEA WHY YOU'RE TRUSTING ME WITH THIS. LOOK—

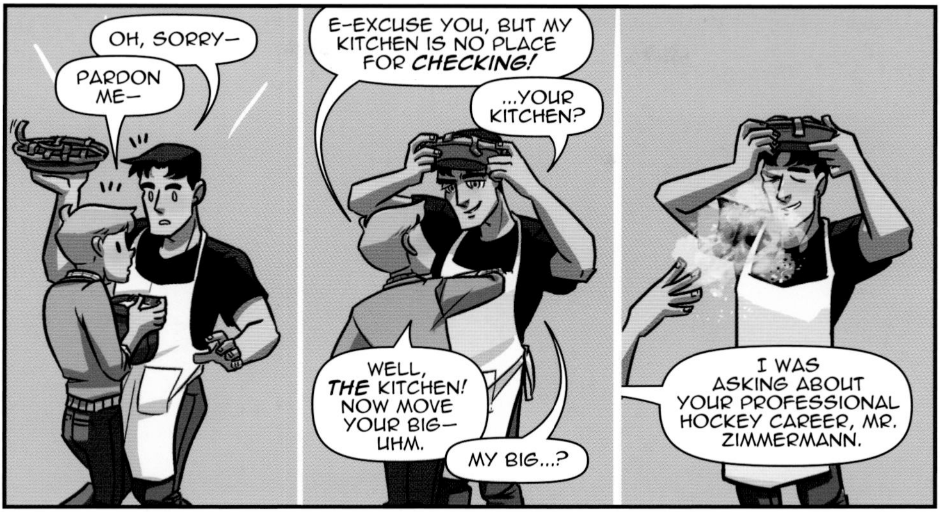
OH, SORRY—
PARDON ME—
E-EXCUSE YOU, BUT MY KITCHEN IS NO PLACE FOR CHECKING!
...YOUR KITCHEN?
WELL, THE KITCHEN! NOW MOVE YOUR BIG— UHM.
MY BIG...?
I WAS ASKING ABOUT YOUR PROFESSIONAL HOCKEY CAREER, MR. ZIMMERMANN.

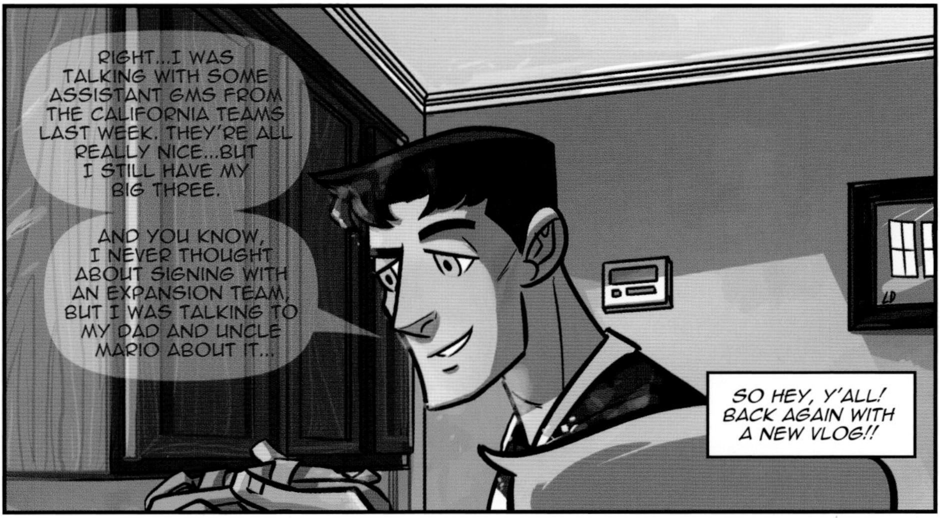
RIGHT...I WAS TALKING WITH SOME ASSISTANT GMS FROM THE CALIFORNIA TEAMS LAST WEEK. THEY'RE ALL REALLY NICE...BUT I STILL HAVE MY BIG THREE.
AND YOU KNOW, I NEVER THOUGHT ABOUT SIGNING WITH AN EXPANSION TEAM, BUT I WAS TALKING TO MY DAD AND UNCLE MARIO ABOUT IT...
SO HEY, Y'ALL! BACK AGAIN WITH A NEW VLOG!!

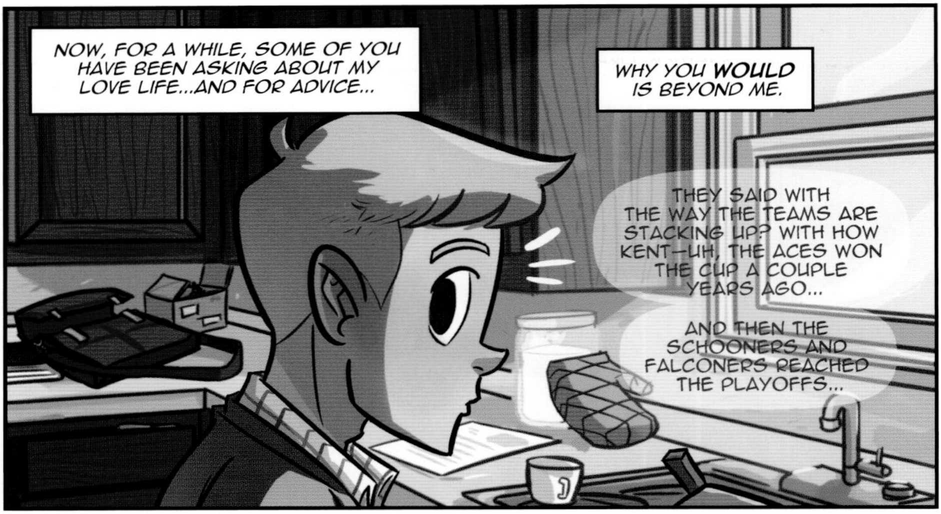
NOW, FOR A WHILE, SOME OF YOU HAVE BEEN ASKING ABOUT MY LOVE LIFE...AND FOR ADVICE...
WHY YOU **WOULD** IS BEYOND ME.
THEY SAID WITH THE WAY THE TEAMS ARE STACKING UP? WITH HOW KENT—UH, THE ACES WON THE CUP A COUPLE YEARS AGO...
AND THEN THE SCHOONERS AND FALCONERS REACHED THE PLAYOFFS...

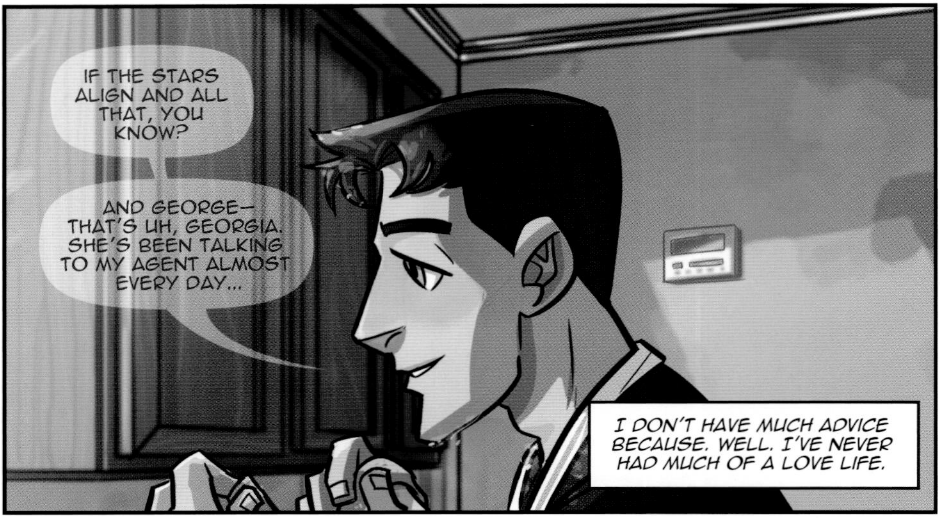
IF THE STARS ALIGN AND ALL THAT, YOU KNOW?
AND GEORGE— THAT'S UH, GEORGIA. SHE'S BEEN TALKING TO MY AGENT ALMOST EVERY DAY...
I DON'T HAVE MUCH ADVICE BECAUSE. WELL. I'VE NEVER HAD MUCH OF A LOVE LIFE.

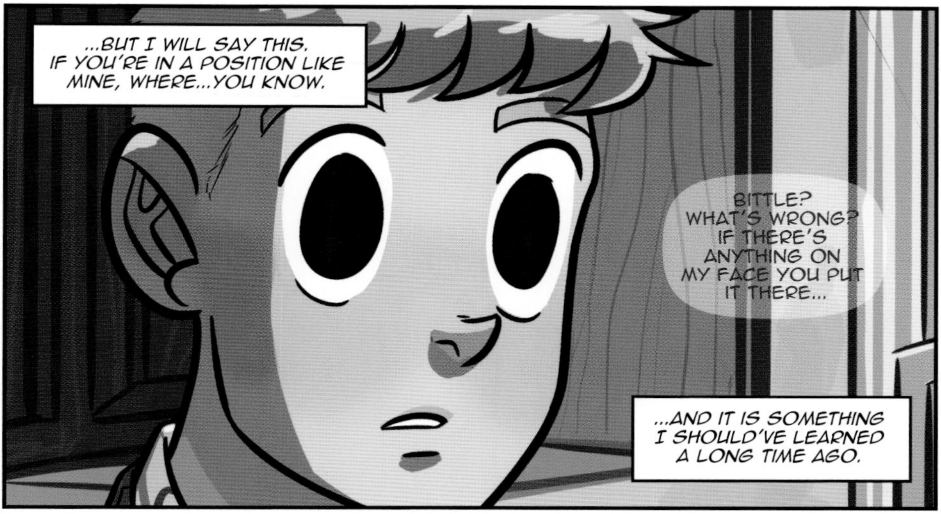
...BUT I WILL SAY THIS. IF YOU'RE IN A POSITION LIKE MINE, WHERE...YOU KNOW.
BITTLE? WHAT'S WRONG? IF THERE'S ANYTHING ON MY FACE YOU PUT IT THERE...
...AND IT IS SOMETHING I SHOULD'VE LEARNED A LONG TIME AGO.

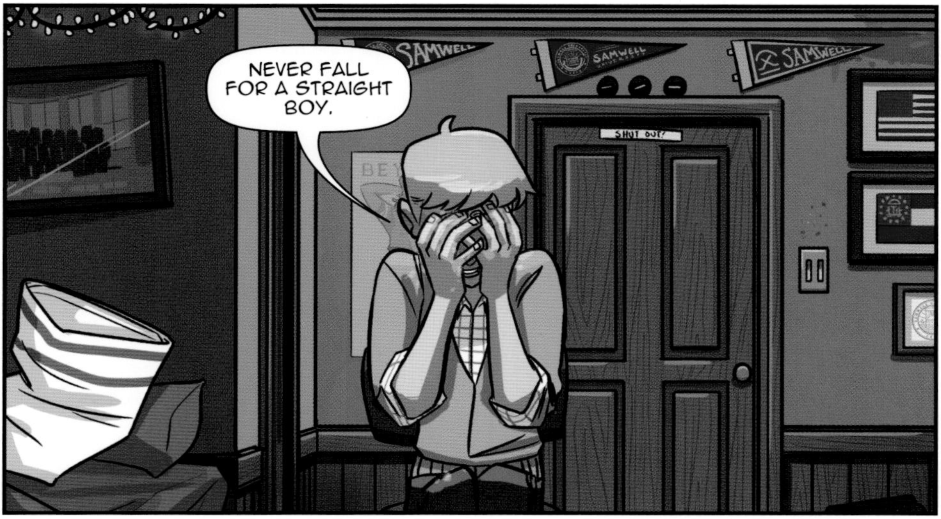
SAMWELL
SAMWELL
SAMWELL
NEVER FALL FOR A STRAIGHT BOY.
SHUT OUT?

7

PARSE — I

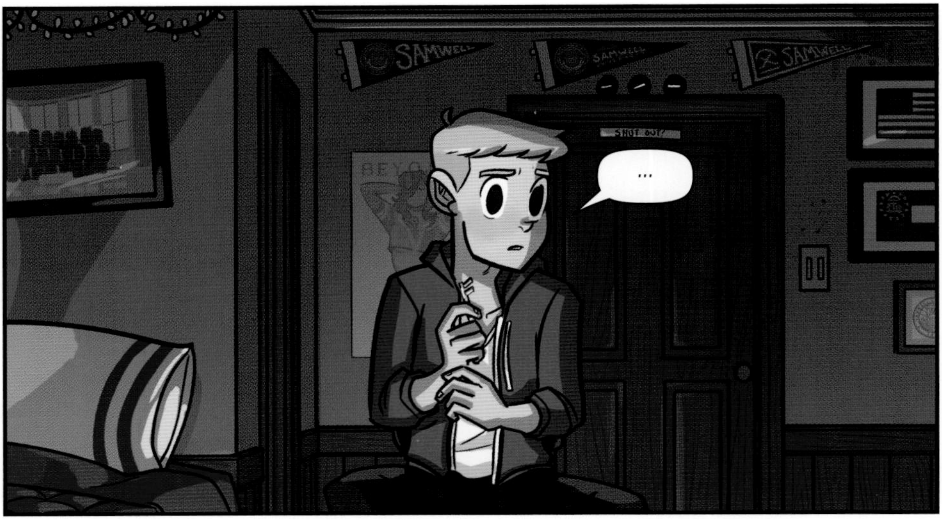
SAMWELL
SAMWELL
SAMWELL
SHUT OUT!
...

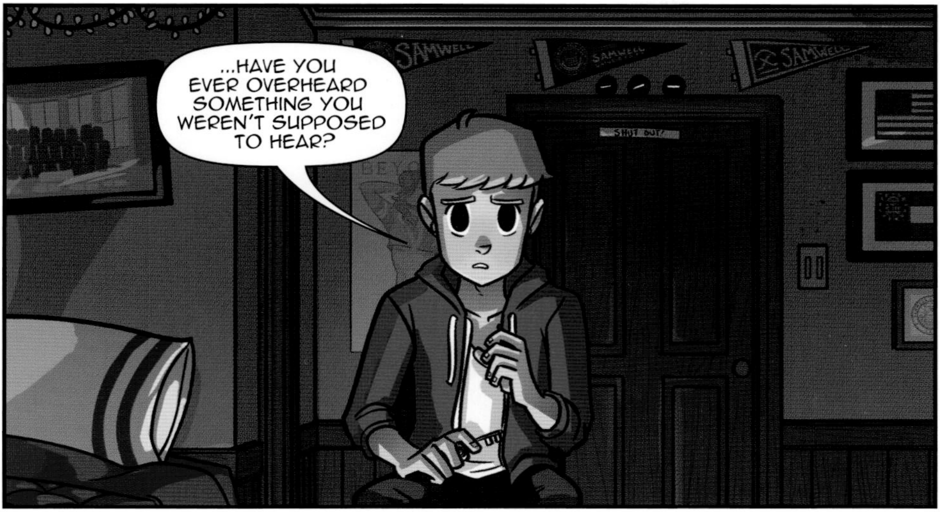
...HAVE YOU EVER OVERHEARD SOMETHING YOU WEREN'T SUPPOSED TO HEAR?

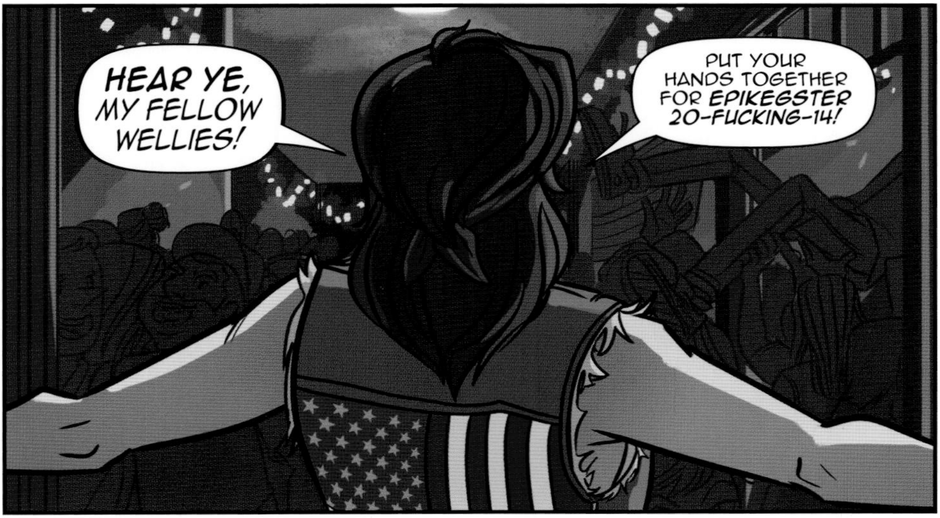
HEAR YE, MY FELLOW WELLIES!
PUT YOUR HANDS TOGETHER FOR EPIKEGSTER 20-FUCKING-14!

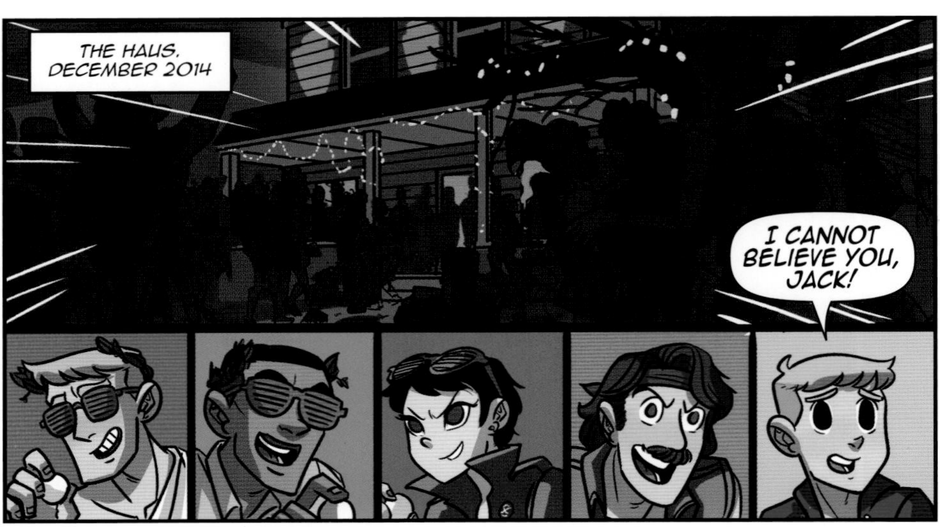
THE HAUS. DECEMBER 2014
I CANNOT BELIEVE YOU, JACK!

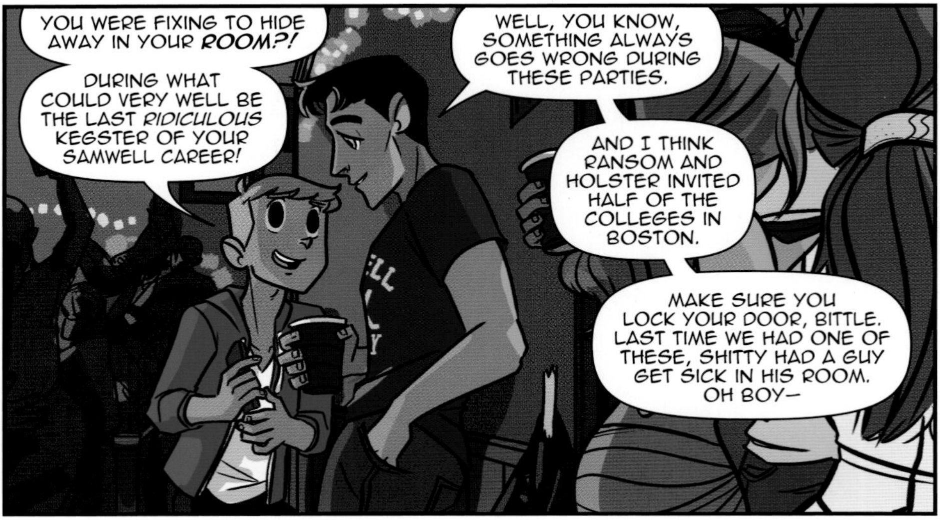
YOU WERE FIXING TO HIDE AWAY IN YOUR *ROOM?!*
DURING WHAT COULD VERY WELL BE THE LAST *RIDICULOUS* KEGSTER OF YOUR SAMWELL CAREER!
WELL, YOU KNOW, SOMETHING ALWAYS GOES WRONG DURING THESE PARTIES.
AND I THINK RANSOM AND HOLSTER INVITED HALF OF THE COLLEGES IN BOSTON.
MAKE SURE YOU LOCK YOUR DOOR, BITTLE. LAST TIME WE HAD ONE OF THESE, SHITTY HAD A GUY GET SICK IN HIS ROOM. OH BOY—

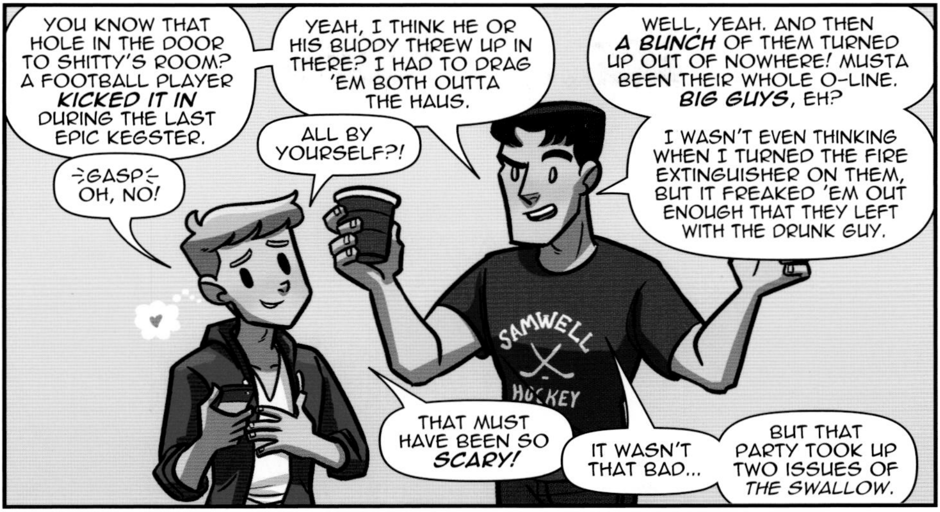
YOU KNOW THAT HOLE IN THE DOOR TO SHITTY'S ROOM? A FOOTBALL PLAYER **KICKED IT IN** DURING THE LAST EPIC KEGSTER.
GASP OH, NO!
YEAH, I THINK HE OR HIS BUDDY THREW UP IN THERE? I HAD TO DRAG 'EM BOTH OUTTA THE HAUS.
ALL BY YOURSELF?!
WELL, YEAH. AND THEN **A BUNCH** OF THEM TURNED UP OUT OF NOWHERE! MUSTA BEEN THEIR WHOLE O-LINE. **BIG GUYS**, EH?
I WASN'T EVEN THINKING WHEN I TURNED THE FIRE EXTINGUISHER ON THEM, BUT IT FREAKED 'EM OUT ENOUGH THAT THEY LEFT WITH THE DRUNK GUY.
SAMWELL HOCKEY
THAT MUST HAVE BEEN SO ***SCARY!***
IT WASN'T THAT BAD...
BUT THAT PARTY TOOK UP TWO ISSUES OF *THE SWALLOW*.

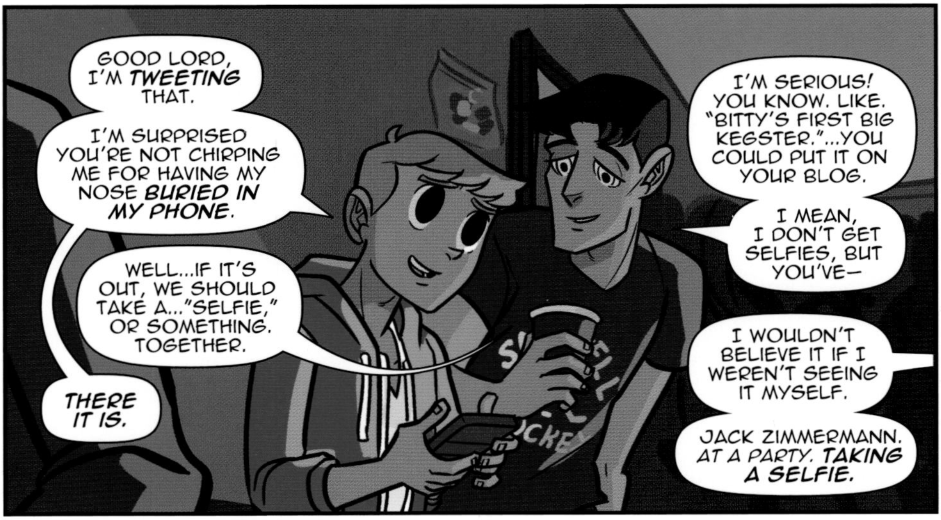
GOOD LORD, I'M ***TWEETING*** THAT.
I'M SURPRISED YOU'RE NOT CHIRPING ME FOR HAVING MY NOSE ***BURIED IN MY PHONE***.
WELL...IF IT'S OUT, WE SHOULD TAKE A..."SELFIE," OR SOMETHING. TOGETHER.
THERE IT IS.
I'M SERIOUS! YOU KNOW. LIKE. "BITTY'S FIRST BIG KEGSTER."...YOU COULD PUT IT ON YOUR BLOG.
I MEAN, I DON'T GET SELFIES, BUT YOU'VE—
I WOULDN'T BELIEVE IT IF I WEREN'T SEEING IT MYSELF.
JACK ZIMMERMANN. *AT A PARTY.* ***TAKING A SELFIE.***

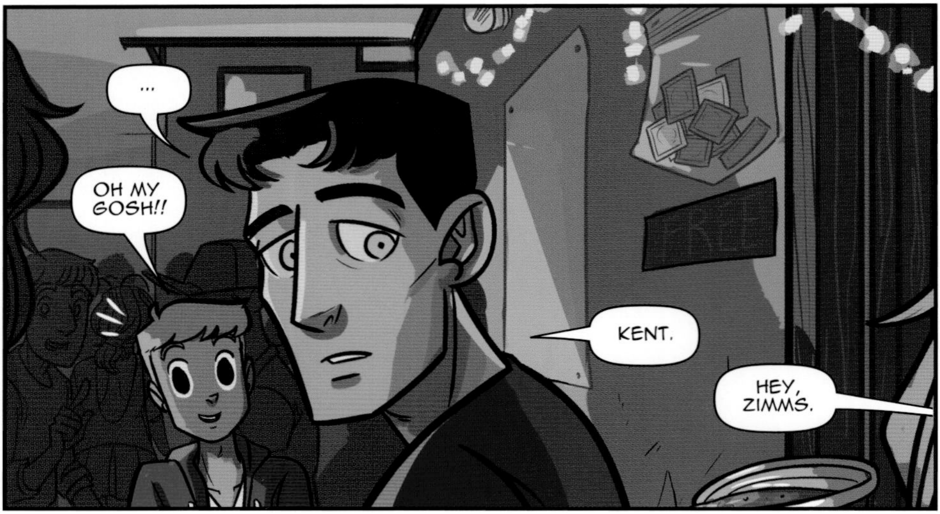
...
OH MY GOSH!!
KENT.
HEY, ZIMMS.

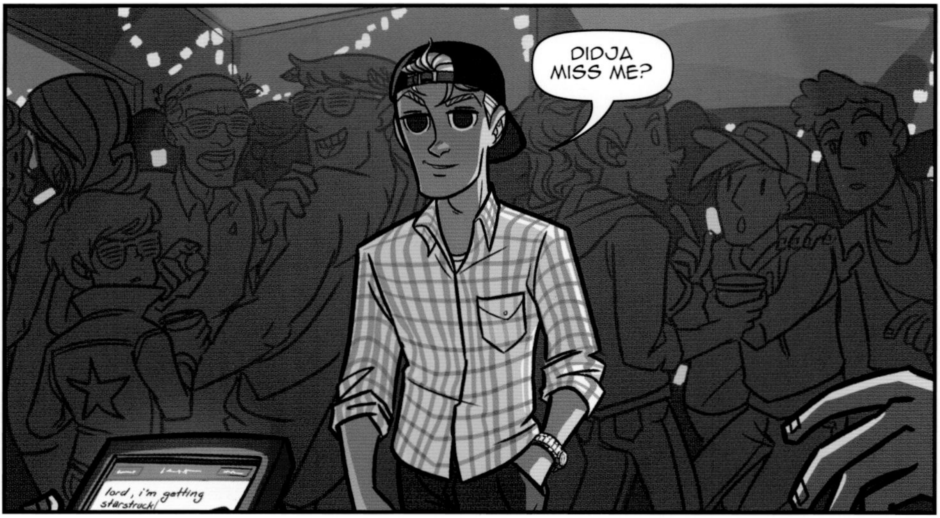
DIDJA MISS ME?
lord, i'm getting starstruck!

8

PARSE — II

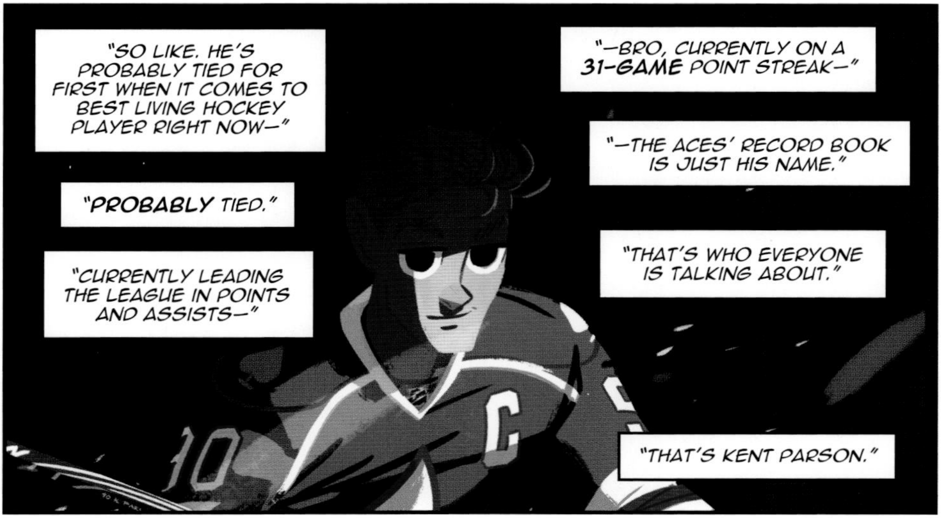
"SO LIKE. HE'S PROBABLY TIED FOR FIRST WHEN IT COMES TO BEST LIVING HOCKEY PLAYER RIGHT NOW—"
"PROBABLY TIED."
"CURRENTLY LEADING THE LEAGUE IN POINTS AND ASSISTS—"
"—BRO, CURRENTLY ON A 31-GAME POINT STREAK—"
"—THE ACES' RECORD BOOK IS JUST HIS NAME."
"THAT'S WHO EVERYONE IS TALKING ABOUT."
"THAT'S KENT PARSON."
C
10

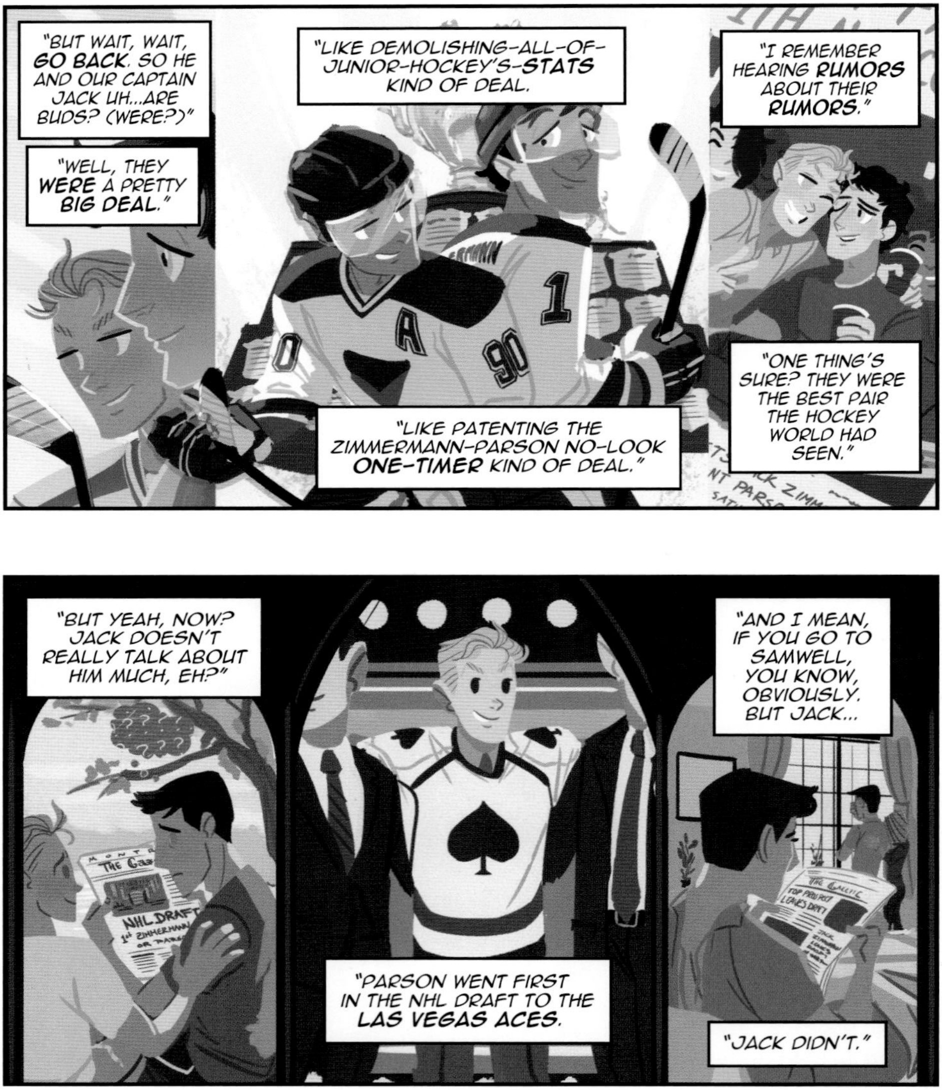
"BUT WAIT, WAIT, GO BACK. SO HE AND OUR CAPTAIN JACK UH...ARE BUDS? (WERE?)"
"WELL, THEY WERE A PRETTY BIG DEAL."
"LIKE DEMOLISHING-ALL-OF-JUNIOR-HOCKEY'S-STATS KIND OF DEAL.
"LIKE PATENTING THE ZIMMERMANN-PARSON NO-LOOK ONE-TIMER KIND OF DEAL."
"I REMEMBER HEARING RUMORS ABOUT THEIR RUMORS."
"ONE THING'S SURE? THEY WERE THE BEST PAIR THE HOCKEY WORLD HAD SEEN."
"BUT YEAH, NOW? JACK DOESN'T REALLY TALK ABOUT HIM MUCH, EH?"
NHL DRAFT
"PARSON WENT FIRST IN THE NHL DRAFT TO THE LAS VEGAS ACES.
"AND I MEAN, IF YOU GO TO SAMWELL, YOU KNOW, OBVIOUSLY. BUT JACK...
"JACK DIDN'T."

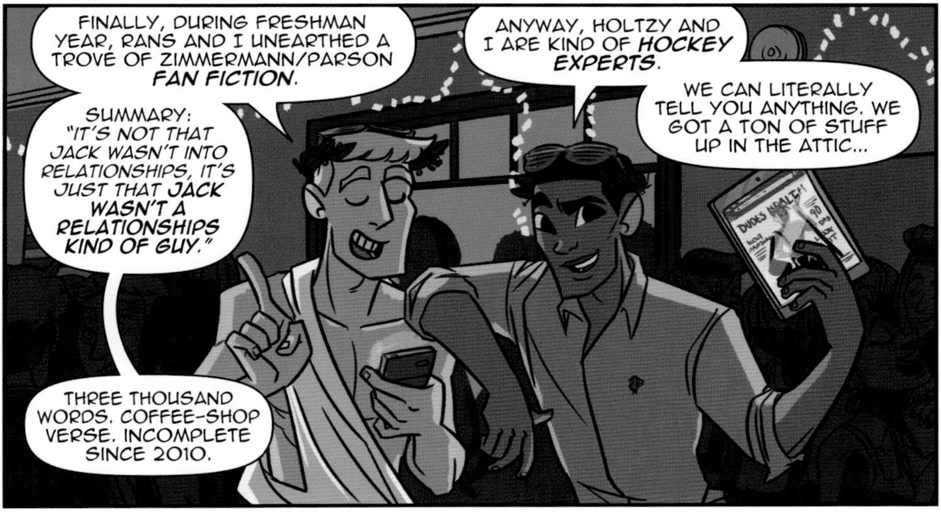
FINALLY, DURING FRESHMAN YEAR, RANS AND I UNEARTHED A TROVE OF ZIMMERMANN/PARSON FAN FICTION.
SUMMARY: "IT'S NOT THAT JACK WASN'T INTO RELATIONSHIPS, IT'S JUST THAT JACK WASN'T A RELATIONSHIPS KIND OF GUY."
THREE THOUSAND WORDS. COFFEE-SHOP VERSE. INCOMPLETE SINCE 2010.
ANYWAY, HOLTZY AND I ARE KIND OF HOCKEY EXPERTS.
WE CAN LITERALLY TELL YOU ANYTHING. WE GOT A TON OF STUFF UP IN THE ATTIC...

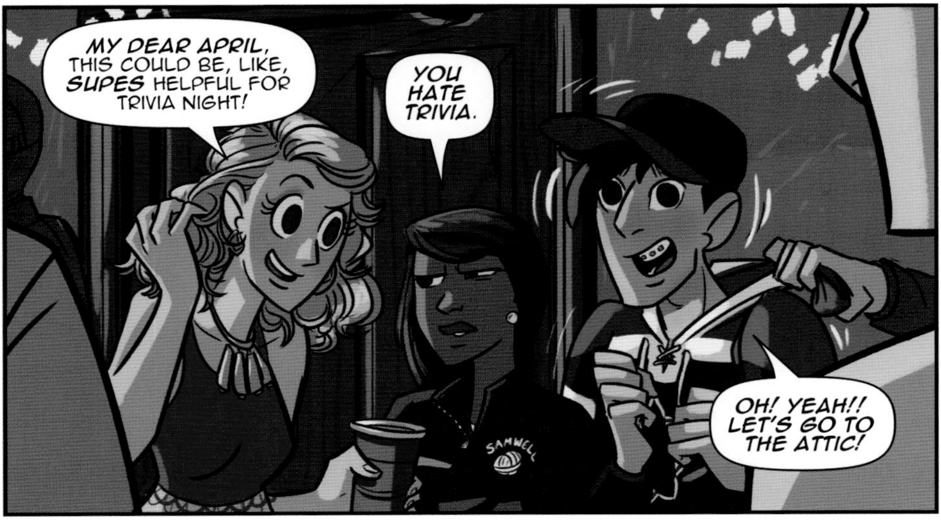
MY DEAR APRIL, THIS COULD BE, LIKE, SUPES HELPFUL FOR TRIVIA NIGHT!
YOU HATE TRIVIA.
OH! YEAH!! LET'S GO TO THE ATTIC!
SAMWELL

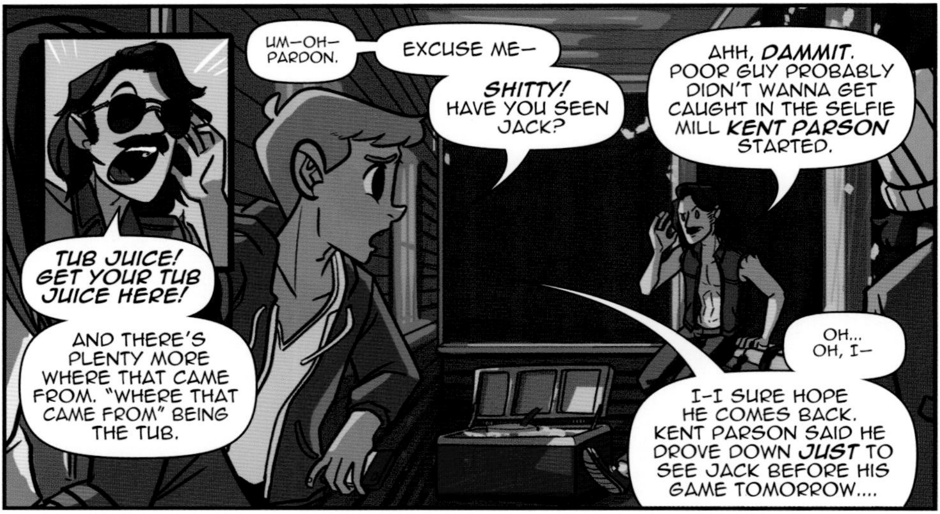
TUB JUICE! GET YOUR TUB JUICE HERE!
AND THERE'S PLENTY MORE WHERE THAT CAME FROM. "WHERE THAT CAME FROM" BEING THE TUB.
UM—OH— PARDON.
EXCUSE ME—
SHITTY! HAVE YOU SEEN JACK?
AHH, DAMMIT. POOR GUY PROBABLY DIDN'T WANNA GET CAUGHT IN THE SELFIE MILL KENT PARSON STARTED.
OH... OH, I—
I-I SURE HOPE HE COMES BACK. KENT PARSON SAID HE DROVE DOWN JUST TO SEE JACK BEFORE HIS GAME TOMORROW....

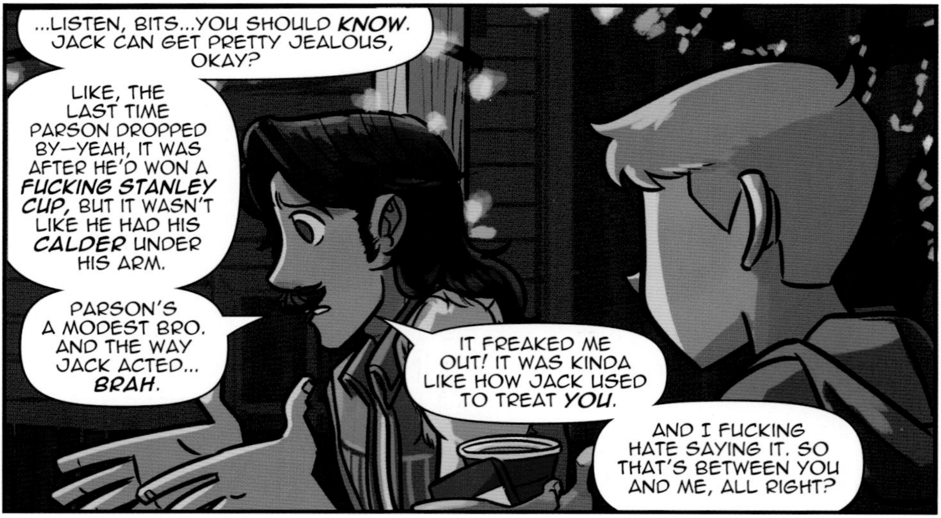
...LISTEN, BITS...YOU SHOULD KNOW. JACK CAN GET PRETTY JEALOUS, OKAY?
LIKE, THE LAST TIME PARSON DROPPED BY—YEAH, IT WAS AFTER HE'D WON A FUCKING STANLEY CUP, BUT IT WASN'T LIKE HE HAD HIS CALDER UNDER HIS ARM.
PARSON'S A MODEST BRO. AND THE WAY JACK ACTED... BRAH.
IT FREAKED ME OUT! IT WAS KINDA LIKE HOW JACK USED TO TREAT YOU.
AND I FUCKING HATE SAYING IT. SO THAT'S BETWEEN YOU AND ME, ALL RIGHT?

...BITS.
...I *SWEAR* I WASN'T SHARING THAT.
⫶SIGH⫶ I'M GONNA PUT THIS THING IN MY ROOM BEFORE I TWEET ANYTHING STUPID.
IF YOU SEE JACK... TELL HIM TO COME FIND ME, OKAY?
SURE, BITS. AND ***LAY OFF THAT FUCKING TUB JUICE***. IT'S MAGICALLY MALICIOUS!
HEY!! AND FUCKING ***LOCK UP***. 'ROUND TWO AM ***THE CHUNKS START TO BLOW.*** LAST EPIKEGSTER—
OH LORD, SHITTY, YES, JACK WARNED ME.
OH! HEY, SUP, LARDS?
YEEEEEEP. JUST CRUSHED PARSON AT FLIP CUP.
PRETTY SURE IT'S ON YOUTUBE.
OH, AND SOMEONE RALPHED IN YOUR ROOM AGAIN.
PROBS THE TUB JUICE.
GODDAMMIT!

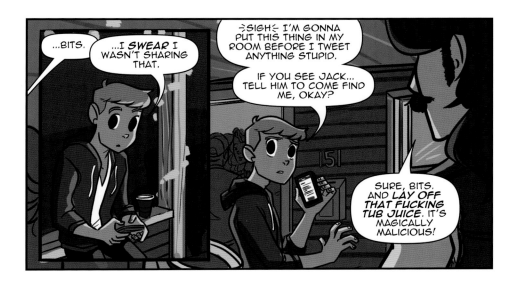

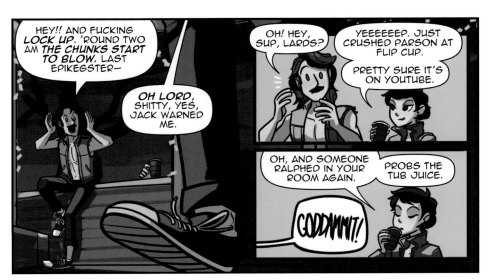

9

PARSE — III

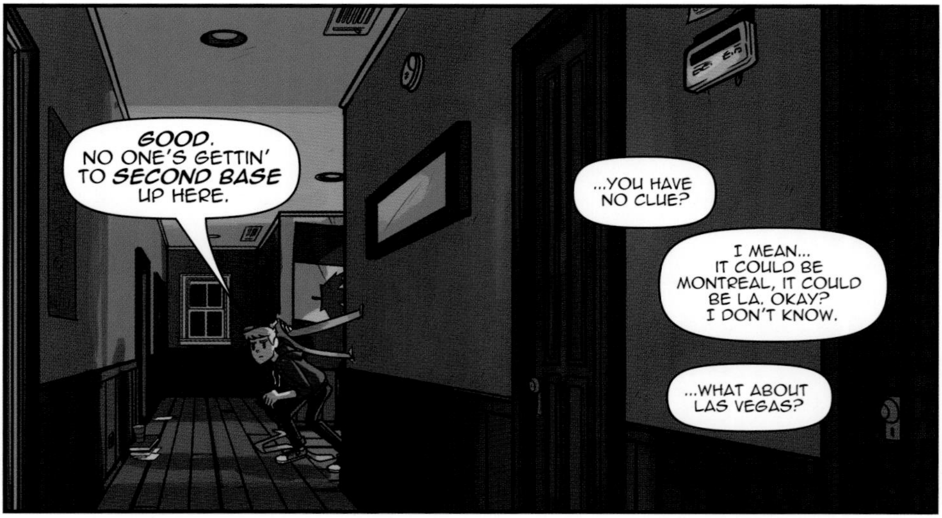
GOOD. NO ONE'S GETTIN' TO SECOND BASE UP HERE.
...YOU HAVE NO CLUE?
I MEAN... IT COULD BE MONTREAL, IT COULD BE LA, OKAY? I DON'T KNOW.
...WHAT ABOUT LAS VEGAS?

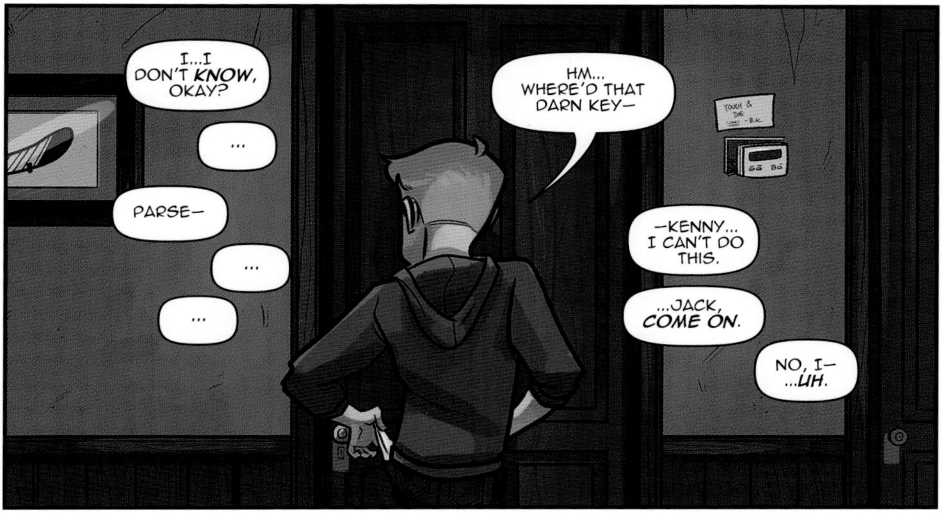
I...I DON'T *KNOW*, OKAY?
HM... WHERE'D THAT DARN KEY—
...
PARSE—
...
...
—KENNY... I CAN'T DO THIS.
...JACK, *COME ON*.
NO, I— ...*UH*.

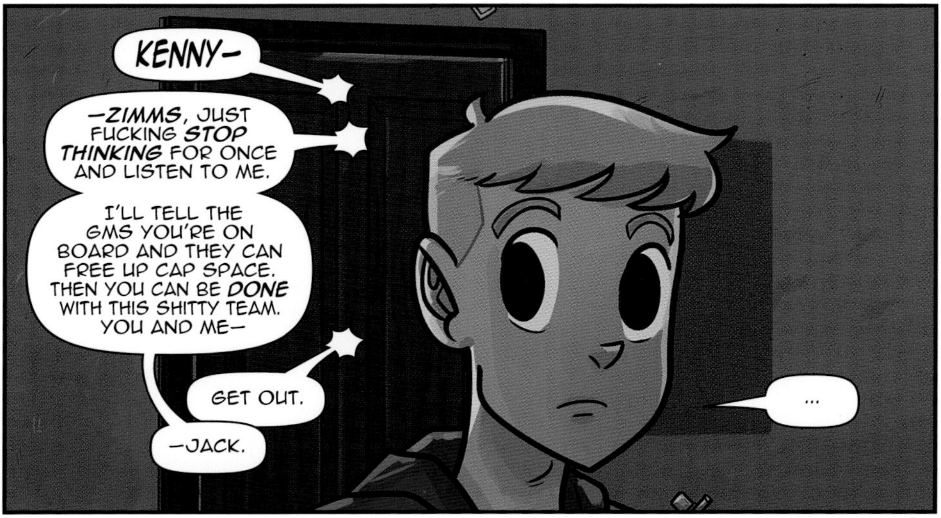
KENNY—
—*ZIMMS*, JUST FUCKING *STOP THINKING* FOR ONCE AND LISTEN TO ME.
I'LL TELL THE GMS YOU'RE ON BOARD AND THEY CAN FREE UP CAP SPACE. THEN YOU CAN BE *DONE* WITH THIS SHITTY TEAM. YOU AND ME—
GET OUT.
—JACK.
...

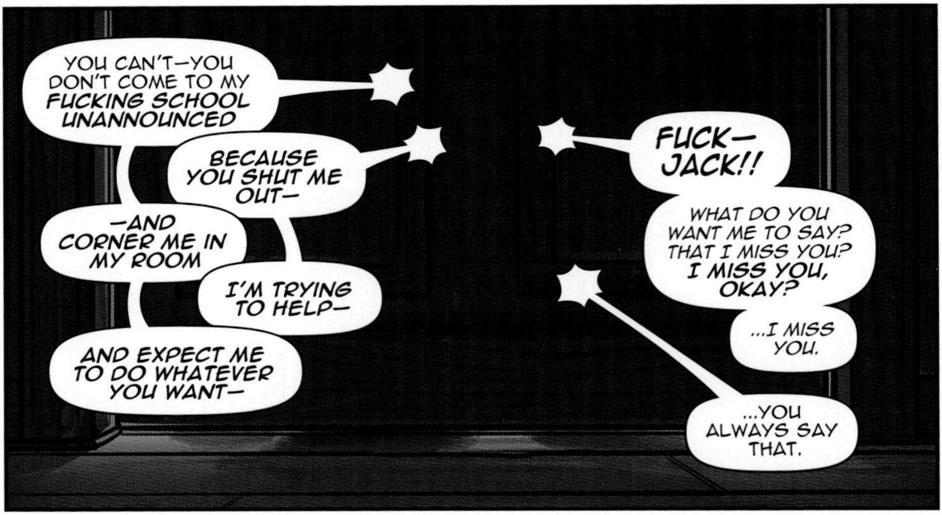
YOU CAN'T—YOU DON'T COME TO MY FUCKING SCHOOL UNANNOUNCED
BECAUSE YOU SHUT ME OUT—
—AND CORNER ME IN MY ROOM
I'M TRYING TO HELP—
AND EXPECT ME TO DO WHATEVER YOU WANT—
FUCK—JACK!!
WHAT DO YOU WANT ME TO SAY? THAT I MISS YOU? I MISS YOU, OKAY?
...I MISS YOU.
...YOU ALWAYS SAY THAT.

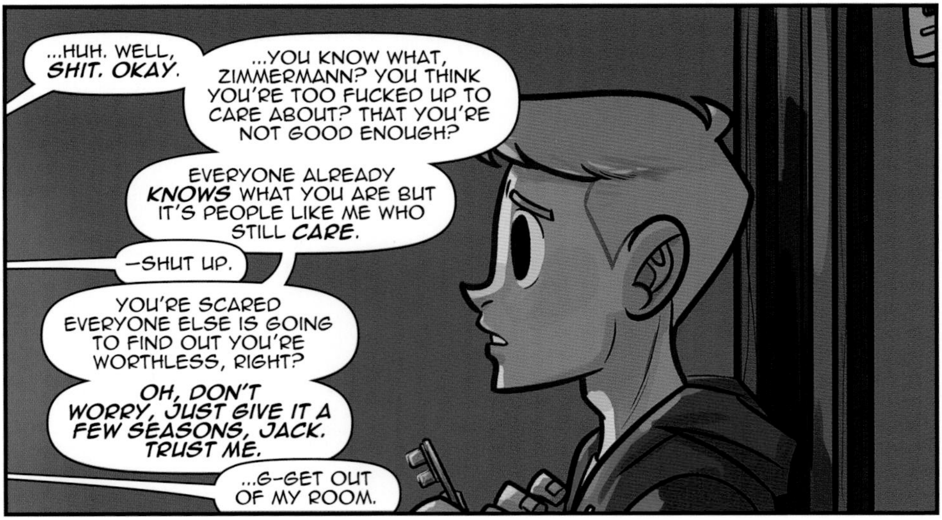
...HUH. WELL, SHIT. OKAY.
...YOU KNOW WHAT, ZIMMERMANN? YOU THINK YOU'RE TOO FUCKED UP TO CARE ABOUT? THAT YOU'RE NOT GOOD ENOUGH?
EVERYONE ALREADY KNOWS WHAT YOU ARE BUT IT'S PEOPLE LIKE ME WHO STILL CARE.
—SHUT UP.
YOU'RE SCARED EVERYONE ELSE IS GOING TO FIND OUT YOU'RE WORTHLESS, RIGHT?
OH, DON'T WORRY, JUST GIVE IT A FEW SEASONS, JACK. TRUST ME.
...G-GET OUT OF MY ROOM.

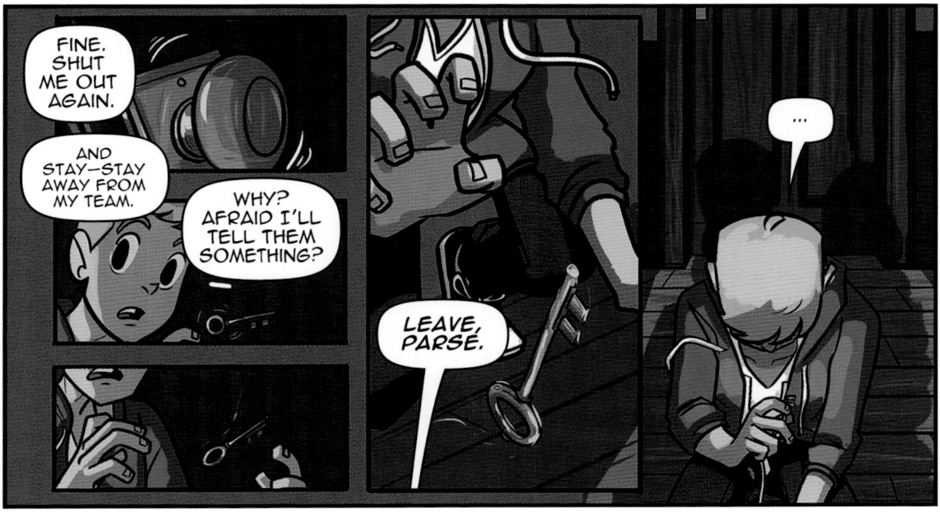
FINE. SHUT ME OUT AGAIN.
AND STAY—STAY AWAY FROM MY TEAM.
WHY? AFRAID I'LL TELL THEM SOMETHING?
LEAVE, PARSE.
...

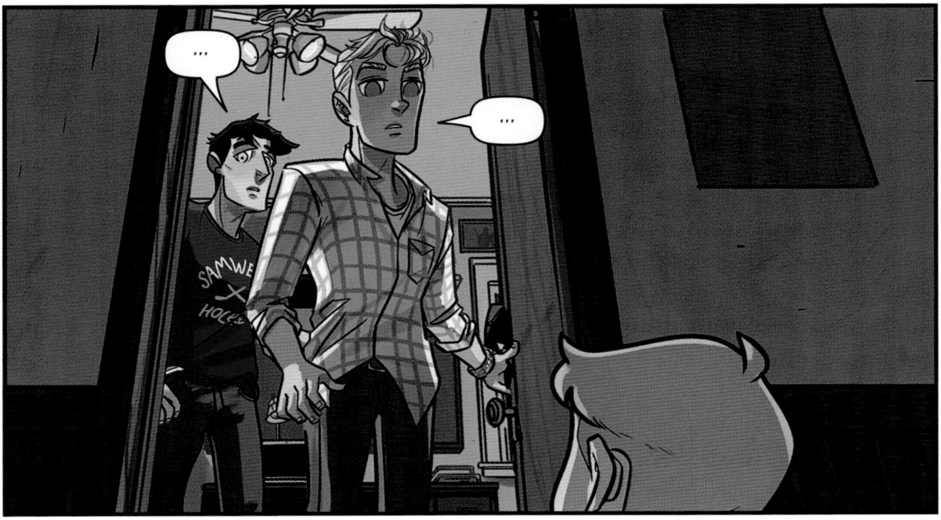
...
...

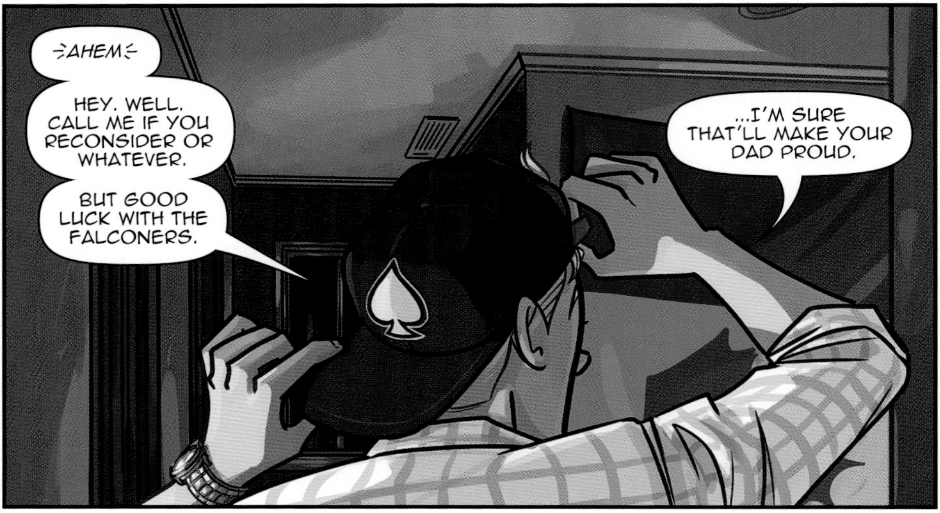
=AHEM=
HEY. WELL. CALL ME IF YOU RECONSIDER OR WHATEVER.
BUT GOOD LUCK WITH THE FALCONERS.
...I'M SURE THAT'LL MAKE YOUR DAD PROUD.

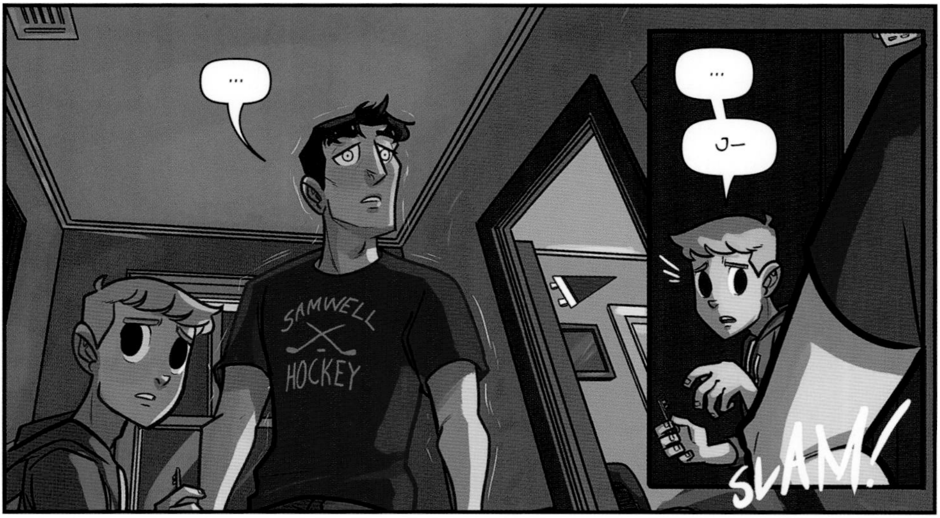
...
...
J—
SAMWELL HOCKEY
SLAM!

10

SHINNY

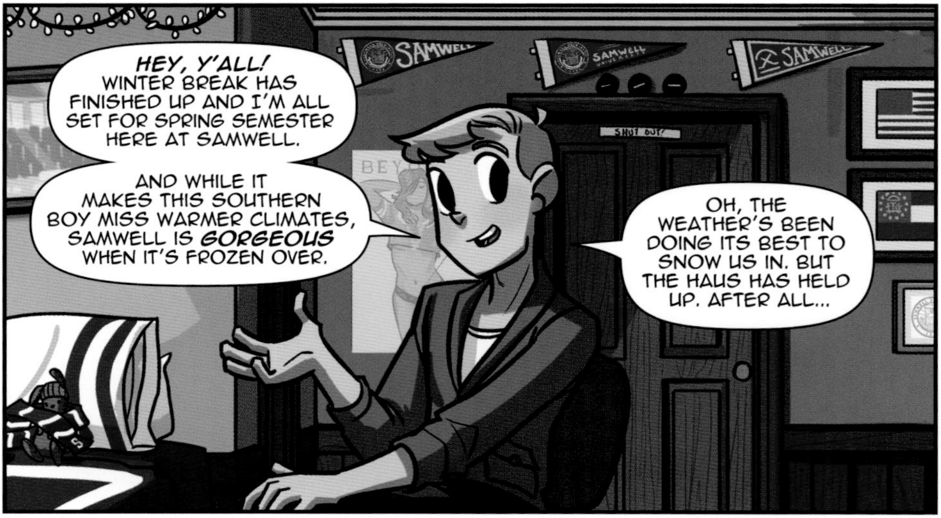

HEY, Y'ALL! WINTER BREAK HAS FINISHED UP AND I'M ALL SET FOR SPRING SEMESTER HERE AT SAMWELL.
AND WHILE IT MAKES THIS SOUTHERN BOY MISS WARMER CLIMATES, SAMWELL IS GORGEOUS WHEN IT'S FROZEN OVER.
OH, THE WEATHER'S BEEN DOING ITS BEST TO SNOW US IN. BUT THE HAUS HAS HELD UP. AFTER ALL...
SAMWELL
SAMWELL
SAMWELL

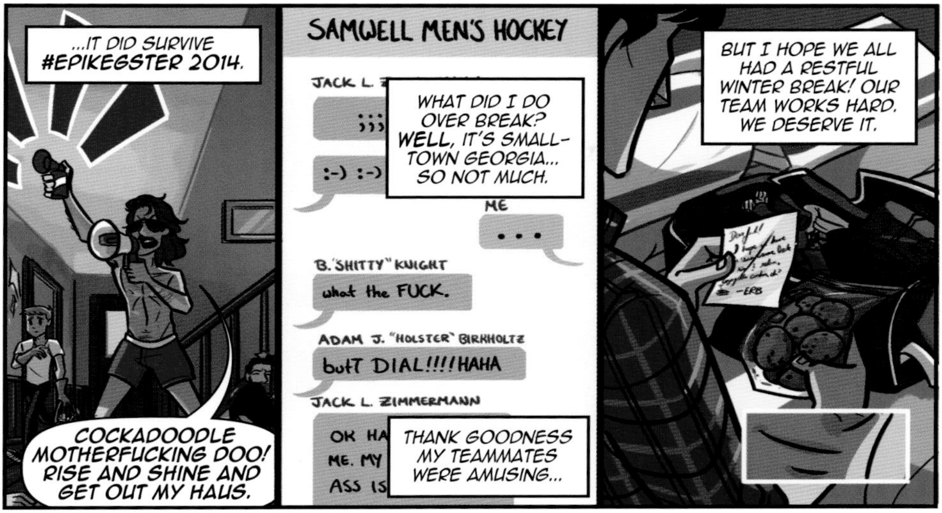
...IT DID SURVIVE #EPIKEGSTER 2014.
COCKADOODLE MOTHERFUCKING DOO! RISE AND SHINE AND GET OUT MY HAUS.
SAMWELL MEN'S HOCKEY
WHAT DID I DO OVER BREAK? WELL, IT'S SMALL-TOWN GEORGIA... SO NOT MUCH.
:-) :-)
ME
...
B. "SHITTY" KNIGHT
what the FUCK.
ADAM J. "HOLSTER" BIRKHOLTZ
butT DIAL!!!! HAHA
JACK L. ZIMMERMANN
THANK GOODNESS MY TEAMMATES WERE AMUSING...
BUT I HOPE WE ALL HAD A RESTFUL WINTER BREAK! OUR TEAM WORKS HARD. WE DESERVE IT.

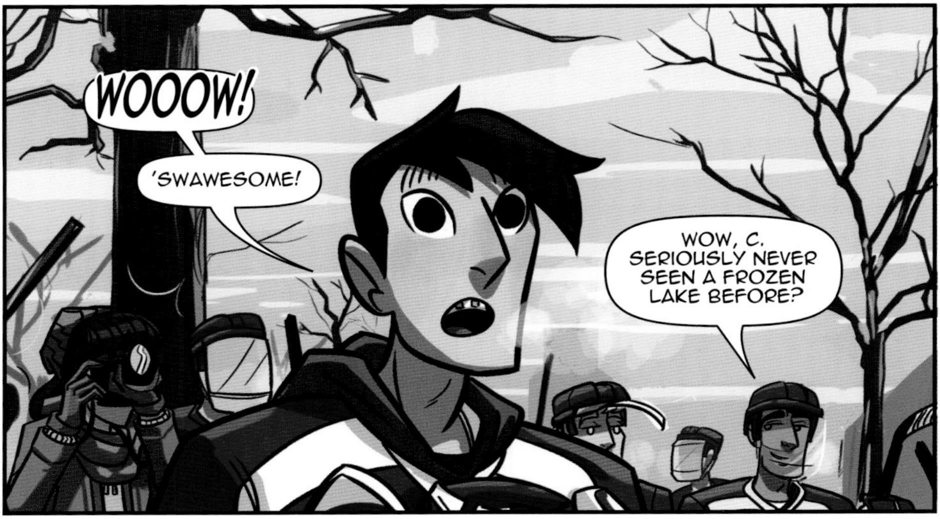
WOOOW!
'SWAWESOME!
WOW, C. SERIOUSLY NEVER SEEN A FROZEN LAKE BEFORE?

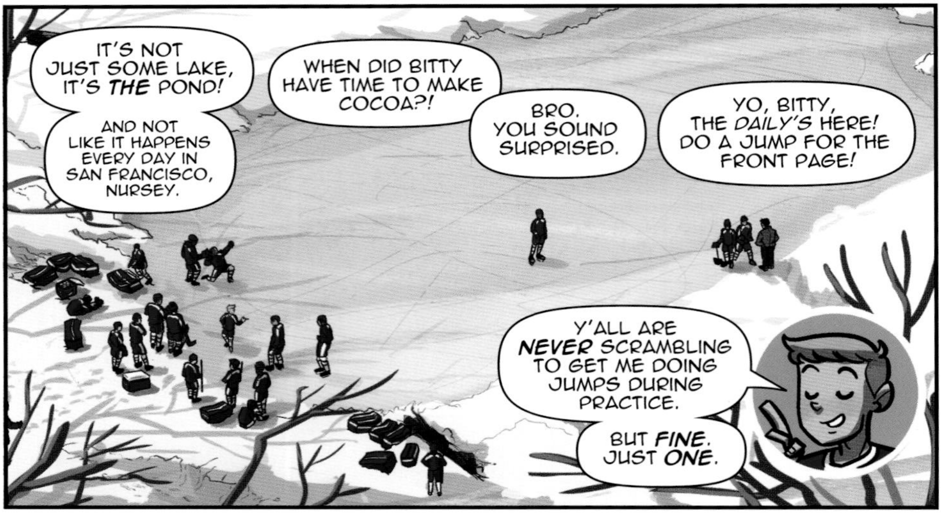
IT'S NOT JUST SOME LAKE, IT'S ***THE*** POND!
AND NOT LIKE IT HAPPENS EVERY DAY IN SAN FRANCISCO, NURSEY.
WHEN DID BITTY HAVE TIME TO MAKE COCOA?!
BRO. YOU SOUND SURPRISED.
YO, BITTY, THE *DAILY'S* HERE! DO A JUMP FOR THE FRONT PAGE!
Y'ALL ARE **NEVER** SCRAMBLING TO GET ME DOING JUMPS DURING PRACTICE.
BUT **FINE**. JUST **ONE**.

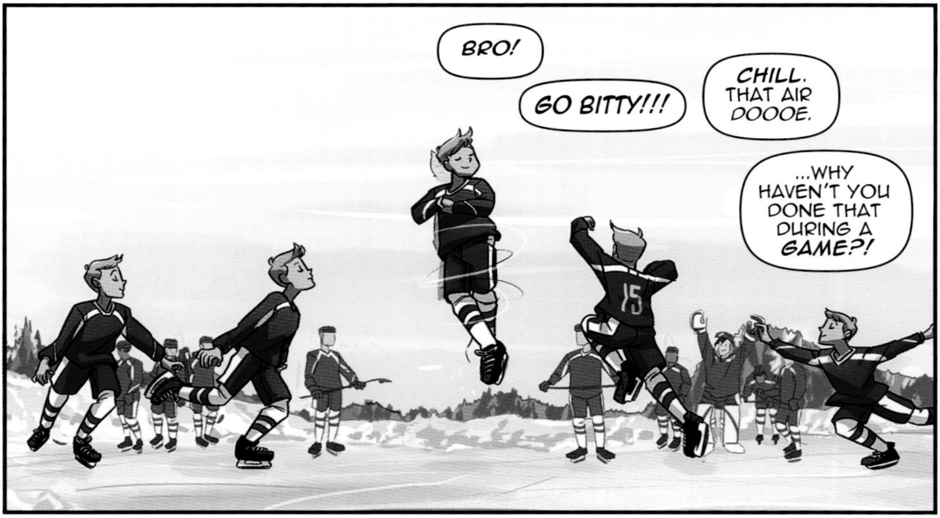
BRO!
GO BITTY!!!
CHILL. THAT AIR *DOOOE*.
...WHY HAVEN'T YOU DONE THAT DURING A ***GAME?!***

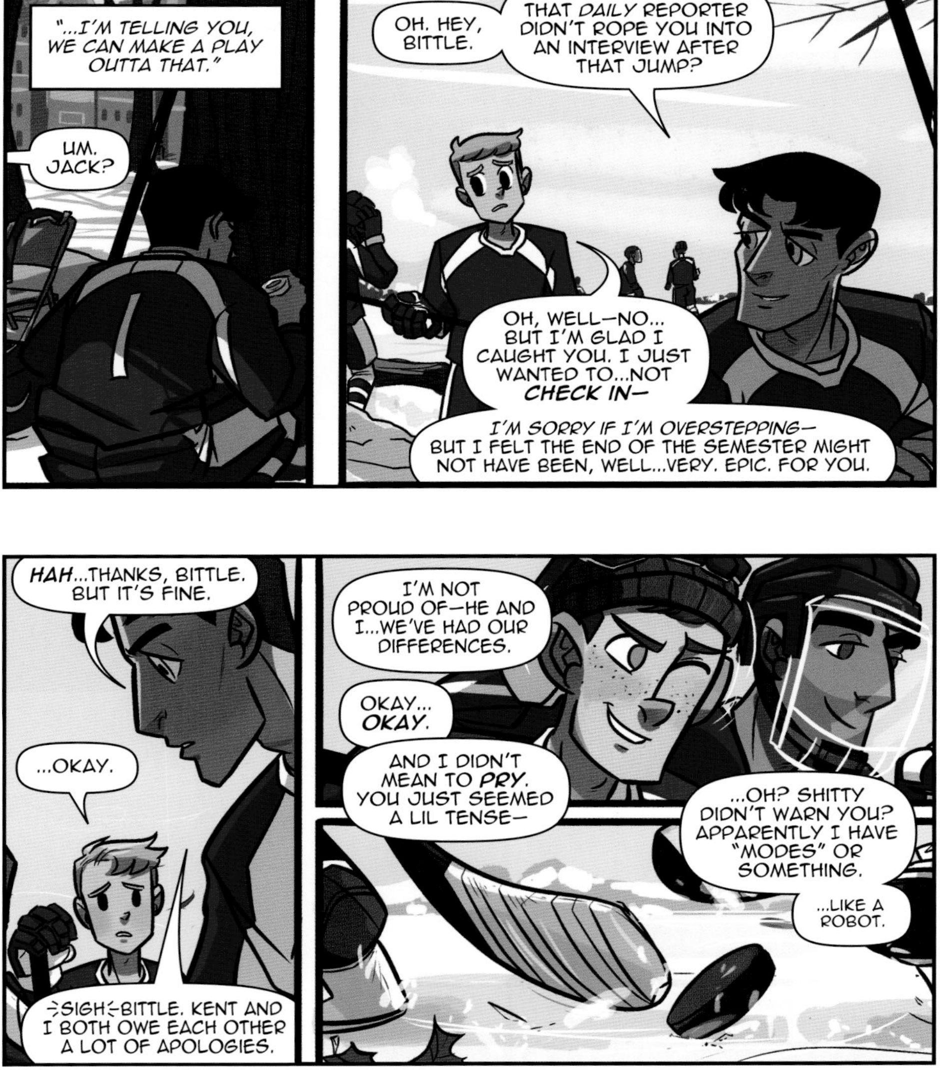
"...I'M TELLING YOU, WE CAN MAKE A PLAY OUTTA THAT."
UM. JACK?
OH. HEY, BITTLE.
THAT DAILY REPORTER DIDN'T ROPE YOU INTO AN INTERVIEW AFTER THAT JUMP?
OH, WELL—NO... BUT I'M GLAD I CAUGHT YOU. I JUST WANTED TO...NOT CHECK IN—
I'M SORRY IF I'M OVERSTEPPING— BUT I FELT THE END OF THE SEMESTER MIGHT NOT HAVE BEEN, WELL...VERY. EPIC. FOR YOU.
HAH...THANKS, BITTLE. BUT IT'S FINE.
...OKAY.
⥽SIGH⥼BITTLE. KENT AND I BOTH OWE EACH OTHER A LOT OF APOLOGIES.
I'M NOT PROUD OF—HE AND I...WE'VE HAD OUR DIFFERENCES.
OKAY... OKAY.
AND I DIDN'T MEAN TO PRY. YOU JUST SEEMED A LIL TENSE—
...OH? SHITTY DIDN'T WARN YOU? APPARENTLY I HAVE "MODES" OR SOMETHING.
...LIKE A ROBOT.

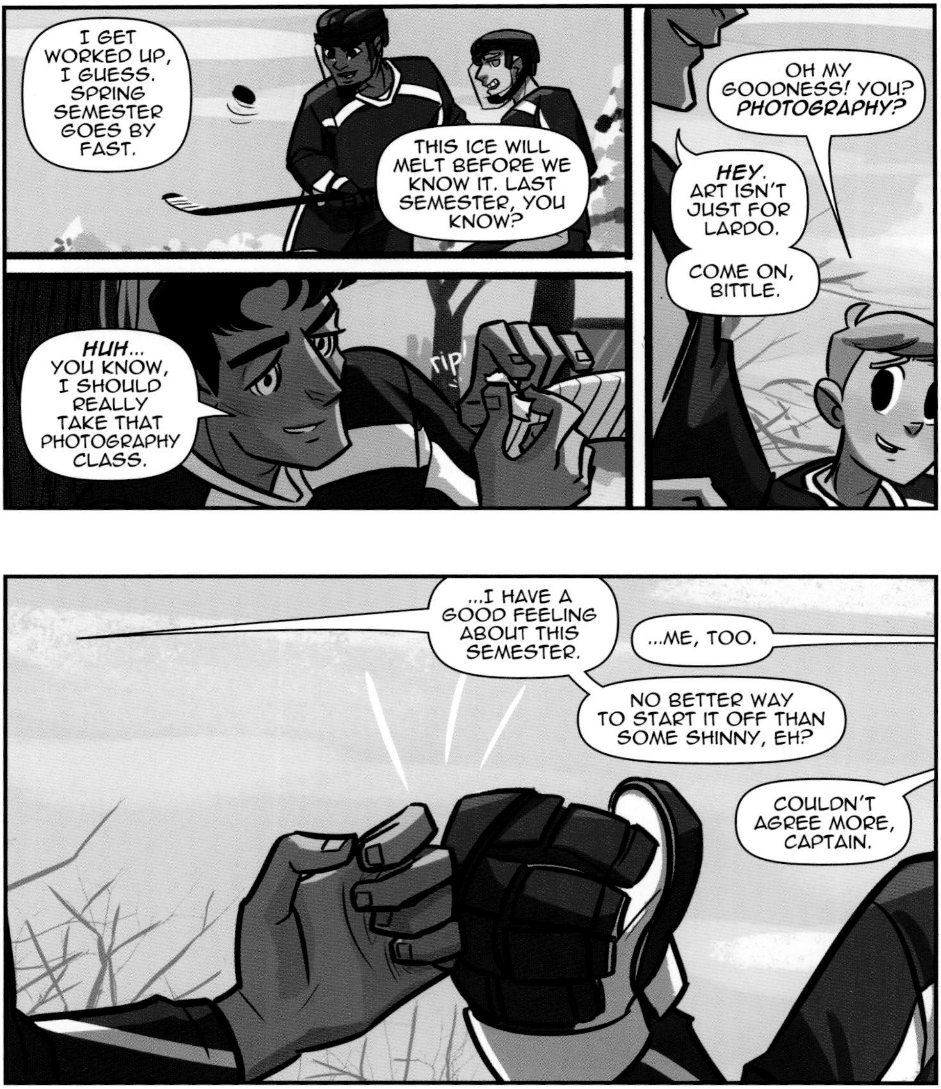
I GET WORKED UP, I GUESS. SPRING SEMESTER GOES BY FAST.
THIS ICE WILL MELT BEFORE WE KNOW IT. LAST SEMESTER, YOU KNOW?
HUH... YOU KNOW, I SHOULD REALLY TAKE THAT PHOTOGRAPHY CLASS.
rip!
OH MY GOODNESS! YOU? PHOTOGRAPHY?
HEY. ART ISN'T JUST FOR LARDO.
COME ON, BITTLE.
...I HAVE A GOOD FEELING ABOUT THIS SEMESTER.
...ME, TOO.
NO BETTER WAY TO START IT OFF THAN SOME SHINNY, EH?
COULDN'T AGREE MORE, CAPTAIN.

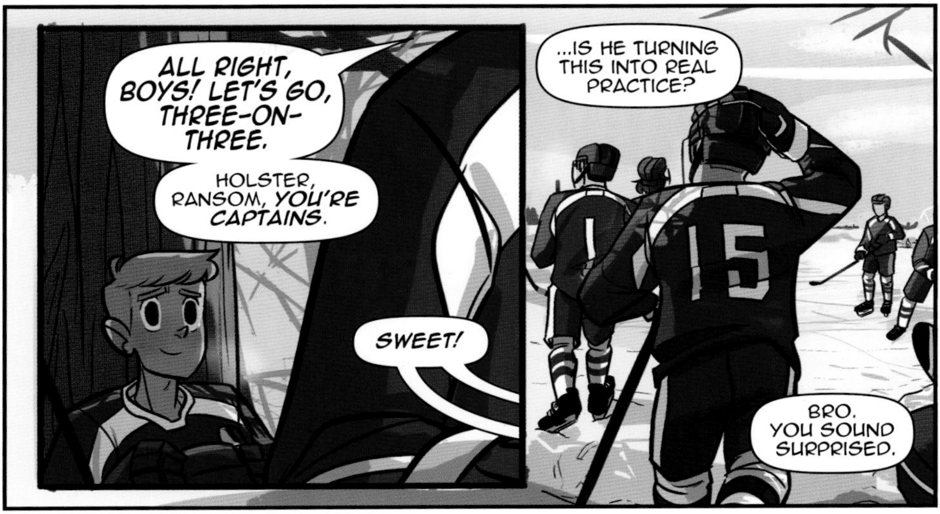
ALL RIGHT, BOYS! LET'S GO, THREE-ON-THREE.
HOLSTER, RANSOM, YOU'RE CAPTAINS.
SWEET!
...IS HE TURNING THIS INTO REAL PRACTICE?
BRO. YOU SOUND SURPRISED.

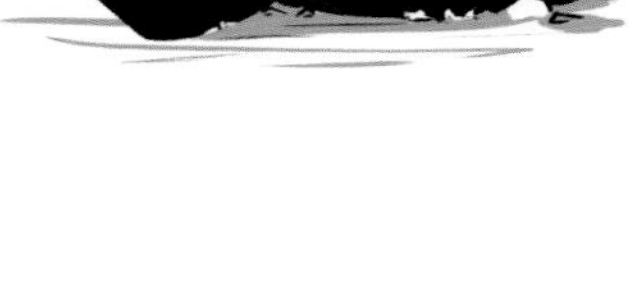

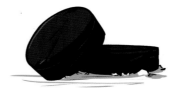

11

JUNIOR SHOW

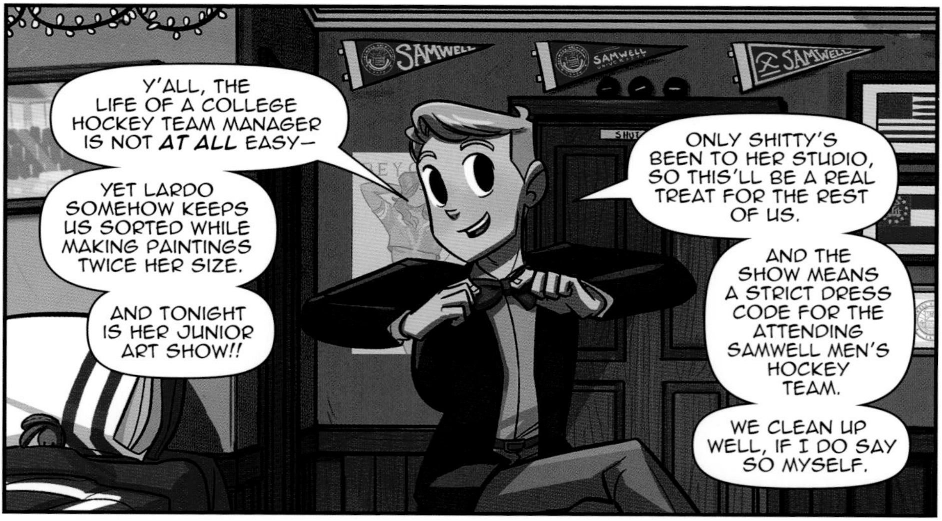

Y'ALL, THE LIFE OF A COLLEGE HOCKEY TEAM MANAGER IS NOT *AT ALL* EASY—
YET LARDO SOMEHOW KEEPS US SORTED WHILE MAKING PAINTINGS TWICE HER SIZE.
AND TONIGHT IS HER JUNIOR ART SHOW!!
ONLY SHITTY'S BEEN TO HER STUDIO, SO THIS'LL BE A REAL TREAT FOR THE REST OF US.
AND THE SHOW MEANS A STRICT DRESS CODE FOR THE ATTENDING SAMWELL MEN'S HOCKEY TEAM.
WE CLEAN UP WELL, IF I DO SAY SO MYSELF.

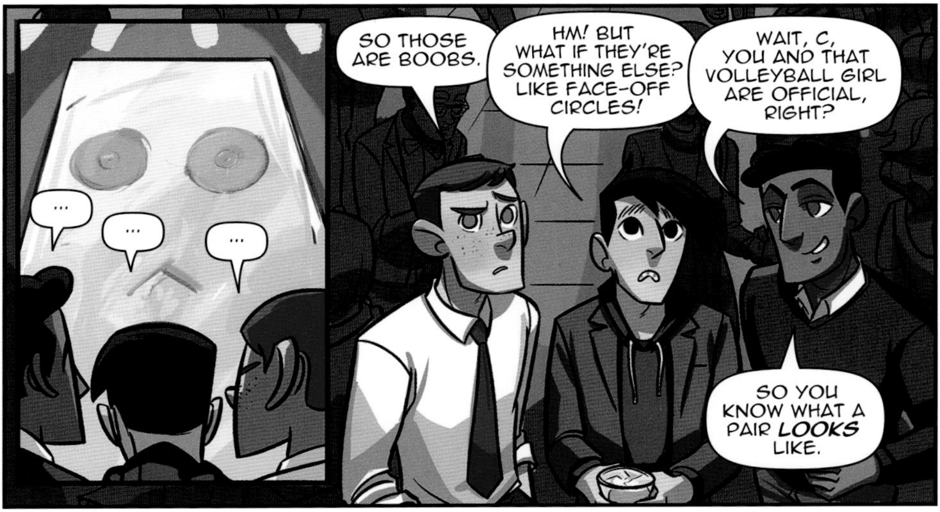
...
...
...
SO THOSE ARE BOOBS.
HM! BUT WHAT IF THEY'RE SOMETHING ELSE? LIKE FACE-OFF CIRCLES!
WAIT, C, YOU AND THAT VOLLEYBALL GIRL ARE OFFICIAL, RIGHT?
SO YOU KNOW WHAT A PAIR LOOKS LIKE.

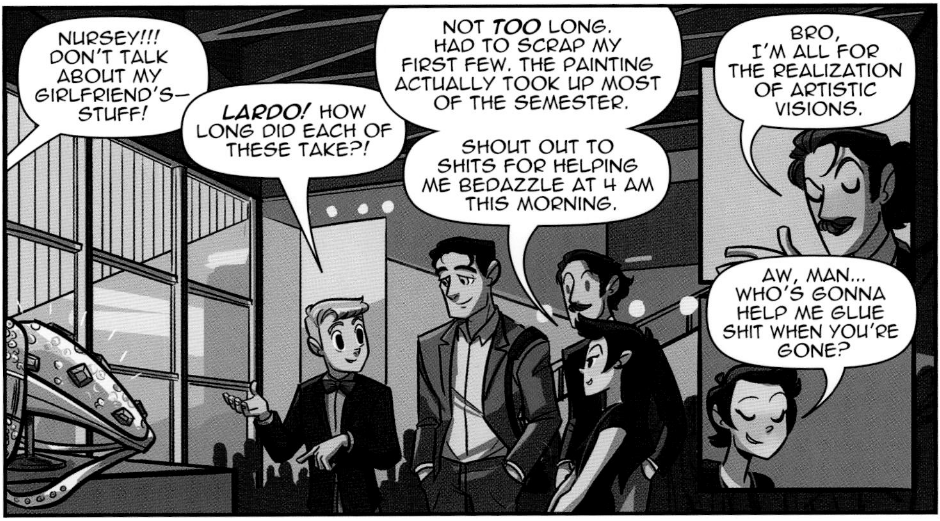
NURSEY!!! DON'T TALK ABOUT MY GIRLFRIEND'S— STUFF!
LARDO! HOW LONG DID EACH OF THESE TAKE?!
NOT TOO LONG. HAD TO SCRAP MY FIRST FEW. THE PAINTING ACTUALLY TOOK UP MOST OF THE SEMESTER.
SHOUT OUT TO SHITS FOR HELPING ME BEDAZZLE AT 4 AM THIS MORNING.
BRO, I'M ALL FOR THE REALIZATION OF ARTISTIC VISIONS.
AW, MAN... WHO'S GONNA HELP ME GLUE SHIT WHEN YOU'RE GONE?

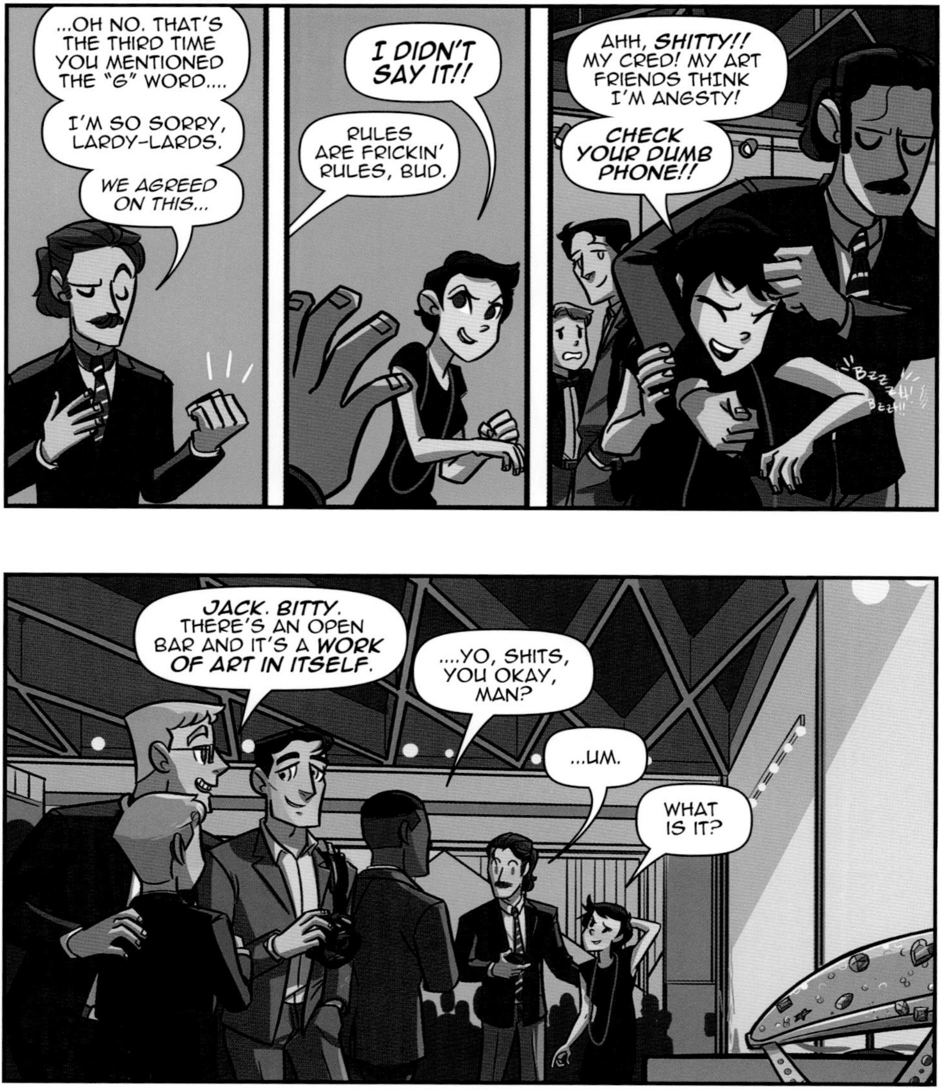
...OH NO. THAT'S THE THIRD TIME YOU MENTIONED THE "G" WORD....
I'M SO SORRY, LARDY-LARDS.
WE AGREED ON THIS...
I DIDN'T SAY IT!!
RULES ARE FRICKIN' RULES, BUD.
AHH, SHITTY!! MY CRED! MY ART FRIENDS THINK I'M ANGSTY!
CHECK YOUR DUMB PHONE!!
JACK. BITTY. THERE'S AN OPEN BAR AND IT'S A WORK OF ART IN ITSELF.
...YO, SHITS, YOU OKAY, MAN?
...UM.
WHAT IS IT?

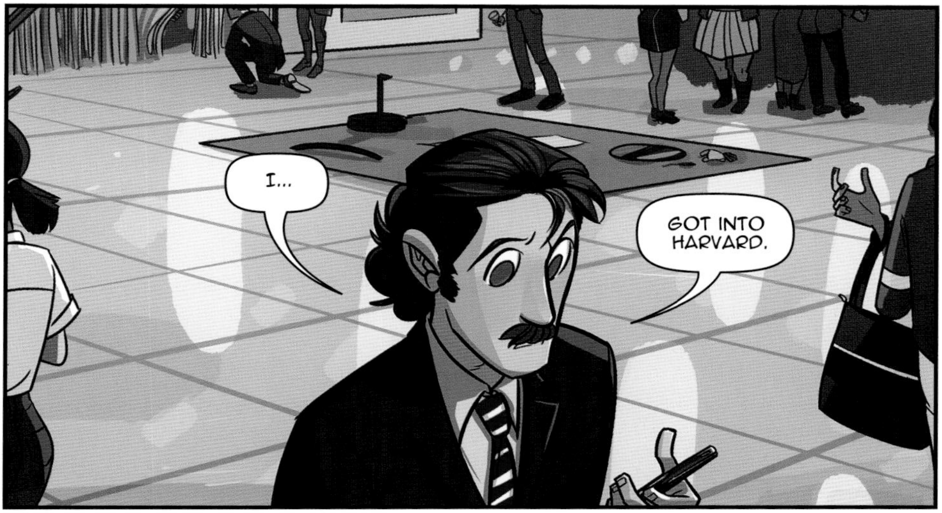
I...
GOT INTO HARVARD.

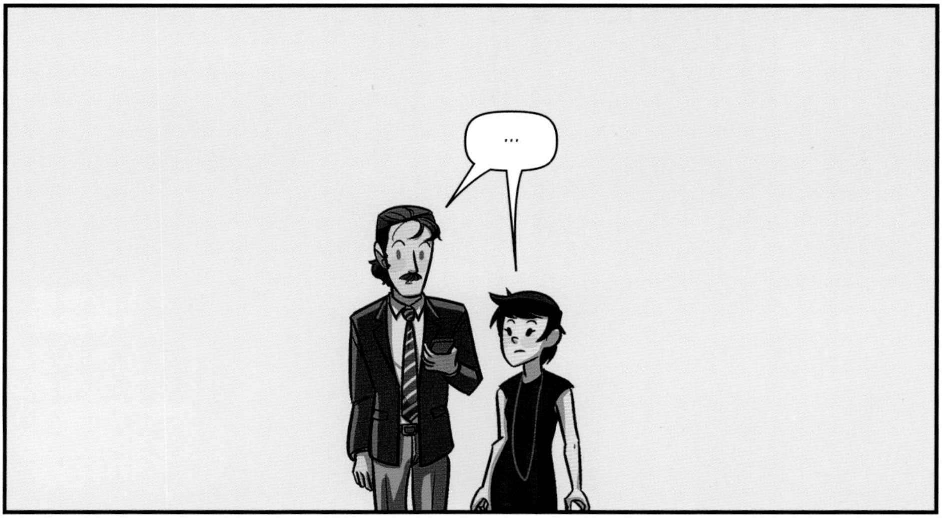
...

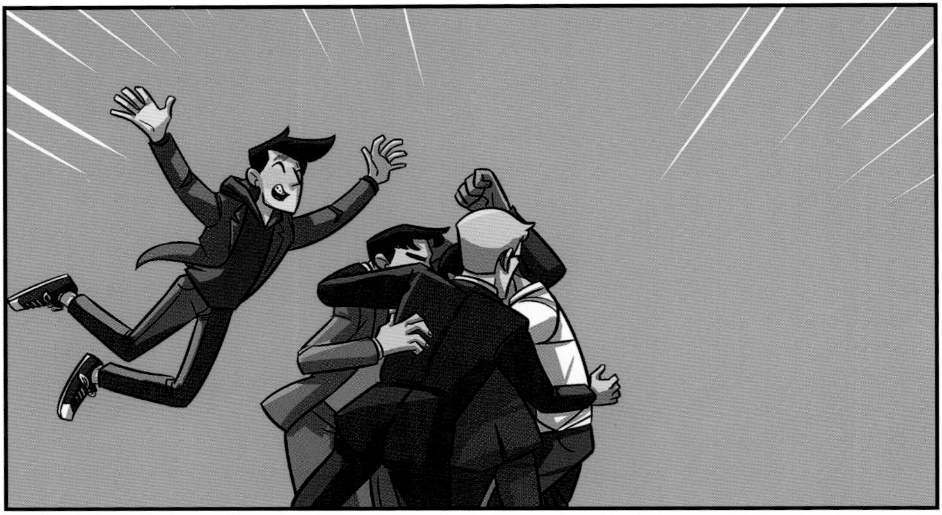

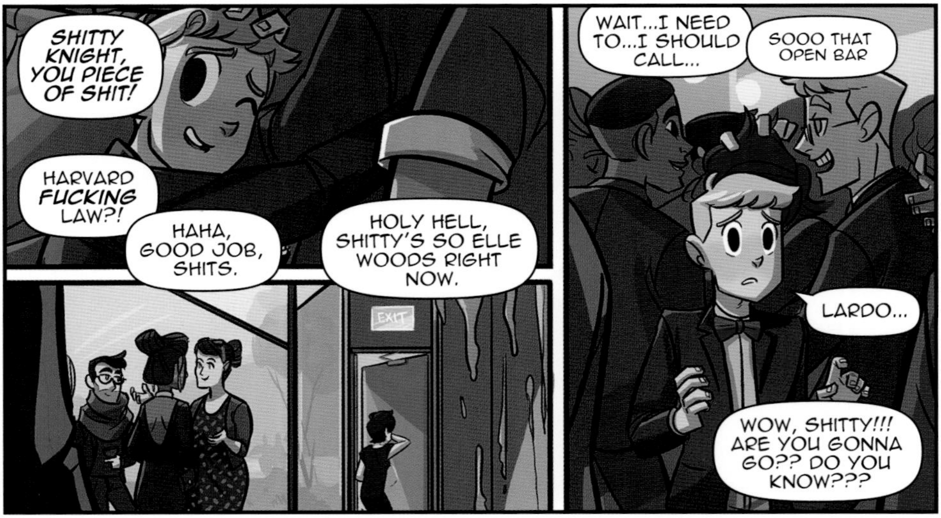
SHITTY KNIGHT, YOU PIECE OF SHIT!
HARVARD FUCKING LAW?!
HAHA, GOOD JOB, SHITS.
HOLY HELL, SHITTY'S SO ELLE WOODS RIGHT NOW.
EXIT
WAIT...I NEED TO...I SHOULD CALL...
SOOO THAT OPEN BAR
LARDO...
WOW, SHITTY!!! ARE YOU GONNA GO?? DO YOU KNOW???

12

POST I: ROADIE

I KNOW I'VE BEEN PROMISING AN EPISODE ON THE GREAT PIE VS. CRUMBLE DEBATE, BUT QUICK UPDATE ON THE ATHLETIC PART OF MY LIFE!
SAMWELL JUST FINISHED UP THE REGULAR SEASON WITH A FOUR-GAME WIN STREAK! WHICH WE'RE TAKING INTO THE PLAYOFFS.
AND BEING ON A TEAM THAT'S DOING WELL—
⇒SIGH⇐ Y'ALL, I'M JUST PROUD OF MY TEAMMATES.
NOW BACK TO *PIES* AND *CRUMBLES*. IF IT'S FRUIT AND BUTTER, *THEN YES*.

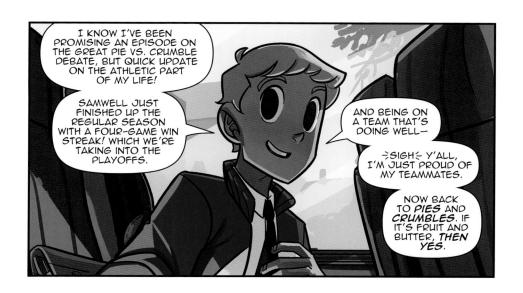

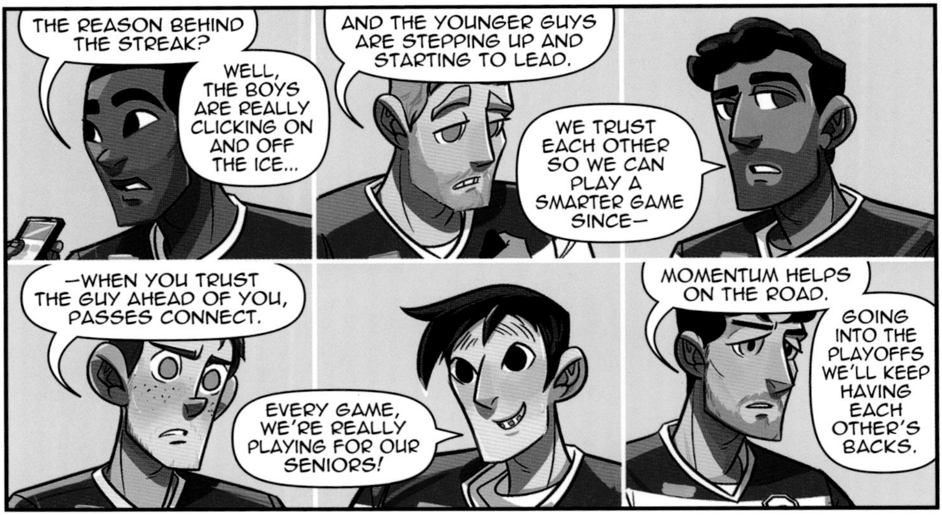
THE REASON BEHIND THE STREAK?
WELL, THE BOYS ARE REALLY CLICKING ON AND OFF THE ICE...
AND THE YOUNGER GUYS ARE STEPPING UP AND STARTING TO LEAD.
WE TRUST EACH OTHER SO WE CAN PLAY A SMARTER GAME SINCE—
—WHEN YOU TRUST THE GUY AHEAD OF YOU, PASSES CONNECT.
EVERY GAME, WE'RE REALLY PLAYING FOR OUR SENIORS!
MOMENTUM HELPS ON THE ROAD.
GOING INTO THE PLAYOFFS WE'LL KEEP HAVING EACH OTHER'S BACKS.

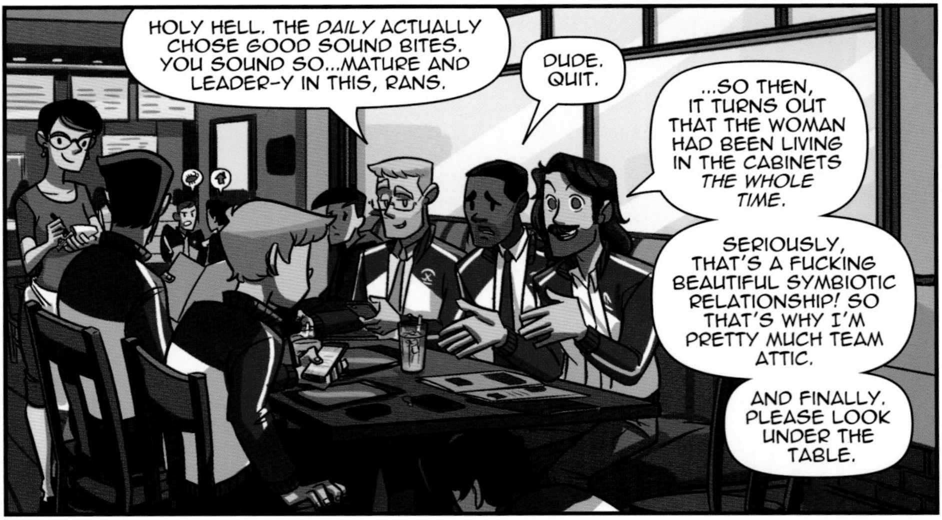
HOLY HELL. THE *DAILY* ACTUALLY CHOSE GOOD SOUND BITES. YOU SOUND SO...MATURE AND LEADER-Y IN THIS, RANS.
DUDE. QUIT.
...SO THEN, IT TURNS OUT THAT THE WOMAN HAD BEEN LIVING IN THE CABINETS *THE WHOLE TIME*.
SERIOUSLY, THAT'S A FUCKING BEAUTIFUL SYMBIOTIC RELATIONSHIP! SO THAT'S WHY I'M PRETTY MUCH TEAM ATTIC.
AND FINALLY. PLEASE LOOK UNDER THE TABLE.

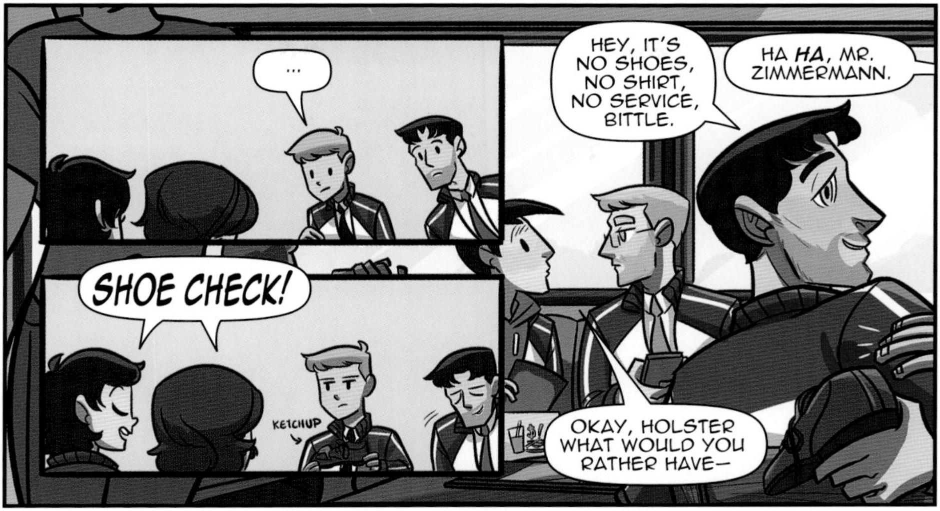
...
SHOE CHECK!
KETCHUP
HEY, IT'S NO SHOES, NO SHIRT, NO SERVICE, BITTLE.
HA *HA*, MR. ZIMMERMANN.
OKAY, HOLSTER WHAT WOULD YOU RATHER HAVE—

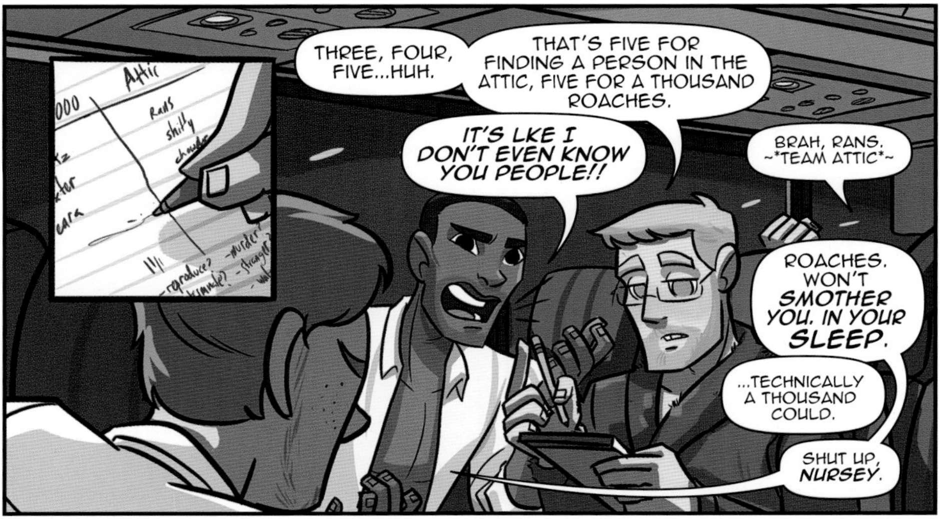
Attic
THREE, FOUR, FIVE...HUH.
THAT'S FIVE FOR FINDING A PERSON IN THE ATTIC, FIVE FOR A THOUSAND ROACHES.
IT'S LKE I DON'T EVEN KNOW YOU PEOPLE!!
BRAH, RANS. ~*TEAM ATTIC*~
ROACHES. WON'T *SMOTHER* YOU. IN YOUR *SLEEP*.
...TECHNICALLY A THOUSAND COULD.
SHUT UP, *NURSEY*.

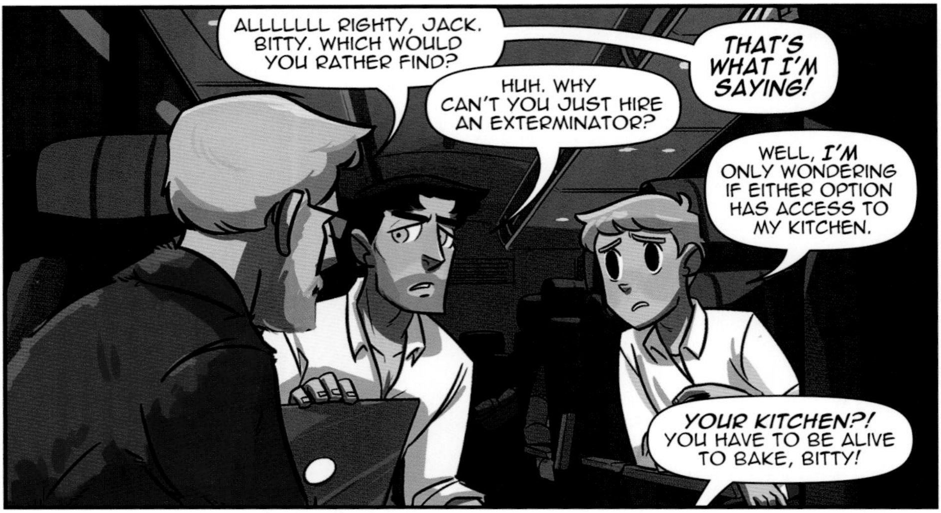
ALLLLLLL RIGHTY, JACK. BITTY. WHICH WOULD YOU RATHER FIND?
THAT'S WHAT I'M SAYING!
HUH. WHY CAN'T YOU JUST HIRE AN EXTERMINATOR?
WELL, I'M ONLY WONDERING IF EITHER OPTION HAS ACCESS TO MY KITCHEN.
YOUR KITCHEN?! YOU HAVE TO BE ALIVE TO BAKE, BITTY!

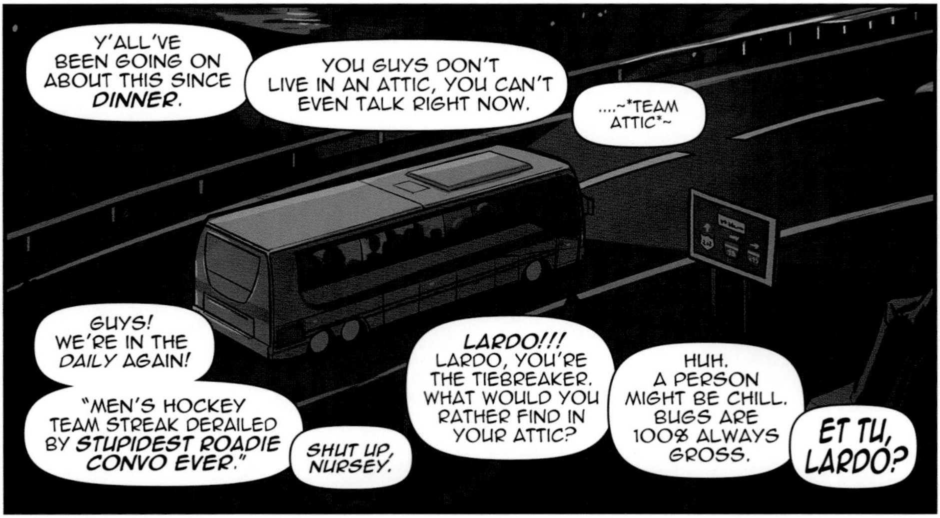
Y'ALL'VE BEEN GOING ON ABOUT THIS SINCE DINNER.
YOU GUYS DON'T LIVE IN AN ATTIC, YOU CAN'T EVEN TALK RIGHT NOW.
....~*TEAM ATTIC*~
GUYS! WE'RE IN THE DAILY AGAIN!
"MEN'S HOCKEY TEAM STREAK DERAILED BY STUPIDEST ROADIE CONVO EVER."
SHUT UP, NURSEY.
LARDO!!! LARDO, YOU'RE THE TIEBREAKER. WHAT WOULD YOU RATHER FIND IN YOUR ATTIC?
HUH. A PERSON MIGHT BE CHILL. BUGS ARE 100% ALWAYS GROSS.
ET TU, LARDO?

13

POST II: FROZEN FOUR

"FEW EXPECTED THIS LITTLE SCHOOL FROM MASSACHUSETTS TO RETURN FOR YET ANOTHER FROZEN FOUR APPEARANCE...

"...BUT SAMWELL UNIVERSITY IS *YET AGAIN* IN THE NCAA CHAMPIONSHIPS AFTER AN UNBELIEVABLE RUN THROUGH THE PLAYOFFS."

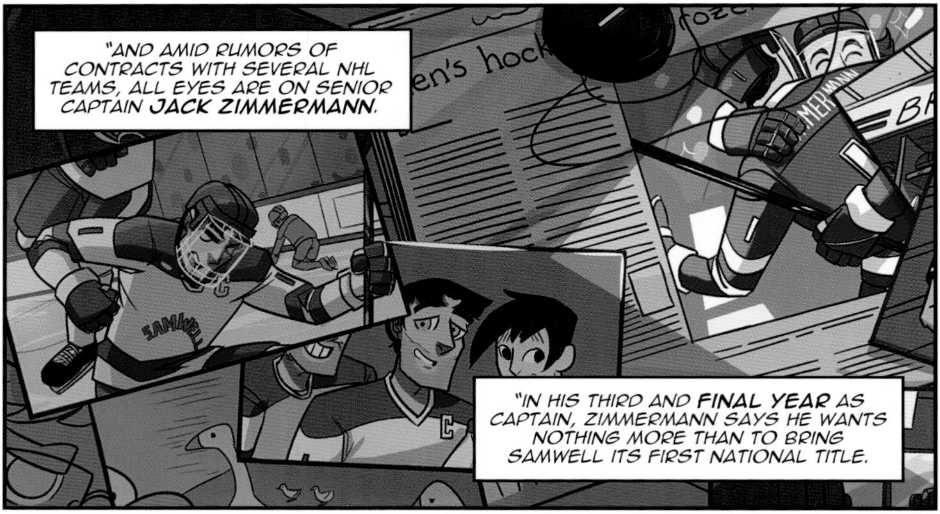
"AND AMID RUMORS OF CONTRACTS WITH SEVERAL NHL TEAMS, ALL EYES ARE ON SENIOR CAPTAIN **JACK ZIMMERMANN**.
"IN HIS THIRD AND **FINAL YEAR** AS CAPTAIN, ZIMMERMANN SAYS HE WANTS NOTHING MORE THAN TO BRING SAMWELL ITS FIRST NATIONAL TITLE.

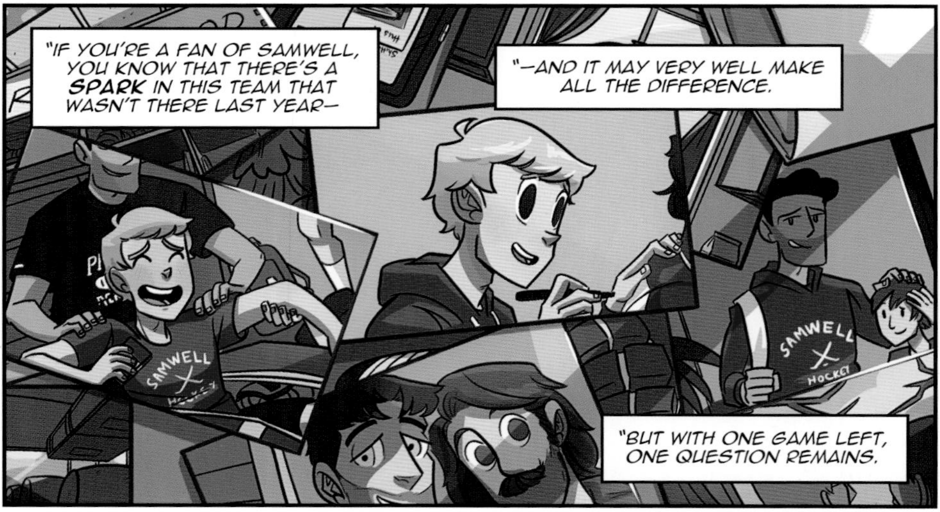
"IF YOU'RE A FAN OF SAMWELL, YOU KNOW THAT THERE'S A **SPARK** IN THIS TEAM THAT WASN'T THERE LAST YEAR—
"—AND IT MAY VERY WELL MAKE ALL THE DIFFERENCE.
"BUT WITH ONE GAME LEFT, ONE QUESTION REMAINS.

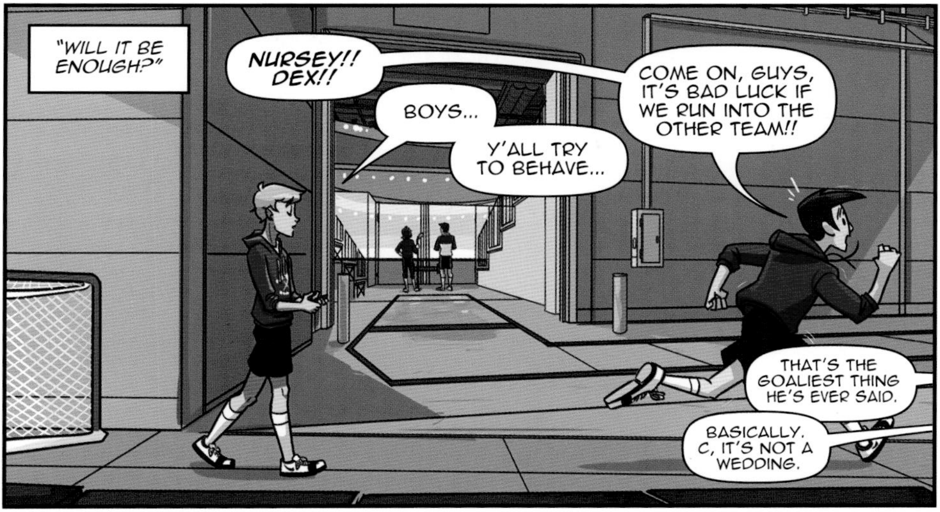
"WILL IT BE ENOUGH?"
NURSEY!! DEX!!
COME ON, GUYS, IT'S BAD LUCK IF WE RUN INTO THE OTHER TEAM!!
BOYS...
Y'ALL TRY TO BEHAVE...
THAT'S THE GOALIEST THING HE'S EVER SAID.
BASICALLY. C, IT'S NOT A WEDDING.

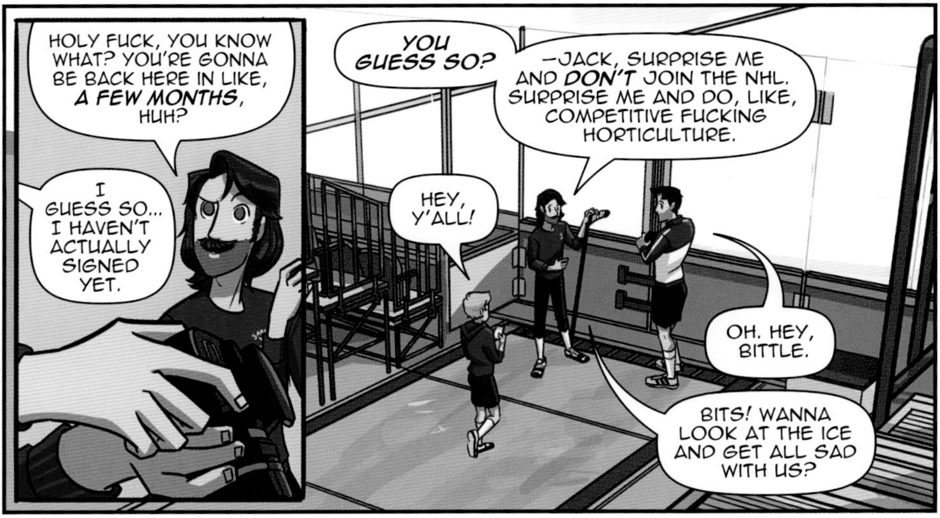
HOLY FUCK, YOU KNOW WHAT? YOU'RE GONNA BE BACK HERE IN LIKE, A FEW MONTHS, HUH?
I GUESS SO... I HAVEN'T ACTUALLY SIGNED YET.
YOU GUESS SO?
—JACK, SURPRISE ME AND DON'T JOIN THE NHL. SURPRISE ME AND DO, LIKE, COMPETITIVE FUCKING HORTICULTURE.
HEY, Y'ALL!
OH. HEY, BITTLE.
BITS! WANNA LOOK AT THE ICE AND GET ALL SAD WITH US?

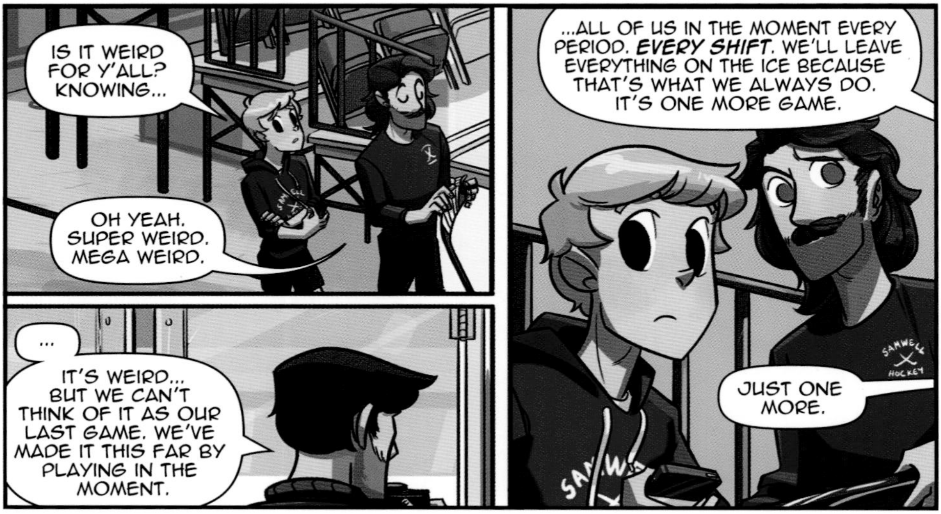
IS IT WEIRD FOR Y'ALL? KNOWING...
OH YEAH. SUPER WEIRD. MEGA WEIRD.
...
IT'S WEIRD... BUT WE CAN'T THINK OF IT AS OUR LAST GAME. WE'VE MADE IT THIS FAR BY PLAYING IN THE MOMENT.
...ALL OF US IN THE MOMENT EVERY PERIOD. ***EVERY SHIFT***. WE'LL LEAVE EVERYTHING ON THE ICE BECAUSE THAT'S WHAT WE ALWAYS DO. IT'S ONE MORE GAME.
JUST ONE MORE.
SAMWELL HOCKEY

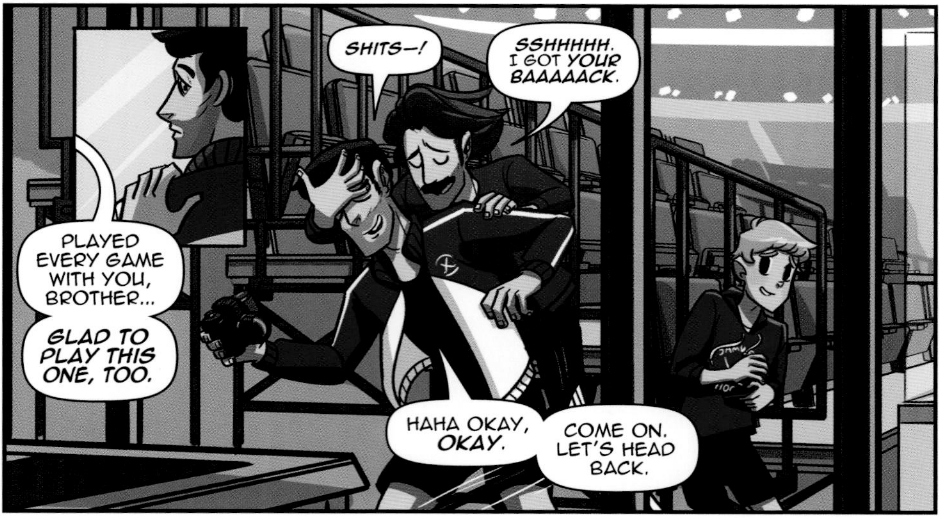
PLAYED EVERY GAME WITH YOU, BROTHER...
GLAD TO PLAY THIS ONE, TOO.
SHITS—!
SSHHHHH. I GOT ***YOUR BAAAAACK***.
HAHA OKAY, ***OKAY***.
COME ON. LET'S HEAD BACK.

BRAH, IF WE WIN TOMORROW I GET A LIFETIME SUPPLY OF ZIMMERMANN HUGS! NO QUESTIONS!
YOU GET THAT SHOT YOU WANTED?
YEAH....
COME ON, BITTLE.
OH! WAIT UP!

15

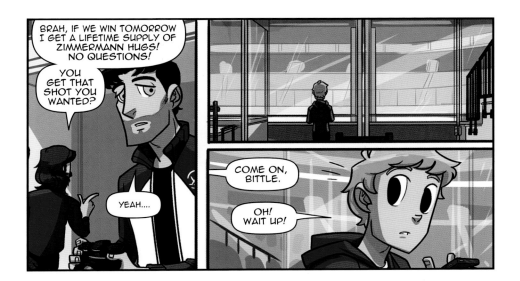

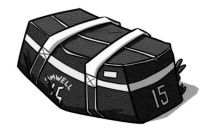

14

POST III: LAST GAME

CHOW
55
4
28

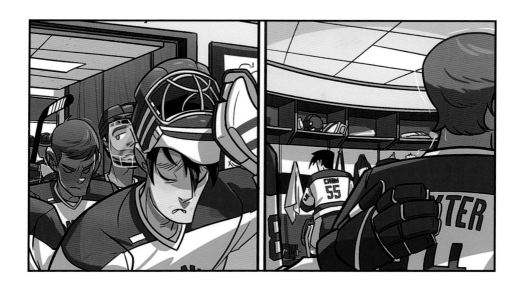

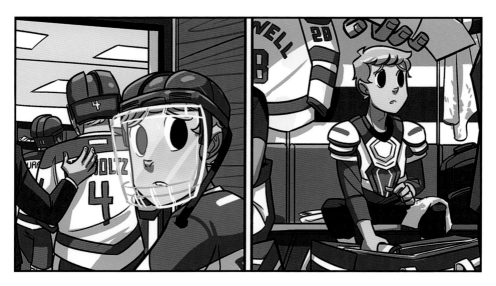

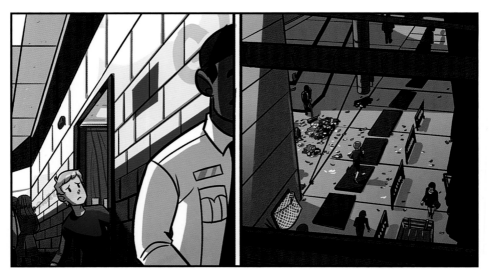

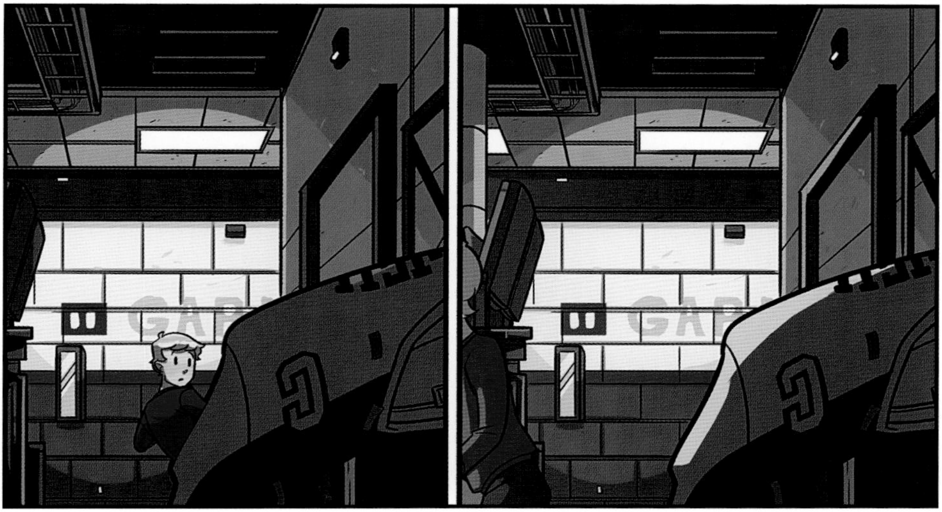

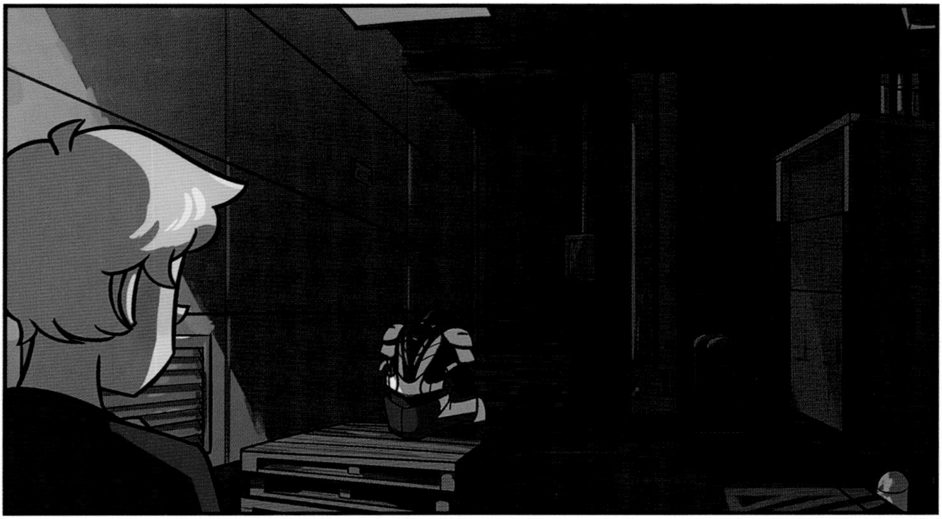

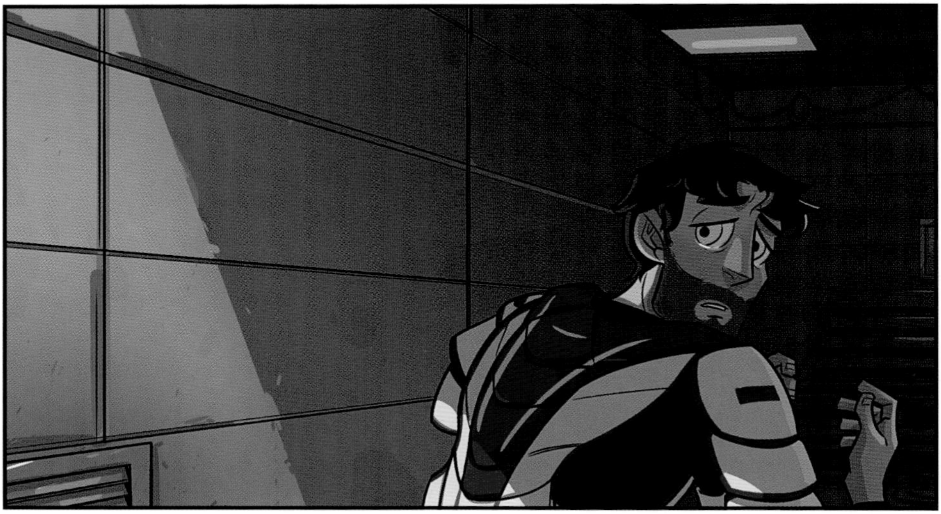

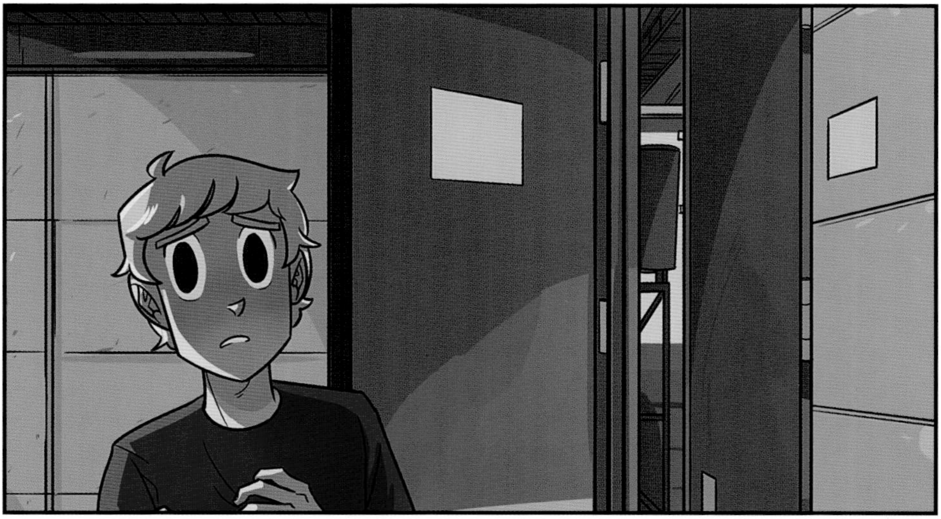

15

"A"

I DUNNO, BRO. I'M NOT SAYING YOU'RE A SHOO-IN, BUT.
WHAT?! I THOUGHT YOU THOUGHT YOU WERE.
OH, DUDE. NO, DUDE. ME? OH, MAN.
WAIT, HOW MANY BOXES OF PIE TINS DID BITTY BRING WITH HIM?
...THERE'S STILL, LIKE, FIVE IN THE CAR.
TO DO LIST
- CHORE WHEEL
- GROCERY RUNS
- JACK'S B-DAY
(- COUCH)
BAKING 3/10

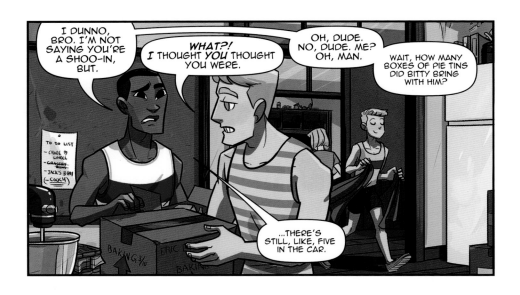

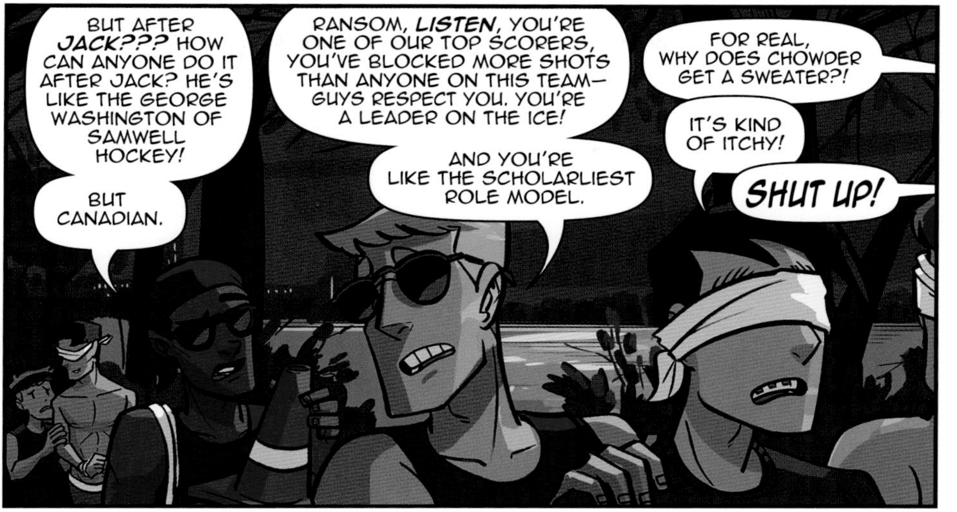
BUT AFTER JACK??? HOW CAN ANYONE DO IT AFTER JACK? HE'S LIKE THE GEORGE WASHINGTON OF SAMWELL HOCKEY!
BUT CANADIAN.
RANSOM, LISTEN, YOU'RE ONE OF OUR TOP SCORERS, YOU'VE BLOCKED MORE SHOTS THAN ANYONE ON THIS TEAM— GUYS RESPECT YOU. YOU'RE A LEADER ON THE ICE!
AND YOU'RE LIKE THE SCHOLARLIEST ROLE MODEL.
FOR REAL, WHY DOES CHOWDER GET A SWEATER?!
IT'S KIND OF ITCHY!
SHUT UP!

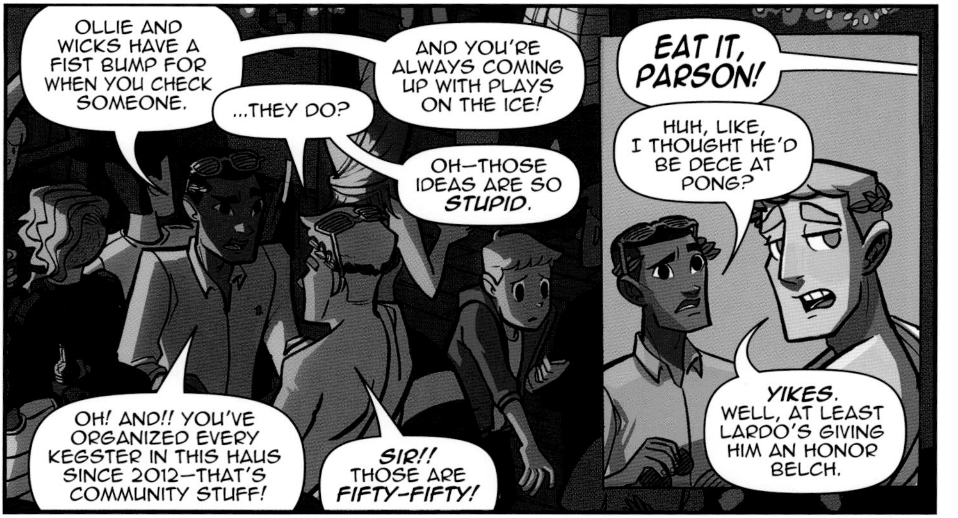
OLLIE AND WICKS HAVE A FIST BUMP FOR WHEN YOU CHECK SOMEONE.
...THEY DO?
AND YOU'RE ALWAYS COMING UP WITH PLAYS ON THE ICE!
OH—THOSE IDEAS ARE SO STUPID.
OH! AND!! YOU'VE ORGANIZED EVERY KEGSTER IN THIS HAUS SINCE 2012—THAT'S COMMUNITY STUFF!
SIR!! THOSE ARE FIFTY-FIFTY!
EAT IT, PARSON!
HUH, LIKE, I THOUGHT HE'D BE DECE AT PONG?
YIKES. WELL, AT LEAST LARDO'S GIVING HIM AN HONOR BELCH.

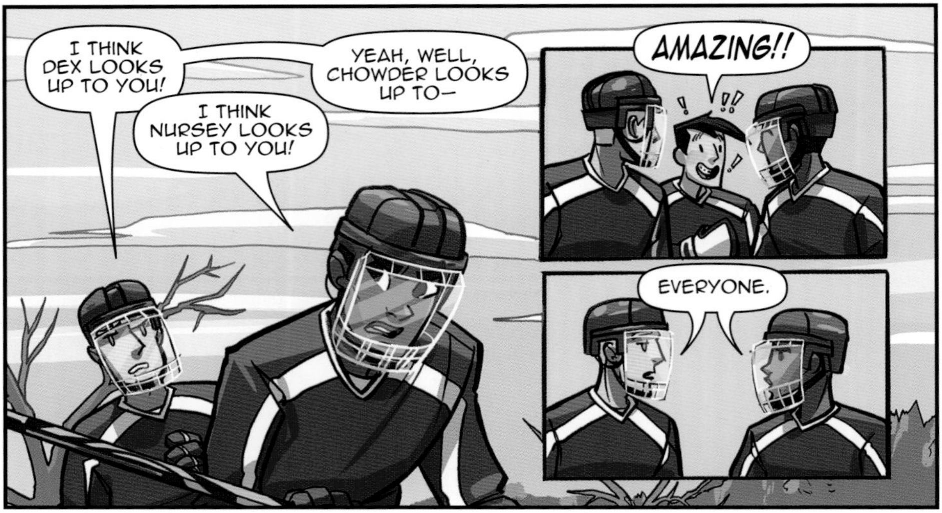
I THINK DEX LOOKS UP TO YOU!
YEAH, WELL, CHOWDER LOOKS UP TO—
I THINK NURSEY LOOKS UP TO YOU!
AMAZING!!
EVERYONE.

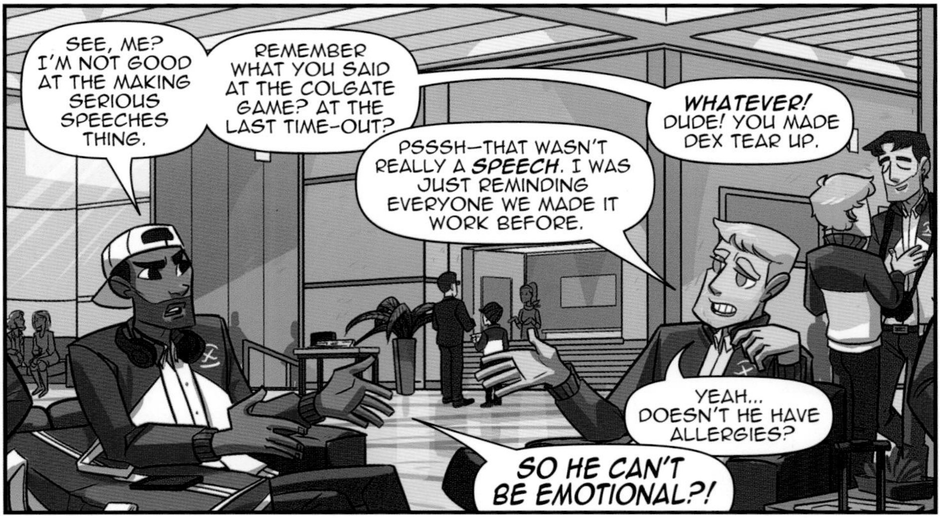
SEE, ME? I'M NOT GOOD AT THE MAKING SERIOUS SPEECHES THING.
REMEMBER WHAT YOU SAID AT THE COLGATE GAME? AT THE LAST TIME-OUT?
PSSSH—THAT WASN'T REALLY A *SPEECH*. I WAS JUST REMINDING EVERYONE WE MADE IT WORK BEFORE.
WHATEVER! DUDE! YOU MADE DEX TEAR UP.
YEAH... DOESN'T HE HAVE ALLERGIES?
SO HE CAN'T BE EMOTIONAL?!

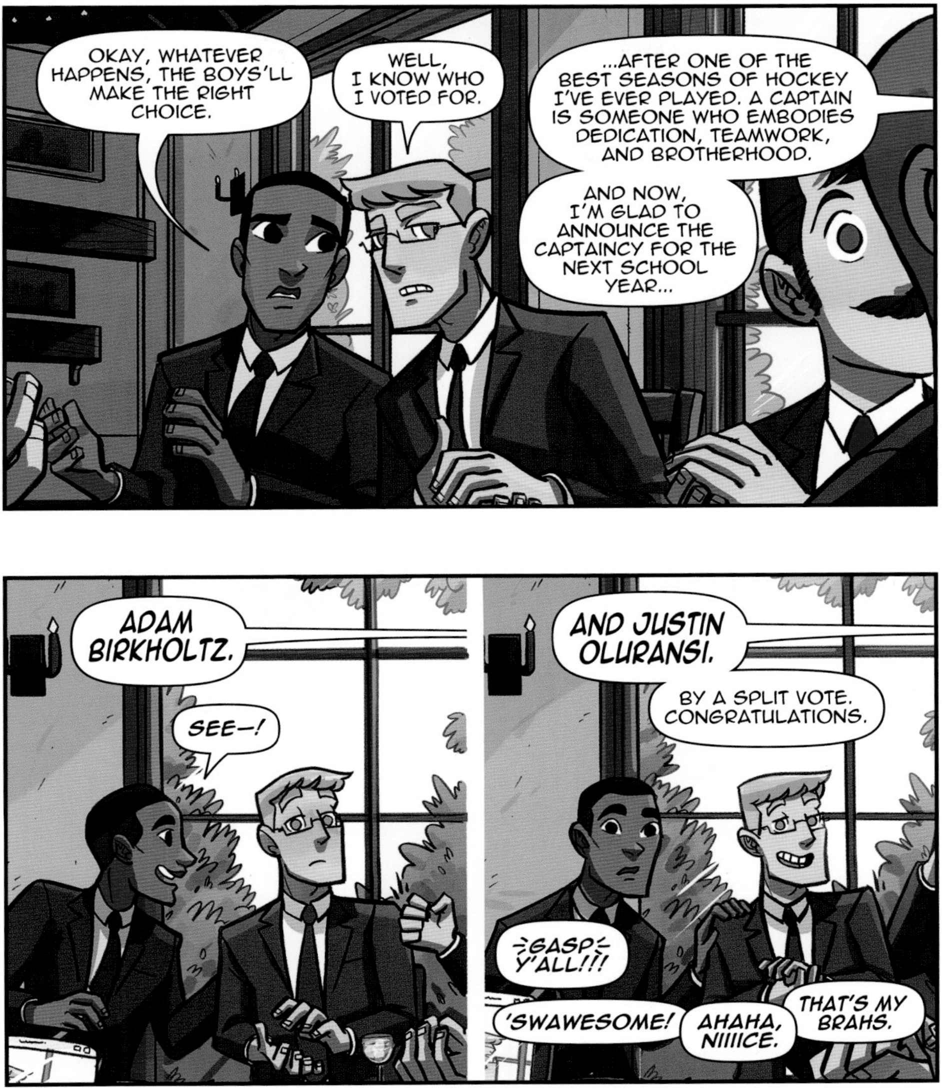
OKAY, WHATEVER HAPPENS, THE BOYS'LL MAKE THE RIGHT CHOICE.
WELL, I KNOW WHO I VOTED FOR.
...AFTER ONE OF THE BEST SEASONS OF HOCKEY I'VE EVER PLAYED. A CAPTAIN IS SOMEONE WHO EMBODIES DEDICATION, TEAMWORK, AND BROTHERHOOD.
AND NOW, I'M GLAD TO ANNOUNCE THE CAPTAINCY FOR THE NEXT SCHOOL YEAR...
ADAM BIRKHOLTZ.
SEE—!
AND JUSTIN OLURANSI.
BY A SPLIT VOTE. CONGRATULATIONS.
=GASP= Y'ALL!!!
'SWAWESOME!
AHAHA, NIIIICE.
THAT'S MY BRAHS.

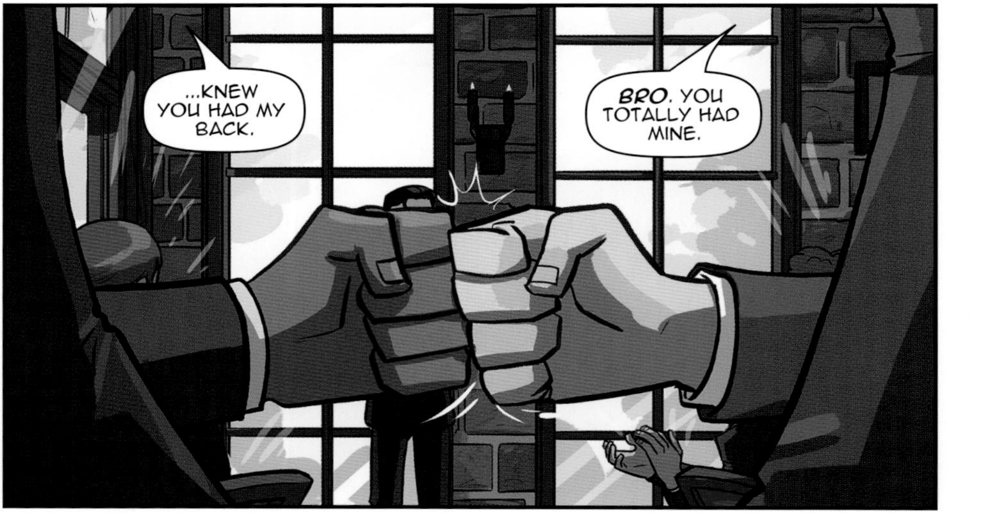
...KNEW YOU HAD MY BACK.
BRO. YOU TOTALLY HAD MINE.

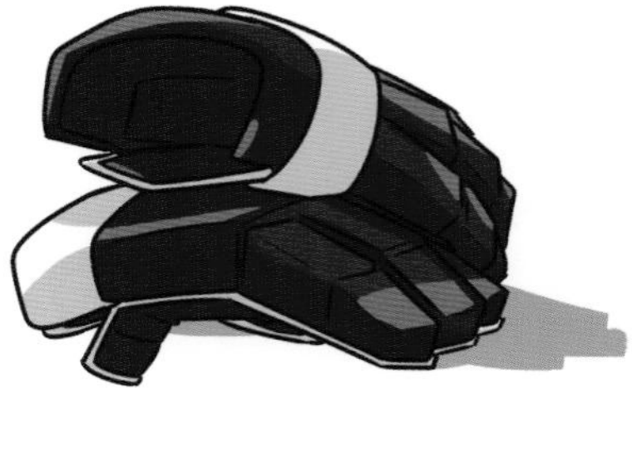

16

KISS THE ICE

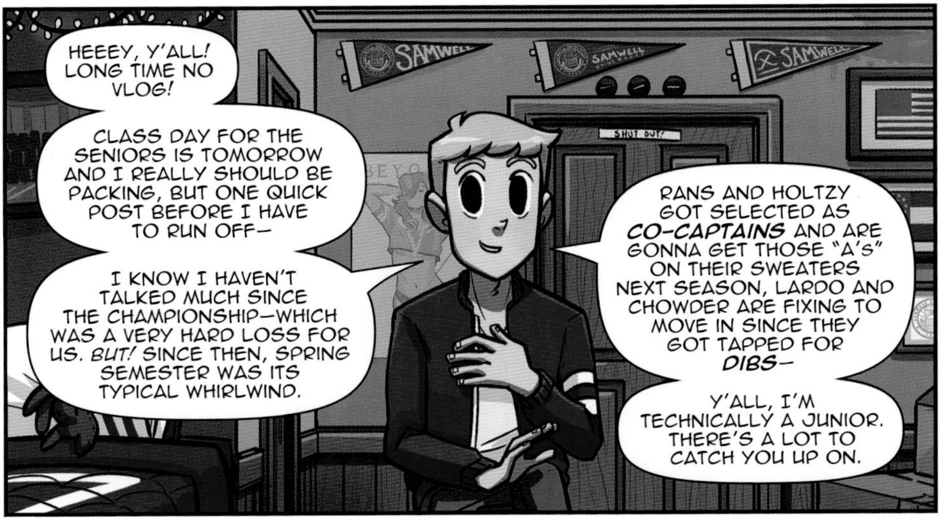
HEEEY, Y'ALL! LONG TIME NO VLOG!
CLASS DAY FOR THE SENIORS IS TOMORROW AND I REALLY SHOULD BE PACKING, BUT ONE QUICK POST BEFORE I HAVE TO RUN OFF—
I KNOW I HAVEN'T TALKED MUCH SINCE THE CHAMPIONSHIP—WHICH WAS A VERY HARD LOSS FOR US. *BUT!* SINCE THEN, SPRING SEMESTER WAS ITS TYPICAL WHIRLWIND.
RANS AND HOLTZY GOT SELECTED AS ***CO-CAPTAINS*** AND ARE GONNA GET THOSE "A'S" ON THEIR SWEATERS NEXT SEASON, LARDO AND CHOWDER ARE FIXING TO MOVE IN SINCE THEY GOT TAPPED FOR ***DIBS***—
Y'ALL, I'M TECHNICALLY A JUNIOR. THERE'S A LOT TO CATCH YOU UP ON.
SAMWELL
SAMWELL
SAMWELL
SHUT OUT!

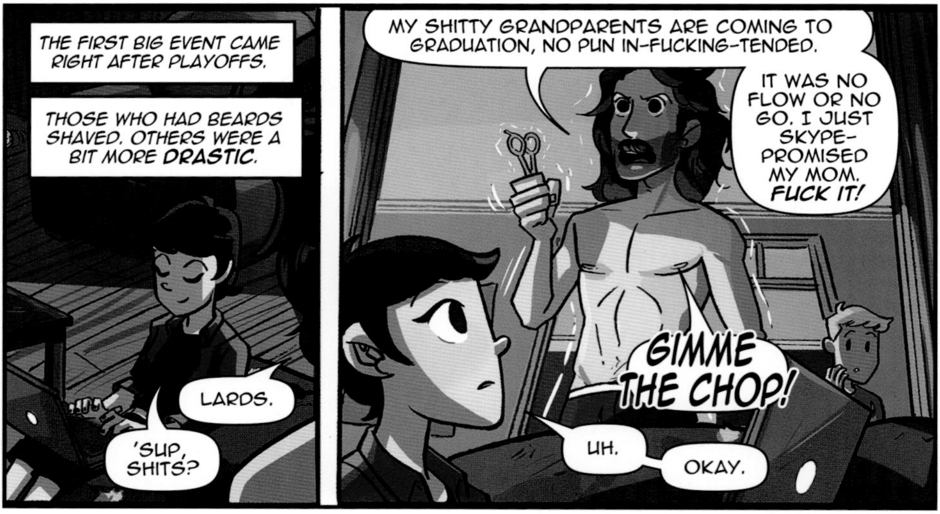
THE FIRST BIG EVENT CAME RIGHT AFTER PLAYOFFS.
THOSE WHO HAD BEARDS SHAVED. OTHERS WERE A BIT MORE **DRASTIC**.
LARDS.
'SUP, SHITS?
MY SHITTY GRANDPARENTS ARE COMING TO GRADUATION, NO PUN IN-FUCKING-TENDED.
IT WAS NO FLOW OR NO GO. I JUST SKYPE-PROMISED MY MOM. ***FUCK IT!***
GIMME THE CHOP!
UH.
OKAY.

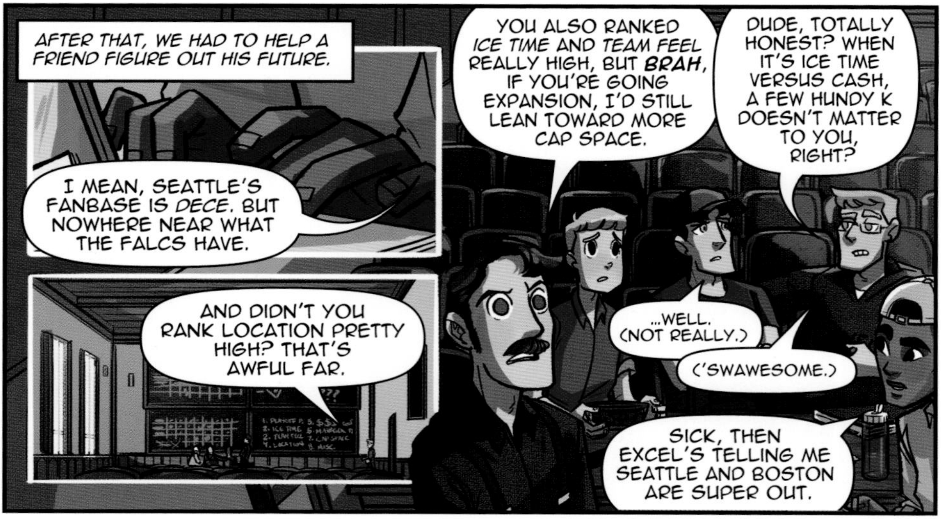
AFTER THAT, WE HAD TO HELP A FRIEND FIGURE OUT HIS FUTURE.
I MEAN, SEATTLE'S FANBASE IS *DECE*. BUT NOWHERE NEAR WHAT THE FALCS HAVE.
AND DIDN'T YOU RANK LOCATION PRETTY HIGH? THAT'S AWFUL FAR.
YOU ALSO RANKED *ICE TIME* AND *TEAM FEEL* REALLY HIGH, BUT ***BRAH***, IF YOU'RE GOING EXPANSION, I'D STILL LEAN TOWARD MORE CAP SPACE.
DUDE, TOTALLY HONEST? WHEN IT'S ICE TIME VERSUS CASH, A FEW HUNDY K DOESN'T MATTER TO YOU, RIGHT?
...WELL. (NOT REALLY.)
('SWAWESOME.)
SICK, THEN EXCEL'S TELLING ME SEATTLE AND BOSTON ARE SUPER OUT.

BRAH.

WHY'D I HAVE TO FIND OUT FROM NHL.COM THAT YOU JUST SIGNED WITH PROVIDENCE?

OH.

I WOULD'VE TOLD YOU SOONER BUT.

I HAD A LECTURE.

WITH JACK SIGNING, THE SENIORS GRADUATING SUDDENLY BECAME TOO REAL... ⸗SIGH⸗

AND THEN Y'ALL OF COURSE HEARD ALL ABOUT MY TRIALS AND TRIBULATIONS WITH THE PASSING OF BETSY.

OH, BETSY ISN'T A PERSON— SHE'S THAT OLD WORKHORSE OF AN OVEN THAT I DROVE TO AN **EARLY GRAVE.**

(BLESS HER HEART.)

...YOU CAN ACTUALLY TELL WHAT'S WRONG WITH IT?

...WELL, YEAH.

AND **SORRY**, BITTY. IF SOMEONE BROUGHT THIS INTO MY UNCLE'S SHOP WE'D PROBABLY SUGGEST SELLING HER FOR SCRAP.

...OH LORD. AND TO THINK THE LAST THING I MADE IN HER WAS **BAGEL BITES.**

IF ONLY I'D KNOWN.

BUT Y'ALL KNOW WHAT? SHAME ON ME FOR FORGETTING SAMWELL HOCKEY'S NUMBER ONE MOTTO.

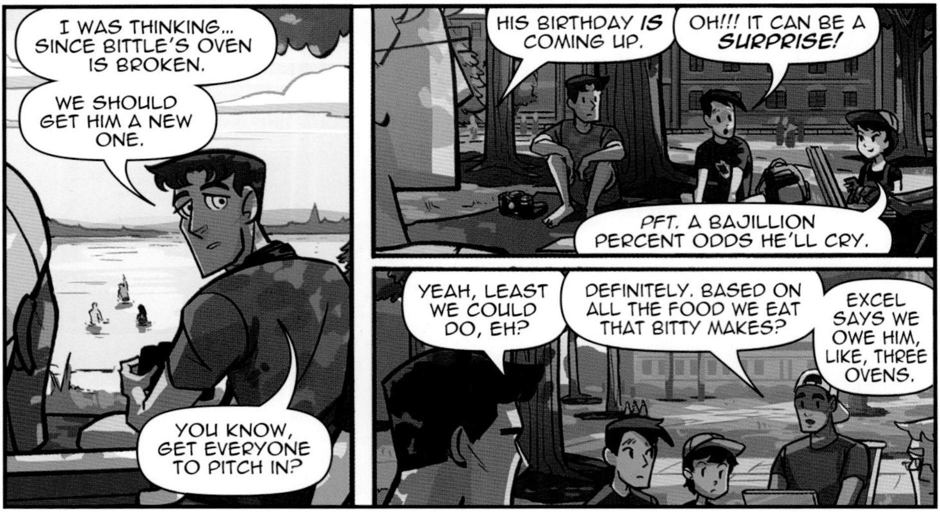
I WAS THINKING... SINCE BITTLE'S OVEN IS BROKEN.
WE SHOULD GET HIM A NEW ONE.
YOU KNOW, GET EVERYONE TO PITCH IN?
HIS BIRTHDAY *IS* COMING UP.
OH!!! IT CAN BE A *SURPRISE!*
PFT. A BAJILLION PERCENT ODDS HE'LL CRY.
YEAH, LEAST WE COULD DO, EH?
DEFINITELY. BASED ON ALL THE FOOD WE EAT THAT BITTY MAKES?
EXCEL SAYS WE OWE HIM, LIKE, THREE OVENS.

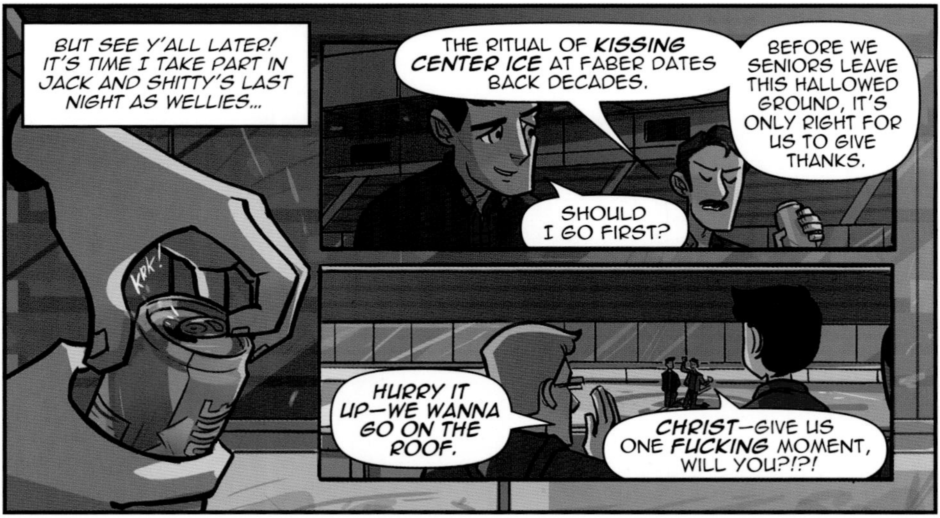
BUT SEE Y'ALL LATER! IT'S TIME I TAKE PART IN JACK AND SHITTY'S LAST NIGHT AS WELLIES...
KRK!
THE RITUAL OF **KISSING CENTER ICE** AT FABER DATES BACK DECADES.
BEFORE WE SENIORS LEAVE THIS HALLOWED GROUND, IT'S ONLY RIGHT FOR US TO GIVE THANKS.
SHOULD I GO FIRST?
HURRY IT UP—WE WANNA GO ON THE ROOF.
CHRIST—GIVE US ONE **FUCKING** MOMENT, WILL YOU?!?!

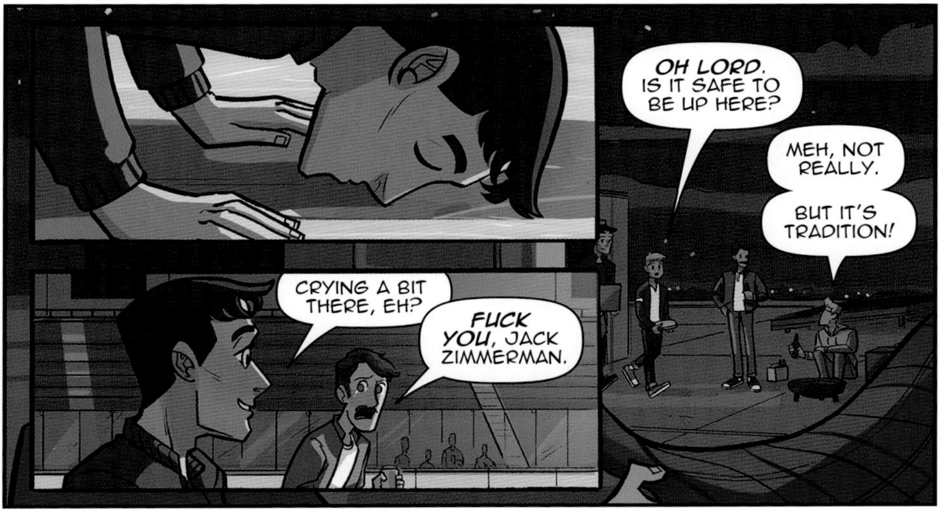
OH LORD. IS IT SAFE TO BE UP HERE?
MEH, NOT REALLY.
BUT IT'S TRADITION!
CRYING A BIT THERE, EH?
FUCK YOU, JACK ZIMMERMAN.

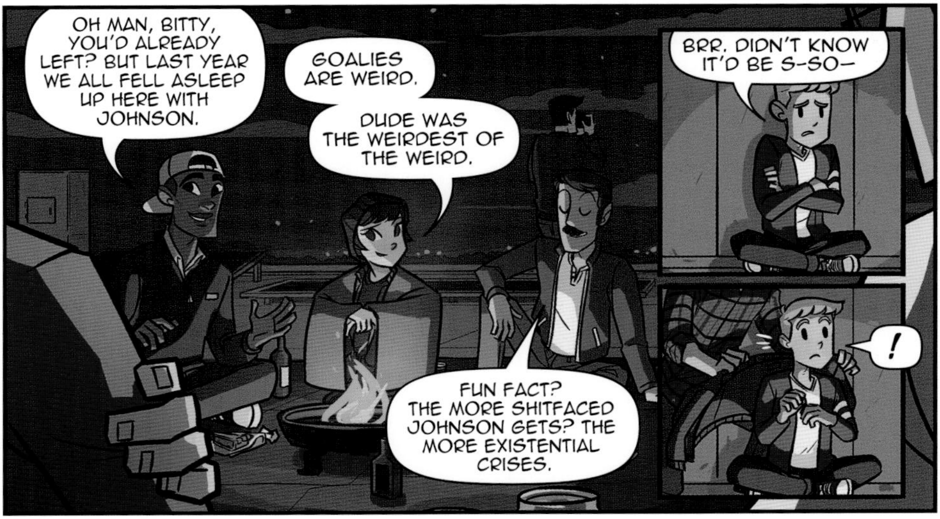
OH MAN, BITTY, YOU'D ALREADY LEFT? BUT LAST YEAR WE ALL FELL ASLEEP UP HERE WITH JOHNSON.
GOALIES ARE WEIRD.
DUDE WAS THE WEIRDEST OF THE WEIRD.
BRR. DIDN'T KNOW IT'D BE S-SO—
FUN FACT? THE MORE SHITFACED JOHNSON GETS? THE MORE EXISTENTIAL CRISES.
!

OH! THANKS, JACK!
NO PROBLEM.
TO THE SAMWELL CLASS OF 2015!
JACK. SHITS. IT'S SECRET TIME. WE GET TO ASK YOU ANYTHING.
DUDE, CAN WE PLEASE KNOW WHAT HAPPENED AT THE DRAFT.
NO, NO, NO, WAIT. HOW ABOUT SHITTY TELL US HIS FIRST NAME!
WHAT?! YOU GUYS DON'T KNOW MY FIRST NAME??
NO!

S

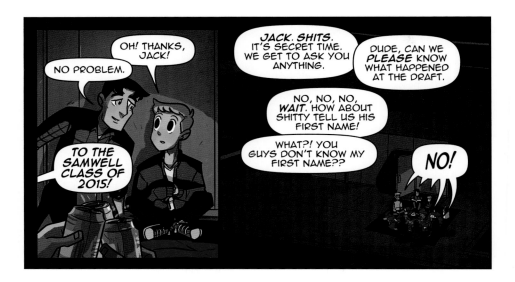

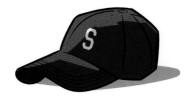

17

GRADUATION

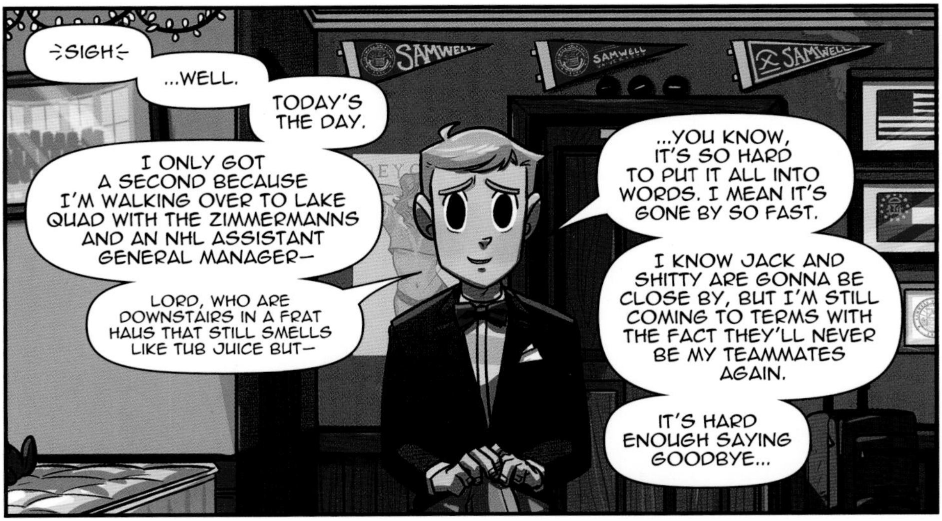

⸗SIGH⸗
...WELL.
TODAY'S THE DAY.
I ONLY GOT A SECOND BECAUSE I'M WALKING OVER TO LAKE QUAD WITH THE ZIMMERMANNS AND AN NHL ASSISTANT GENERAL MANAGER—
LORD, WHO ARE DOWNSTAIRS IN A FRAT HAUS THAT STILL SMELLS LIKE TUB JUICE BUT—
...YOU KNOW, IT'S SO HARD TO PUT IT ALL INTO WORDS. I MEAN IT'S GONE BY SO FAST.
I KNOW JACK AND SHITTY ARE GONNA BE CLOSE BY, BUT I'M STILL COMING TO TERMS WITH THE FACT THEY'LL NEVER BE MY TEAMMATES AGAIN.
IT'S HARD ENOUGH SAYING GOODBYE...

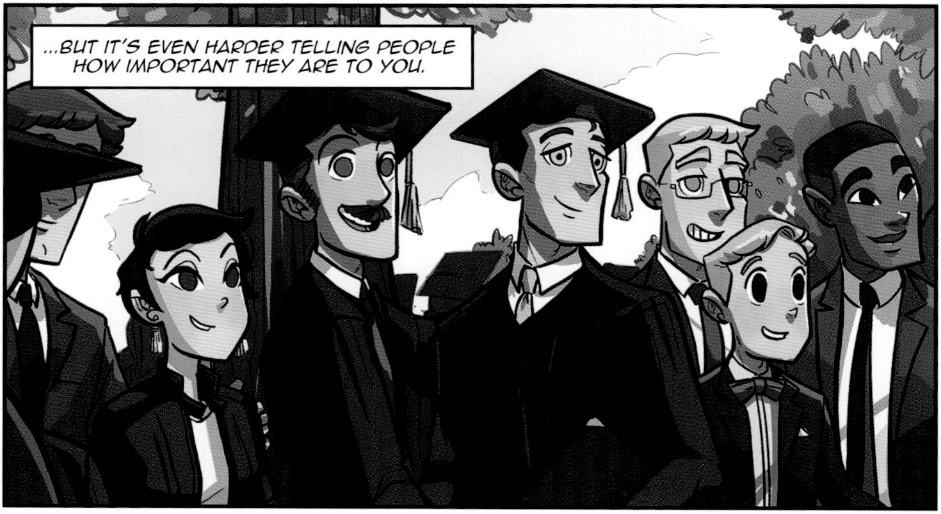
...BUT IT'S EVEN HARDER TELLING PEOPLE HOW IMPORTANT THEY ARE TO YOU.

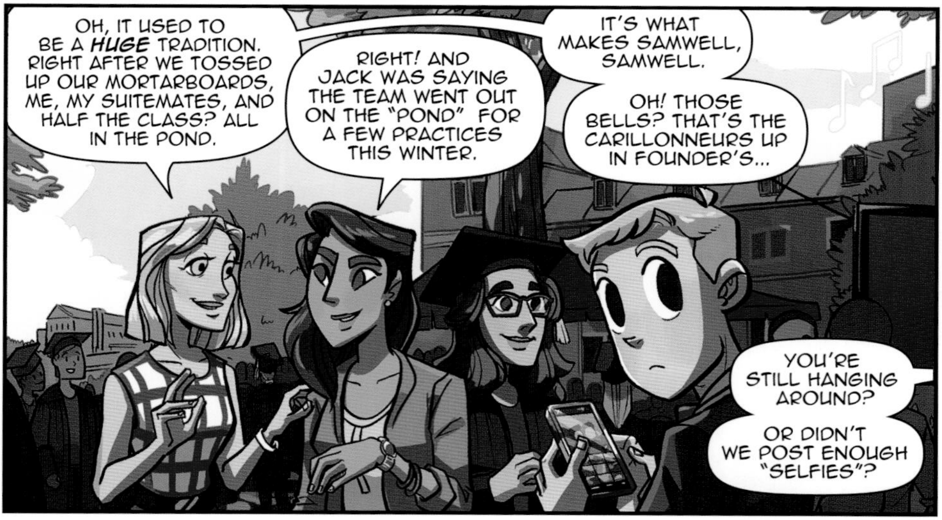
OH, IT USED TO BE A ***HUGE*** TRADITION. RIGHT AFTER WE TOSSED UP OUR MORTARBOARDS, ME, MY SUITEMATES, AND HALF THE CLASS? ALL IN THE POND.
RIGHT! AND JACK WAS SAYING THE TEAM WENT OUT ON THE "POND" FOR A FEW PRACTICES THIS WINTER.
IT'S WHAT MAKES SAMWELL, SAMWELL.
OH! THOSE BELLS? THAT'S THE CARILLONNEURS UP IN FOUNDER'S...
YOU'RE STILL HANGING AROUND?
OR DIDN'T WE POST ENOUGH "SELFIES"?

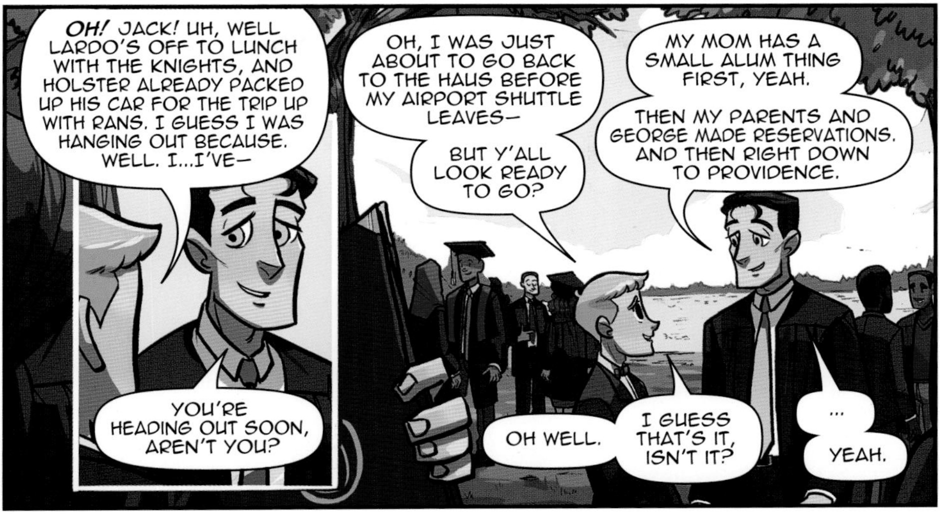
OH! JACK! UH, WELL LARDO'S OFF TO LUNCH WITH THE KNIGHTS, AND HOLSTER ALREADY PACKED UP HIS CAR FOR THE TRIP UP WITH RANS. I GUESS I WAS HANGING OUT BECAUSE. WELL. I...I'VE—
YOU'RE HEADING OUT SOON, AREN'T YOU?
OH, I WAS JUST ABOUT TO GO BACK TO THE HAUS BEFORE MY AIRPORT SHUTTLE LEAVES—
BUT Y'ALL LOOK READY TO GO?
MY MOM HAS A SMALL ALUM THING FIRST, YEAH.
THEN MY PARENTS AND GEORGE MADE RESERVATIONS. AND THEN RIGHT DOWN TO PROVIDENCE.
OH WELL.
I GUESS THAT'S IT, ISN'T IT?
...
YEAH.

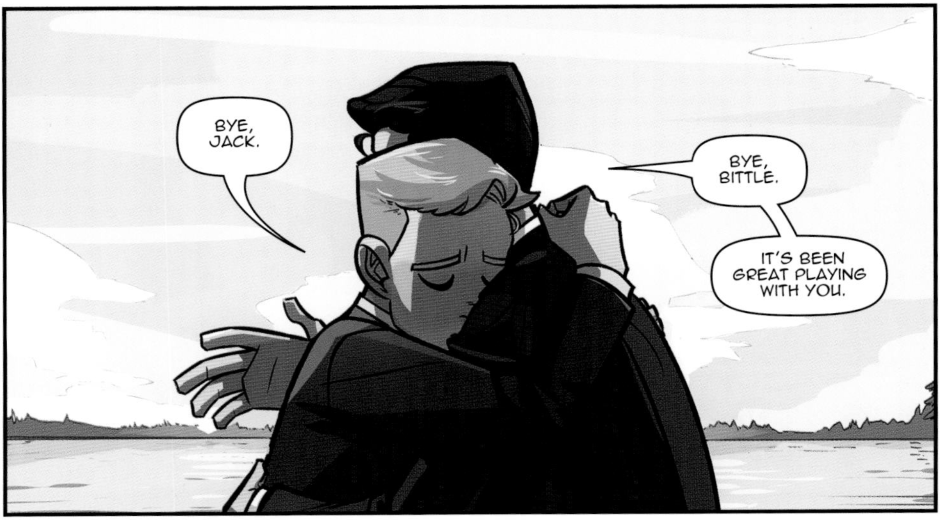
BYE, JACK.
BYE, BITTLE.
IT'S BEEN GREAT PLAYING WITH YOU.

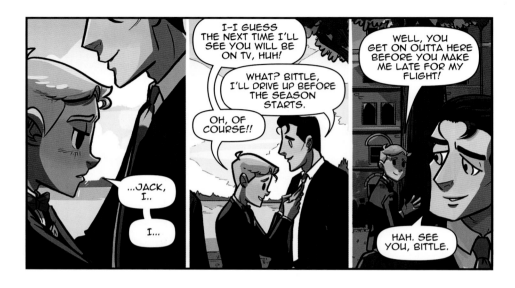

I–I GUESS THE NEXT TIME I'LL SEE YOU WILL BE ON TV, HUH!

WHAT? BITTLE, I'LL DRIVE UP BEFORE THE SEASON STARTS.

OH, OF COURSE!!

...JACK, I..

I...

WELL, YOU GET ON OUTTA HERE BEFORE YOU MAKE ME LATE FOR MY FLIGHT!

HAH. SEE YOU, BITTLE.

A HANDFUL OF GOODBYES LATER...

THOSE ALUMNI EVENTS GET LONGER EVERY YEAR! READY TO HEAD BACK TO THE HOTEL?

YEAH. ALMOST.

I JUST UH...

I FEEL LIKE... I HAVEN'T REALLY SAID GOODBYE TO EVERYONE.

WELL, IT'S A BIT TOO LATE TO TAKE ANOTHER LAP AROUND THE RINK!

NO... NOT THAT.

...

AH.
<YOU KNOW WHAT YOUR UNCLE ALWAYS SAYS. "YOU MISS 100% OF THE SHOTS YOU DON'T TAKE.">
<WHAT DO YOU MEAN?>
<I MEAN. ***GO SAY GOODBYE***. YOU WON'T BE BACK HERE FOR SOME TIME, YOU KNOW?>
<IF THAT'S WHAT YOUR HEART IS TELLING YOU, YOU SHOULD GO.>
<GO REALLY SAY GOODBYE.>
...
OH.

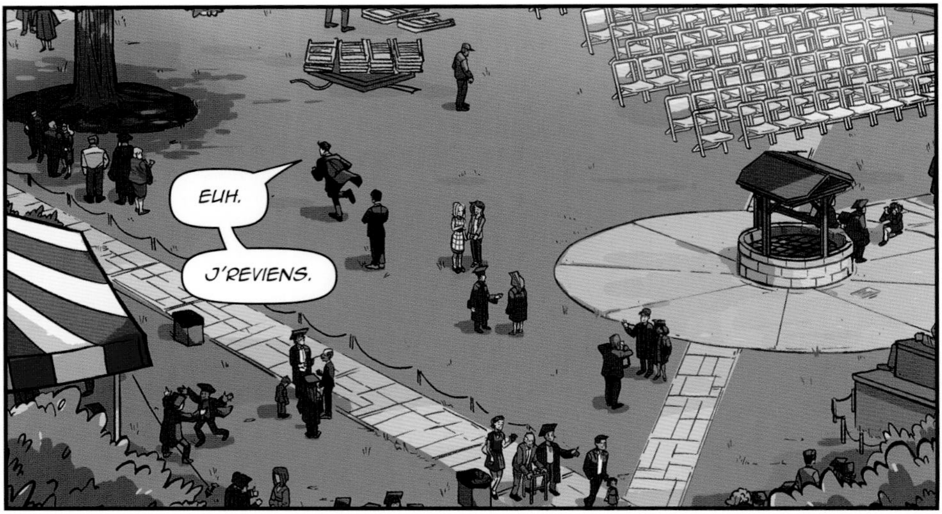
EUH.
J'REVIENS.

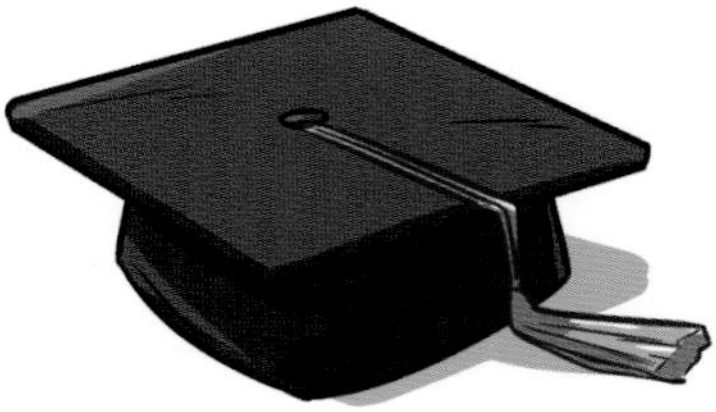

18

GOODBYE FOR THE SUMMER — I

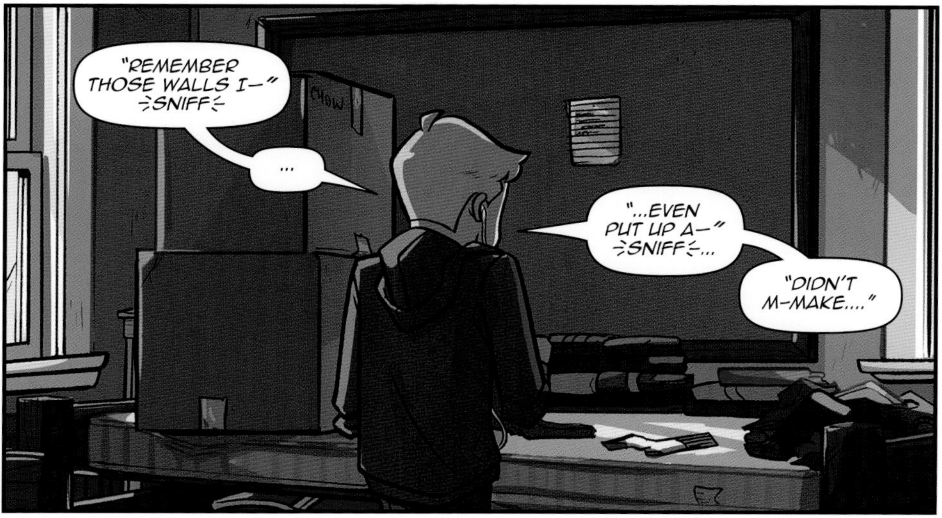
"REMEMBER THOSE WALLS I—" ⇒SNIFF⇐
...
"...EVEN PUT UP A—" ⇒SNIFF⇐...
"DIDN'T M-MAKE...."

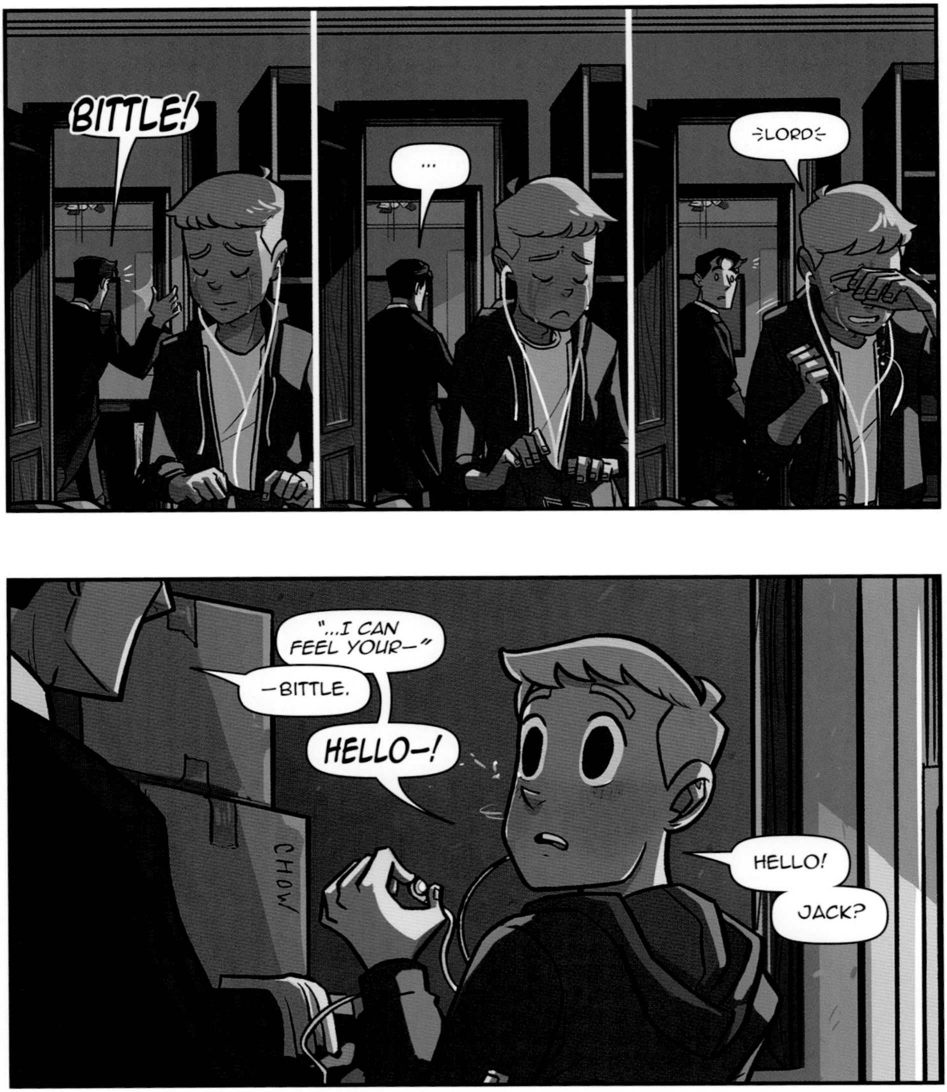
BITTLE!
...
LORD
"...I CAN FEEL YOUR—"
—BITTLE.
HELLO—!
CHOW
HELLO!
JACK?

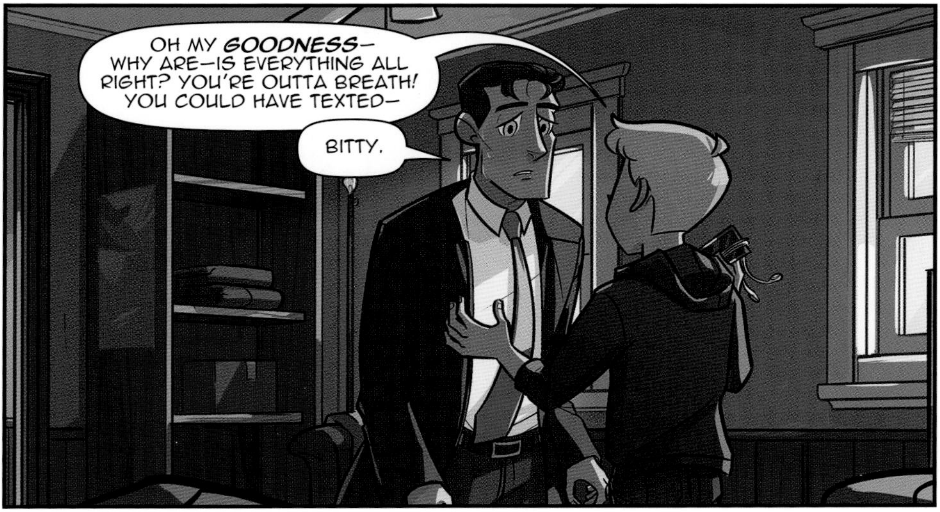
OH MY GOODNESS— WHY ARE—IS EVERYTHING ALL RIGHT? YOU'RE OUTTA BREATH! YOU COULD HAVE TEXTED—
BITTY.

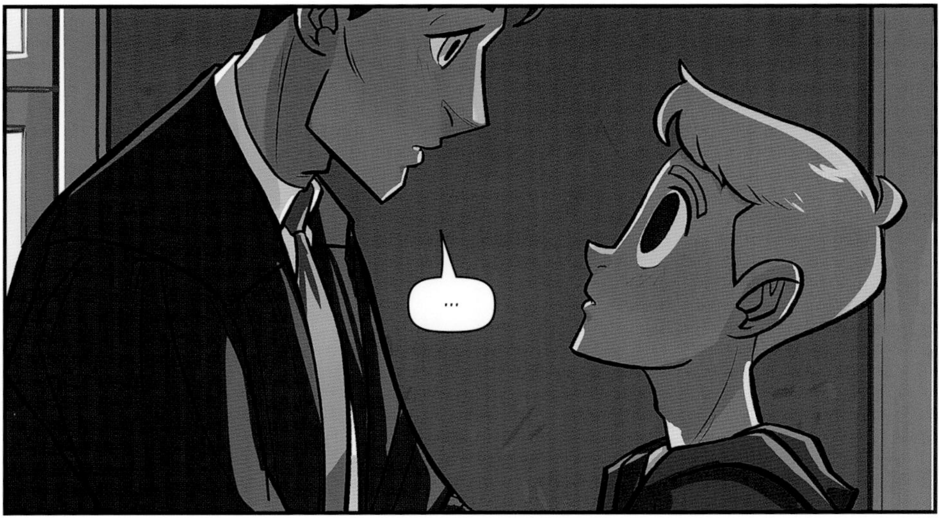
...

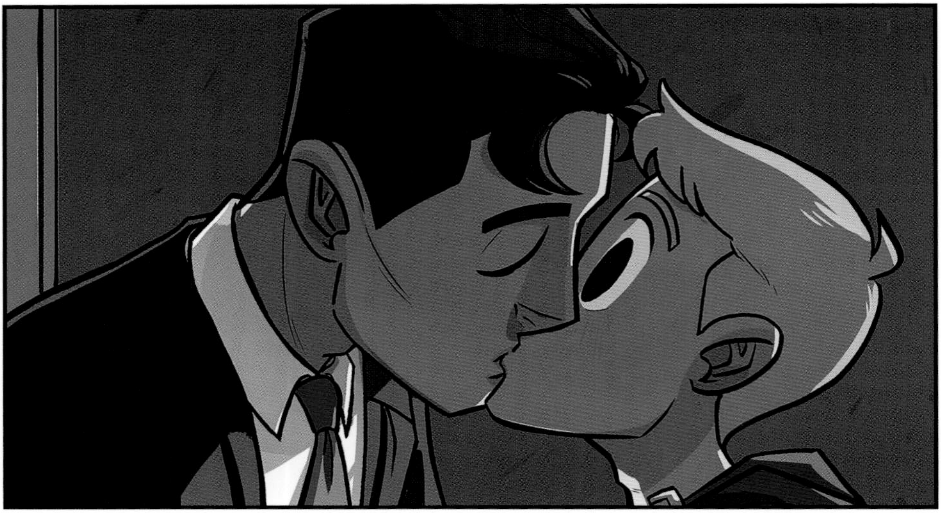

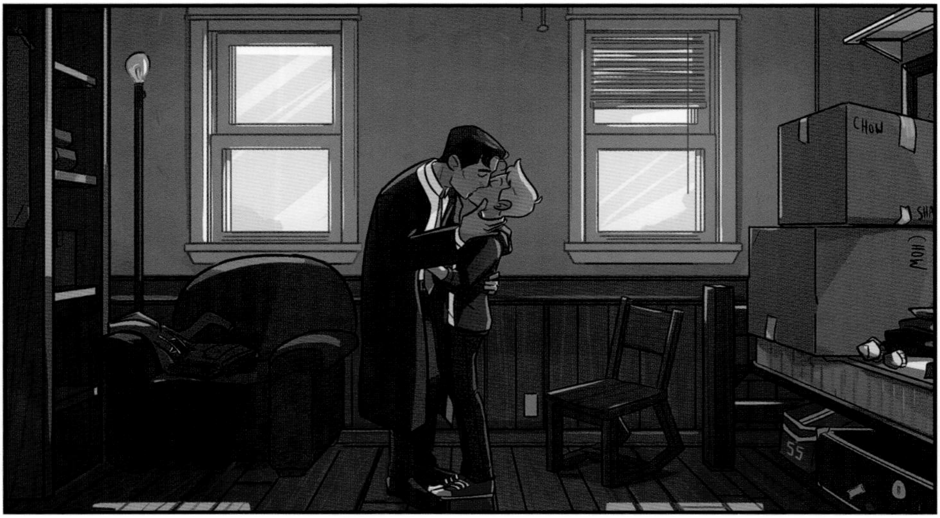
CHOW

19

GOODBYE FOR THE SUMMER — II

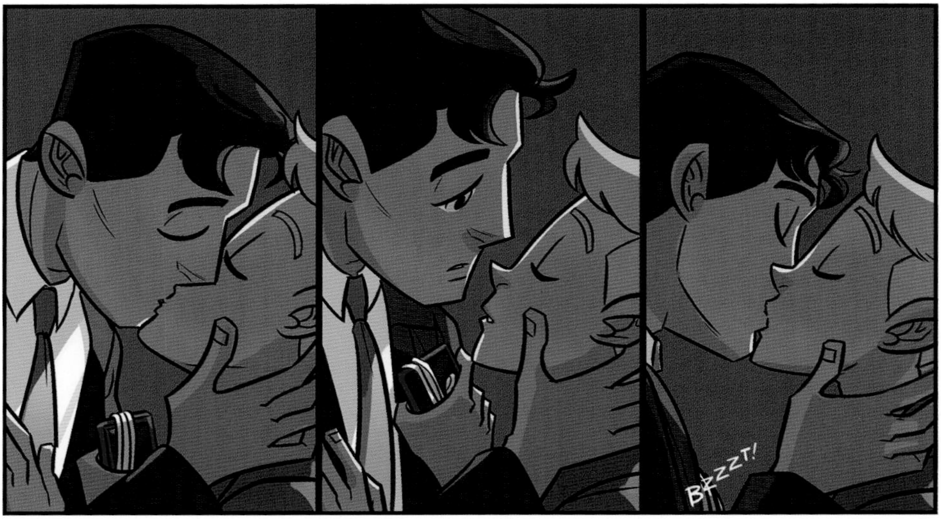
BZZZT!

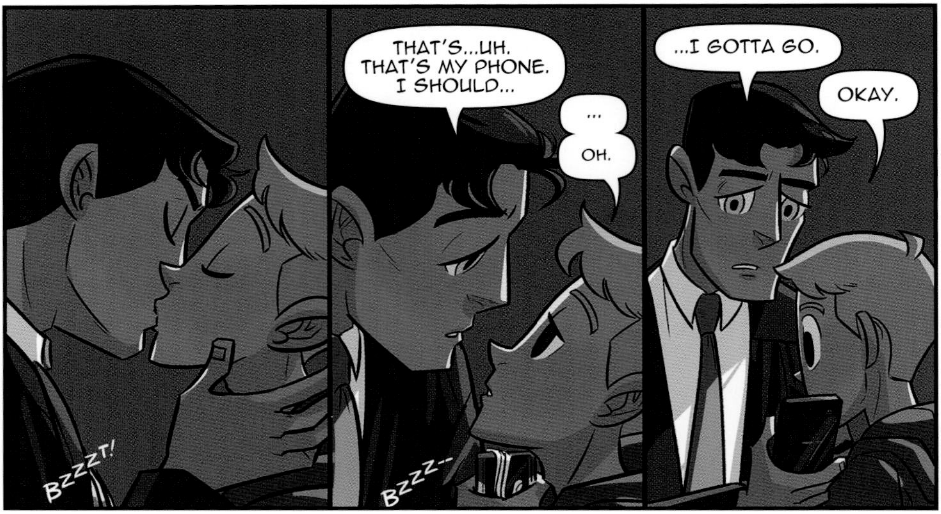
BZZZT!
BZZZ--
THAT'S...UH. THAT'S MY PHONE. I SHOULD...
...
OH.
...I GOTTA GO.
OKAY.

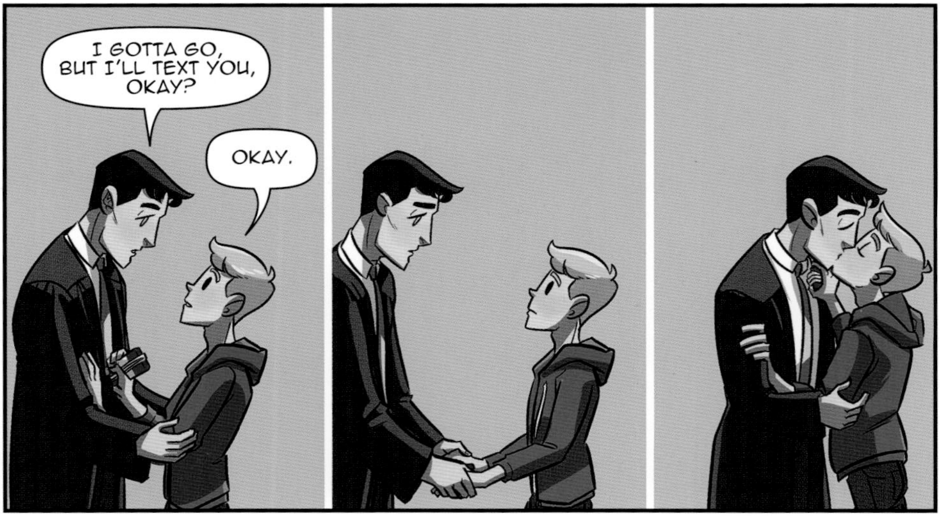
I GOTTA GO, BUT I'LL TEXT YOU, OKAY?
OKAY.

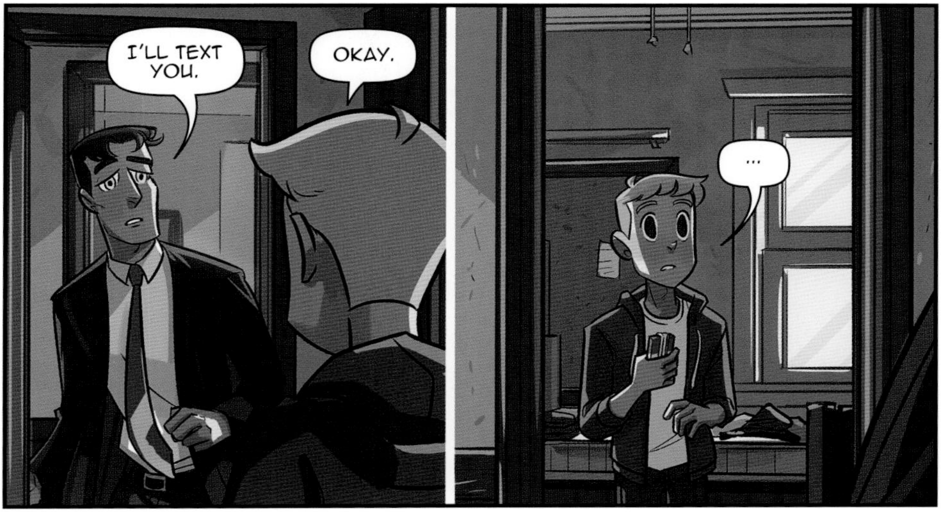
I'LL TEXT YOU.
OKAY.
...

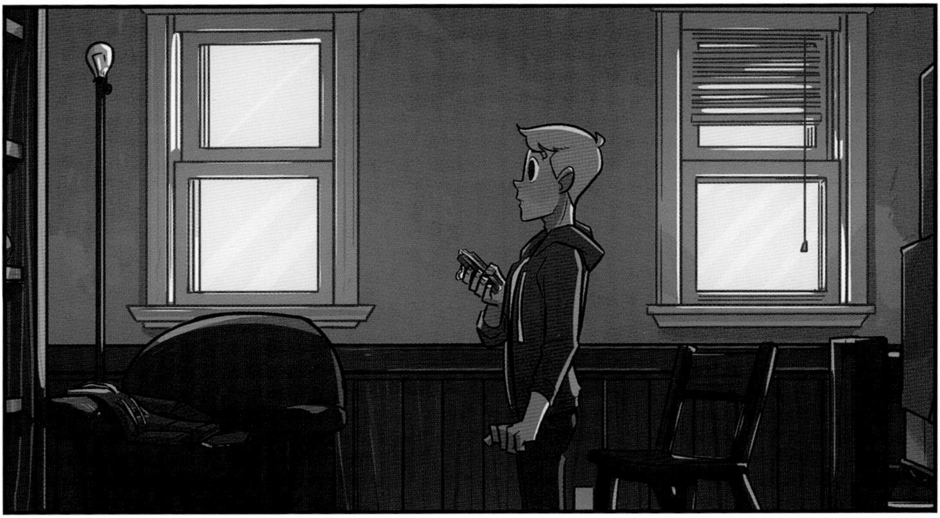

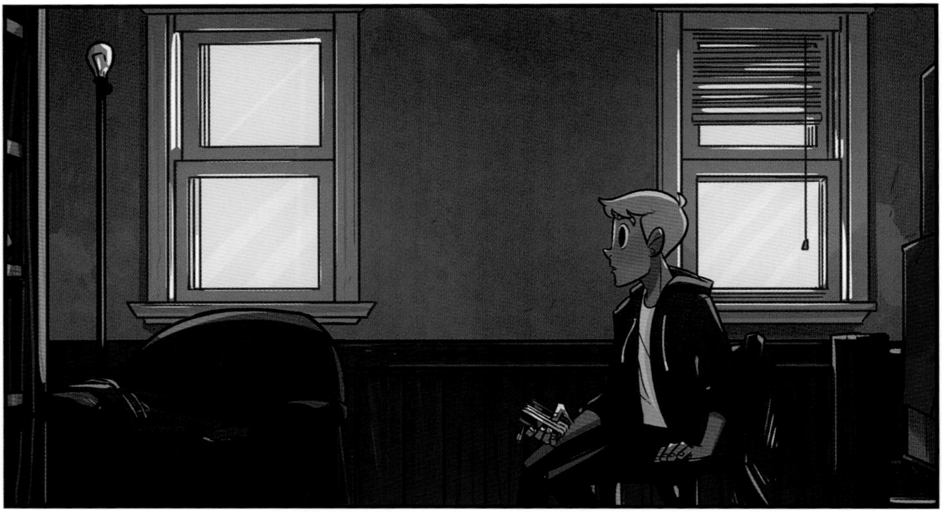

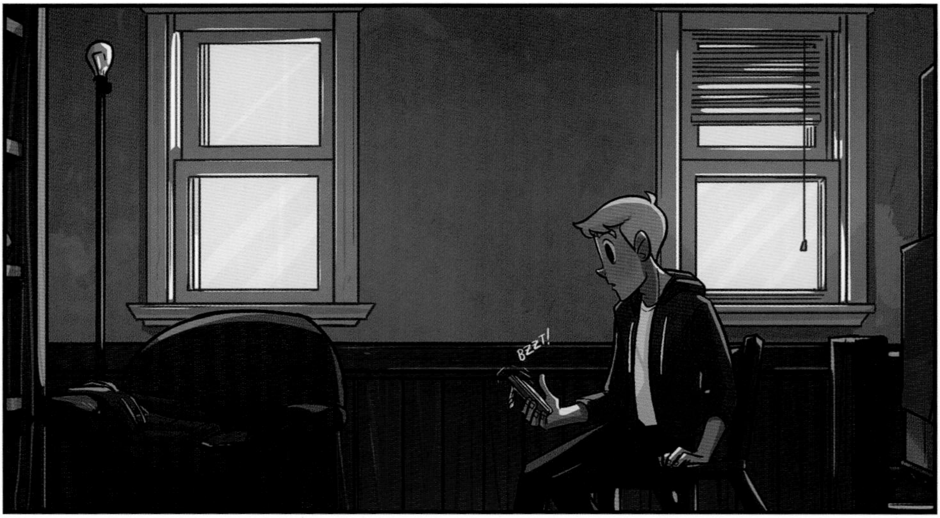
BZZT!

TO BE CONTINUED IN...

CHECK

Book 2: Sticks and Scones

PLEASE!

EXTRA COMICS

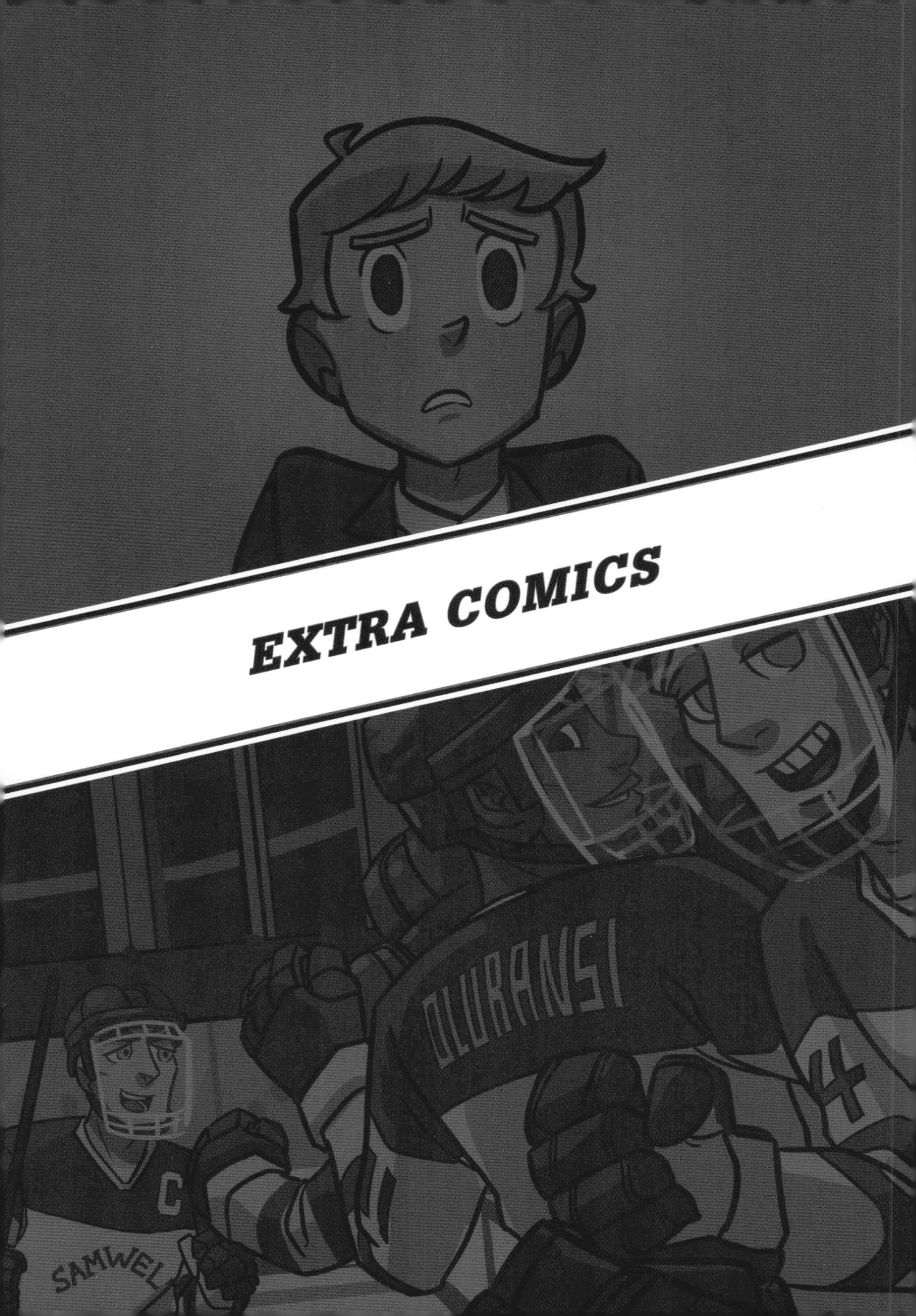
OLURANSI
SAMWEL

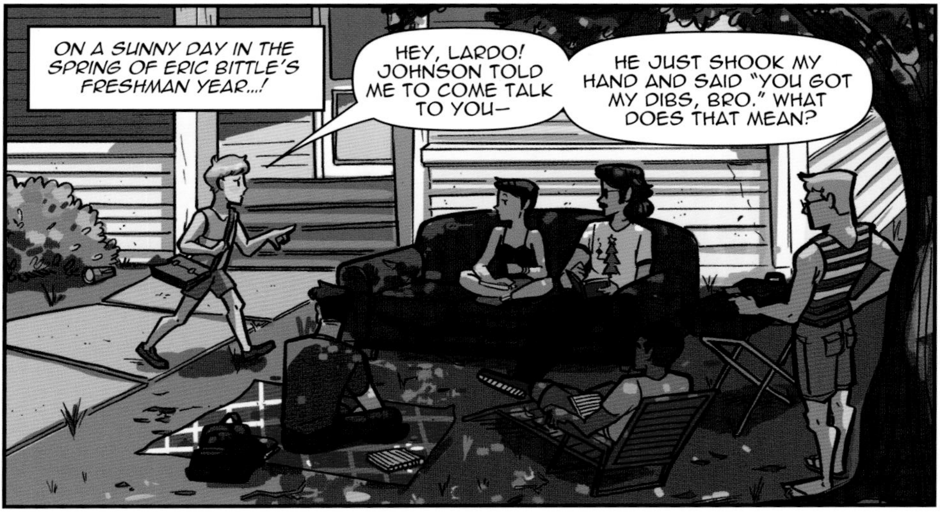
ON A SUNNY DAY IN THE SPRING OF ERIC BITTLE'S FRESHMAN YEAR...!
HEY, LARDO! JOHNSON TOLD ME TO COME TALK TO YOU—
HE JUST SHOOK MY HAND AND SAID "YOU GOT MY DIBS, BRO." WHAT DOES THAT MEAN?

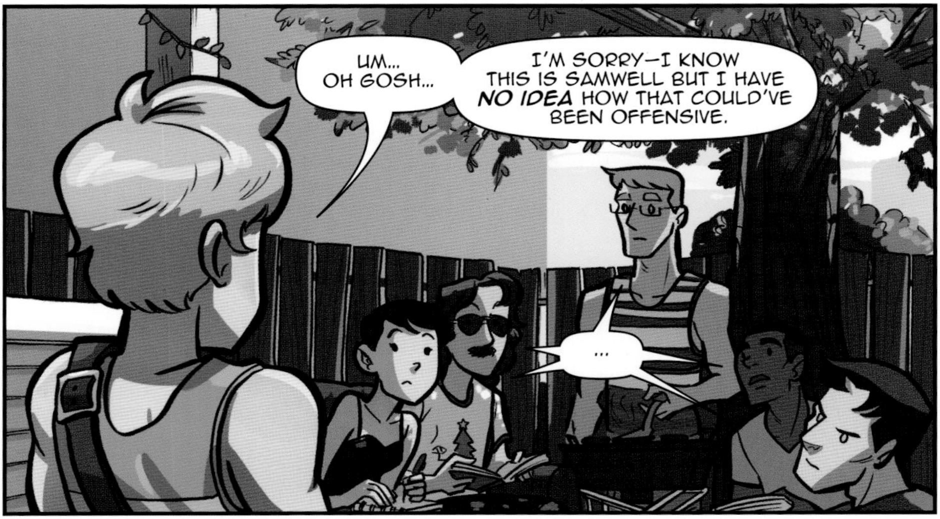
UM... OH GOSH...
I'M SORRY—I KNOW THIS IS SAMWELL BUT I HAVE NO IDEA HOW THAT COULD'VE BEEN OFFENSIVE.
...

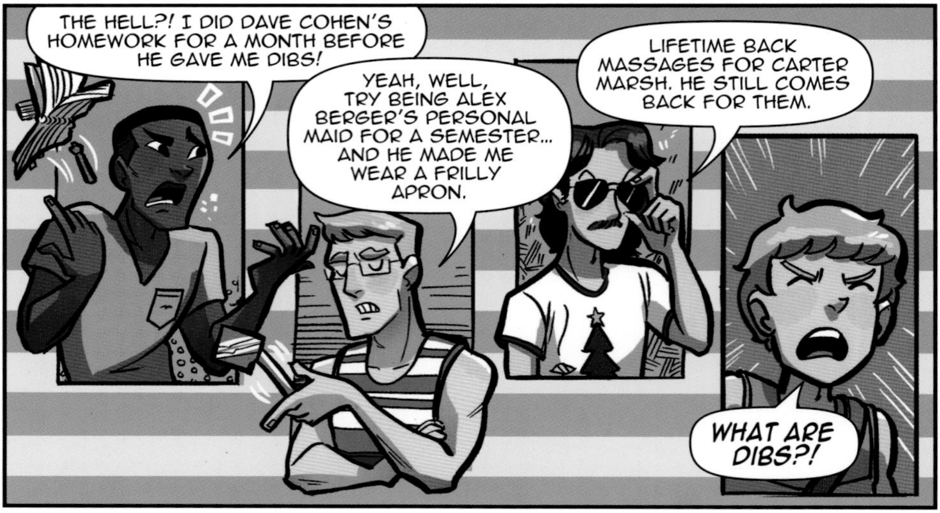
THE HELL?! I DID DAVE COHEN'S HOMEWORK FOR A MONTH BEFORE HE GAVE ME DIBS!
YEAH, WELL, TRY BEING ALEX BERGER'S PERSONAL MAID FOR A SEMESTER... AND HE MADE ME WEAR A FRILLY APRON.
LIFETIME BACK MASSAGES FOR CARTER MARSH. HE STILL COMES BACK FOR THEM.
WHAT ARE DIBS?!

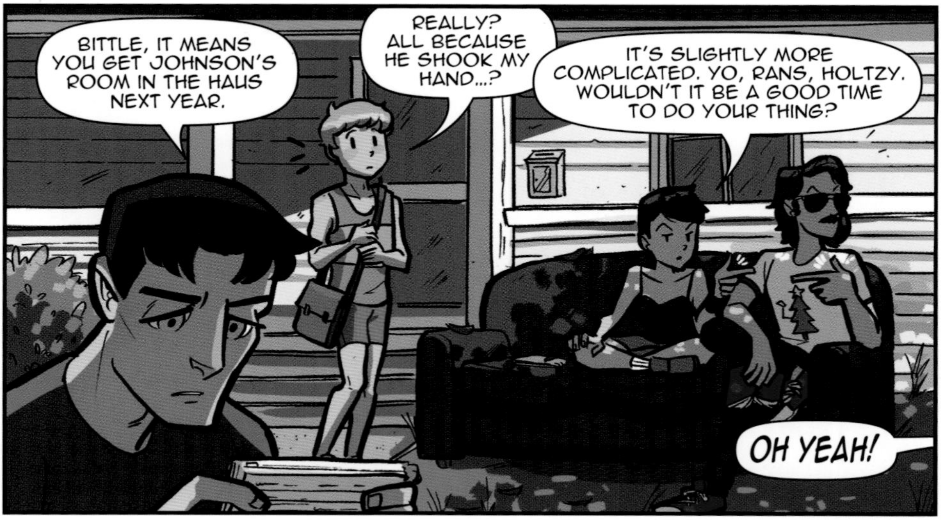
BITTLE, IT MEANS YOU GET JOHNSON'S ROOM IN THE HAUS NEXT YEAR.
REALLY? ALL BECAUSE HE SHOOK MY HAND...?
IT'S SLIGHTLY MORE COMPLICATED. YO, RANS, HOLTZY. WOULDN'T IT BE A GOOD TIME TO DO YOUR THING?
OH YEAH!

HOCKEY SHIT

with RANSOM $\frac{1}{3}$ HOLSTER

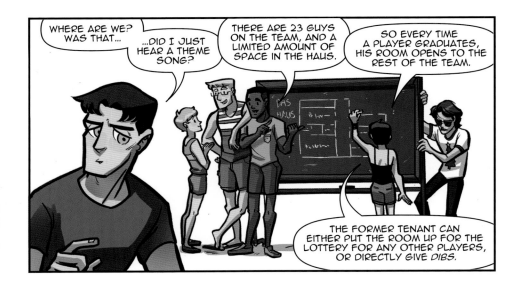

WHERE ARE WE? WAS THAT...

...DID I JUST HEAR A THEME SONG?

THERE ARE 23 GUYS ON THE TEAM, AND A LIMITED AMOUNT OF SPACE IN THE HAUS.

SO EVERY TIME A PLAYER GRADUATES, HIS ROOM OPENS TO THE REST OF THE TEAM.

THE FORMER TENANT CAN EITHER PUT THE ROOM UP FOR THE LOTTERY FOR ANY OTHER PLAYERS, OR DIRECTLY GIVE *DIBS*.

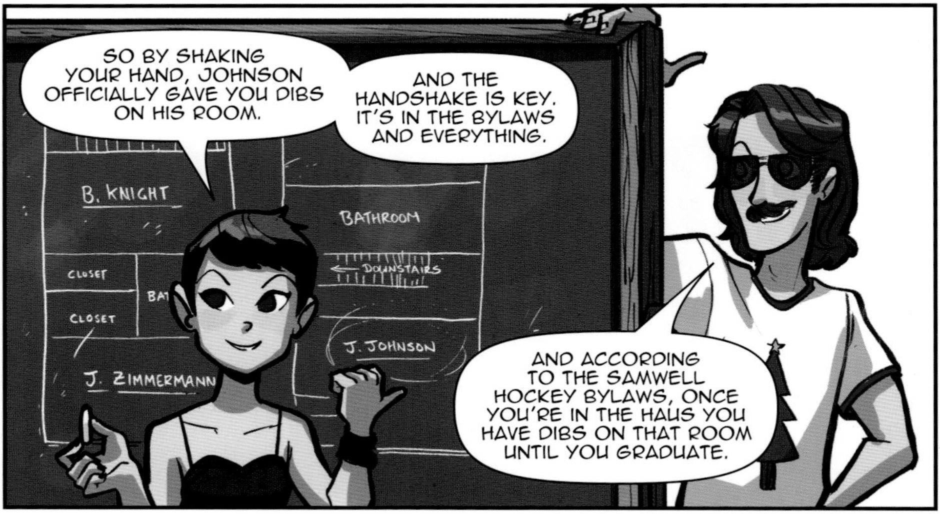
SO BY SHAKING YOUR HAND, JOHNSON OFFICIALLY GAVE YOU DIBS ON HIS ROOM.
AND THE HANDSHAKE IS KEY. IT'S IN THE BYLAWS AND EVERYTHING.
B. KNIGHT
BATHROOM
CLOSET
DOWNSTAIRS
CLOSET
J. JOHNSON
J. ZIMMERMANN
AND ACCORDING TO THE SAMWELL HOCKEY BYLAWS, ONCE YOU'RE IN THE HAUS YOU HAVE DIBS ON THAT ROOM UNTIL YOU GRADUATE.

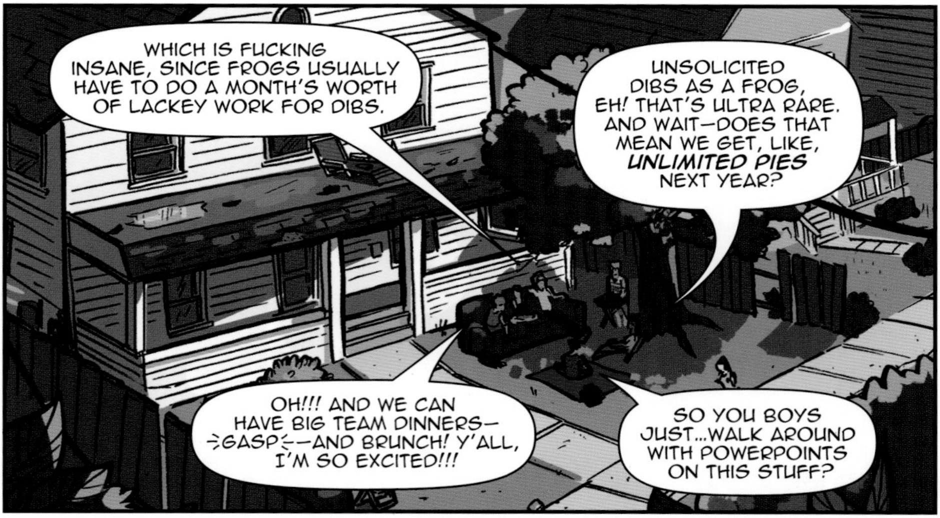
WHICH IS FUCKING INSANE, SINCE FROGS USUALLY HAVE TO DO A MONTH'S WORTH OF LACKEY WORK FOR DIBS.
UNSOLICITED DIBS AS A FROG, EH! THAT'S ULTRA RARE. AND WAIT—DOES THAT MEAN WE GET, LIKE, ***UNLIMITED PIES*** NEXT YEAR?
OH!!! AND WE CAN HAVE BIG TEAM DINNERS—⋝GASP⋜—AND BRUNCH! Y'ALL, I'M SO EXCITED!!!
SO YOU BOYS JUST...WALK AROUND WITH POWERPOINTS ON THIS STUFF?

flow, n.

1. the majestic mane that fluxes forth from the helmets of hockey bros. Widely considered to be the most glorious of all athletic 'dos.

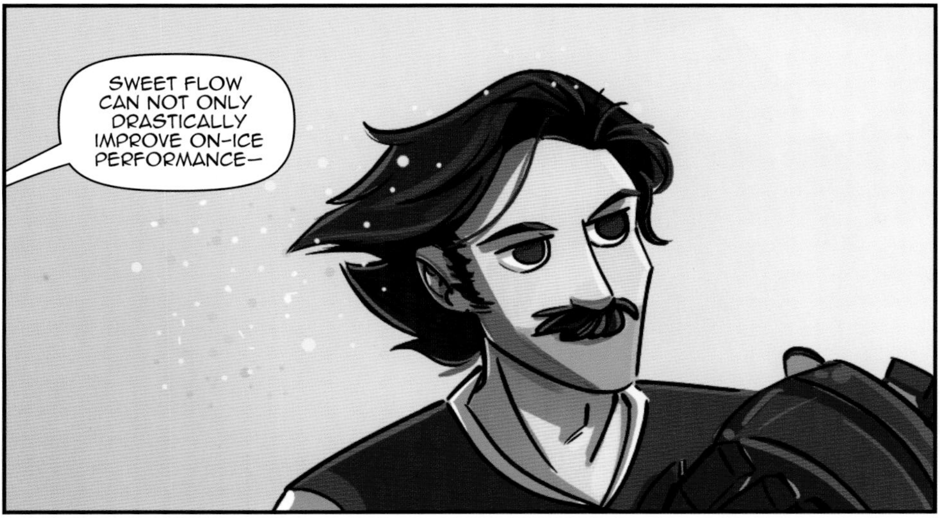
SWEET FLOW CAN NOT ONLY DRASTICALLY IMPROVE ON-ICE PERFORMANCE—

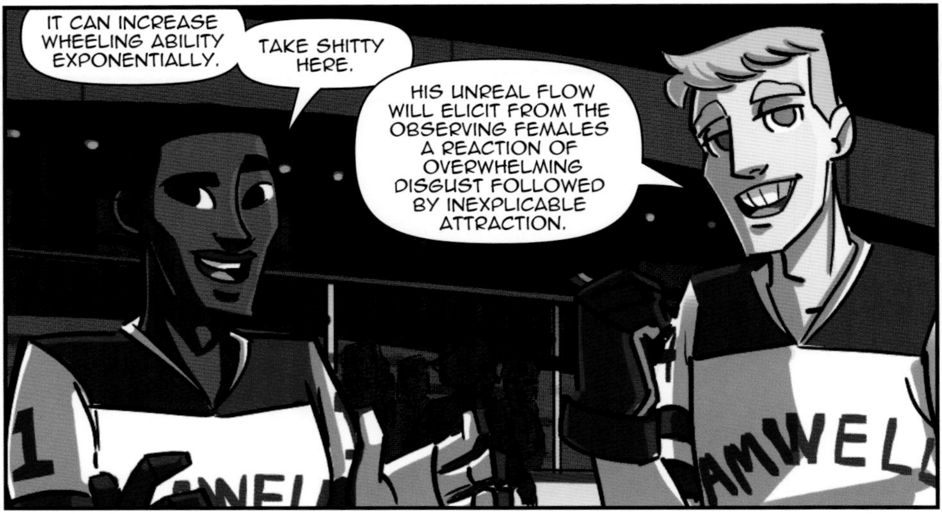
IT CAN INCREASE WHEELING ABILITY EXPONENTIALLY.
TAKE SHITTY HERE.
HIS UNREAL FLOW WILL ELICIT FROM THE OBSERVING FEMALES A REACTION OF OVERWHELMING DISGUST FOLLOWED BY INEXPLICABLE ATTRACTION.

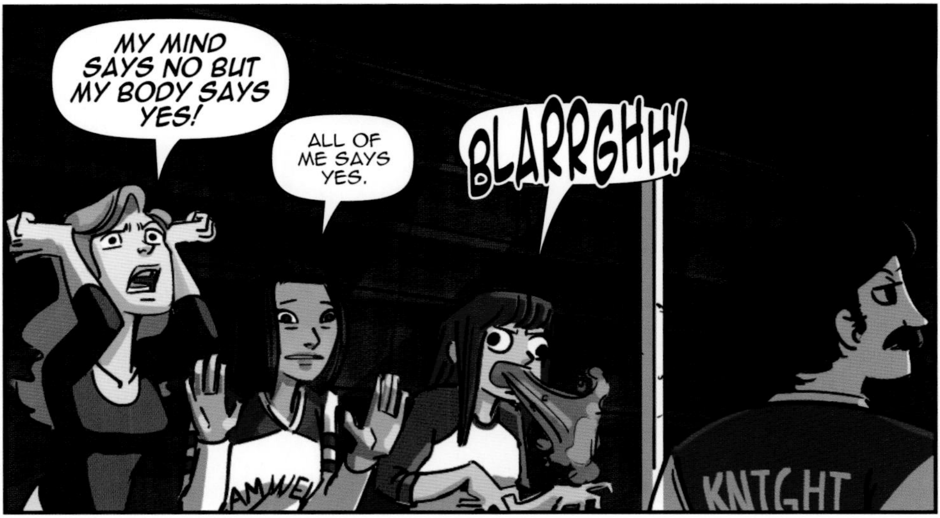
MY MIND SAYS NO BUT MY BODY SAYS YES!
ALL OF ME SAYS YES.
BLARRGHH!
KNIGHT

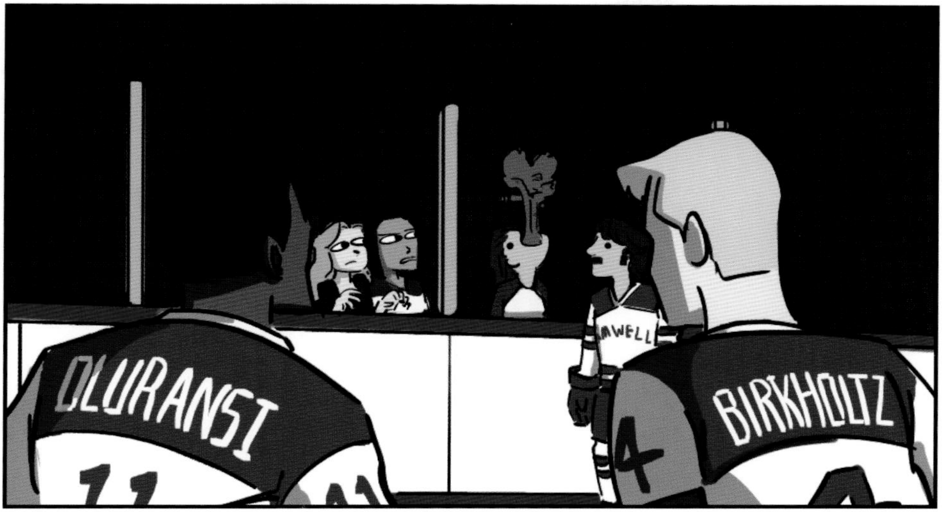
SAMWELL
OLURANSI
11
BIRKHOLTZ
4

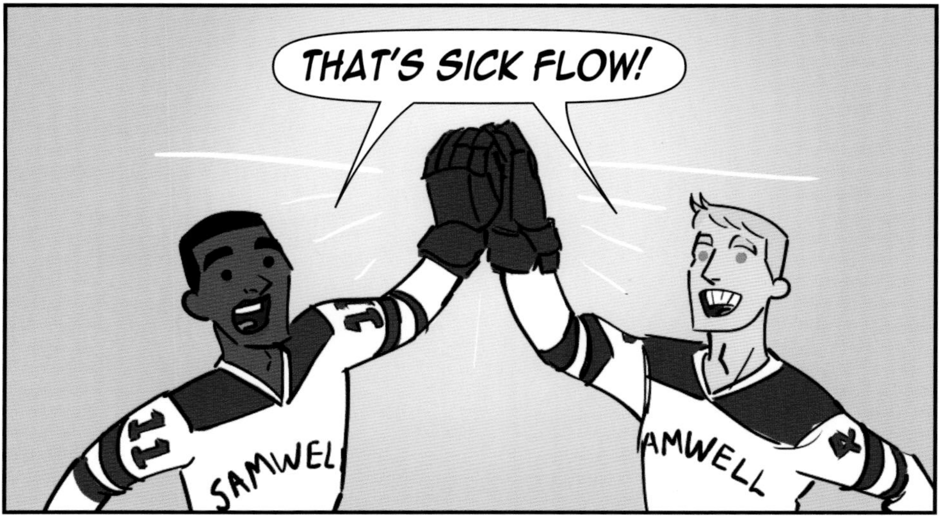
THAT'S SICK FLOW!
11
SAMWEL
AMWELL

chirp, v.

1. to dispatch the competition with witticisms that lower esteem, assert dominance, and put benders in place.

   Quite simply—to talk smack.

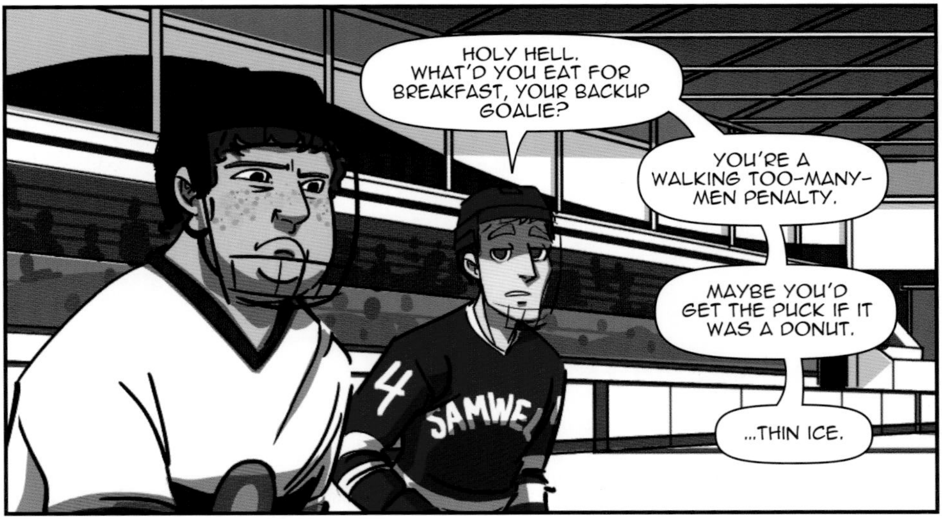
HOLY HELL. WHAT'D YOU EAT FOR BREAKFAST, YOUR BACKUP GOALIE?
YOU'RE A WALKING TOO-MANY-MEN PENALTY.
MAYBE YOU'D GET THE PUCK IF IT WAS A DONUT.
...THIN ICE.
4
SAMWE

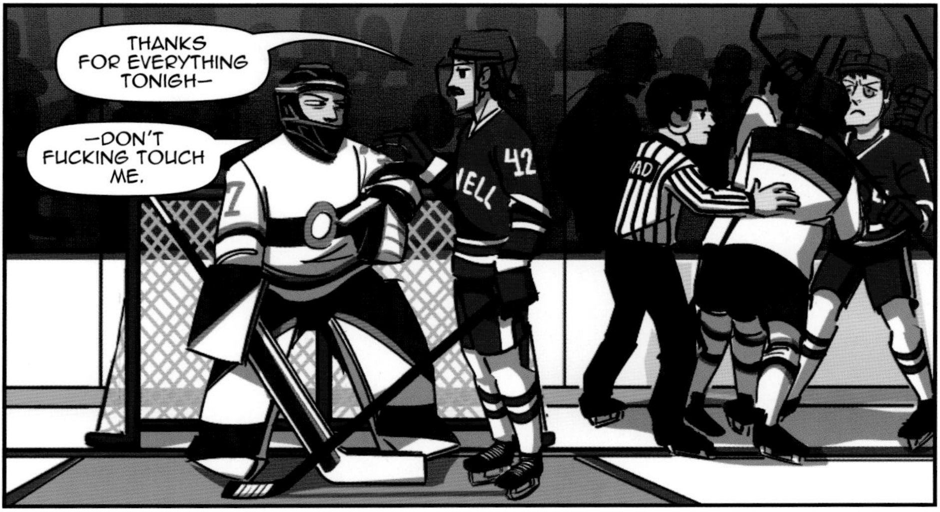
THANKS FOR EVERYTHING TONIGH—
—DON'T FUCKING TOUCH ME.

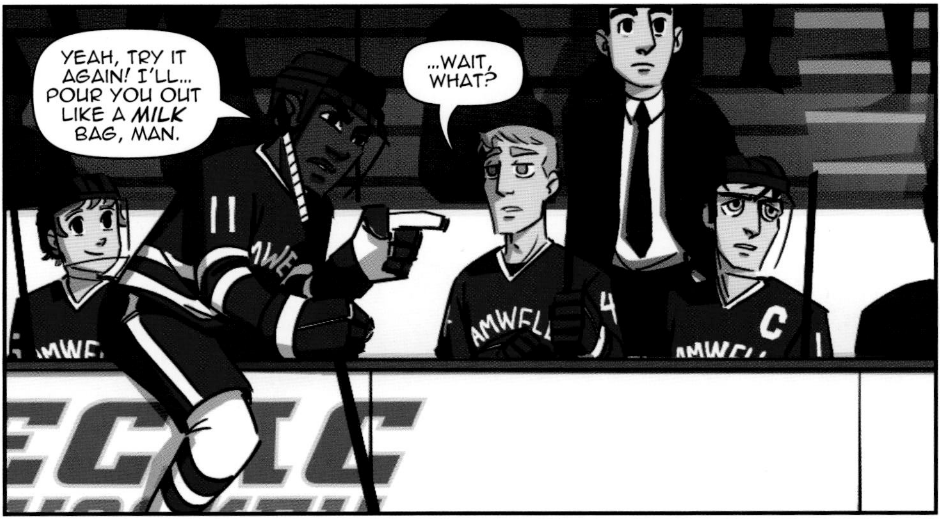
YEAH, TRY IT AGAIN! I'LL... POUR YOU OUT LIKE A *MILK* BAG, MAN.
...WAIT, WHAT?

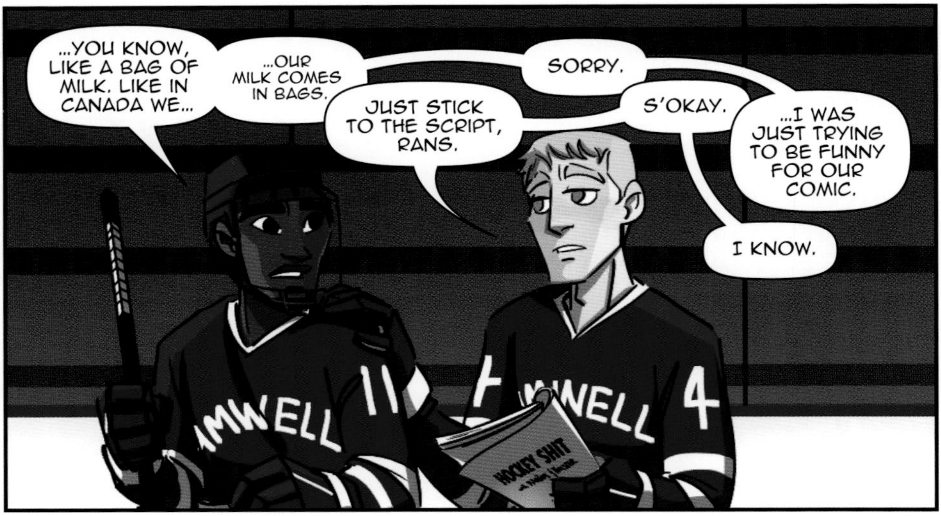
...YOU KNOW, LIKE A BAG OF MILK. LIKE IN CANADA WE...
...OUR MILK COMES IN BAGS.
JUST STICK TO THE SCRIPT, RANS.
SORRY.
S'OKAY.
...I WAS JUST TRYING TO BE FUNNY FOR OUR COMIC.
I KNOW.
11
4
HOCKEY SHIT

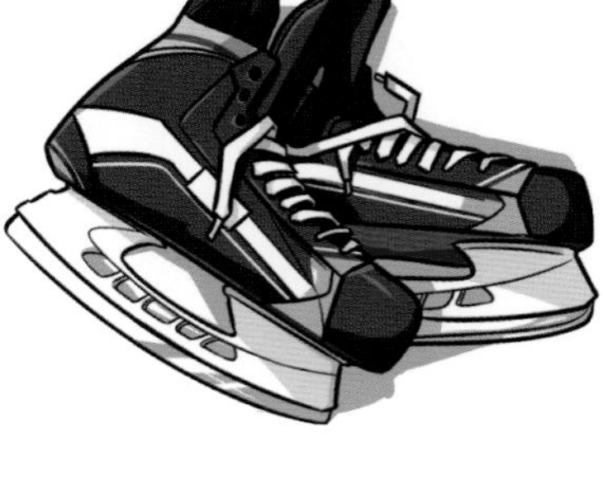

nicknames, n.

1. the noble titles hockey bros give to other hockey bros, representing trust and brotherhood. A hockey player learns a teammate's first name from his gravestone.

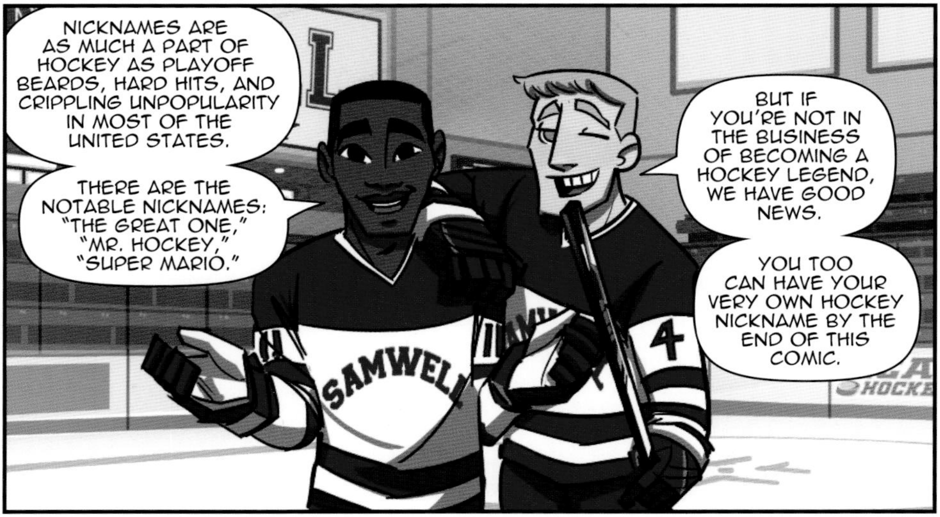
NICKNAMES ARE AS MUCH A PART OF HOCKEY AS PLAYOFF BEARDS, HARD HITS, AND CRIPPLING UNPOPULARITY IN MOST OF THE UNITED STATES.
THERE ARE THE NOTABLE NICKNAMES: "THE GREAT ONE," "MR. HOCKEY," "SUPER MARIO."
BUT IF YOU'RE NOT IN THE BUSINESS OF BECOMING A HOCKEY LEGEND, WE HAVE GOOD NEWS.
YOU TOO CAN HAVE YOUR VERY OWN HOCKEY NICKNAME BY THE END OF THIS COMIC.
SAMWELL
4

NICKNAMES WERE INVENTED IN 1944 WHEN DRUNK CANADIAN SCIENTISTS DERIVED A REVOLUTIONARY FORMULA FOR NAME FISSION.
NATIONAL SOCIALIST PARTY. WELL, SHOOT, THAT'S LONG.
SHIT, JEAN CLAUDE, LET'S JUST CALL 'EM NAZIS, EH?
HOLY SHIT, NICHOLAS, THAT'S GENIUS!
NOW GET THIS...JUST CALL ME ***NICK***.
HOLY EH!
RIGHT, EH?
IT GOES LIKE THIS:

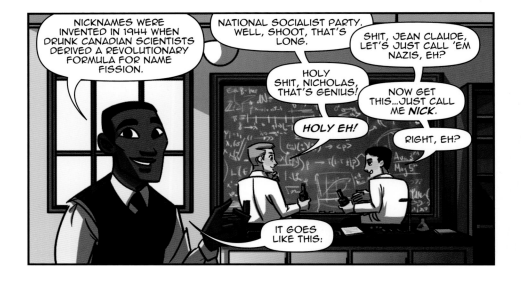

1. Take a syllable from your last (or first) name.
2. Add one of the following:

-ie	-zy
-y	-er
-sy	-s

3. ***'Swawesome!*** You're now the proud owner of a totally sick hockey nickname.* It's so easy, an idiot can do it! An idiot like you!

*Depending on the syllables in your name and the off-chance your name will produce a noun, results may vary from epically legendary to "Patsy."

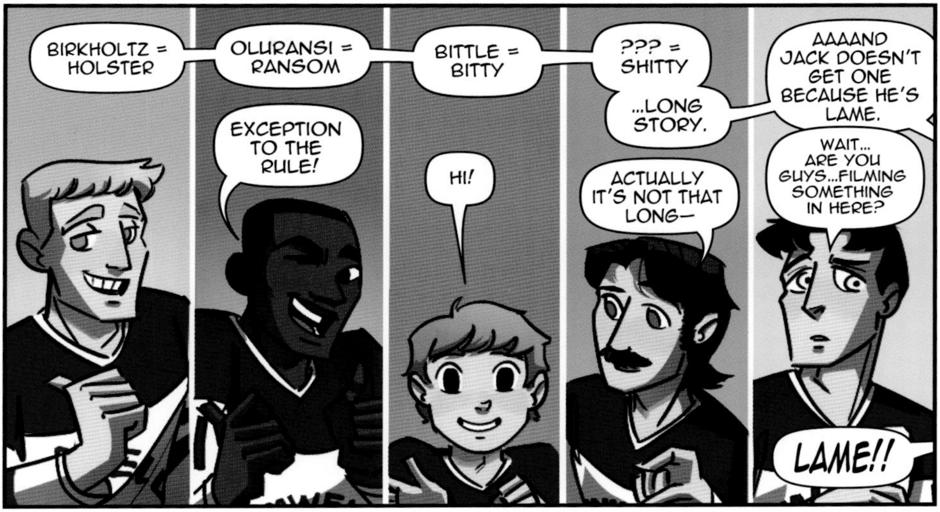
BIRKHOLTZ = HOLSTER
OLURANSI = RANSOM
EXCEPTION TO THE RULE!
BITTLE = BITTY
HI!
??? = SHITTY
...LONG STORY.
ACTUALLY IT'S NOT THAT LONG—
AAAAND JACK DOESN'T GET ONE BECAUSE HE'S LAME.
WAIT... ARE YOU GUYS...FILMING SOMETHING IN HERE?
LAME!!

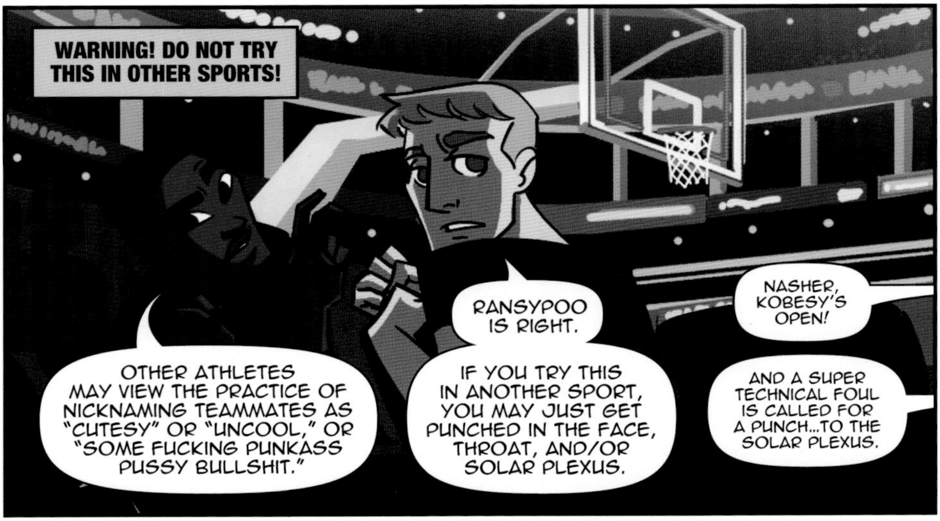
WARNING! DO NOT TRY THIS IN OTHER SPORTS!
OTHER ATHLETES MAY VIEW THE PRACTICE OF NICKNAMING TEAMMATES AS "CUTESY" OR "UNCOOL," OR "SOME FUCKING PUNKASS PUSSY BULLSHIT."
RANSYPOO IS RIGHT.
IF YOU TRY THIS IN ANOTHER SPORT, YOU MAY JUST GET PUNCHED IN THE FACE, THROAT, AND/OR SOLAR PLEXUS.
NASHER, KOBESY'S OPEN!
AND A SUPER TECHNICAL FOUL IS CALLED FOR A PUNCH...TO THE SOLAR PLEXUS.

hockey butt, n.

1. the totally rockin' medius, maximus, and minimus gluteal muscles that are resultant of hours of hard practice and gritty shifts on the ice.

*Used to destroy enemies and attract mates.

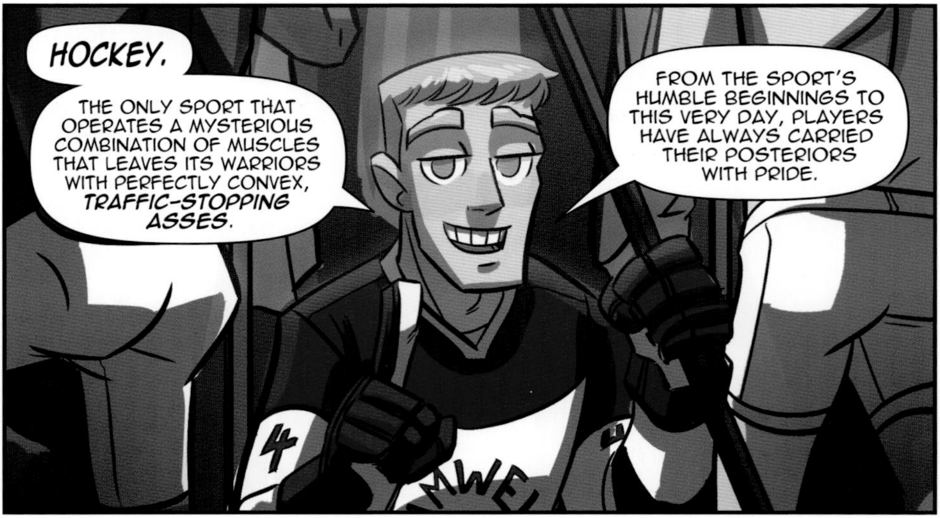
HOCKEY.
THE ONLY SPORT THAT OPERATES A MYSTERIOUS COMBINATION OF MUSCLES THAT LEAVES ITS WARRIORS WITH PERFECTLY CONVEX, *TRAFFIC-STOPPING ASSES*.
FROM THE SPORT'S HUMBLE BEGINNINGS TO THIS VERY DAY, PLAYERS HAVE ALWAYS CARRIED THEIR POSTERIORS WITH PRIDE.

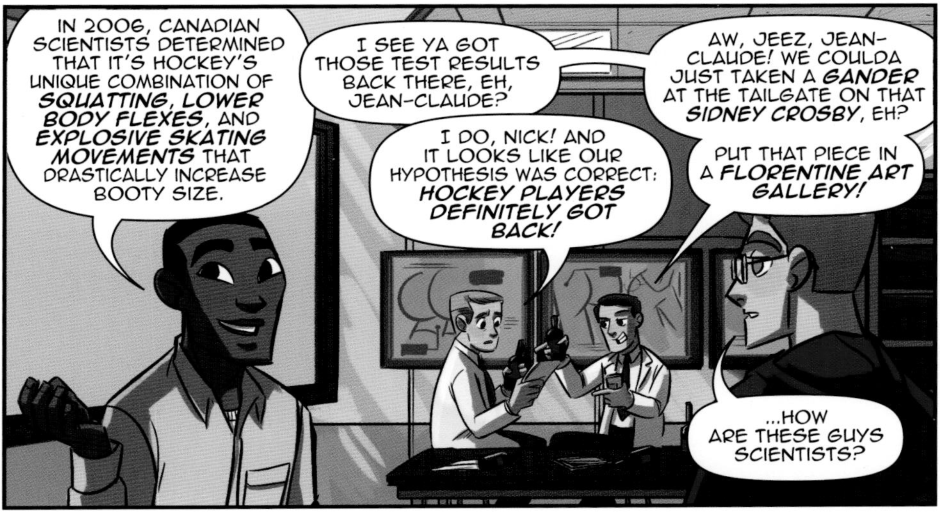
IN 2006, CANADIAN SCIENTISTS DETERMINED THAT IT'S HOCKEY'S UNIQUE COMBINATION OF SQUATTING, LOWER BODY FLEXES, AND EXPLOSIVE SKATING MOVEMENTS THAT DRASTICALLY INCREASE BOOTY SIZE.
I SEE YA GOT THOSE TEST RESULTS BACK THERE, EH, JEAN-CLAUDE?
I DO, NICK! AND IT LOOKS LIKE OUR HYPOTHESIS WAS CORRECT: HOCKEY PLAYERS DEFINITELY GOT BACK!
AW, JEEZ, JEAN-CLAUDE! WE COULDA JUST TAKEN A GANDER AT THE TAILGATE ON THAT SIDNEY CROSBY, EH?
PUT THAT PIECE IN A FLORENTINE ART GALLERY!
...HOW ARE THESE GUYS SCIENTISTS?

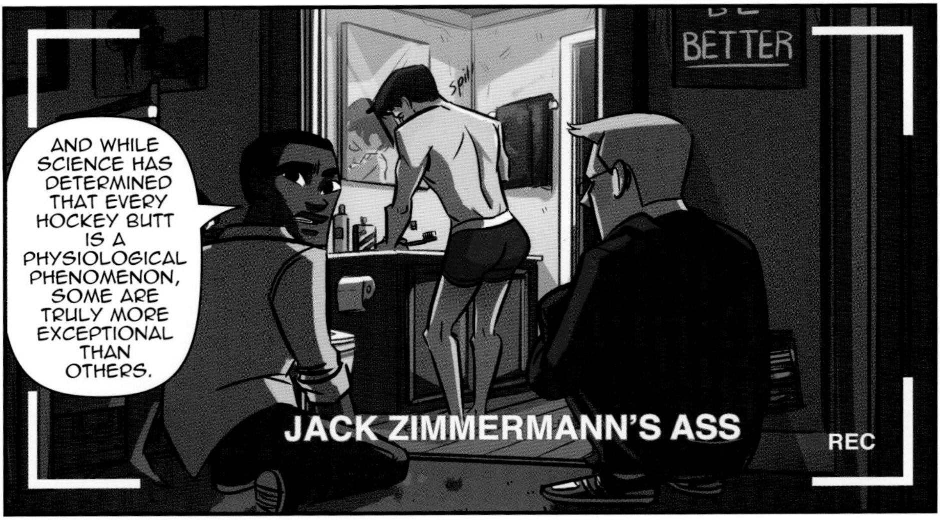
BETTER
spit
AND WHILE SCIENCE HAS DETERMINED THAT EVERY HOCKEY BUTT IS A PHYSIOLOGICAL PHENOMENON, SOME ARE TRULY MORE EXCEPTIONAL THAN OTHERS.
JACK ZIMMERMANN'S ASS
REC

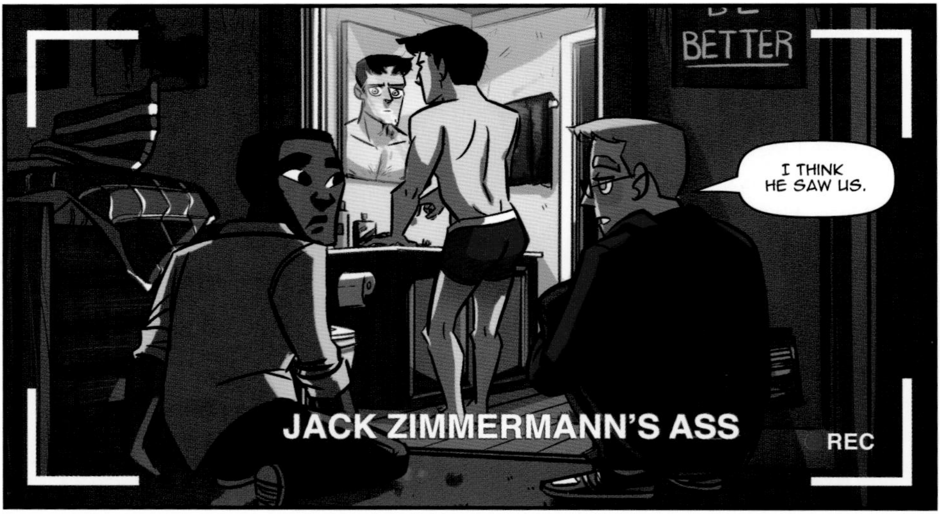
BETTER
I THINK HE SAW US.
JACK ZIMMERMANN'S ASS
REC

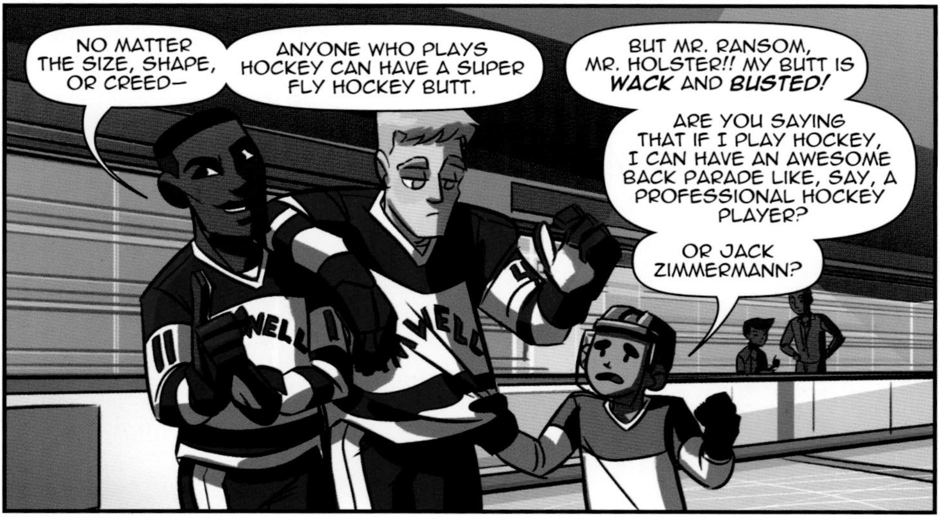
NO MATTER THE SIZE, SHAPE, OR CREED—
ANYONE WHO PLAYS HOCKEY CAN HAVE A SUPER FLY HOCKEY BUTT.
BUT MR. RANSOM, MR. HOLSTER!! MY BUTT IS *WACK* AND *BUSTED!*
ARE YOU SAYING THAT IF I PLAY HOCKEY, I CAN HAVE AN AWESOME BACK PARADE LIKE, SAY, A PROFESSIONAL HOCKEY PLAYER?
OR JACK ZIMMERMANN?

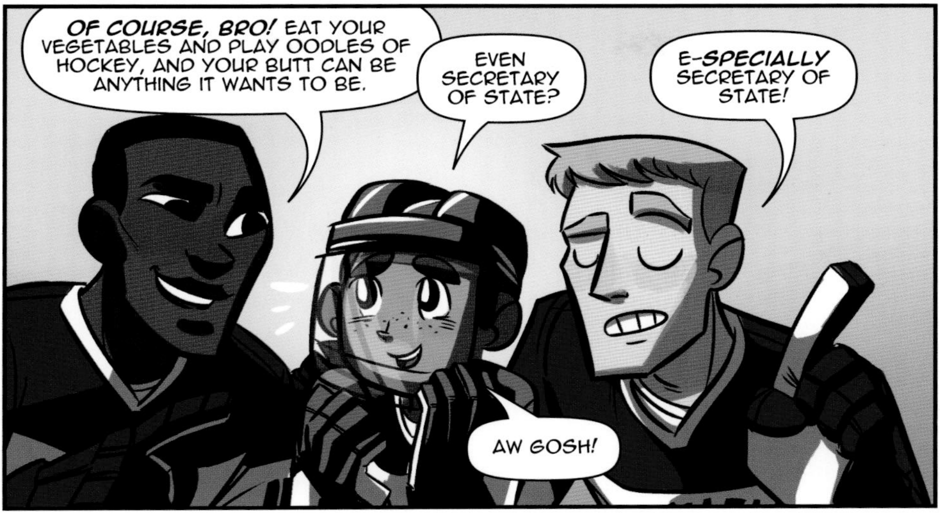
OF COURSE, BRO! EAT YOUR VEGETABLES AND PLAY OODLES OF HOCKEY, AND YOUR BUTT CAN BE ANYTHING IT WANTS TO BE.
EVEN SECRETARY OF STATE?
E-SPECIALLY SECRETARY OF STATE!
AW GOSH!

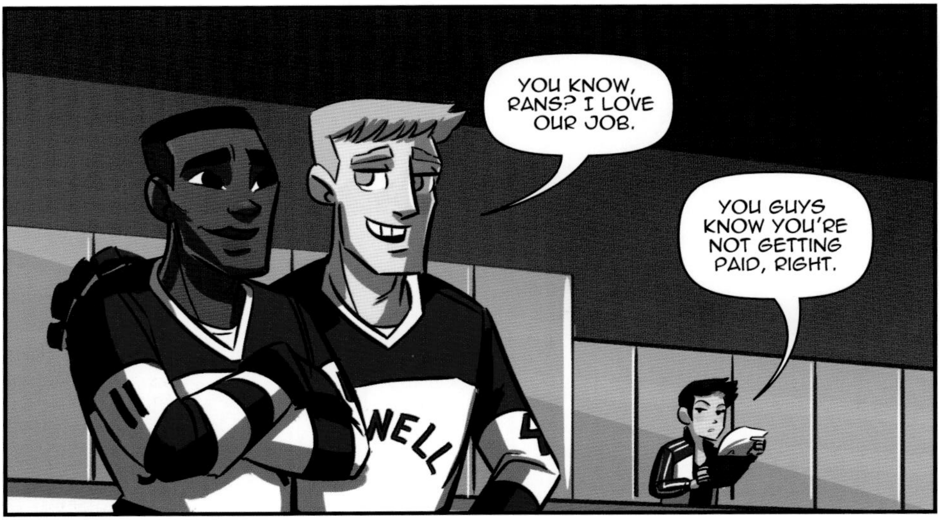
YOU KNOW, RANS? I LOVE OUR JOB.
YOU GUYS KNOW YOU'RE NOT GETTING PAID, RIGHT.

celly, n.

1. The cathartic release of energy catalyzed by a goal. Characterized by ebullient noise-making and loosely choreographed motion. Often accompanied by hugs.

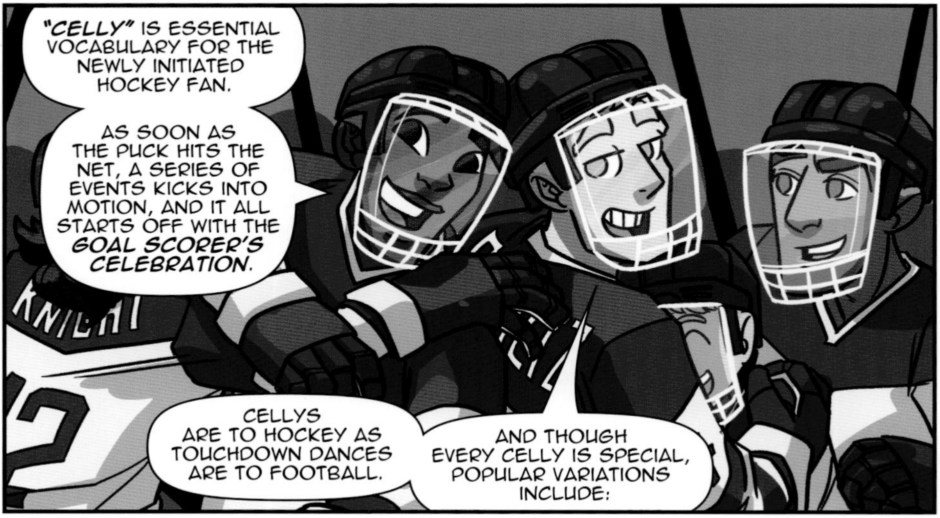
"CELLY" IS ESSENTIAL VOCABULARY FOR THE NEWLY INITIATED HOCKEY FAN.
AS SOON AS THE PUCK HITS THE NET, A SERIES OF EVENTS KICKS INTO MOTION, AND IT ALL STARTS OFF WITH THE GOAL SCORER'S CELEBRATION.
CELLYS ARE TO HOCKEY AS TOUCHDOWN DANCES ARE TO FOOTBALL.
AND THOUGH EVERY CELLY IS SPECIAL, POPULAR VARIATIONS INCLUDE:
KNIGHT

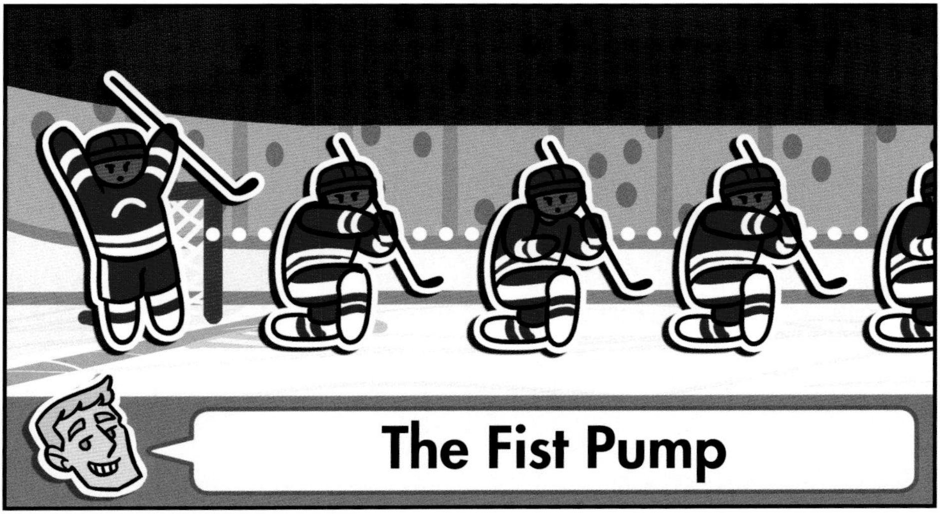
The Fist Pump

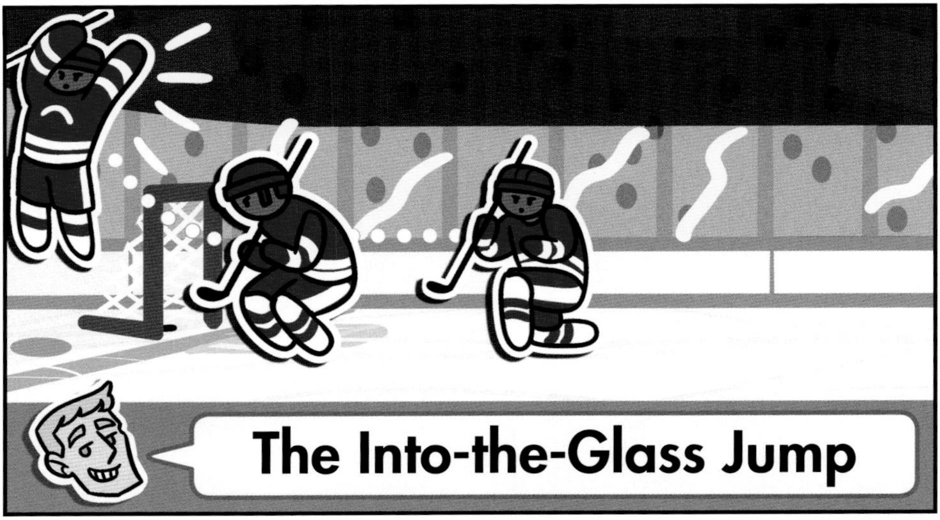
The Into-the-Glass Jump

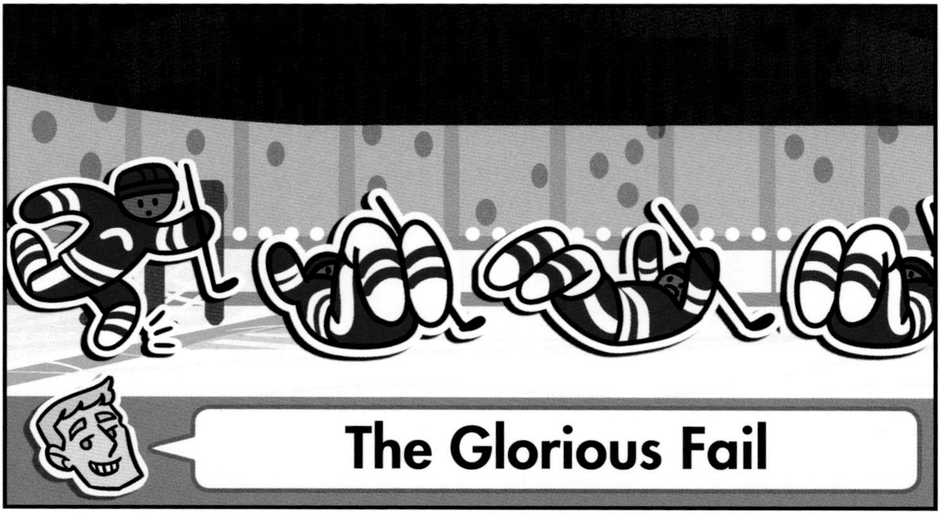
The Glorious Fail

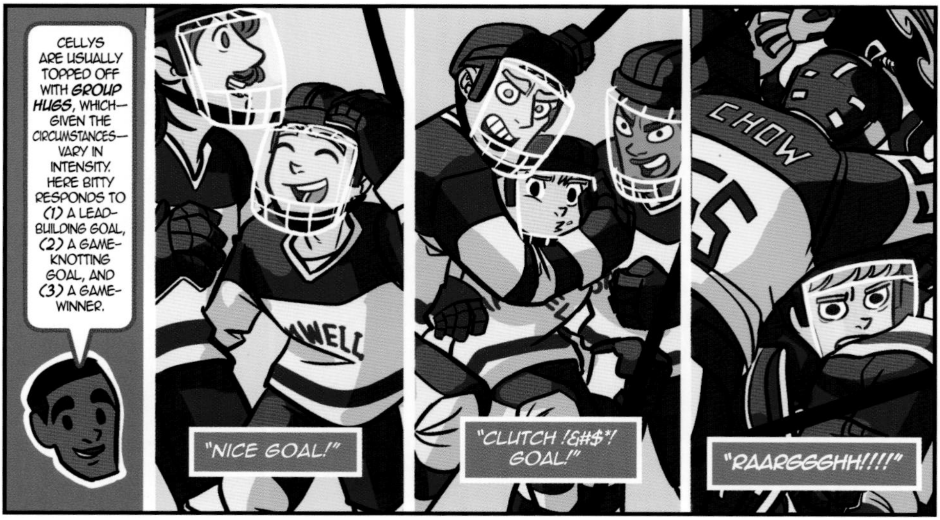
CELLYS ARE USUALLY TOPPED OFF WITH GROUP HUGS, WHICH—GIVEN THE CIRCUMSTANCES—VARY IN INTENSITY. HERE BITTY RESPONDS TO (1) A LEAD-BUILDING GOAL, (2) A GAME-KNOTTING GOAL, AND (3) A GAME-WINNER.
"NICE GOAL!"
"CLUTCH !&#$*! GOAL!"
CHOW
"RAARGGGHH!!!!"

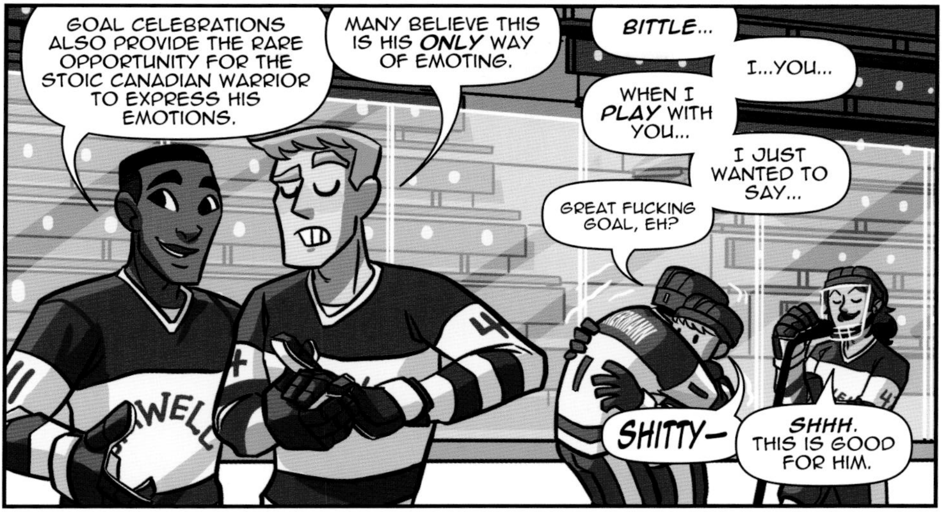
GOAL CELEBRATIONS ALSO PROVIDE THE RARE OPPORTUNITY FOR THE STOIC CANADIAN WARRIOR TO EXPRESS HIS EMOTIONS.
MANY BELIEVE THIS IS HIS *ONLY* WAY OF EMOTING.
BITTLE...
I...YOU...
WHEN I *PLAY* WITH YOU...
I JUST WANTED TO SAY...
GREAT FUCKING GOAL, EH?
SHITTY—
SHHH. THIS IS GOOD FOR HIM.

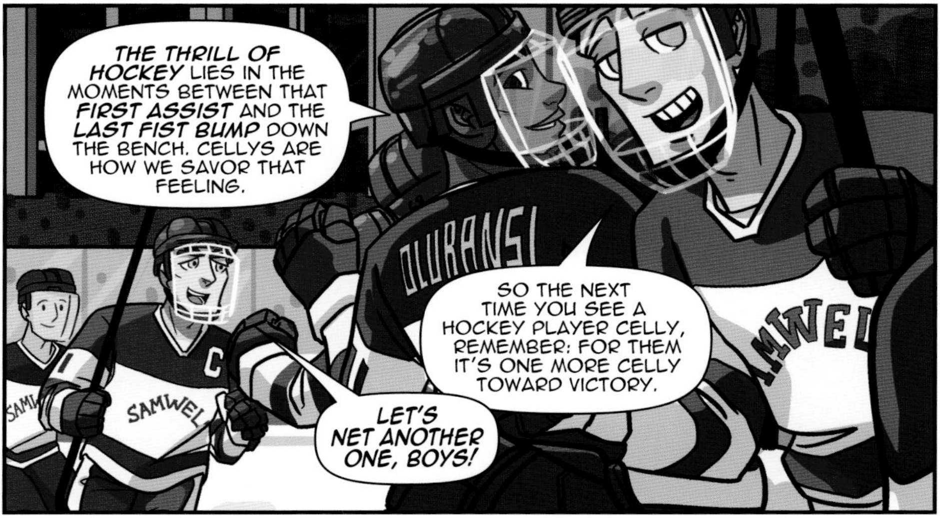
THE THRILL OF HOCKEY LIES IN THE MOMENTS BETWEEN THAT *FIRST ASSIST* AND THE *LAST FIST BUMP* DOWN THE BENCH. CELLYS ARE HOW WE SAVOR THAT FEELING.
OLURANSI
SO THE NEXT TIME YOU SEE A HOCKEY PLAYER CELLY, REMEMBER: FOR THEM IT'S ONE MORE CELLY TOWARD VICTORY.
LET'S NET ANOTHER ONE, BOYS!
SAMWEL

14.5

WINTER SCREW

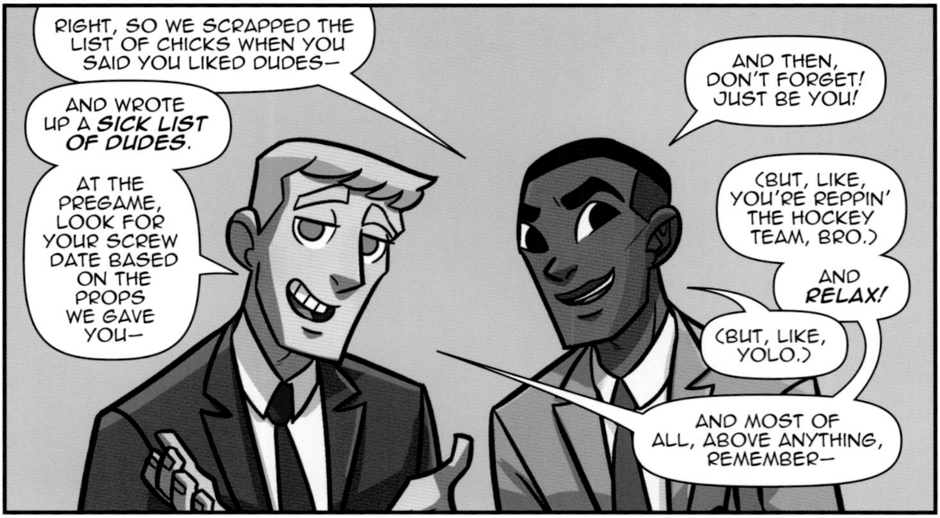

RIGHT, SO WE SCRAPPED THE LIST OF CHICKS WHEN YOU SAID YOU LIKED DUDES—
AND WROTE UP A **SICK LIST OF DUDES**.
AT THE PREGAME, LOOK FOR YOUR SCREW DATE BASED ON THE PROPS WE GAVE YOU—
AND THEN, DON'T FORGET! JUST BE YOU!
(BUT, LIKE, YOU'RE REPPIN' THE HOCKEY TEAM, BRO.)
AND **RELAX!**
(BUT, LIKE, YOLO.)
AND MOST OF ALL, ABOVE ANYTHING, REMEMBER—

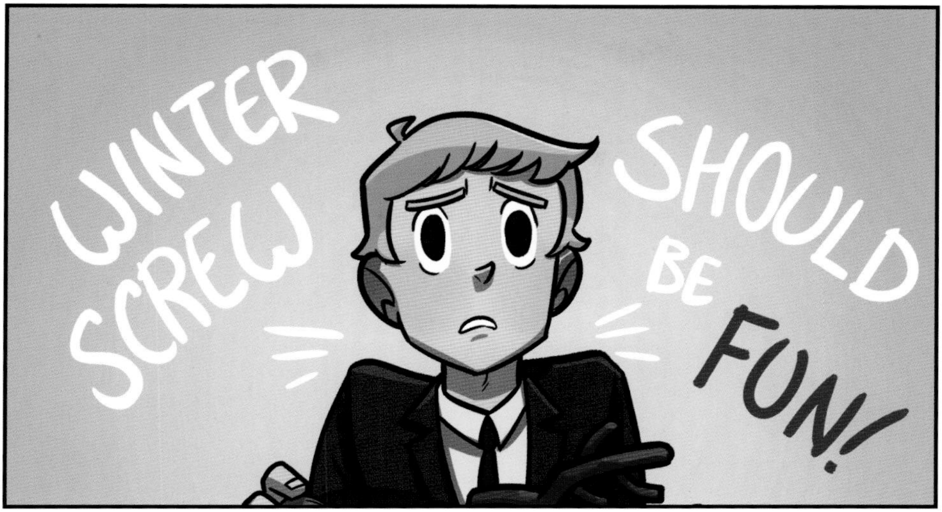
WINTER SCREW SHOULD BE FUN!

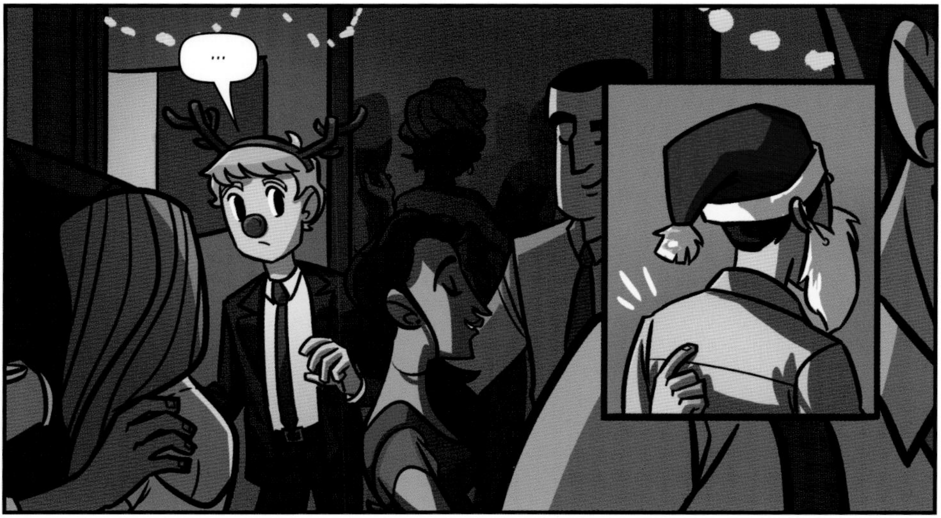
...

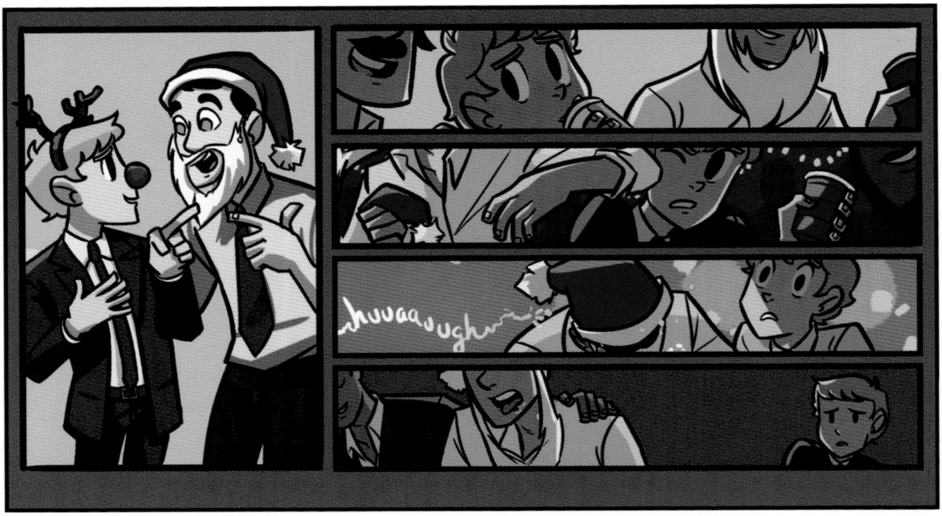
huuaaough

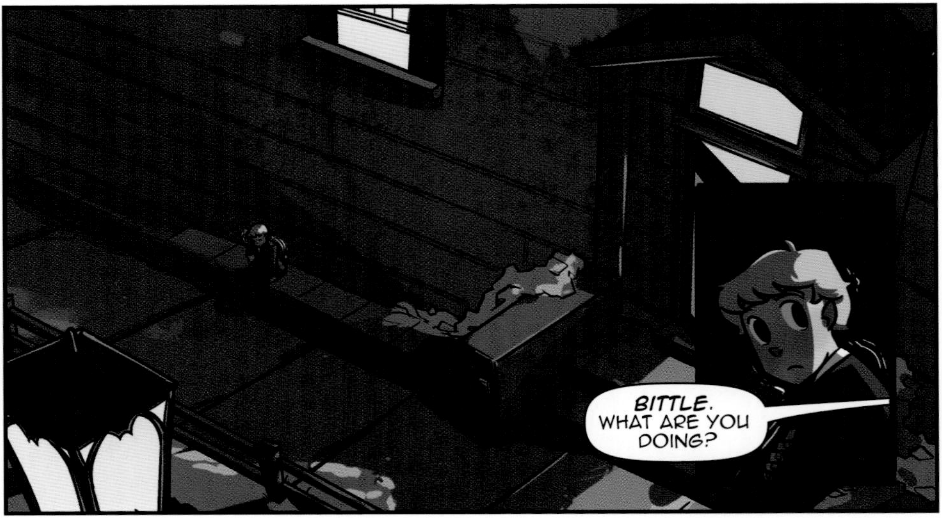
BITTLE. WHAT ARE YOU DOING?

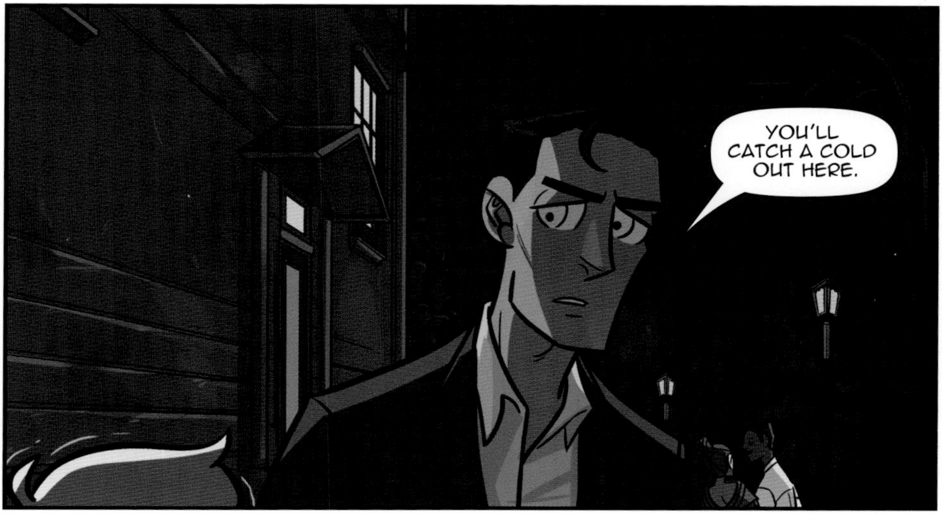
YOU'LL CATCH A COLD OUT HERE.

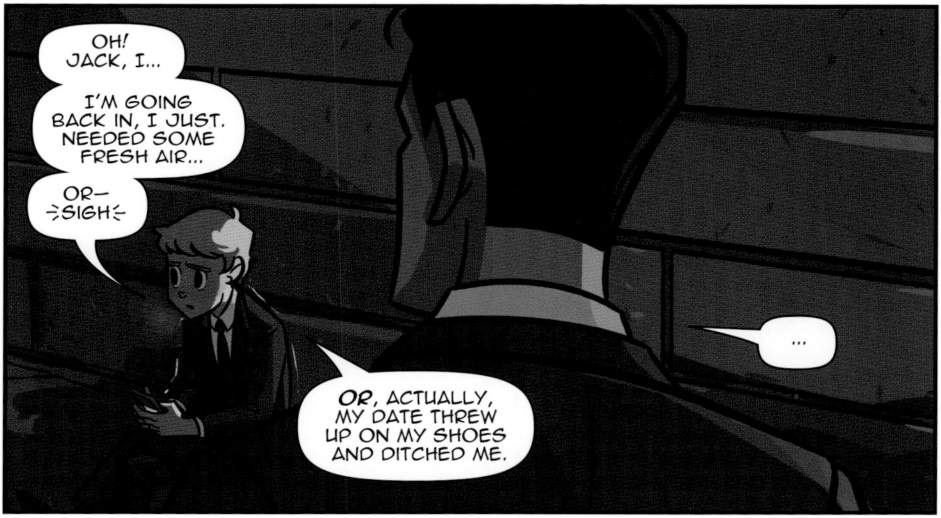
OH! JACK, I...
I'M GOING BACK IN, I JUST. NEEDED SOME FRESH AIR...
OR— ⇥SIGH⇤
...
OR, ACTUALLY, MY DATE THREW UP ON MY SHOES AND DITCHED ME.

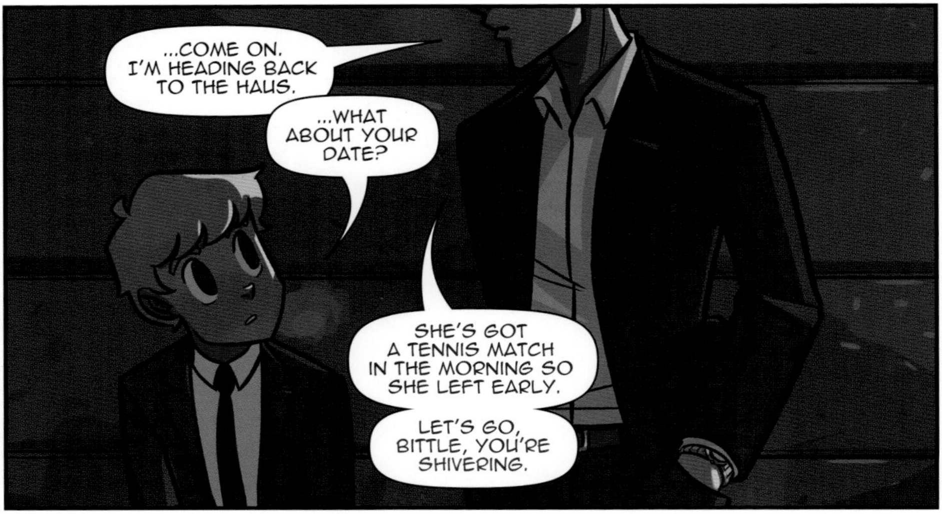
...COME ON. I'M HEADING BACK TO THE HAUS.
...WHAT ABOUT YOUR DATE?
SHE'S GOT A TENNIS MATCH IN THE MORNING SO SHE LEFT EARLY.
LET'S GO, BITTLE, YOU'RE SHIVERING.

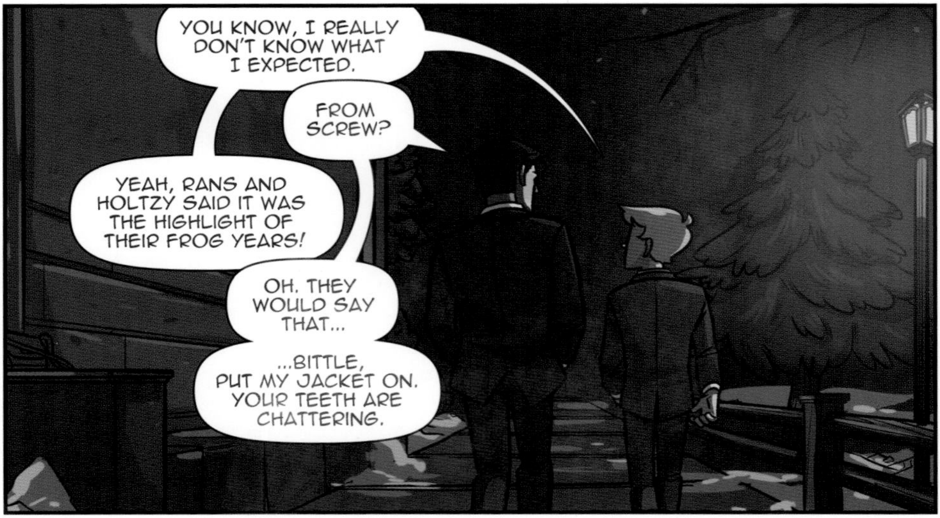
YOU KNOW, I REALLY DON'T KNOW WHAT I EXPECTED.
FROM SCREW?
YEAH, RANS AND HOLTZY SAID IT WAS THE HIGHLIGHT OF THEIR FROG YEARS!
OH. THEY WOULD SAY THAT...
...BITTLE, PUT MY JACKET ON. YOUR TEETH ARE CHATTERING.

SHITTY AND JACK'S DIBS

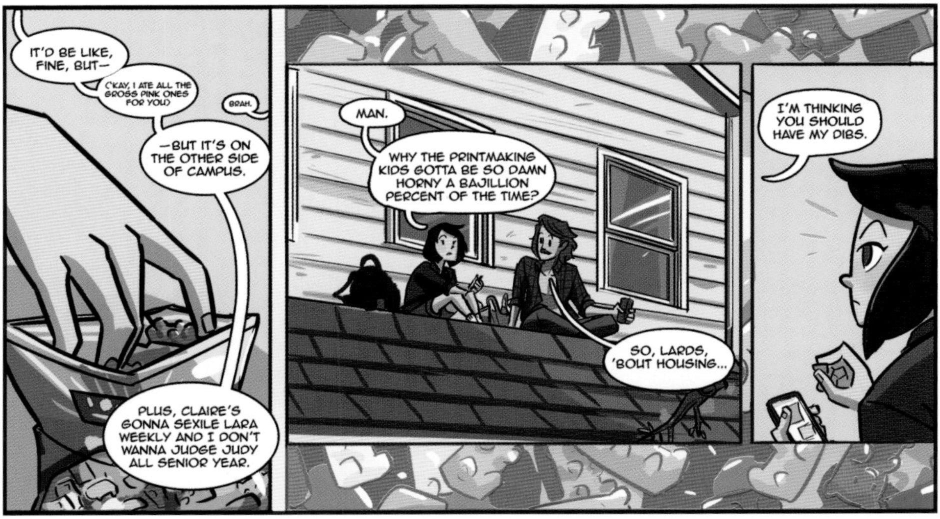

IT'D BE LIKE, FINE, BUT—
('KAY, I ATE ALL THE GROSS PINK ONES FOR YOU)
BRAH.
—BUT IT'S ON THE OTHER SIDE OF CAMPUS.
PLUS, CLAIRE'S GONNA SEXILE LARA WEEKLY AND I DON'T WANNA JUDGE JUDY ALL SENIOR YEAR.
MAN.
WHY THE PRINTMAKING KIDS GOTTA BE SO DAMN HORNY A BAJILLION PERCENT OF THE TIME?
SO, LARDS, 'BOUT HOUSING...
I'M THINKING YOU SHOULD HAVE MY DIBS.

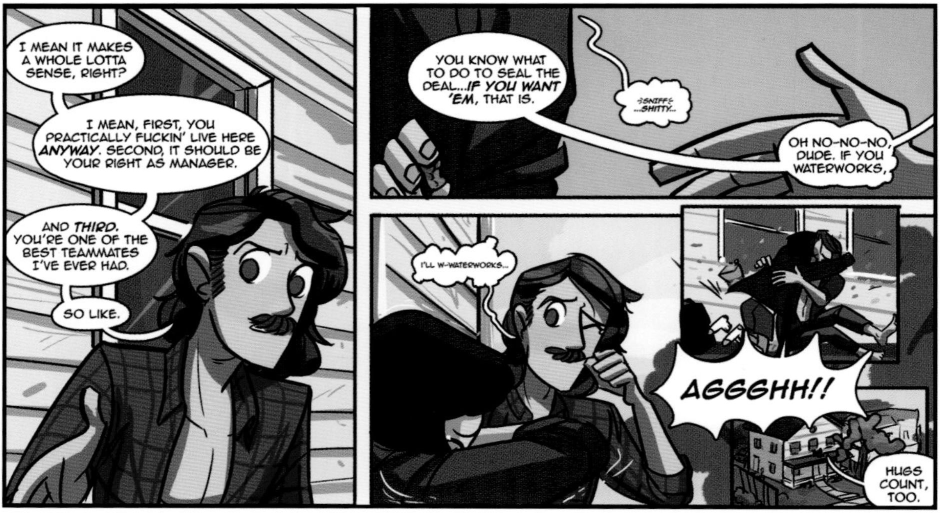
I MEAN IT MAKES A WHOLE LOTTA SENSE, RIGHT?
I MEAN, FIRST, YOU PRACTICALLY FUCKIN' LIVE HERE ANYWAY. SECOND, IT SHOULD BE YOUR RIGHT AS MANAGER.
AND THIRD. YOU'RE ONE OF THE BEST TEAMMATES I'VE EVER HAD.
SO LIKE.
YOU KNOW WHAT TO DO TO SEAL THE DEAL...IF YOU WANT 'EM, THAT IS.
SNIFF ...SHITTY...
OH NO-NO-NO, DUDE. IF YOU WATERWORKS,
I'LL W-WATERWORKS...
AGGGHH!!
HUGS COUNT, TOO.

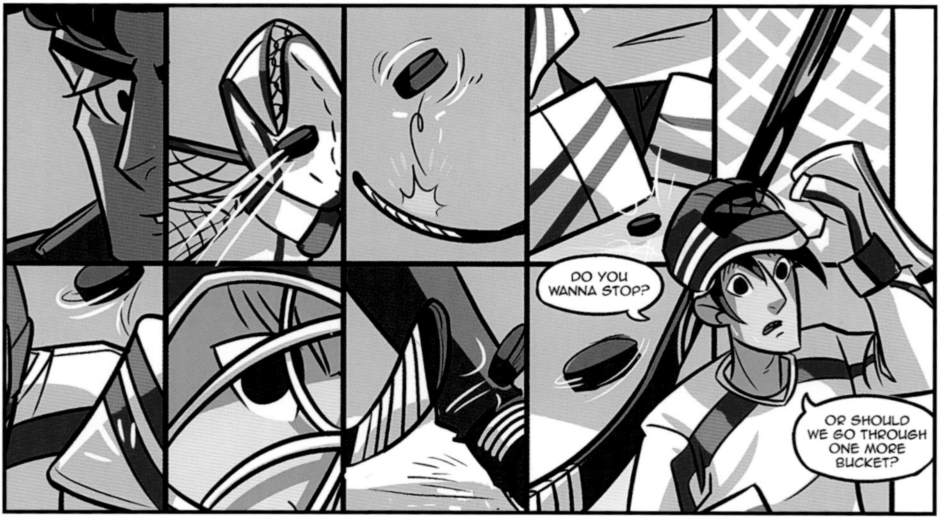
DO YOU WANNA STOP?
OR SHOULD WE GO THROUGH ONE MORE BUCKET?

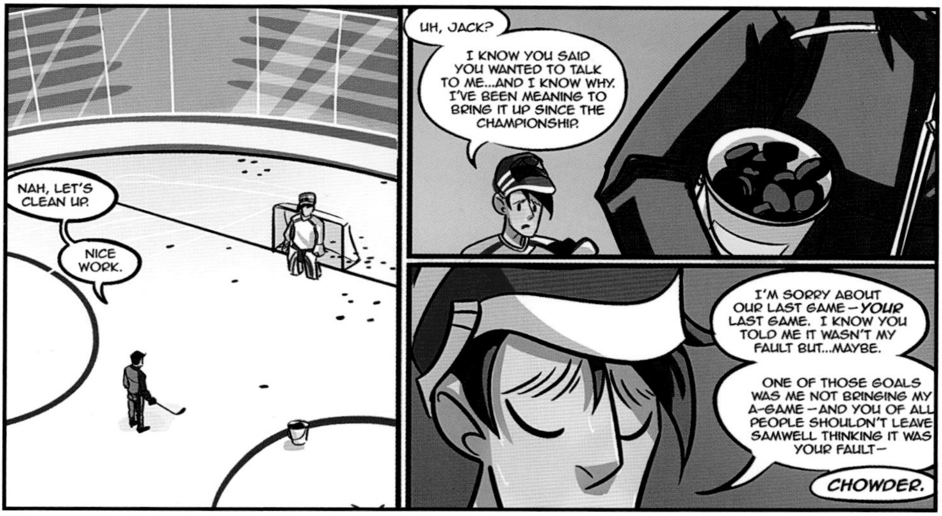
NAH, LET'S CLEAN UP.
NICE WORK.
UH, JACK?
I KNOW YOU SAID YOU WANTED TO TALK TO ME...AND I KNOW WHY. I'VE BEEN MEANING TO BRING IT UP SINCE THE CHAMPIONSHIP.
I'M SORRY ABOUT OUR LAST GAME—YOUR LAST GAME. I KNOW YOU TOLD ME IT WASN'T MY FAULT BUT...MAYBE.
ONE OF THOSE GOALS WAS ME NOT BRINGING MY A-GAME—AND YOU OF ALL PEOPLE SHOULDN'T LEAVE SAMWELL THINKING IT WAS YOUR FAULT—
CHOWDER.

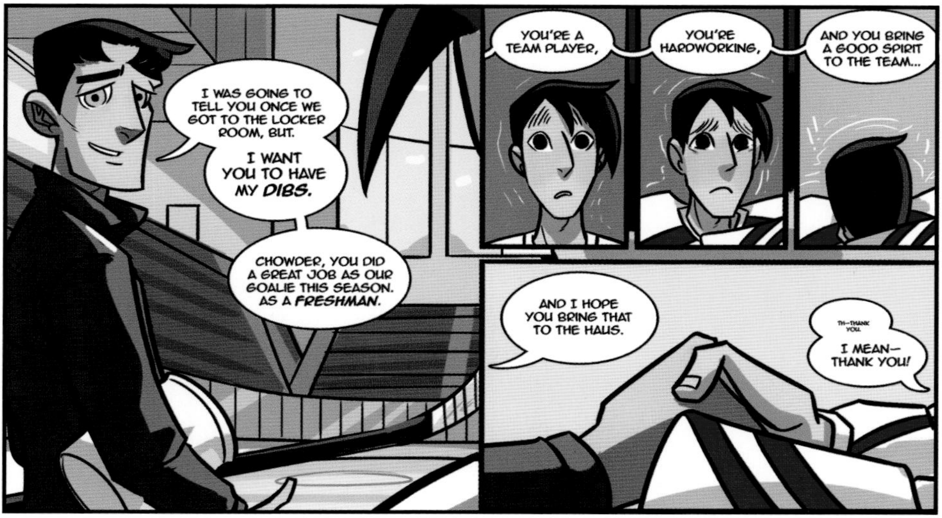
I WAS GOING TO TELL YOU ONCE WE GOT TO THE LOCKER ROOM, BUT.
I WANT YOU TO HAVE MY DIBS.
CHOWDER, YOU DID A GREAT JOB AS OUR GOALIE THIS SEASON. AS A FRESHMAN.
YOU'RE A TEAM PLAYER,
YOU'RE HARDWORKING,
AND YOU BRING A GOOD SPIRIT TO THE TEAM...
AND I HOPE YOU BRING THAT TO THE HAUS.
TH—THANK YOU.
I MEAN— THANK YOU!

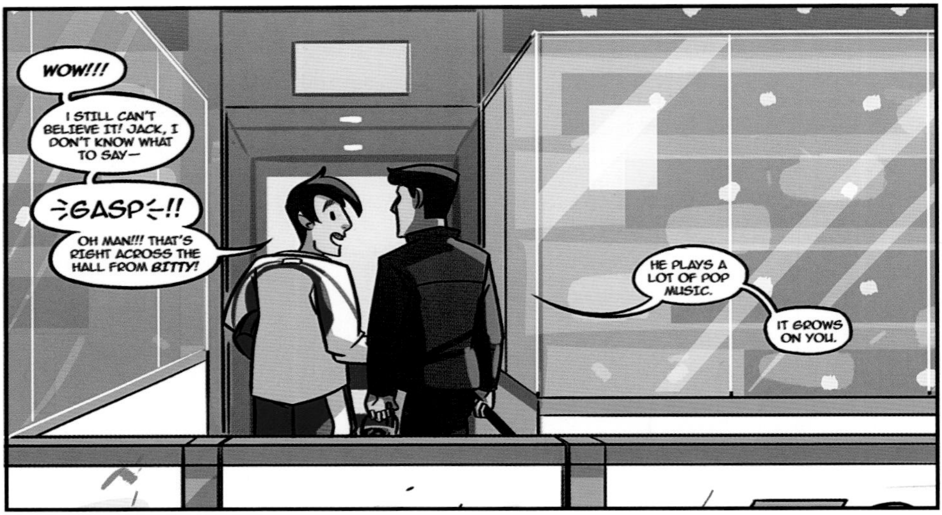
WOW!!!
I STILL CAN'T BELIEVE IT! JACK, I DON'T KNOW WHAT TO SAY—
GASP!!
OH MAN!!! THAT'S RIGHT ACROSS THE HALL FROM BITTY!
HE PLAYS A LOT OF POP MUSIC.
IT GROWS ON YOU.

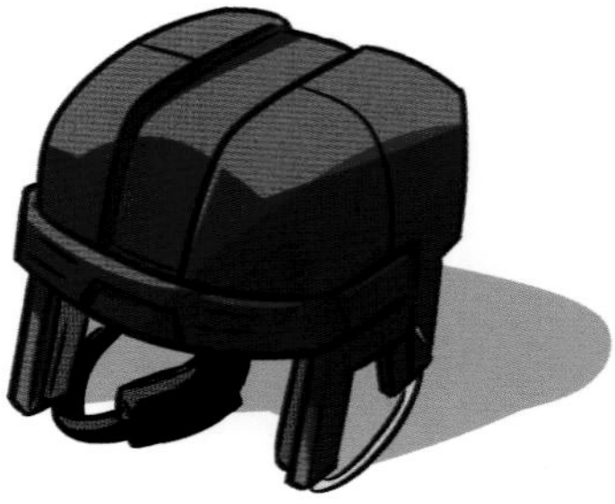

TWEETS

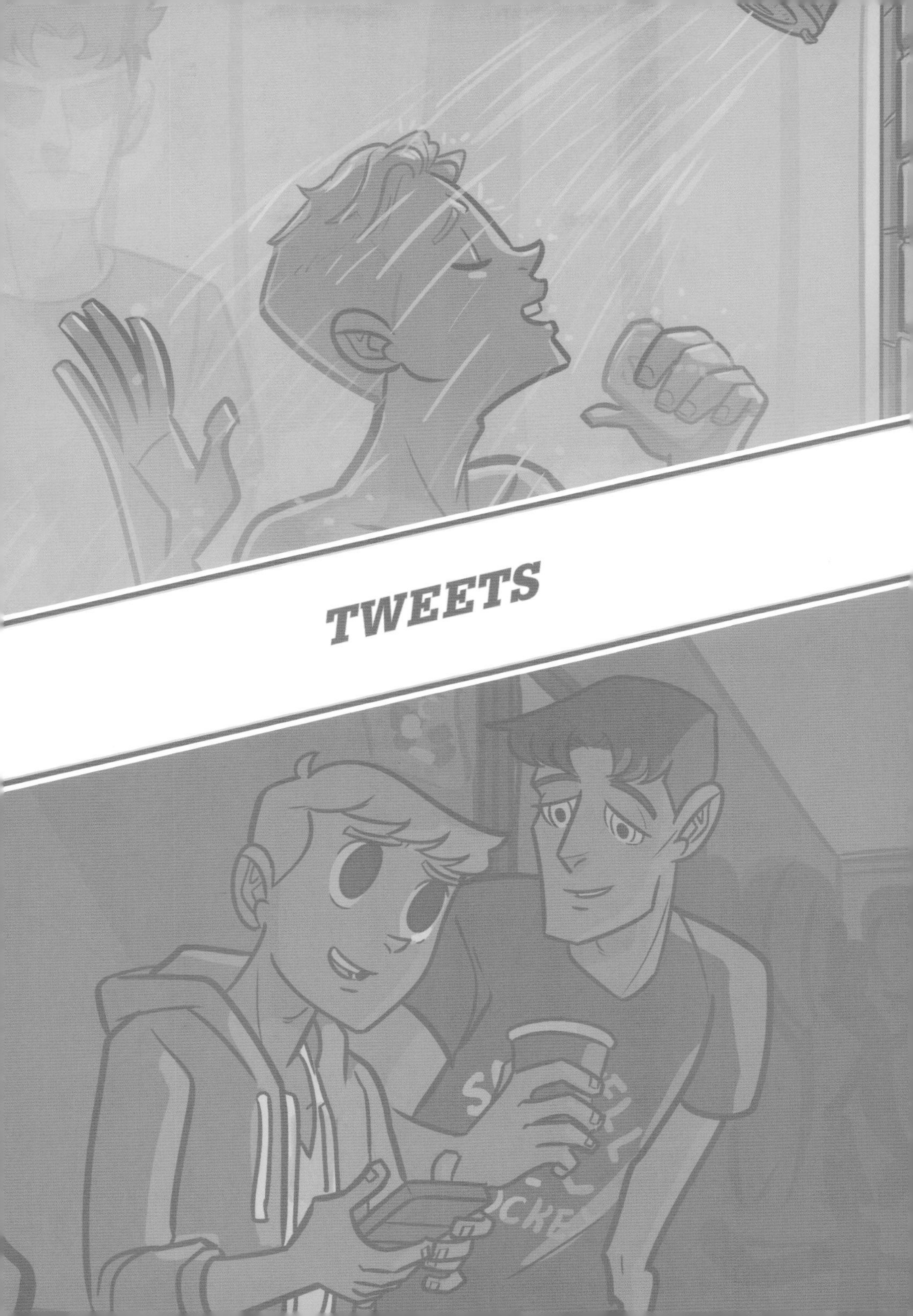

#HOCKEY

HEY, Y'ALL! Oh my gosh, you've worked through my vlog already? Well!! I hope you aren't planning to catch up on every single post I make on social media. Honestly, I talk about everything: what I'm baking, what homework I'm not doing, the lives and goings-ons of ALL of Samwell men's hockey, #TeamBreakfast, our games, what I #OverheardAtSamwell, and sometimes my hopes and dreams! Getting through all those tweets? *Lord*. Instead of having you read all my silly thoughts on pastries and every worry I've had about a teammate, I've found the essentials. . . . Maybe Jack was right, I do tweet a lot.

Also, that tweet I have about flirting and chirping . . . pay attention to that one! ⎯/✓ ♥

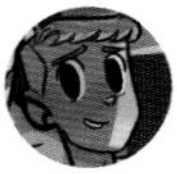

Eric Bittle @omgcheckplease · Tue, Jun 17, 2014 | 8:16 PM
Hey, y'all! Guess it's about time I started tweeting! But I feel like I'm just gonna tweet a whole bunch of pie recipes. #omgcheckplease

---

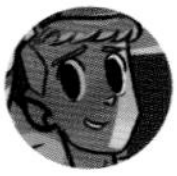

Eric Bittle @omgcheckplease · Tue, Jun 17, 2014 | 8:29 PM
I do love being at home, but Madison, GA can be a bit of a hot mess during these June months. How I miss the breeze off the Samwell River!

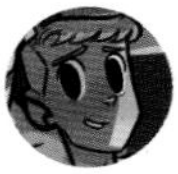

Eric Bittle @omgcheckplease · Tue, Jun 17, 2014 | 8:32 PM
And if it weren't obvious, I love being at home because of my kitchen. <3 <3 <3 Which makes me wonder how things at the Haus are going...

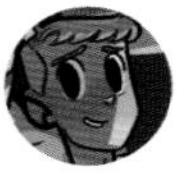

Eric Bittle @omgcheckplease · Mon, Jun 23, 2014 | 9:44 PM
Skyped Shitty today; he just got back from his dad's place in Boston—apparently there's an ultimatum to get rid of his flow by graduation?

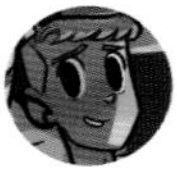

Eric Bittle @omgcheckplease · Thu, Jul 10, 2014 | 11:20 PM
Got a check-in text from Jack. What a good captain. :) It's crazy how your relationship with someone can change so much in a year.

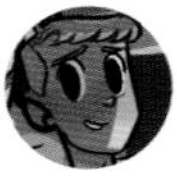

Eric Bittle @omgcheckplease · Tue, Jul 15, 2014 | 1:27 PM
FB chat w\ Chowder today: "lol those mini pies were great!! do you think you'll bake a lot when we get back to samwell?" oh, you sweet child.

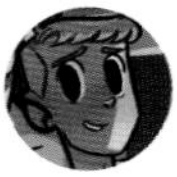

Eric Bittle @omgcheckplease · Wed, Jul 16, 2014 | 12:50 PM
ANYWAY I mention all this since I'm making a maple sugar crusted apple pie for Our Dear Captain's B-day & am testing out a recipe tonight!!!

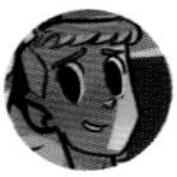

Eric Bittle @omgcheckplease · Tue, Jul 29, 2014 | 2:30 PM
THE SAMWELL 2014–2015 COURSE SCHEDULE IS OUT!! brb looking for courses about food \(~o~)/

Eric Bittle @omgcheckplease · Tue, Jul 29, 2014 | 2:45 PM

LARDO TEXT: "Bitty! WGSS120/HIST376 : Women, Food & American Culture!!" HOLY FUCKING SHIT.

Eric Bittle @omgcheckplease · Tue, Jul 29, 2014 | 9:32 PM

...So seniors get priority for 300-level history classes. I asked the boys via group text. The only class on food taught at Samwell. T_T

Eric Bittle @omgcheckplease · Tue, Jul 29, 2014 | 9:40 PM

I have to get in that class. I'm not above playing dirty. I'll bake a bribery pie. Wouldn't be my first.

Eric Bittle @omgcheckplease · Tue, Aug 5, 2014 | 7:04 PM

Please don't scare the freshmen. We can't make new ones.

Eric Bittle @omgcheckplease · Tue, Aug 5, 2014 | 7:08 PM

I worry immensely about my adopted son, the sweet baby Chowder. If the frogs' 1st Haus party is anything like mine, he might actually die.

Eric Bittle @omgcheckplease · Tue, Aug 12, 2014 | 2:44 PM

Finally ready for school! #newhaircut

Eric Bittle @omgcheckplease · Wed, Aug 13, 2014 | 10:50 PM
Haus Sweet Haus. :)

Eric Bittle @omgcheckplease · Wed, Aug 13, 2014 | 10:51 PM
First (Birthday) Pie of Sophomore Year
Maple Sugar Crusted Apple Pie
#BittleBakes

Eric Bittle @omgcheckplease · Thu, Aug 14, 2014 | 3:16 PM
Those curtains? Got em today with #MamaBittle. AND we threw
SO many things away. Lord, I can pay my tuition from recycling
those beer cans.

Eric Bittle @omgcheckplease · Mon, Aug 25, 2014 | 1:01 PM
Jack just told me the coaches might move practice to a slightly diff.
time...
"Which means you could take that Food & Culture Class?" 0_0

Eric Bittle @omgcheckplease · Mon, Aug 25, 2014 | 1:05 PM
"If you even get in that is"
Don't you even play games with my heart, Jack Zimmermann.

Eric Bittle @omgcheckplease · Mon, Aug 25, 2014 | 5:06 PM
"...We're all fucking sexy. Why the FUCK are we all single?"—Shitty.
I just stress baked a rhubarb over that same thought, Mr. Knight.

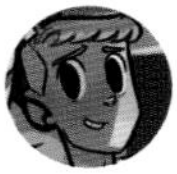

Eric Bittle @omgcheckplease · Mon, Aug 25, 2014 | 5:09 PM
Shitty just asked Jack why the fuck he's single.
As of tweet, Jack is still stuttering out a convoluted response.

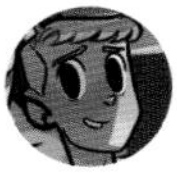

Eric Bittle @omgcheckplease · Mon, Aug 25, 2014 | 5:09 PM
"um" count: 6
"hockey" count: 18

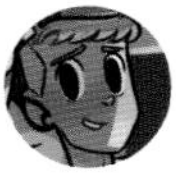

Eric Bittle @omgcheckplease · Tue, Aug 26, 2014 | 1:36 PM
Jack: ...Bittle, have you been transcribing all of our conversations on your phone?
Me: No.
(Yes.)

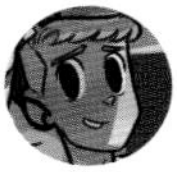

Eric Bittle @omgcheckplease · Wed, Aug 27, 2014 | 1:26 PM
—food class update—this morning, i walked into a senior history seminar with only my bribery pie and a dream. i left victorious.

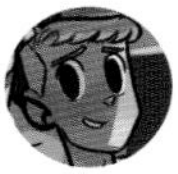

Eric Bittle @omgcheckplease · Wed, Aug 27, 2014 | 1:26 PM
Jack: I can't believe you bribed your way into my senior history seminar
Jack: are you tweeting what I'm saying

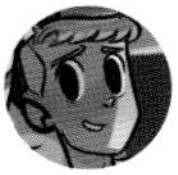

Eric Bittle @omgcheckplease · Thu, Aug 28, 2014 | 9:21 PM
I'm worried about our oven...It's stressing me out & I bake when I'm stressed but I can't bake if it's broken & i'm stressed out.

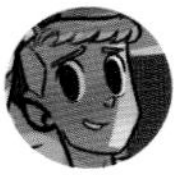

Eric Bittle @omgcheckplease · Tue, Sep 2, 2014 | 3:32 PM
DEX CAN FIX MY OVEN

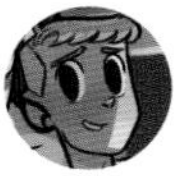

Eric Bittle @omgcheckplease · Tue, Sep 2, 2014 | 3:32 PM
*OUR OVEN WHATEVER WE ALL KNOW IT'S MINE

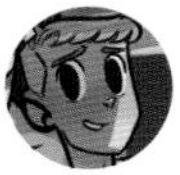

Eric Bittle @omgcheckplease · Tue, Sep 2, 2014 | 3:34 PM
Dex: As long as there isn't anyone chirping over my shoulder, sure I think I can
IF YOU'RE ASKING ME TO KILL NURSEY
I'LL DO IT

Eric Bittle @omgcheckplease · Tue, Sep 2, 2014 | 9:22 PM

Jack: you're starting a pie now?...We have practice and then Food Seminar in the morning.
Me: Why're you still surprised by my behavior?

Eric Bittle @omgcheckplease · Tue, Sep 2, 2014 | 9:26 PM

Jack just asked if I vlog about him.

Eric Bittle @omgcheckplease · Tue, Sep 2, 2014 | 9:28 PM

Hm. I don't know why I tweet and vlog about my teammates so much. I mean, people find it interesting. It's like an open diary.

Eric Bittle @omgcheckplease · Tue, Sep 2, 2014 | 9:30 PM

"When you get YouTube famous don't go out and chirp me all over the internet, eh? 'Night."

Eric Bittle @omgcheckplease · Wed, Sep 3, 2014 | 8:41 AM

OMFG I think the girl sitting across from us tried to take a picture of Jack on her phone. #LordHelpUs #WGSS120

Eric Bittle @omgcheckplease · Wed, Sep 3, 2014 | 8:48 AM

Phone Girl, please, you're not even being subtle. Try Tortoise Shell Glasses Girl's approach instead: blatantly staring at Jack dreamily.

Eric Bittle @omgcheckplease · Wed, Sep 3, 2014 | 3:31 PM

"The Haus is closer to my bio seminar than the dining halls..." Chowder stopped by just to see if I had baked anything. U_U

Eric Bittle @omgcheckplease · Wed, Sep 3, 2014 | 3:31 PM

"Bitty, when do you ever do homework?" Shut up and eat the damn pie.

Eric Bittle @omgcheckplease · Thu, Sep 4, 2014 | 10:06 AM

Why do I have class on a national holiday. #HappyBirthdayBeyonce

---

Eric Bittle @omgcheckplease · Thu, Sep 4, 2014 | 2:40 PM

Jack's thoughts on our Food Seminar: "Uuuh. I like it. It's interesting stuff. Yeah." Ladies and gentlemen he can hardly contain himself.

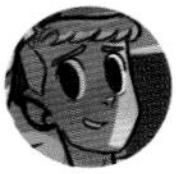

Eric Bittle @omgcheckplease · Sun, Sep 7, 2014 | 4:53 PM

Sorry...I was thinking about people leaving Samwell... Shitty has a bad habit of walking into rooms & going "OH BALLS, I'M GRADUATING."

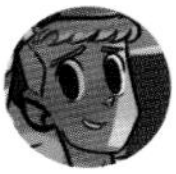

Eric Bittle @omgcheckplease · Thu, Sep 11, 2014 | 9:44 AM

Nursey & Dex are mature, intelligent young men. Yet when together: "stop it" "I'm not even touching you" "I said—NURSEY" "OW QUIT" "BITTY"

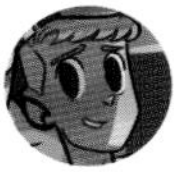

Eric Bittle @omgcheckplease · Thu, Sep 11, 2014 | 9:49 AM

And Chowder tries to interject but he's too nice and usually just gets hit in the face. Pray for these frogs, y'all.

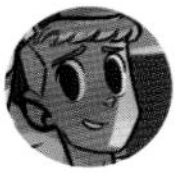

Eric Bittle @omgcheckplease · Sun, Sep 14, 2014 | 2:01 PM

Ha ha—have you ever accidentally called a teammate sweetheart <_<

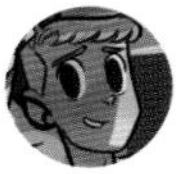

Eric Bittle @omgcheckplease · Sun, Sep 14, 2014 | 2:03 PM

I was brave enough to say I did it? But I'm not brave enough to say to whom I did it? ~_~

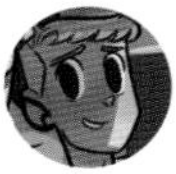

Eric Bittle @omgcheckplease · Wed, Sep 17, 2014 | 2:17 PM

Jack wants to start checking practice with me again. I already got hit really bad...why can't I just avoid checks until I graduate. ;~;

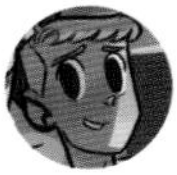

Eric Bittle @omgcheckplease · Fri, Sep 19, 2014 | 10:29 AM

Jack on the phone w/ his dad a while ago: french french french I'm with Bittle french french Bittle ha ha french french no...okay, bye. ._.?

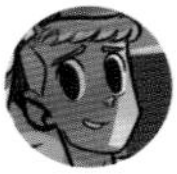

Eric Bittle @omgcheckplease · Sat, Sep 20, 2014 | 3:07 PM

My newborn goalie lamb Chowder came by looking for cookies. I started a batch right away.

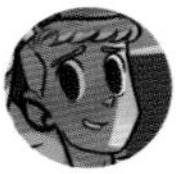

Eric Bittle @omgcheckplease · Sat, Sep 20, 2014 | 3:16 PM

"You know, people just give me stuff all the time? Dex gave me his jacket today because I said it was chilly." 0_0 He's just using me.

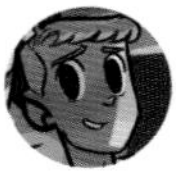

Eric Bittle @omgcheckplease · Sat, Sep 20, 2014 | 4:36 PM

Jack: how many of those tweets do you start with "oh my god y'all"?
He thinks he's so funny.

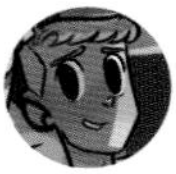

Eric Bittle @omgcheckplease · Sat, Sep 20, 2014 | 5:15 PM

Me: I'll stop tweeting when you quit teasing me
Jack: I guess you'll never stop tweeting
(This one.)

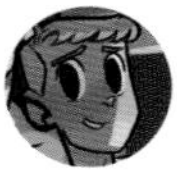

Eric Bittle @omgcheckplease · Sun, Sep 21, 2014 | 1:42 PM

Y'all...I'm still sore from getting checked a million times at 4 in the morning.U_U...Jack doesn't think it's early. –_–

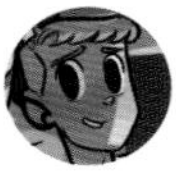

Eric Bittle @omgcheckplease · Sun, Sep 21, 2014 | 9:09 PM

I mean...I guess he doesn't have to help me...and I am getting better....

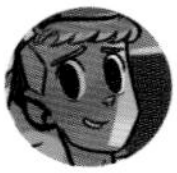

Eric Bittle @omgcheckplease · Mon, Sep 22, 2014 | 1:15 PM

I don't have *time* to date. My life's already filled up w/ school, hockey, baking, running a vlog & keeping these poor freshmen alive.

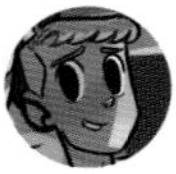

Eric Bittle @omgcheckplease · Mon, Sep 22, 2014 | 1:19 PM

Crushes are stressful. Dating is disappointing. Every relationship, you either break up or get married & then divorced. Pies can't hurt you.

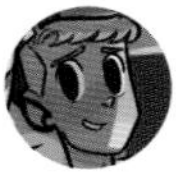

Eric Bittle @omgcheckplease · Mon, Sep 22, 2014 | 1:24 PM

...And then parents. "I'm sure you'll find a nice girl up there." >_<

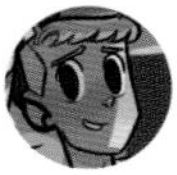

Eric Bittle @omgcheckplease · Tue, Sep 23, 2014 | 7:36 PM

Sitting in the Norris library with Jack. Trying to do an essay response for food class...and why am I tweeting under the table.

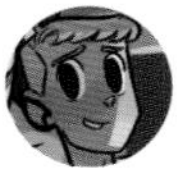

Eric Bittle @omgcheckplease · Tue, Sep 23, 2014 | 7:45 PM

oh god, so Jack just went to use the bathroom and tossed a note on my laptop. Yes I'm live-tweeting this; my life is not exciting.

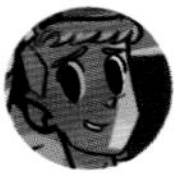

Eric Bittle @omgcheckplease · Tue, Sep 23, 2014 | 7:46 PM
it's in french OF COURSE. the girl in the corner of this reading room is looking at me like I'm an idiot. sorry, i'm giggling this is so stupid.

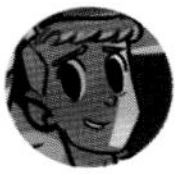

Eric Bittle @omgcheckplease · Tue, Sep 23, 2014 | 7:50 PM
translation: "write your essay response" oh Lord.

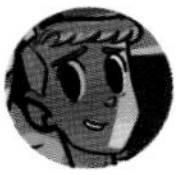

Eric Bittle @omgcheckplease · Tue, Sep 23, 2014 | 7:52 PM
Okay, he's back. I left a note on his backpack. I've never seen Jack have to stifle a laugh before. #NoteGameStrong

---

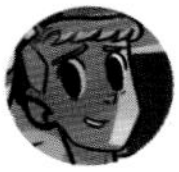

Eric Bittle @omgcheckplease · Fri, Oct 3, 2014 | 5:38 PM
Out on Lake Quad. Talking to Lardo about boys.

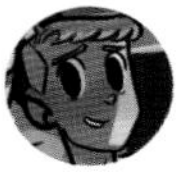

Eric Bittle @omgcheckplease · Fri, Oct 3, 2014 | 5:40 PM
Lardo: Boys are dumb.
Me: It's true; we are.
Lardo: Aren't I like, super eloquent.
Me: You're succinct and I like that.

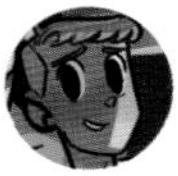

Eric Bittle @omgcheckplease · Fri, Oct 3, 2014 | 10:30 PM
You know how all people wear pants most of the time? Shitty's not most people all of the time.

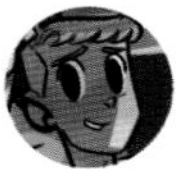

Eric Bittle @omgcheckplease · Sat, Oct 4, 2014 | 8:04 PM
Going to get froyo with a slightly baked Shitty and Lardo. #SamwellSuperBerry

---

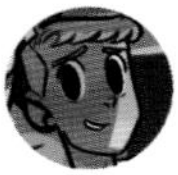

Eric Bittle @omgcheckplease · Sat, Oct 4, 2014 | 8:08 PM
& Jack if Shitty can drag him out of his room. We're out on the front lawn. Shitty's yelling at us from Jack's window. "HE'S PUTTING ON PANTS."

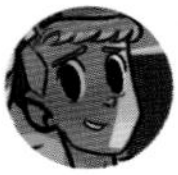

Eric Bittle @omgcheckplease · Sat, Oct 4, 2014 | 8:15 PM
From Jack's window—
Jack: Is Bittle going? If he tweets about this I'm taking his phone.
Lardo: bro hates your tweet game, bits.

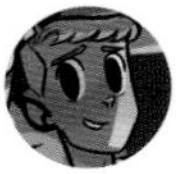

Eric Bittle @omgcheckplease · Sun, Oct 5, 2014 | 2:14 AM

how to use twitter

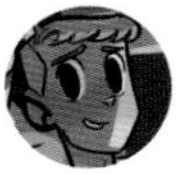

Eric Bittle @omgcheckplease · Sun, Oct 5, 2014 | 7:51 AM

I'm never deleting that last tweet. #youtried

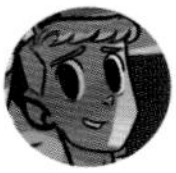

Eric Bittle @omgcheckplease · Sun, Oct 12, 2014 | 6:56 PM

Looking forward to: long bus rides w/ the boys
Not looking forward to: a marked increase in bathroom humor during long bus rides w/ the boys

---

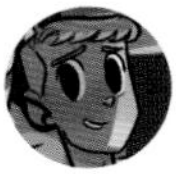

Eric Bittle @omgcheckplease · Sun, Oct 12, 2014 | 6:58 PM

You'd think there'd only be so many dirty jokes. But OH no! Never underestimate the humor of boys ages 18 to 23...And Lardo!

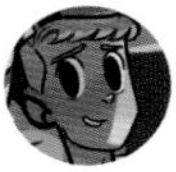

Eric Bittle @omgcheckplease · Tue, Oct 14, 2014 | 8:54 PM

Shitty: Dex, brah. If you grew your hair out you'd have some flamin' flow. Sick carroty lettuce, maaaan.
Dex: I cut my hair once a month.

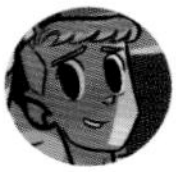

Eric Bittle @omgcheckplease · Wed, Oct 15, 2014 | 8:23 AM

Me: Jack! You wanna get a Pumpkin Spice Latte with me before class? :) :) :)
Jack: You shouldn't be drinking those.
Me: :(:(:(

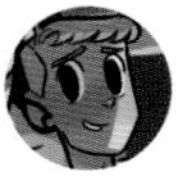

Eric Bittle @omgcheckplease · Wed, Oct 15, 2014 | 9:11 AM

Dragging Jack to Annie's before class. Without caffeine I am not a southern gentleman.

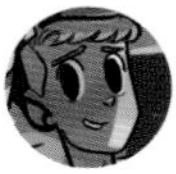

Eric Bittle @omgcheckplease · Wed, Oct 15, 2014 | 9:32 AM

OMFG few things are funnier than watching Jack guess who's playing on the radio in here. I can't breathe.

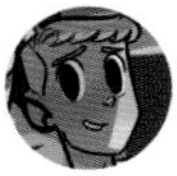

Eric Bittle @omgcheckplease · Wed, Oct 15, 2014 | 9:35 AM

TOO HARD TO TWEET. He keeps guessing TAYLOR SWIFT. HELP

Eric Bittle @omgcheckplease · Wed, Oct 15, 2014 | 9:41 AM

Jack: It's way too easy to make you laugh. Make sure you tweet that.

Eric Bittle @omgcheckplease · Fri, Oct 17, 2014 | 8:09 AM

Getting called into Coach Hall's office is like being sent to the principal...Let's get this over with...

Eric Bittle @omgcheckplease · Fri, Oct 17, 2014 | 8:12 AM

...I didn't have the best practice today. You can't throw someone off a team after one awful practice, right?...ugh.

Eric Bittle @omgcheckplease · Mon, Oct 20, 2014 | 6:50 PM

Our final for Food Class will involve creating a dish from an old recipe and thus:
Jack:...I might need your help.
>:)

Eric Bittle @omgcheckplease · Mon, Oct 20, 2014 | 9:15 PM

Chowder: we tried to get Nursey to take intro programming with us!
Dex: he said he's more of a "poetry guy."
Dex's eye roll was AUDIBLE.

Eric Bittle @omgcheckplease · Tue, Oct 21, 2014 | 10:20 AM

Chirping and flirting are variants on the same idea.

Eric Bittle @omgcheckplease · Thu, Oct 23, 2014 | 8:41 AM

Oh, okay, I think Nursey's trying to set Dex up with one of his friends from Andover for a screw date or something.

Eric Bittle @omgcheckplease · Thu, Oct 23, 2014 | 8:43 AM

Nursey: She does experimental theater & makes her own clothes. Sick, riiiight?
Chowder: wow!
Dex: That entire sentence was frustrating.

Eric Bittle @omgcheckplease · Fri, Oct 24, 2014 | 7:01 PM

Shitty: WHELP. My Last First-Game at Samwell Ever is next week.

Eric Bittle @omgcheckplease · Mon, Oct 27, 2014 | 10:05 AM
text: "stay hydrated this week"
Jack Zimmermann is a special combination of thoughtful and
awkward.

Eric Bittle @omgcheckplease · Tue, Oct 28, 2014 | 9:13 AM
Hockey is important, but MUST we have a game on Halloween???
I'm gonna miss SO many trick-or-treating babies in SO many
pumpkin costumes.

Eric Bittle @omgcheckplease · Fri, Oct 31, 2014 | 1:43 PM
#naptime Oh no...This is what dorms are for...
#SweetBabyChowder

Eric Bittle @omgcheckplease · Fri, Oct 31, 2014 | 2:35 PM
I swear I'm going to get rid of that couch before I graduate...it's
seen the worst of humanity.

Eric Bittle @omgcheckplease · Fri, Oct 31, 2014 | 4:27 PM
Lardo: sup boys
Lardo: wreck shit tonight (^o^)/
~*best manager*~

Eric Bittle @omgcheckplease · Fri, Oct 31, 2014 | 4:49 PM
After this I'm putting away my phone. Thanks for all the support!!
#SamwellMensHockey #LetsGoBoys

Eric Bittle @omgcheckplease · Fri, Oct 31, 2014 | 9:15 PM

Samwell 3-1!! Samwell Halloween 2014!

Eric Bittle @omgcheckplease · Mon, Nov 3, 2014 | 1:07 PM

Nursey's so cool, but then he drops a whole plate of pasta on some poor bio major in the dhall and then I remember he's just a frog.

Eric Bittle @omgcheckplease · Mon, Nov 3, 2014 | 11:08 PM

I was falling asleep until Jack shouted "Shits! Sleep in your OWN BED" and then several words in French.

Eric Bittle @omgcheckplease · Mon, Nov 3, 2014 | 11:13 PM

(Shitty just shrieked "OW." Jack's laughing.)
(Oh my goodness, how are we a functioning hockey team.)

Eric Bittle @omgcheckplease · Tue, Nov 4, 2014 | 8:11 PM

At the library with The Captain.

Eric Bittle @omgcheckplease · Tue, Nov 4, 2014 | 10:02 PM

Jack: You only tweeted twice while we were working, Bittle. That's a record.
Jack's Chirp Game's Strong.

Eric Bittle @omgcheckplease · Tue, Nov 4, 2014 | 10:04 PM

(To be fair, it's hard to goof off when you're in Jack's peripheral vision.)

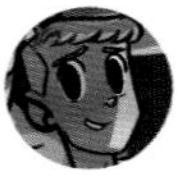

Eric Bittle @omgcheckplease · Tue, Nov 4, 2014 | 10:07 PM
Jack wants to walk past Faber.
Taking the long way back to the #HausSweetHaus.

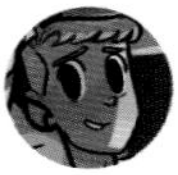

Eric Bittle @omgcheckplease · Mon, Nov 10, 2014 | 8:01 PM
Things I Talk to My Father About: — My Ice Time — My Diet ("More Protein") — My Stats — If I'm feeling OK/"toughin it out" — Jack Zimmermann

---

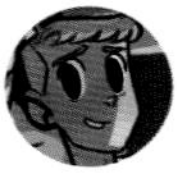

Eric Bittle @omgcheckplease · Mon, Nov 10, 2014 | 8:03 PM
...You know, I should be happy. He actually cares abt something I'm doing. He's even watching more hockey & listens to WSMC for our games.

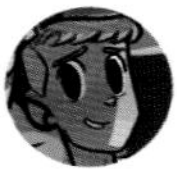

Eric Bittle @omgcheckplease · Mon, Nov 10, 2014 | 8:05 PM
And he asks about Jack because...well, my father LOVES sports. He's just as fascinated as everyone else about what team Jack'll choose.

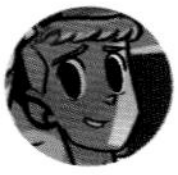

Eric Bittle @omgcheckplease · Thu, Nov 13, 2014 | 8:28 AM
There are people who sit on Lake Quad benches? And then there's Nursey. "CHILL. Why would we neglect this obscene pile of leaves? Man."

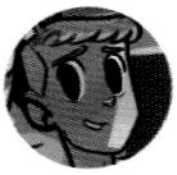

Eric Bittle @omgcheckplease · Thu, Nov 13, 2014 | 2:50 PM
Do you ever think about being with someone but realize it's impossible and then get really sad so you bake a pie instead.

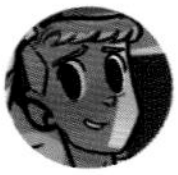

Eric Bittle @omgcheckplease · Thu, Nov 13, 2014 | 3:00 PM
(I tweet a lot abt being single, but I'm OK, really. I'm on a great team w/ all my best friends + I go to a wonderful school. I'm thankful.)

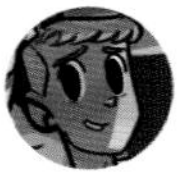

Eric Bittle @omgcheckplease · Thu, Nov 13, 2014 | 3:01 PM
(I wish I could tell high school Eric Bittle all of this. It gets so much better.)

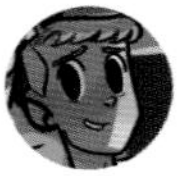

Eric Bittle @omgcheckplease · Thu, Nov 13, 2014 | 9:21 PM
Cleaning the kitchen while listening to Jack talk about the nuances of power plays. :)

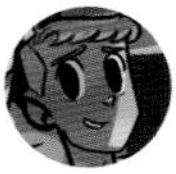

Eric Bittle @omgcheckplease · Sun, Nov 16, 2014 | 2:40 PM
Getting texts from Jack Zimmermann himself who is sitting in a room mere FEET away from mine.

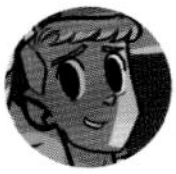

Eric Bittle @omgcheckplease · Sun, Nov 16, 2014 | 2:40 PM
Jack: we need to cook for class :/

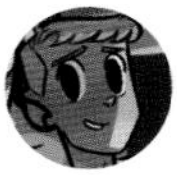

Eric Bittle @omgcheckplease · Sun, Nov 16, 2014 | 2:42 PM
Jack: we can go to stop & shop today. have a skype call with a GM @ 6. can we go before then

---

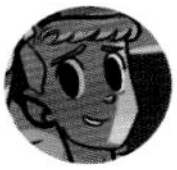

Eric Bittle @omgcheckplease · Sun, Nov 16, 2014 | 2:46 PM
Jack's Sunday To-Do List: (1) Negotiate Multi-Million Dollar NHL Contracts (2) Go Grocery Shopping with Bittle

---

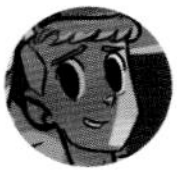

Eric Bittle @omgcheckplease · Tue, Nov 25, 2014 | 6:33 PM
quick nursey or dex for a piggyback ride race!! shitty is on the other side of river quad officiating!!

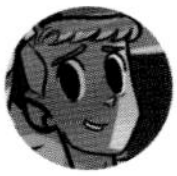

Eric Bittle @omgcheckplease · Tue, Nov 25, 2014 | 6:34 PM
okay wish us luck!!!!

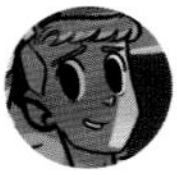

Eric Bittle @omgcheckplease · Tue, Nov 25, 2014 | 6:40 PM
we lost. :(

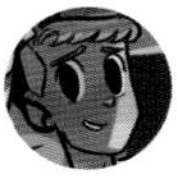

Eric Bittle @omgcheckplease · Tue, Nov 25, 2014 | 6:42 PM
BUT Dex tripped over the sidewalk and he and Chowder went careening into half the women's volleyball team i am still laughing

---

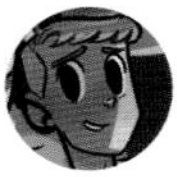

Eric Bittle @omgcheckplease · Tue, Nov 25, 2014 | 6:43 PM
chowder is mortified he keeps asking the same girl if she's okay (they were both in the same pile of leaves for a second there)

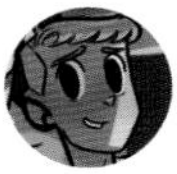

Eric Bittle @omgcheckplease · Tue, Nov 25, 2014 | 10:59 PM
Chowder Text: "I HAVE A DATE!!!!!!!!...(FOR SCREW!!!!!!!!)" Ransom and Holster work quickly.

Eric Bittle @omgcheckplease · Fri, Nov 28, 2014 | 1:55 AM
"Hockey players baking. My brother won't let me live this down."
So that happened. Dex w/ the asst. Happy Thanksgiving!! (Y'all!)
#Hausgiving.

Eric Bittle @omgcheckplease · Sat, Nov 29, 2014 | 9:40 AM
What is homework? What is finals? -_-! I'd like to pour one out for
my GPA this semester.

Eric Bittle @omgcheckplease · Sat, Nov 29, 2014 | 9:48 AM
Transcribing the following interaction across the hall:
Jack: get the @$% out my room SHITS
Shitty: good morning man it's 9:30 you slept in

Eric Bittle @omgcheckplease · Sat, Nov 29, 2014 | 9:59 AM
[5 min. of Jack & Shitty talking quietly]...[10 sec. of Shitty laughing
uproariously]...[3 sec. of Jack chuckling]

Eric Bittle @omgcheckplease · Tue, Dec 2, 2014 | 10:27 AM
RIP My GPA. Did y'all know I was taking a calc course this
semester? I apparently didn't either.

Eric Bittle @omgcheckplease · Tue, Dec 2, 2014 | 1:46 PM
I was freaking out to Jack about finals and he just looked at me
and said "17."

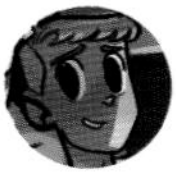

Eric Bittle @omgcheckplease · Tue, Dec 2, 2014 | 2:59 PM
Jack: That's the number of pies you baked in September. In case you were wondering where your time went. #ChirpGameStrong

---

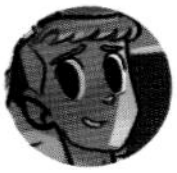

Eric Bittle @omgcheckplease · Sat, Dec 6, 2014 | 11:45 PM
It's #SamwellWinterScrew. There's a lot of things I want to say right now, but it's raining, and I told my date I was going to the restroom 10 minutes ago.

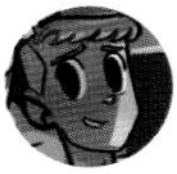

Eric Bittle @omgcheckplease · Sat, Dec 6, 2014 | 11:52 PM
And though opinions vary among the #SamwellMensHockey team, let the record show: Jack Zimmermann is not a terrible dancer. #SamwellWinterScrew

---

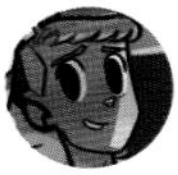

Eric Bittle @omgcheckplease · Sunday, Dec 7, 2014 | 1:57 PM
Things I'll miss next year: hearing the aftermath of Shitty barging into Jack's room in the mornings.

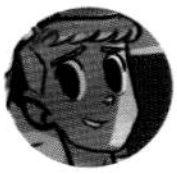

Eric Bittle @omgcheckplease · Sunday, Dec 7, 2014 | 1:59 PM
Shitty: DEETS DEETS DEETS DEETS WINTERSCREW??
Jack: ...I have no deets, man.

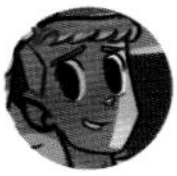

Eric Bittle @omgcheckplease · Sunday, Dec 7, 2014 | 2:03 PM
Shitty: don't give me any of that dumbass zimmermanns don't kiss and tell bullshit.
Jack: get out. OF MY BED

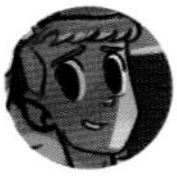

Eric Bittle @omgcheckplease · Sunday, Dec 7, 2014 | 2:11 PM
Shitty: no one will do this with you in the NHL
Shitty: shhhh don't fight ow ow ow
Shitty: why do you resist my snuggles

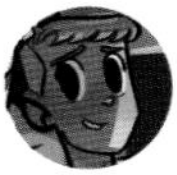

Eric Bittle @omgcheckplease · Sunday, Dec 7, 2014 | 7:06 PM
Dex's expression 60% of the time is "how do these people exist"

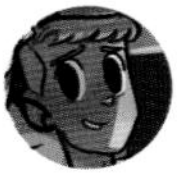

Eric Bittle @omgcheckplease · Sunday, Dec 7, 2014 | 9:42 PM
Ransom: it's reading week
Holster: yup gotta study
Ransom: how many kegsters can we throw
Holster: probably 9

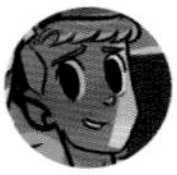

Eric Bittle @omgcheckplease · Sunday, Dec 7, 2014 | 9:44 PM
(After I started complaining)
Ransom: My dear Bits. If you're drunk when you're studying, all you have to do is take the test drunk.

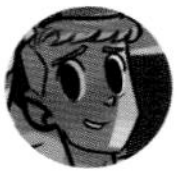

Eric Bittle @omgcheckplease · Tue, Dec 9, 2014 | 10:40 PM
Jack finished his essay for our history seminar already. HOW????

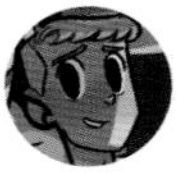

Eric Bittle @omgcheckplease · Tue, Dec 9, 2014 | 10:43 PM
Jack: I'm sure you'd be done too if you had tweeted it.
Jack: Is that an option?
Jack Zimmermann: :^)

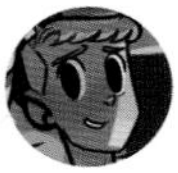

Eric Bittle @omgcheckplease · Tue, Dec 9, 2014 | 10:47 PM
I try to prepare myself for Jack Zimmermann's chirping but I am never ready.

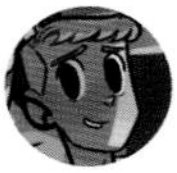

Eric Bittle @omgcheckplease · Tue, Dec 9, 2014 | 10:50 PM
He's so happy with himself right now. And Jack doesn't have that many expressions.

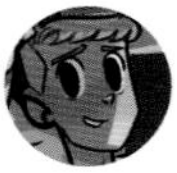

Eric Bittle @omgcheckplease · Fri, Dec 12, 2014 | 12:13 PM
I'm going to throw out that couch before I graduate.

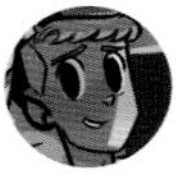

Eric Bittle @omgcheckplease · Fri, Dec 12, 2014 | 4:38 PM
Apparently Jack is in "Procrastinate by Bothering Bittle Mode." I'm not a fan.

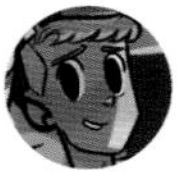

Eric Bittle @omgcheckplease · Fri, Dec 12, 2014 | 4:39 PM
Doesn't he have important hockey related activities to attend to???

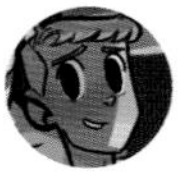

Eric Bittle @omgcheckplease · Fri, Dec 12, 2014 | 4:42 PM
Jack: what are you blogging about
Jack: is that the camera you use
Jack: oh wow you write a script

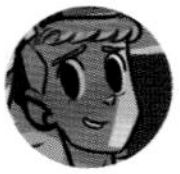

Eric Bittle @omgcheckplease · Fri, Dec 12, 2014 | 4:44 PM
Jack: what're you texting
shows him tweets
Jack: I said "where'd you get that camera" not "is that the camera you use." Come on, Bittle.

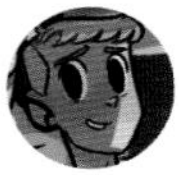

Eric Bittle @omgcheckplease · Fri, Dec 12, 2014 | 4:46 PM
Give this boy back to Montreal.

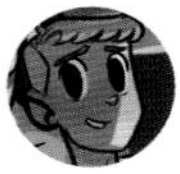

Eric Bittle @omgcheckplease · Fri, Dec 12, 2014 | 11:25 PM
Holster: KEGSTER
Ransom: TOMORROW
Holster: THE HAUS
Ransom: WE INVITED 1000 PEOPLE ON FACEBOOK.....#EPIKEGSTER

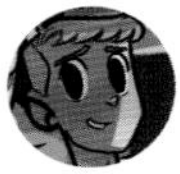

Eric Bittle @omgcheckplease · Fri, Dec 12, 2014 | 11:25 PM
D:...I'm just...#Terrified.

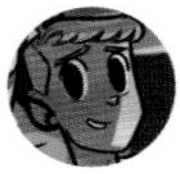

Eric Bittle @omgcheckplease · Sat, Dec 13, 2014 | 8:05 PM
Rans and Holster have an excel sheet for this kegster. I don't know what's on it but its very existence scares me.

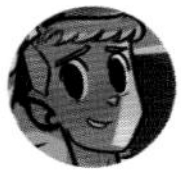

Eric Bittle @omgcheckplease · Sat, Dec 13, 2014 | 8:09 PM
If I do have a good time it'll be thanks to whatever Shitty and Lardo ARE BREWING IN OUR BATHTUB.

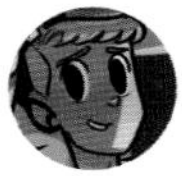

Eric Bittle @omgcheckplease · Sat, Dec 13, 2014 | 8:10 PM
Me: what're y'all making in the tub?
Shitty: kegster punch
Me: what're y'all making the frogs do?
Lardo: kegster chores

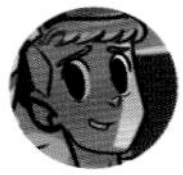

Eric Bittle @omgcheckplease · Sat, Dec 13, 2014 | 11:05 PM
Have you ever had 40 people walk into your house at once. #Epikegster

---

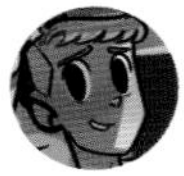

Eric Bittle @omgcheckplease · Sat, Dec 13, 2014 | 11:28 PM
[a wild Jack Zimmermann appears]

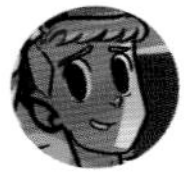

Eric Bittle @omgcheckplease · Sat, Dec 13, 2014 | 11:31 PM
Me: *talks to senior hockey captain so he won't be an awkward wallflower at #Epikegster*
Senior Hockey Captain: *seems grateful*

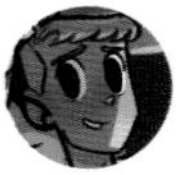

Eric Bittle @omgcheckplease · Sat, Dec 13, 2014 | 11:51 PM

Jack: I've only experienced one #EpiKegster
Jack: it took up two issues of the Swallow
Jack: no I'm not kidding

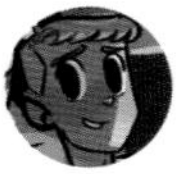

Eric Bittle @omgcheckplease · Sun, Dec 14, 2014 | 12:14 AM

Shitty: JACK ZIMMERMANN HAVING FUN AT A COLLEGE PARTY
Shitty: IT'S AN #EPIKEGSTERMAS MIRACLE

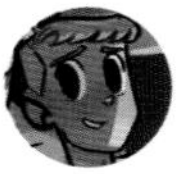

Eric Bittle @omgcheckplease · Sun, Dec 14, 2014 | 12:28 AM

"Oh my fucking GOD that's FUCKING Kent Parson!" —Some Drunk Lax Bro at #EpiKegster (probably).

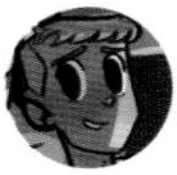

Eric Bittle @omgcheckplease · Sun, Dec 14, 2014 | 12:28 AM

No, sweetheart, that's Jack Zimmermann. #Bless...But. hmm. Should I be worried about Nursey crowdsurfing?

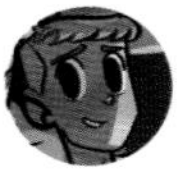

Eric Bittle @omgcheckplease · Sun, Dec 14, 2014 | 12:50 AM

Oh. It was Kent Parson!!

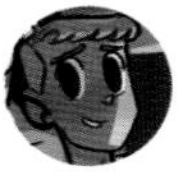

Eric Bittle @omgcheckplease · Sun, Dec 14, 2014 | 1:07 AM

lord, I'm getting starstruck

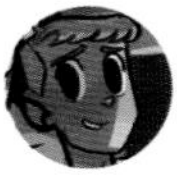

Eric Bittle @omgcheckplease · Sun, Dec 14, 2014 | 1:33 AM

Had to get a pic w/ NHL star Kent Parson!! #SamwellUniversity #TypicalSamwellParty #EpiKegster #NHL #omgcheckplease

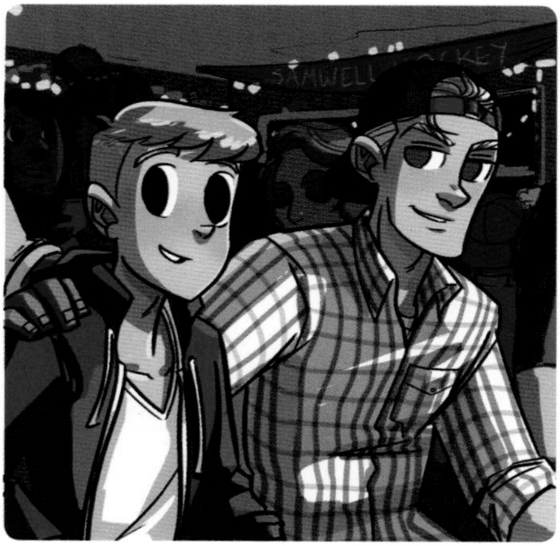

Eric Bittle @omgcheckplease · Sun, Dec 14, 2014 | 1:33 AM

!!!! HE'S SO NICE!!!!!

Eric Bittle @omgcheckplease · Sun, Dec 14, 2014 | 1:38 AM

Where is Jack?

Eric Bittle @omgcheckplease · Sun, Dec 14, 2014 | 10:21 AM

Well, the frogs survived.

Eric Bittle @omgcheckplease · Sun, Dec 14, 2014 | 10:23 AM

(survived is being generous)
Me: good morning!
Nursey: hhhhmmmmnngggggrrgghhhhhhhhhhh

Eric Bittle @omgcheckplease · Mon, Dec 15, 2014 | 9:57 AM

Oh Dear God.
All of the frogs are in the Swallow.

Eric Bittle @omgcheckplease · Mon, Dec 15, 2014 | 9:59 AM

Rans:...is this what new fathers feel like? *whispers* Hashtag
EpiKegster.

Eric Bittle @omgcheckplease · Mon, Dec 15, 2014 | 3:03 PM

Okay, Jack & Shitty are fixing to head out. I'm going on a very
dangerous mission. Wish me luck.

Eric Bittle @omgcheckplease · Mon, Dec 15, 2014 | 3:24 PM

MISSION ACCOMPLISHED And now to wait for him to find
them... [cookies!]

Eric Bittle @omgcheckplease · Tue, Dec 16, 2014 | 12:34 PM

Text from Jack: i'm surprised your cookies got through customs,
Bittle
UvU He found them.

Eric Bittle @omgcheckplease · Sat, Dec 20, 2014 | 9:12 PM

Dear Santa, for Christmas I'd like my hockey butt, thank you. —ERB
(Well. My birthday's in May. Maybe I'll get it by then. :/)

Eric Bittle @omgcheckplease · Thu, Dec 25, 2014 | 11:41 AM

Merry Christmas, y'all! (^o^)/

Eric Bittle @omgcheckplease · Thu, Dec 25, 2014 | 6:06 PM

SMH Group Text:
Jack: Merry Christmas
Jack: We have a game next week.

Eric Bittle @omgcheckplease · Fri, Dec 26, 2014 | 6:08 PM

Once we get back to Samwell, which of my teammates would do squats with me every day? (a) Chowder (b) Lardo (c) Holster (d) Other

---

Eric Bittle @omgcheckplease · Fri, Dec 26, 2014 | 6:09 PM

Ransom: #FlyBittyBooty2015

Eric Bittle @omgcheckplease · Sun, Dec 28, 2014 | 5:14 PM

My baby-child, my son and ward, the warm ray of sunshine that is the net-minder Chris "Chowder" Chow...no longer appears to be single.

Eric Bittle @omgcheckplease · Sun, Dec 28, 2014 | 5:16 PM

Apparently he and Volleyball Girl are both from California....

Eric Bittle @omgcheckplease · Mon, Dec 29, 2014 | 10:51 PM

YES. Jack butt-texted the group TEXT. My day is made. He shouldn't've admitted to it. Rookie Mistake.

Eric Bittle @omgcheckplease · Mon, Dec 29, 2014 | 10:52 PM

My phone won't stop vibrating from the CONSTANT CHIRPING. #GotYourBack

---

Eric Bittle @omgcheckplease · Mon, Dec 29, 2014 | 10:52 PM

If Holster were a shark, this faux pas would be a wounded sea lion. #HolsterHasBeenWaitingForThisDay

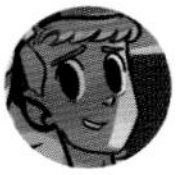

Eric Bittle @omgcheckplease · Mon, Dec 29, 2014 | 10:58 PM
SMH Group Text:
Jack: ok haha very funny
Jack: you got me
Jack: my ass is big i get it
Holster: and it miSSES US MORE THAN you DO

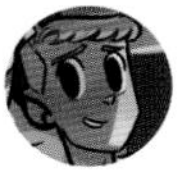

Eric Bittle @omgcheckplease · Mon, Dec 29, 2014 | 11:09 PM
(What he texted:
Jack: edijdia;;;;;;;;;;;;:-):-):-):-)
Jack: :-):-)
Shitty: WHAT THE FUCK)

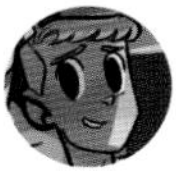

Eric Bittle @omgcheckplease · Fri, Jan 2, 2015 | 7:45 PM
enters Haus
immediately do squats w/ Rans
#BetterBittyBootyBureau2015

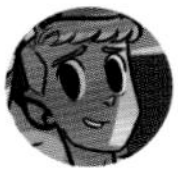

Eric Bittle @omgcheckplease · Fri, Jan 2, 2015 | 7:51 PM
"Hey, Bittle. Oh, squats. Good."
—Jack Zimmermann

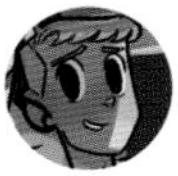

Eric Bittle @omgcheckplease · Sat, Jan 3, 2015 | 12:15 PM
Chowder's reaction to coming back to Samwell: "Wow!! It's like I never left! But I totally did because I really missed you guys!!" #SweetBabyChowder

---

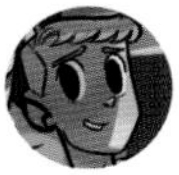

Eric Bittle @omgcheckplease · Sat, Jan 3, 2015 | 12:21 PM
Nursey: You miss me, Poindexter?
Dex: No.
Nursey: You're always free to skype me.

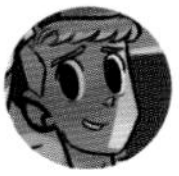

Eric Bittle @omgcheckplease · Sat, Jan 3, 2015 | 8:21 PM
"That food seminar was something, eh?"
—Jack Zimmermann

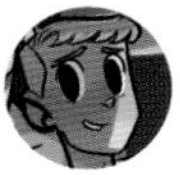

Eric Bittle @omgcheckplease · Sun, Jan 4, 2015 | 11:38 AM
Afternoon game! #LetsGoBoys

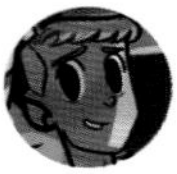

Eric Bittle @omgcheckplease · Sun, Jan 4, 2015 | 4:27 PM
Good win, even if I got banged up a little! Spears over body checks any day imho.

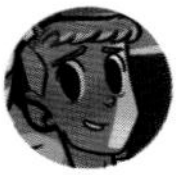

Eric Bittle @omgcheckplease · Mon, Jan 5, 2015 | 11:15 AM
The Psychology, Biology & Politics of Food WAS AMAZING. Ugggh, a perfect lecture class. I will take EVERY food class at Samwell!

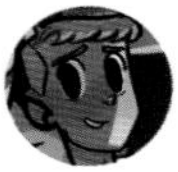

Eric Bittle @omgcheckplease · Fri, Jan 9, 2015 | 10:12 PM
Rans:...bro. every game of words with friends can easily turn into words with enemies
Hoslter:...*bro*

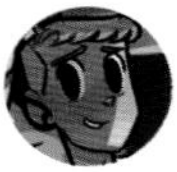

Eric Bittle @omgcheckplease · Sat, Jan 10, 2015 | 5:16 PM
jack's hatty tho

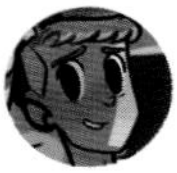

Eric Bittle @omgcheckplease · Sat, Jan 10, 2015 | 7:01 PM
Dex: Jack, how often do you do that?
Jack: do what?
Jack: ...oh...you mean get hat tric-
Shitty: HE SAID IT
EVERYONE THROWS HATS AT JACK

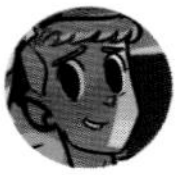

Eric Bittle @omgcheckplease · Sat, Jan 10, 2015 | 7:02 PM
Jack Zimmermann is covered in hats and laughing. We're going to get kicked out of this restaurant. #RoadieAdventures

---

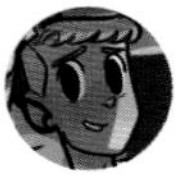

Eric Bittle @omgcheckplease · Thu, Jan 15, 2015 | 1:56 PM
Holster: WAIT BITS is that food lecture a science credit?
Nursey: hold up, it's a science credit???
Lardo: did someone say science credit

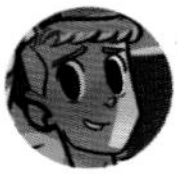

Eric Bittle @omgcheckplease · Thu, Jan 15, 2015 | 1:58 PM
If half this hockey team takes this class with me I'm going to be somewhat uncomfortable. I see you people EVERY DAY ALREADY.

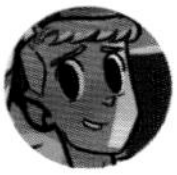

Eric Bittle @omgcheckplease · Sun, Jan 18, 2015 | 2:12 PM
THANK GOODNESS Shitty forced me to look out the window with him. Jack is taking photos of the tree in our front yard with a DSLR.

Eric Bittle @omgcheckplease · Sun, Jan 18, 2015 | 2:20 PM
Shitty: Yaaa it's for his photography class, but I like to pretend he's going nuts. Hashtag Jack As Second-Semester Senior.

Eric Bittle @omgcheckplease · Sun, Jan 18, 2015 | 2:27 PM
He's showing Lardo his photos. I think they're talking composition. Aaaand now Shitty's shouting at him to take a picture of us.

Eric Bittle @omgcheckplease · Sun, Jan 18, 2015 | 2:32 PM
So I'm probably going to be in Jack's homework assignment.

Eric Bittle @omgcheckplease · Thu, Jan 22, 2015 | 9:31 AM
I've always baked to cope with the fact that I've been single for most of my life. (...Maybe that's why I'm good at it? Hm.)

Eric Bittle @omgcheckplease · Mon, Jan 26, 2015 | 12:14 PM
So. Blizzards, eh?

Eric Bittle @omgcheckplease · Tue, Jan 27, 2015 | 12:44 PM
"Yeeep, Bits. That's a metric shit ton of snow." —Shitty, partially clothed, looking out at our front yard, w/ a mug full of hot cocoa.

Eric Bittle @omgcheckplease · Tue, Jan 27, 2015 | 12:48 PM
Shitty: Dex is texting about Dibs for shoveling us out. Christ I love that ambitious little butt nugget.

Eric Bittle @omgcheckplease · Wed, Jan 28, 2015 | 11:59 AM
"I'm gonna go take some pictures for class," said Jack Zimmermann casually traipsing into two feet of snow.

Eric Bittle @omgcheckplease · Thu, Jan 29, 2015 | 12:20 AM
Banging on my door.
"Bittle. Team practice tomorrow afternoon."
"...I took some cool pictures today."

Eric Bittle @omgcheckplease · Thu, Jan 29, 2015 | 12:22 AM
Jack is either somber and concerned about us making playoffs? or in this...strange senior mood. That's what I'm calling it.

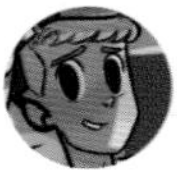

Eric Bittle @omgcheckplease · Thu, Jan 29, 2015 | 12:26 AM

Jack: there were some kids nordic skiing down elm street
Jack: neat eh. they didn't even see me

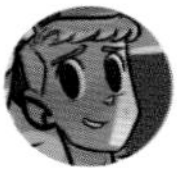

Eric Bittle @omgcheckplease · Thu, Jan 29, 2015 | 12:28 AM

Jack: I like that, you know? they didn't even know I was there

---

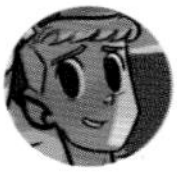

Eric Bittle @omgcheckplease · Sat, Jan 31, 2015 | 12:22 PM

Dex: [fixes broken chair. stops fridge door from squeaking. saves Betsy.] ;o;

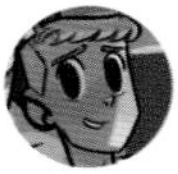

Eric Bittle @omgcheckplease · Sun, Feb 1, 2015 | 2:17 PM

Ransom's doing homework in the kitchen because "Holtzy won't stop singing this STUPID Wuthering Heights song."

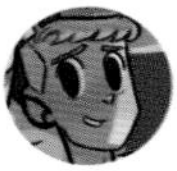

Eric Bittle @omgcheckplease · Sun, Feb 1, 2015 | 2:21 PM

Ransom: i have no idea how Holster's voice gets so high, like the pitch is OH WAIT BITS DO YOU NEED A DATE FOR VALENTINE'S DAY???????

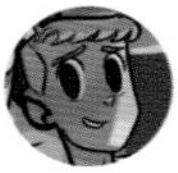

Eric Bittle @omgcheckplease · Sun, Feb 1, 2015 | 2:34 PM

Shitty: what are you guys doing
Rans: finding Bitty a date
Jack: why is Bittle under the table

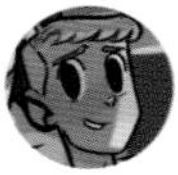

Eric Bittle @omgcheckplease · Sun, Feb 1, 2015 | 2:41 PM

um please do not photograph me while i'm down here.
Jack: while you're down there do you want to see some photos, Bittle?
DEAR GOD!!!!!!!!

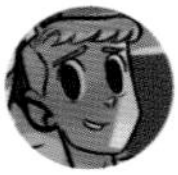

Eric Bittle @omgcheckplease · Wed, Feb 4, 2015 | 12:26 AM

Me: [sneezes]
Jack: [across the hall] bless you
Jack: go to sleep
Jack: we have practice

Eric Bittle @omgcheckplease · Thu, Feb 5, 2015 | 2:31 PM

Me: [sees jack across River quad]
Me: [waves]
Jack: [waves]
Jack: [walks across quad]
Jack: [jumps over snowbank]
Jack: do you want coffee?

Eric Bittle @omgcheckplease · Thu, Feb 5, 2015 | 3:06 PM

Jack: oh yeah, Bittle, I wanted to show—[pulls out camera and knocks into my coffee and spills entire contents on my Samwell hoodie]

Eric Bittle @omgcheckplease · Thu, Feb 5, 2015 | 3:09 PM

what is wrong with this boy

Eric Bittle @omgcheckplease · Fri, Feb 6, 2015 | 11:50 AM

My pregame ritual involves getting pumped with my favorite playlist! Others like to get broody / eat pb&j sandwiches instead w/e.

Eric Bittle @omgcheckplease · Mon, Feb 16, 2015 | 11:41 AM

Overheard at Samwell
girl 1: half the hockey team is in the class
girl 2: ugh they would
girl 1: they're so loud

Eric Bittle @omgcheckplease · Wed, Feb 18, 2015 | 11:29 AM

"HOW? HOW can you be 'CLOSE TO DONE'???" shouts Shitty re: Jack's thesis. We're at Norris library but of course that doesn't matter.

Eric Bittle @omgcheckplease · Wed, Feb 18, 2015 | 11:31 AM

Shitty: BRAH. Where do you find TIME?
Jack:...I do a little every night?
Shitty: That's???? Not??? Real???

Eric Bittle @omgcheckplease · Wed, Feb 18, 2015 | 11:32 AM

if it isn't obvious, half of my tweets are done while cackling

Eric Bittle @omgcheckplease · Wed, Feb 18, 2015 | 11:37 AM
"I don't really procrastinate, I guess."
—Jack Zimmermann
#ThingsIWillNeverSay

Eric Bittle @omgcheckplease · Thu, Feb 19, 2015 | 5:33 PM
When you're crossing the River and realize the guy taking pictures of a goose is the captain of the hockey team.

Eric Bittle @omgcheckplease · Thu, Feb 19, 2015 | 10:10 PM
:) Game tomorrow!

Eric Bittle @omgcheckplease · Sat, Feb 21, 2015 | 10:50 AM
sigh Nursey definitely just hit a kid in the face with his hockey bag. #MostDangerousDman #RoadieAdventures

Eric Bittle @omgcheckplease · Sat, Feb 21, 2015 | 10:58 AM
Dear Lord, this child is like 8 and he just said, "nah, it's cool. Good luck with your game, bro." #MoreChillThanDerekNurse

Eric Bittle @omgcheckplease · Sat, Feb 21, 2015 | 11:07 AM
Jack: Nice check, Nurse. (All of SMH: [CACKLES])

Eric Bittle @omgcheckplease · Tue, Feb 24, 2015 | 9:26 AM
Holster: "MEN'S HOCKEY: Wellies finish weekend w/ road sweep; clinch ECAC playoff spot." you know sometimes the Daily isn't a piece of crap.

Eric Bittle @omgcheckplease · Tue, Feb 24, 2015 | 9:39 AM
Holster: "'We're a close knit group of guys. We look out for each other on the ice,' forward and team capt. Jack Zimmermann '15 said."

Eric Bittle @omgcheckplease · Tue, Feb 24, 2015 | 9:43 AM
Holster: Guys, Jack loves us! SAY YOU LOVE US!
Jack: I love you.
#TeamBreakfast

Eric Bittle @omgcheckplease · Thu, Feb 26, 2015 | 2:42 PM

Lardo's art show is this weekend! Excited to mingle with the art majors! I hope they like hockey players.

Eric Bittle @omgcheckplease · Thu, Feb 26, 2015 | 11:31 PM

Jack has a critique tomorrow and wants feedback on photos. It is SO past his bedtime. Also? I'm NO Lardo...

Eric Bittle @omgcheckplease · Thu, Feb 26, 2015 | 11:38 PM

Jack: I figured you'd be up baking a pie or three. (???????? I'm making TWO.)

Eric Bittle @omgcheckplease · Thu, Feb 26, 2015 | 11:58 PM

Jack: this goose one isn't dumb?
Me: no, it's charming!

Eric Bittle @omgcheckplease · Fri, Feb 27, 2015 | 12:10 AM

I did NOT ask for so many chirps this late at night

Eric Bittle @omgcheckplease · Fri, Feb 27, 2015 | 8:18 PM

Current location: Koetter Art & Student Center, right on the Pond.

Eric Bittle @omgcheckplease · Fri, Feb 27, 2015 | 8:59 PM

Have you ever heard five college hockey players earnestly trying to dissect modern art?

Eric Bittle @omgcheckplease · Fri, Feb 27, 2015 | 9:00 PM

Shitty: Ah yes, Lardo, brilliant visual metaphor this
Holster: ah yes indeed
Rans: ah yes rather indeed
Lardo: you guys are idiots

Eric Bittle @omgcheckplease · Fri, Feb 27, 2015 | 9:30 PM

!!!!!!!!!!! SHITTY GOT INTO LAW SCHOOL

Eric Bittle @omgcheckplease · Sat, Feb 28, 2015 | 1:32 AM

...late night froyo with Lardo. game tomorrow. we're gonna regret it in the morning, but I honestly couldn't care <3

Eric Bittle @omgcheckplease · Tue, Mar 3, 2015 | 11:29 PM

My teammates deserve everything. Every last one of us works so hard.

Eric Bittle @omgcheckplease · Tue, Mar 3, 2015 | 11:38 PM

For them, I couldn't bake a pie big enough. (Which sounds sweet, but seriously they're all bottomless pits.)

Eric Bittle @omgcheckplease · Sun, Mar 8, 2015 | 1:01 PM

Jack:...i probably can't do much photography when i'm playing professionally
Me: offseason, jack
Lardo: plz be that one artsy hipster NHL bro

Eric Bittle @omgcheckplease · Sat, Mar 21, 2015 | 9:04 PM

It's always #OneMoreGame.

Eric Bittle @omgcheckplease · Fri, Mar 27, 2015 | 6:25 PM

\(^o^)/ LET'S GO BOYS!

Eric Bittle @omgcheckplease · Sat, Mar 28, 2015 | 12:18 PM

Happy 22nd, Rans!

Eric Bittle @omgcheckplease · Sat, Mar 28, 2015 | 10:08 PM

we're moving on :)

Eric Bittle @omgcheckplease · Sun, Apr 5, 2015 | 11:50 PM

I'm almost done with my second season of hockey at Samwell...

Eric Bittle @omgcheckplease · Thu, Apr 9, 2015 | 11:07 PM

#OneMoreGame

Eric Bittle @omgcheckplease · Sun, Apr 12, 2015 | 8:22 PM

home.

Eric Bittle @omgcheckplease · Sat, Apr 18, 2015 | 8:33 AM

do you ever call your mama first thing in the morning because the ancient oven in your sport team's Haus is on the fritz lol

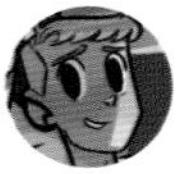
Eric Bittle @omgcheckplease · Sat, Apr 18, 2015 | 8:39 AM
I'm on the ground with my forehead against this oven's door

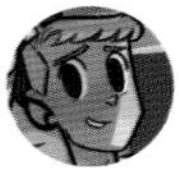
Eric Bittle @omgcheckplease · Sat, Apr 18, 2015 | 8:42 AM
Jack: ...did something happen
Me: betsy's not well
Jack: oh. is that. . . an aunt

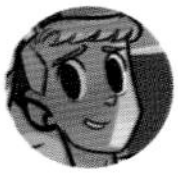
Eric Bittle @omgcheckplease · Sat, Apr 18, 2015 | 10:34 AM
Waiting outside of Dex's class to tell him everything again but in person for the third time.

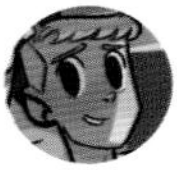
Eric Bittle @omgcheckplease · Sat, Apr 18, 2015 | 12:04 PM
Dex: have you ever considered baking less?
Me: I don't understand your question?

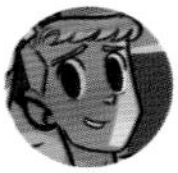
Eric Bittle @omgcheckplease · Sat, Apr 18, 2015 | 11:08 PM
pies baked today: 0

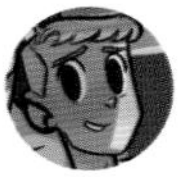
Eric Bittle @omgcheckplease · Sat, Apr 18, 2015 | 11:11 PM
Sometimes the things you love in your life just go away. You just have to take a deep breath and keep going.

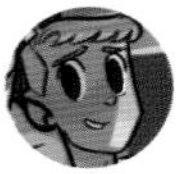
Eric Bittle @omgcheckplease · Sat, Apr 18, 2015 | 11:18 PM
Well, congrats to Jack Zimmermann for signing. It's official...

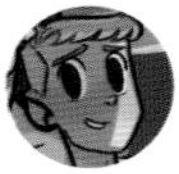
Eric Bittle @omgcheckplease · Sun, Apr 19, 2015 | 8:17 AM
Another Samwell morning. Jack and Shitty are across the hall talking about Dibs...

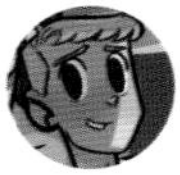
Eric Bittle @omgcheckplease · Sun, Apr 19, 2015 | 1:52 PM
I got one batch of cookies done, but B. shut off halfway through the second. *sigh*

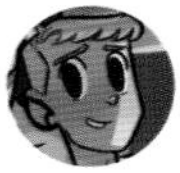
Eric Bittle @omgcheckplease · Sun, Apr 19, 2015 | 5:10 PM
Trying to pay for my own froyo at Superberry but this boy: "It's on me, Bittle. I think I'm good for it."

Eric Bittle @omgcheckplease · Sun, Apr 19, 2015 | 5:11 PM
my mother has sent me at least 5 articles about jack signing

Eric Bittle @omgcheckplease · Sat, Apr 25, 2015 | 6:54 PM
Bittle and Shitty #SpringC

Eric Bittle @omgcheckplease · Mon, May 4, 2015 | 3:17 PM
Holster and Ransom both just texted me to see if I had lunch plans tomorrow. Separately...Something's fishy.

Eric Bittle @omgcheckplease · Mon, May 4, 2015 | 3:31 PM
SMH Group Text:
Me: I love y'all but no festive baking, please. The oven's fragile. Thx!
Holster: Wouldn't worry bout that!

Eric Bittle @omgcheckplease · Mon, May 4, 2015 | 10:59 PM
Things I Should Be Doing: studying for a final tomorrow
Things I Should Not Be Doing: thinking about tres leches

Eric Bittle @omgcheckplease · Tue, May 5, 2015 | 7:55 AM
Woke up to birthday wishes from #MamaBittle. Lovely AM phone call. What more could a boy ask for? (^_^)

Eric Bittle @omgcheckplease · Tue, May 5, 2015 | 8:04 AM
Lardo was at my door with a party horn! "Put on pants and get breakfast with me, grandpa."

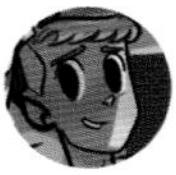

Eric Bittle @omgcheckplease · Tue, May 5, 2015 | 8:05 AM

Lardo: You're so OOOOLD!
Me: I'm ancienntttt!!!

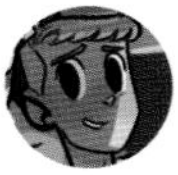

Eric Bittle @omgcheckplease · Tue, May 5, 2015 | 9:22 AM

HM. So I guess I won't be heading back to the Haus anytime soon.

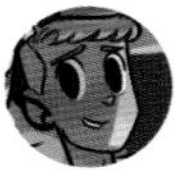

Eric Bittle @omgcheckplease · Tue, May 5, 2015 | 9:28 AM

Lardo won't let me go back to get my notes for my final. "How do they look like? Jack can bring them." (ALL OF THEM ARE IN ON THIS!!!)

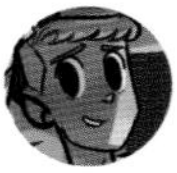

Eric Bittle @omgcheckplease · Tue, May 5, 2015 | 9:32 AM

WHAT IF THEY'RE THROWING AWAY THAT FILTHY COUCH!!!!!! #GOTYOURBACK #SAMWELLMENSHOCKEY #TRUEBROS #MYONLYWISH

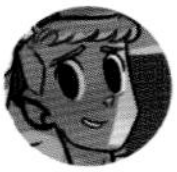

Eric Bittle @omgcheckplease · Tue, May 5, 2015 | 9:52 AM

Me: I know y'all are up to something.
Jack: What?
Me: For my birthday!
Jack:...today's your birthday?
:(

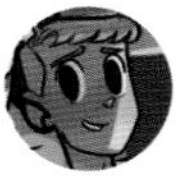

Eric Bittle @omgcheckplease · Tue, May 5, 2015 | 1:14 PM

Well, that final went exactly as planned...And seriously??? Ransom and Holster are waiting outside. I think I'm being escorted.

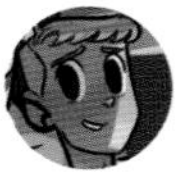

Eric Bittle @omgcheckplease · Tue, May 5, 2015 | 1:22 PM

Me: I'm not gonna head back to the Haus.
Holster: What? We're here to grab lunch with you!
Me: Let's have lunch at the Haus
Rans: Nice try.

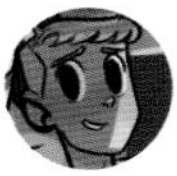

Eric Bittle @omgcheckplease · Tue, May 5, 2015 | 2:38 PM

Lord, how long does it take to move in a couch?...Maybe they're burning the old one...But they'd invite me! Hm. :/

Eric Bittle @omgcheckplease · Tue, May 5, 2015 | 4:06 PM

Does EVERYONE at Samwell know??? I'm being told that I'm allowed to tweet one more thing. And now—

Eric Bittle @omgcheckplease · Tue, May 5, 2015 | 5:17 PM

Testing. Testing. cool

Eric Bittle @omgcheckplease · Tue, May 5, 2015 | 5:19 PM

Hey, everyone! I'm Derek, number 28 for Samwell men's hockey team. I was given instructions to tweet for your favorite vlogger Eric Bittle.

Eric Bittle @omgcheckplease · Tue, May 5, 2015 | 5:20 PM

Bitty says "Don't you wreck my reputation." We're heading back to the Haus! Bittle says "I knew y'all were up to something."

Eric Bittle @omgcheckplease · Tue, May 5, 2015 | 5:22 PM

He totally didn't. About a minute away from the Haus! Unsuspecting Bittle...

Eric Bittle @omgcheckplease · Tue, May 5, 2015 | 5:37 PM

Bitty says "K, y'all. The whole team's here and I haven't baked anything. It's a surprise party. I get it."

Eric Bittle @omgcheckplease · Tue, May 5, 2015 | 5:37 PM

Bitty says "Aren't y'all gonna yell surprise?" He just saw it.

Eric Bittle @omgcheckplease · Tue, May 5, 2015 | 6:26 PM

(Sorry things got kegstery really fast.) Also Bitty probably wouldn't want photos of him crying posted all over the internet.

Eric Bittle @omgcheckplease · Tue, May 5, 2015 | 6:29 PM

Bitty is still crying. "I need to bake something right this second!"

Eric Bittle @omgcheckplease · Tue, May 5, 2015 | 6:32 PM

stop crying first —jack

Eric Bittle @omgcheckplease · Tue, May 5, 2015 | 6:34 PM
He wants his phone back. It was fun! If you're a Wellie, come over for the festivitiessssss. (My name's Derek.)

Eric Bittle @omgcheckplease · Thu, May 7, 2015 | 8:46 PM
Newsflash: I've been baking a lot. :) Jack's chirp of the day: "If we move the kitchen table out, you can bring your bed in." #VeryFunnyMrZimmermann #HarHar

Eric Bittle @omgcheckplease · Fri, May 8, 2015 | 12:57 PM
Well, Jack and Shitty just picked up their graduation robes.

Eric Bittle @omgcheckplease · Sun, May 17, 2015 | 7:42 AM
Class Day! #Samwell2015

Eric Bittle @omgcheckplease · Sun, May 17, 2015 | 10:42 AM
Jack: Hey, nice robes.
Shitty: Nice robes yourself, brother.

Eric Bittle @omgcheckplease · Sun, May 17, 2015 | 12:13 PM
As Rans explained to me "class day is fun & everyone wears cool hats, commencement is boring but you get to throw your hat at the end."

Eric Bittle @omgcheckplease · Sun, May 17, 2015 | 1:27 PM
They set up a few screens around the Quad. Jack and Shitty showed up on one and we made SO MUCH NOISE. Sorry to anyone here! #Samwell2015

Eric Bittle @omgcheckplease · Sun, May 17, 2015 | 1:57 PM
I'm already thinking of how I'll trick out my mortarboard in a few years. Detachable felt pie slice? Or should I go full helmet like Jack...

Eric Bittle @omgcheckplease · Sun, May 17, 2015 | 2:14 PM
Announcing awards for graduating seniors. #Samwell2015

Eric Bittle @omgcheckplease · Sun, May 17, 2015 | 2:32 PM
OH!! "For an unprecedented three years of captaincy and exhibiting outstanding character on and off the field of play." Jack!!

Eric Bittle @omgcheckplease · Sun, May 17, 2015 | 2:37 PM

Samwell 2015's Best Male Athlete! #GotYourBack #Samwell2015

Eric Bittle @omgcheckplease · Sun, May 17, 2015 | 3:52 PM

~Seniors~shitty: so what are we gonna put in your "I Won Samwell" shiny trophy bowl

Eric Bittle @omgcheckplease · Mon, May 18, 2015 | 10:10 AM

Don't know how many times I've said to myself "Keep it together, Bittle." It doesn't seem to be working.

Eric Bittle @omgcheckplease · Mon, May 18, 2015 | 1:27 PM

This boy.

Eric Bittle @omgcheckplease · Fri, Jul 3, 2015 | 3:05 PM

Just in time for the festivities. :)

I LOVE GRAPHIC NOVELS!

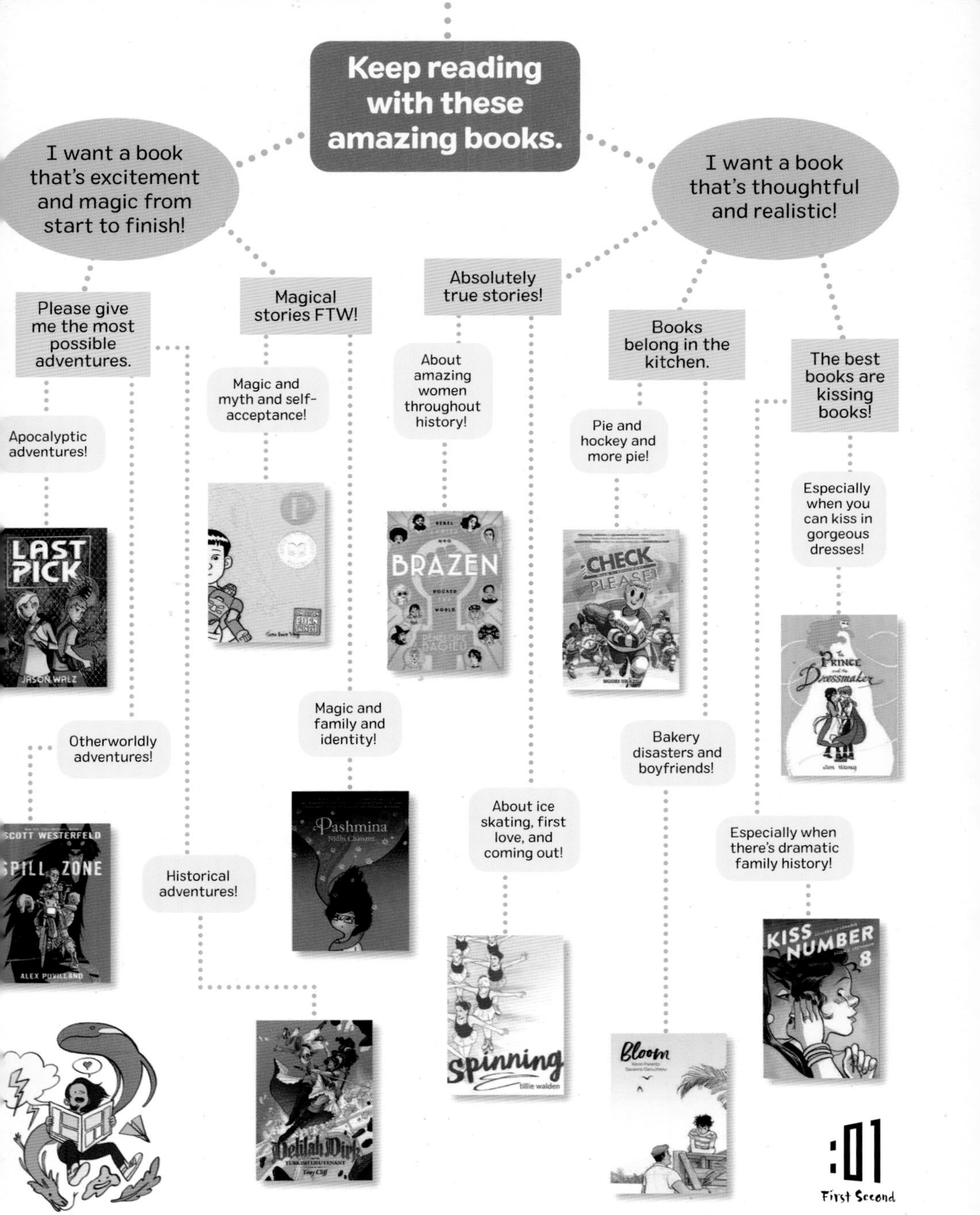

Keep reading with these amazing books.
I want a book that's excitement and magic from start to finish!
I want a book that's thoughtful and realistic!
Please give me the most possible adventures.
Magical stories FTW!
Absolutely true stories!
Books belong in the kitchen.
The best books are kissing books!
Apocalyptic adventures!
Magic and myth and self-acceptance!
About amazing women throughout history!
Pie and hockey and more pie!
Especially when you can kiss in gorgeous dresses!
LAST PICK
JASON WALZ
BRAZEN
CHECK, PLEASE!
The Prince and the Dressmaker
Otherworldly adventures!
Magic and family and identity!
Bakery disasters and boyfriends!
Pashmina
Nidhi Chanani
About ice skating, first love, and coming out!
Especially when there's dramatic family history!
SCOTT WESTERFELD
SPILL ZONE
ALEX PUVILLAND
Historical adventures!
KISS NUMBER 8
spinning
tillie walden
Bloom
Delilah Dirk
Tony Cliff

:01 First Second

First Second

Library of Congress Control Number: 2017957140

Hardcover ISBN: 978-1-250-17795-7
Paperback ISBN: 978-1-250-17796-4

Our books may be purchased in bulk for promotional, educational, or business use.
Please contact your local bookseller or the Macmillan Corporate and Premium Sales Department
at (800) 221-7945 ext. 5442 or by e-mail at MacmillanSpecialMarkets@macmillan.com.

First edition, 2018
Special thanks to Chelle Finkler
Edited by Calista Brill and Kiara Valdez
Book design by Andrew Arnold and Molly Johanson
Printed in China

Paperback: 1   3   5   7   9   10   8   6   4   2
Hardcover: 3   5   7   9   10   8   6   4   2